STIPULATIONS and COMPLICATIONS

The Sisters, Texas Mystery Series

Book Three

BECKI WILLIS

Editing by SJS Editorial Services

ISBN-10: 194768602X
ISBN-13: 978-1-947686-021

CONTENTS

1 1
2 13
3 24
4 43
5 53
6 71
7 86
8 97
9 110
10 124
11 136
12 158
13 162
14 173
15 187
16 198
17 208
18 226
19 237
20 246
21 266
22 279
23 296
24 307
25 321
26 329
Note from Author 336
Questions for Book Club Discussion 337
ABOUT THE AUTHOR 339

1

Life comes with stipulations.

If you want to fit into last year's swimsuit, you can't have ice cream and a Gennydoodle cookie after every meal.

If you want to go to heaven, you can't raise hell on Saturday night and show up in the church pew on Sunday morning, hungover and reeking of cheap perfume.

And if you want your hundred-year-old mansion completely updated and remodeled for free, you have to sacrifice.

Stipulations, my child.

Granny Bert's words of wisdom resonated in Madison Reynold's head.

Not for the first time, her mind balked at the logic. Why did the sacrifices have to include her privacy and what was left of her hard-earned sanity? What had she been thinking?

In just seven short weeks, her life had exploded. Again. And this time, it was on national television.

When Madison agreed to the unprecedented proposal two months ago, she had no idea of the whirlwind she set into motion. Tornadoes were known to touch down with less disruption than the ruckus caused by a TV reality show filmed in The Sisters.

For the price of baring her soul in front of millions of viewers, HOME TV's new make-over series was bringing the old house into the twenty-first century. It would give her a better-than-new, because-it-was-historically-old home, all without spending a dime. All the network required was her life story, splashed across the television screen. Her secrets. What was left of her dignity.

Stipulations, Madison reminded herself. *There are always stipulations.*

She, of course, had stipulations of her own. No filming inside the bedrooms. No filming of private conversations. No disrupting school or church. No encouraging the dramatic exploits of the town and members of her own family. No sneaking in footage without her consent. She had a half dozen other stipulations, some of which were actually met.

Today was a perfect example of the chaos she had created. The *Home Again: Starting Over* film crew was on scene, shooting a segment about the outside of the old mansion. While show host and head carpenter Nick Vilardi explained the process, a crew of five men worked behind him, replacing rotted wood, nailing down loose boards, and preparing the house for its first new coat of paint in over thirty years. To the delight of the mostly female crowd gathered alongside the elaborate iron fence out front, the usual workers had been replaced by younger, more muscular counterparts sporting broad shoulders and nice behinds, all of which were turned toward the camera. The women crowding along the sidewalk had no qualms about ogling the men so publicly nor, anytime the cameras rested, throwing out crude suggestions, telephone numbers, and enthusiastic catcalls. One went so far as to throw her bra.

Filming stopped twice due to the noise. A third interruption ensued when Abigail Combs broke free of the barriers and ran up the cobblestone path, chasing her wayward kitten. Because the child was only six, her antics were excused. Then her older sister came sauntering up the walk after her, dressed in ridiculously short shorts, a skimpy halter top, and heels high enough to cause a nosebleed. Security officers shooed the teenager away and threatened to clear the sidewalk if they heard another peep from the audience. Even from where she stood across the street, Madison could hear the angry rumble of the crowd, but eventually the people quieted and filming resumed.

This was not the first incident of such nature, nor would it be the last. With all the cameras, crew, and now spectators in town, the residents of the community put on quite the performance. Madison could only imagine the madness to come, once the show aired on a weekly basis.

When Nick asked her to come down to make final color selections for the exterior, the show host neglected to mention it would take place on camera. The moment she turned onto Main and saw the crowd, Madison knew they were filming again. A quick glance down at her outfit had her wishing she had worn something different from khaki capris and a solid navy tee. Not that her limited wardrobe offered much better, but this was just so ... plain.

That's me, plain ol' Maddy.

As owner of the house, she had every right to pull up to the electronic gate and drive inside the premises. But the last time she had done so, an overzealous fan had slipped in alongside her and caused quite the scene. Rather than fight the crowd and call attention to herself, she would stay here and watch from a distance, then quietly slip in among the crowd. She actually preferred to stay on the perimeters of the camera lens; just a few weeks in, but already, she had her fill of stardom.

Madison lounged against the side of her car as she watched the crowd gathered in front of the Big House. That's what locals had called Juliet Randolph Blakely's home since it was built a century ago, dominating an entire city block and then some. Since it was the woman's own town and namesake, she could do anything she wanted, and she wanted the biggest and best house in town. Never mind that an identical one was built across the railroad tracks for her sister, in her own namesake town of Naomi. Even though the homes looked alike, each house was as different as the women themselves.

Three stories tall, the Big House's original structure boasted no less than five porches, two turrets, and three chimneys. Across the front, the old mansion still looked much the same. In the back, however, a porch was sacrificed to add a third turret that housed new bathrooms on all three levels. The years had taken their toll upon the house, but with the help of Nick Vilardi and crew, the stately old mansion was not only getting back into shape, it was shaping up better than ever.

"So? What color did you decide on?"

Absorbed in watching the antics of the town, Madison did not hear her best friend approach. She whirled around when she heard Genesis Baker's voice, her lips already pushing upward in a smile. "Genny! You were able to make it, after all."

"What's the point in owning your own business if you can't slip in and out at will?" Her friend gave a nonchalant shrug, as if escaping the busy restaurant so close to noon were no great feat.

"I know it's bad timing for you, but I appreciate the

support."

"You know I've always got your back, girlfriend." Genny flashed her dimpled smile as she hooked her arm through Madison's.

They stood along the perimeters for a long moment, watching the filming. "Where did all the hot bods come from?" Genesis asked after a moment. "Those aren't the usual carpenters, are they?"

Madison's bark of laughter lacked amusement. "Hardly. These are the on-camera carpenters, the ones that look best with their shirts off and their pants cinched up nice and tight."

"At least we don't have to worry about saying no to crack," Genny quipped. She eyed a few of the men more closely. "Mmm. You gotta admit, though, they are one fine-looking crew. I wonder if we could get these to come every day..."

After a long and wistful moment, the women sighed in unison and dismissed the notion.

"Too distracting," Madison murmured.

"And too tempting. As much as I'd like to, I can't leave every day to come down here and ogle the men. I do have to work, after all."

"Speaking of work, I have a couple of new clients."

"Oh? Who this time?" Even though they carried on a normal conversation, their eyes were on the handsome crew parading around the mansion. With uncanny precision, each time the camera panned toward the house, one of the buff carpenters would strategically bend at the waist or flex his bulging biceps. Even from this distance, it was far easier to focus on the men than on the house.

"Miss Sybille was so pleased with the backyard fence Derron built, that two of her neighbors have hired us to continue the fence along their properties."

Genny bobbed her blond head. "Hiring Derron was

a good move on your part."

This time when Maddy laughed, there was genuine humor in the sound. "To be honest, I'm not sure if I hired him, or he hired me. And even though *In a Pinch Temp Services* is barely solvent at the moment, having Derron has been a tremendous help. I wouldn't know the first thing about building fences."

"And he came with his own tools," Genesis reminded her.

"Definitely a plus. And in a roundabout way, he's also responsible for another potential client, Allen Wynn. Even though Derron closed his mother's business when she died, he still has access to her files, and one of the last properties she surveyed was Allen's. Allen wants to pursue the boundary dispute between him and Hank Adams, and he's hinted at hiring me before going to a lawyer."

"That's wonderful. See, things are starting to fall into place."

"We'll see about that," she murmured skeptically. "Speaking of Derron... With all these good-looking carpenters strutting around, I'm really surprised he's not here himself, getting an eyeful." Madison stood on her tiptoes and stretched her five-foot, seven-inch frame, trying to get a glimpse of Derron Mullins.

"I think you spoke too soon. Isn't that him?"

"Where?"

"Up there." With a wide grin, Genesis pointed to an old pecan tree with low, sweeping limbs. "In the tree."

"Oh, Lordy, that is him!"

The women burst out laughing, amused by the younger man's antics. He enjoyed watching the buff carpenters as much as any female in attendance.

"It looks like they're wrapping up this particular segment," Madison noted. "I guess it will be my turn next."

"Don't sound so excited."

Madison nibbled on her lower lip. "Sometimes I think I made a huge mistake, agreeing to all this." She swept her arm toward the milling crowd. With the cameras off, the jovial heckling began again.

"Maddy, look at that place. Even though Granny Bert practically gave you the house, there's no way you could have fixed it up on your own. You needed a place for you and the twins to start over. You did the only thing you could do under the circumstances."

"I guess. But I didn't just do this to myself. I dragged all of you along into this mess with me. You, the twins, Granny Bert... the whole town, really. Sometimes I feel so guilty."

"For what? In case you haven't noticed, the town is lapping up all this attention like a starved puppy. Blake and Bethani are adjusting, and I've never seen Granny Bert this happy, not even the time Willie Nelson wrote a song about her. She may have retired as mayor, but your grandmother is a people person, and she loves being in front of a camera."

"Which is a problem unto itself, but we won't go there now. But honestly, Genny, I'm sorry if this has made your life harder. I know people are swarming into *New Beginnings* now, hoping to be on camera."

"Hey, it's good for business," the café owner shrugged. "I will admit I'm still getting used to having the camera in there all the time. Reality television can be a little unnerving, never knowing what they'll choose to broadcast to a million or so strangers, but the cash registers are keeping up a nice steady cha-ching." She tossed her head and flashed another dimpled smile. "So it's all good."

Genesis owned *New Beginnings Café*, a popular eatery that resided on the Naomi side of the railroad tracks. Even before fame came to the neighboring communities — collectively known as The Sisters — the café had become the prime gathering spot for both towns. People came for the good food, eclectic menu, friendly atmosphere, and scrumptious desserts; the possible chance at television fame was like getting a delicious side order for free.

"You know, when Nick and Amanda first mentioned the idea of doing a reality television show, I laughed in their faces. There are only two thousand residents in both towns combined. We don't have a Starbucks, there's no McDonald's, not even a Wal-Mart. By all rights, The Sisters is a boring little rural community. Why would anyone want to watch us on TV?" Madison gazed at the array of cameras and technical equipment scattered across the lawn, all a necessary part of broadcasting her private life to the eyes of the public. "Who knew it could be so entertaining? The pilot episode broke some sort of record for the network."

"I think that's part of the charm. We're just a normal, boring little town with normal, boring little people. But Amanda Hooper is a brilliant producer. She did a ton of promoting for the new season. She knows exactly what to play up, exactly what to exploit. If occasionally one of our people becomes famous, it gives hope to all the other little towns out there filled with their own normal, boring citizens. If it can happen to us, it can happen to them."

"I noticed she artfully downplayed how Caress, our most famous citizen and daytime star, was just brutally murdered at the hands of her secret lover," Madison commented wryly.

"Ah, but did you notice how she played up the fact that John Paul Nobles was heartbroken over her death? Interviewing him on the set of his latest movie — in Paris, no less — and having him share memories of The

Sisters was a nice touch."

"Except for the part about him and Caress almost buying the Big House," Madison frowned. "The house has never been on the market, not once in its one-hundred-year history! Miss Juliet built the house, left it to Granny Bert when she died in the 80s, and now I'm only the third person to ever own it. He and Caress may have *wanted* to buy it, but Granny Bert would never have considered selling to them."

"What is it they call that, artistic license? Sort of like pretending Glitter Thompson was originally from here, when everyone knows her Vegas-ceremony husband met her at a show and dragged her back here after their second date. That famous showgirl has roots in Milwaukee, not The Sisters."

"Details," Madison said breezily. "Why clog the issue with pesky little details? She put a nice aw-shucks spin on Brash, too. Local football hero hits the big time when he's drafted by the NFL, gives it up to marry his high school sweetheart, goes on to coach at premier universities, then gives that up, too, to come home to The Sisters and pin on a shiny silver star." She batted her eyelashes for dramatic emphasis.

"And if the woman didn't have an obvious crush on the man, she would be playing up the would-be romance between you and said football hero, instead of trying to insinuate something between you and Nick."

This time when Maddy blinked her lashes, it was in genuine surprise. "You think she has a crush on Brash?" Dismay colored her voice with a husky note.

"Oh, please. The minute she heard he was divorced, her eyes lit up like neon. I genuinely like Amanda, but I'm telling you, she genuinely likes your man."

"Brash deCordova is not my man," Madison fairly snapped.

"Again, details." Genny flashed a smile to soften her

retort. "He's crazy over you, Maddy. And you're crazy over him. You're just afraid to admit it."

"What I'm afraid of is trusting another man so completely, only to have him trample on my heart and soul like it was yesterday's trash." Her voice was hard.

"Brash would never do that, and you know it. He's nothing like Gray. You just have to trust him."

"Says the woman afraid to trust her own knight in shining armor," Madison shot back.

Genny shifted uncomfortably. "We're not talking about me; we're talking about you. And I see Nick coming this way, probably looking for you. It's show-time, sister."

The old mansion had always been white.

The infamous structure, with its pristine elegance and haughty airs, sat alone on its corner lot, as cool and inaccessible as the ghosts said to haunt it. Madison knew the first step in turning the old house into a warm and inviting home started with curb appeal, but she was having trouble committing to a color scheme. It was important to convey the right personality through paint choice.

Madison immediately ruled out yellow, citing the Bumble Bee Hotel on the other side of the tracks. Naomi's version of this same house was painted a robust yellow with black trim and offered a bit too *much* personality for Madison's liking.

Tan was too boring, taupe too trendy.

Green was out.

Browns wouldn't do.

The reds weren't to her liking, and none of the blues had struck her fancy.

One by one, she flipped the color samples over, until the only ones left were shades of white.

"You wanted something warmer," Nick Vilardi reminded her, struggling to keep the impatience from his voice. He had envisioned a color scheme from the beginning, but bringing her around to the same decision was harder than he thought.

"I know, but nothing else seems right…"

"You liked this cream color, didn't you?"

"I'm afraid it might look yellow in certain light."

"This pale gray was nice. Remember, you liked this one. It has the feel of tradition, while still being fresh and modern. Elegant, with warm undertones. It would make an excellent field color."

"Maybe," Madison conceded, chewing on her bottom lip. "I liked it with the off-white trim."

It was the most progress they had made. Encouraging her to keep up the momentum of making a decision, Nick nodded enthusiastically and pressed for an accent color. "What about this for the accent? Or this cranberry color?"

Madison studied the samples he presented. "Could I see it again on the computer model?"

All but grinding his teeth, Nick managed a smile. "Sure."

He punched a few buttons on his iPad, brought up a digital rendition of the Big House, and electronically re-painted the image on the screen. He turned it toward Madison for her approval.

"I don't know…" She chewed on her lip, then turned to her friend. "What do you think, Genny?"

"I like it," her friend said, earning a bright smile from the television host. "Nick is right. It keeps the traditional feel of elegance, especially with the cream trim, but the colors are so much warmer and more inviting than conventional white."

Before Madison could voice a protest, a loud commotion erupted from behind the house. Someone screamed. A door banged shut and something crashed to the ground. The cameraman jerked his focus from the indecisive woman to the ruckus unfolding; it was certainly more interesting.

A worker raced from around the house, running as if a flame crawled up his shirttail. There was plenty of fire in his voice as he yelled, "Help! Call the police! Dear Jesus above, I just found a dead body!

2

Blanching whiter than any of the paint samples, Madison felt the air swish from her lungs. "It's a curse," she lamented beneath her breath. "I'm cursed with dead bodies."

The show was forgotten. Even the cameras knew where the real story was.

An on-duty security officer stopped them before they reached the entrance to the basement.

"I'm sorry, you can't go down there."

Madison's voice brooked no argument. "This is my house. Move out of my way."

"But we need to preserve the scene until the police get here."

Although he blocked the entrance, he occupied the step below her, and his five-foot-something frame was shorter than Madison's to begin with. She all but loomed over him, looking formidable with her hands propped upon her hips and determination flashing in her hazel eyes.

"I watch *CSI* just like you do," she informed him coldly, eying the security badge on his chest with something close to disdain. They both knew he had no real authority in the matter. "You were hired to keep the crowd from disrupting filming, not to keep me, *the owner*, from my own property. Now move, or I'll have you fired."

"You have no authority to do so," the man said, but his voice wavered with uncertainty.

Madison arched a fine eyebrow. "Maybe not, but I can have you banned from the property, which is essentially the same thing." The challenge was clear in her eyes as she stared him down.

He was the first to blink. His eyes darted to Genesis. "Fine, but she stays here."

Ignoring him, Madison grabbed her friend's wrist and tugged. "Come on, Genny. You're with me." The man moved hastily away, lest the women trample him.

Before they cleared the doorway, Nick Vilardi and the cameraman were close on their heels.

Madison had only been in the cellar twice before. It took a moment for her eyes to adjust to the dim lighting of the underground recesses. Electricity had been added at some point over the years, but the receptacles were crude and sparse. She paused to get her bearings. The necessitated support beams and load-bearing pilasters chopped the cavernous space into odd and random rooms, creating a maze effect.

As before, the cellar's size and the number of rooms comprising it astounded Madison. She always thought of a cellar as a cold, cramped space filled with vegetables and spiders, a place to retreat when tornadoes swirled through the stormy Texas skies. At the turn of the twentieth century, however, it seemed that cellars played a much more valuable role.

True, the space was cool and slightly damp, kept naturally insulated with floors and walls made of brick, stone, and mortar. But there was evidence that the many rooms within the underground structure were used for different purposes.

Food storage, certainly. Old bins and baskets still

lined the walls.

One smaller room was dedicated to wine and spirits. It boasted a huge wooden labyrinth tucked against one wall, its rack still half-filled with dusty bottles. A half dozen unopened oak barrels sat around the room. Madison made a mental note to visit the wine cellar again at a more opportune moment.

Another room housed a cistern. Discarded buckets and crude early-century copper plumbing apparatuses scattered around the old casement. Connected to that room was another, obviously used as an early laundry room.

Madison and crew moved into a larger space, a graveyard of sorts where old furniture was brought to die. Genny nudged her friend and pointed out some of the antiques littering the area, but there was no time to dawdle over the would-be treasures. The worker who had discovered the body led the way, clearly still distraught. He wrung his hands as he mumbled a mixture of prayers and panic, words of praise interspersed with vile curses. Half came out in English, half in Spanish.

A second cameraman rushed to get in the lead, eager to capture the looks on the group's faces as they advanced into the cool recesses of the cellar.

Have they no shame? Madison wondered. *No sense of reverence?* She wanted to shout at them to turn off their cameras, but the truth was that she appreciated the additional light proffered. She stumbled on an uneven stone in the floor, barely missing a low overhead beam, but Nick caught her arm and helped her to remain steady.

"Are you sure this is the right way?" she asked their leader. They approached a brick wall that looked like a dead end.

"*Si*, yes. There is a hidden room." The man kept

moving forward, slipping into a shadowed recess. The passageway narrowed, forcing them to move through the space in single file. The floor beneath them dipped. "*Cuidadoso.*Watch your step," he warned.

Maddy and Genny alternately clung to the narrow walls and each other as they took the slippery path to access the lowest level of the cellar. The floor through the tunneling passage sloped downward as the brick gave way to dirt. The air became close, the cloying smell of dank earth crowding in around them.

Madison fought a wave of claustrophobia and memories best left in the past. She belatedly realized the folly of her rash decision to see the body for herself. Wasn't the sight of two dead bodies — in three months, no less — enough for anyone?

This is just a room beneath my house, she reminded herself, *not Ronny Gleason's incinerator. There's plenty of room to move around down here, plenty of air to breathe. No danger.* She swallowed down a gulp of fear.

"Th-There!" the man said, throwing his arm toward the back of the darkened space.

They were in a small room, not more than eight feet wide by ten feet deep, its ceiling low. While the rest of the cellar had finished walls and floors, this deepest underground room was much more crude.

Casting too much light for such a small space, the glare from the cameras bounced off the earthen walls, causing momentary blindness. Madison shielded her eyes, peeking through her fingers as she surveyed the room. A crude wooden bed occupied the far corner. As her eyes adjusted to the light, she saw the skeleton stretched out upon it.

Beside her, Genny gasped softly and moved closer in. Nick Vilardi moved behind both women and put an arm around their shoulders.

"It appears to have been here quite some time," he murmured.

Madison managed a nod. "Thank goodness," she said weakly. "Still, I wish Brash would hurry."

What was taking him so long? She would feel better when the chief of police arrived, even if their questionable relationship was strained at the moment.

"I called Cutter," Genny offered. "He's on his way."

Confusion creased Nick's brow. "Cutter? Isn't that the guy from the fire department?"

Genny's blond head bobbed. "The Volunteer Fire Department helps with a lot more than fires, you know."

"I think it's too late to help our friend here." He nodded to the pile of bones on the platform before shifting his attention to the distraught worker. "Enrique, how did you find this room?"

Still visibly shaken, the man pointed to a narrow step that all but blended into the wall. "I was finding *pasadizos secreto* like you said, Boss. Circle down to here." He made a circular motion with his finger.

"A secret spiral staircase?"

"*Si*. Can I go now, Boss?"

"You may go up, but don't leave. Chief deCordova will want to talk with you."

"*Gracias*, Boss." Already halfway out of the room, the worker tossed the hasty parting over his shoulder.

"What is this room?" Madison breathed, venturing forward a few steps. In addition to the bed, it had a narrow table, a set of rickety shelves, and the hidden staircase. None had been touched in recent decades.

"I think someone lived down here," Genny guessed. Her eyes zeroed in on the collection of bones. For the most part, the skeleton was still intact. Perhaps the person had died in their sleep, or been sick. Or wounded.

"It looks like they died down here, too," Madison murmured. The air grew thinner and the walls seemed to inch inward. She was relieved to know the body was decades old, already fully decayed and rotted. Still, being in the room with any dead body was disturbing, particularly when that room was underground, small, and dark. For all she knew, the person had suffocated for lack of air.

"I think I'd like to go up, too," she announced abruptly.

She suddenly could not escape soon enough.

As they stepped back into the blessed fresh air, Madison noted the crowd out front had grown. When two fire department trucks arrived, a half dozen vehicles followed; people in their small community were just naturally curious. If there had been an actual emergency, they would have gladly pitched in to help. And if there was anything to see, anything to pass along in the form of gossip... well, they would be happy to help in that regard, as well.

"You look rather pale," Genesis told her friend. "You find a spot to rest. I'll show Cutter and his men down."

"Thanks." Without arguing, Madison made her way out to the side yard. She could watch the chaos unfolding from there, no need to be up close and personal. She knew it was ridiculous, but the thought of being in the house right now, even on one of its porches, gave her the willies. This was the house she would eventually live in, and that body had been there for ages. It posed no danger, but she needed to put some distance between herself and it right now.

She found a massive old pecan tree just this side of the fence. The exposed roots offered the perfect perch for her weary body.

She watched as a half dozen men from the fire department took control of the scene. With the help of the security officer on duty, three of the firefighters set up a perimeter, shooing away personnel and any clutter accumulated near the cellar entrance. Nick dismissed the crew for the rest of the day, even though most seemed reluctant to leave. It appeared everyone wanted to know what kind of body had been found, and where. One firefighter talked with Enrique, while Genny led Cutter and another fireman inside the would-be crypt.

A police cruiser arrived on scene, then another. Madison breathed a sigh of relief when she saw a familiar athletic form crawl from the second car. She determined, however, that Brash could start his investigation without her. She was fine right here, thank you.

After a while, Madison became aware of voices behind her. As the crowd grew front and center, the swelling number of people pushed along to the side view of the house. Although the gawkers could not see her sitting on the other side of the large tree, she could easily hear their discussion.

"Been years since we've found a dead body; now *she* shows up, and they're popping up like weeds!" one person harrumphed.

"I wonder who it is this time. First, she finds Ronny Gleason dead in his chicken house, then she watched as Caress Ellingsworth was killed in her own living room. Wonder who she's found this time?"

They could at least get their facts straight, Madison thought sullenly. True, she had witnessed the fight that resulted in the former soap queen's death, but she didn't actually *watch* the murder take place. Secondly, it had been in the actress' dining room, not the living room. And third, she had not been the one to discover this body. *Details, people.*

"This might just be a fancy trick to get more people to watch her TV show," a third person suggested.

"I heard she didn't have a penny to her name, till those TV folks came around and offered her ten thousand dollars to do their show."

There was a discernible sniff. "Why would they pay *her* ten thousand dollars? She's nobody special."

"I heard she and her husband were some sort of fancy socialites in Dallas. Lived in a house almost as big as this one, with a maid for every floor and a cook, too."

Nope, a few thousand feet smaller than this one. No maids, unless you counted the once-a-week cleaning service Gray insisted upon. Definitely no cook. Gray would be pleased with the socialite comment, though, even though it was never my style.

"If she had it so good in Dallas, what's she doing here in Juliet?" one of them asked.

"I heard she's planning on fixing up the Big House, and then selling it to a Japanese couple she knows from Dallas," someone replied.

Huh?

"Humph. That's not what I heard," the sniffing woman said. "I heard her husband had an investment company, but when the housing market went down, so did they. Hard."

A fourth voice spoke with an air of authority. "I heard he was involved in one of those Fonzie schemes. Swindled a bunch of people out of their money. Big, important people, people that were supposed to be their friends. Then the whole pack of them turned on her and she came running back home."

Okay, getting warmer.

"I think you mean Ponzi, not Fonzie. Anyways, Lou Ann Snell said she was fixing up the house on her father's behalf, so he can turn it into a home for troubled youth. Her folks are moving back so they can run it."

"Who would have ever thought Charlie Cessna would become a missionary?" This from the first voice, sounding a bit awed. "He wasn't exactly a bad kid, but he was the only one of Miss Bert's boys to stir up trouble. He tried a little bit of everything, before he found his calling with the Lord."

Another sniff. "If you ask me, it's just a good excuse to run around, traveling the world. Sounds better than to say he gets itchy feet the minute the grass starts to grow beneath them."

You might have a point.

"I hope they don't bring in trouble-makers," one woman fretted. "They had one of those homes over in Navasota, but it closed down after only about a year. They tried to be self-sufficient, but folks got tired of those kids walking around town, trying to pawn off their baked goods and crafts. Always trying to sell you something or get you to pay them for doing odd jobs around the house. When folks finally gave in and did let them fix the fence or paint the porch or cut the grass, they would later notice how things came up missing."

"I certainly hope we don't have to deal with those sorts of shenanigans here."

Still another voice spoke. "I don't think any of you are right. I watched the pilot for the show. It looks like they're fixing up the house for her to live in."

"It's just her and two teenage kids. Why do they need a house this size?"

"To keep it in the family, so to speak. You know Miss Juliet thought of Bertha Hamilton Cessna as her own child. Why else would she have practically given her town to the woman?"

"You're new here. You don't know the whole story."

"I've been here over twenty years," the woman

protested.

"Yes, and thirty years ago Juliet Blakely up and left her estate to her cook's daughter, instead of her most trusted employee like she'd always promised. You can't tell me Bertha Cessna didn't have something on the old woman. Mark my words, she tricked Miss Juliet into leaving her fortune to her."

Ignoring the squabble between the two women, the first person spoke. "I went inside it once, you know. That staircase is absolutely gorgeous, even more so in person than it looks on TV. A half dozen living rooms, sitting rooms, and whatnot. You know Miss Juliet was all about putting on airs. If it was considered proper and dignified, it was in that house."

"Does it really have a famous mural painted on the wall?"

"The artist, at least, was famous. Someone Miss Juliet brought in from Paris, France."

Someone gasped. "Just to paint a wall?"

Miss Sniffster spoke again, her tone disapproving. "I watched the show, too. I think there's something going on between her and that carpenter. I've seen the looks that simmer between them. Shameful, if you ask me. She's a widow, after all, and still in mourning."

Madison strained to hear the turn of conversation, her face coloring.

"I thought she and Brash deCordova are supposed to be an item!"

Another gasp.

A judgmental, "Tsk tsk."

A murmured, "Has she no shame?"

"The chief of police? I thought he was dating the school nurse," someone said.

The first speaker broke in with an informative, "Brash and the nurse broke up months ago. I saw him having dinner the other night with that pretty, blond producer for the show."

He did what? Madison sat up straighter. She pressed her shoulders back against the tree, desperate to hear the conversation, even more desperate to remain invisible.

Oblivious to the crack working its way across Madison's heart, the woman continued to speak. "They looked mighty cozy if you ask me, especially after they finished off that bottle of wine."

Madison forced herself to breathe normally. She had no claim on Brash deCordova. When he said he would wait for her, he had not mentioned whether or not his patience came with a time limit. And even though the man said he was not interested in any woman other than her, he had the right to change his mind.

I don't have time for a man in my life right now, she reminded herself for the hundredth time. It normally took just one look into the chief's soulful brown eyes to forget that fact. *Even his affection came with stipulations. I have to trust him explicitly. No halfway, he said. But I have Blake and Bethani to think of. They are my whole world, and the only thing I need to be concentrating on. Them and this house. If Brash deCordova can't respect that, he can go jump in a lake.*

No, make that a wine barrel. And he can take Amanda Hooper with him!

Brave words, but her heart still smarted.

3

Brash deCordova propped both hands upon jean-clad hips and stood back to survey the scene before him.

Cutter Montgomery and his team of volunteer firefighters slowly worked their way toward the waiting coroner's van, carrying the stretcher with the skeletal remains upon it. A sheet covered the bones and shielded the disturbing sight from curious eyes. Even though the show called it a wrap and sent their crews home for the day, it hardly meant there was no longer a crowd.

News of finding a dead body spread like wildfire through the sister towns of Juliet and Naomi. With just two thousand residents between them, the combustion did not take long. Now dozens of people crowded along the street, pushing against the ornate fence, hoping to get a glimpse of something gossip worthy. The gorier, it seemed, the better.

Along with the cameras from *Home Again,* reporters from the local television channel chronicled the event via a live news feed. Reporters from several nearby newspapers now trampled the grass around the Big House, pushing their way in front of the crowd gathered out front.

Shaking his head in disgust, Brash perused the dozen or so people still scattered about the front of the mansion. He saw Genesis on the front porch, which meant Madison was sure to be nearby... His eyes warmed as he located her off to the left, solemnly watching as the doors closed on the coroner's vehicle. Brash's mouth tugged downward as he noticed the celebrity carpenter hovering close to her side, but there was no time to storm to the porch and stake his claim; Cutter was already calling his name.

Did he even have a claim? Brash wondered as he crossed the lawn. Things were so unsettled between him and Maddy. Weeks ago, he had made his position clear: he wanted a future with her, but he refused to do halfway. He told her to go home, get her head together, and let him know when she was ready to trust him.

He was still waiting for her call.

Maybe she would never call. Maybe she would never trust him. Apparently, her deceased husband had done a real number on her. Maybe the scars went deeper than he imagined. Maybe he was wasting his time, waiting for a call that would never come.

Reluctant to believe that, Brash half-listened to what Cutter had to say. The younger man assured him the fire department had secured the area and would continue to keep the crowd at bay. If Brash could offer a few words to the press, Cutter and his men would take care of the rest.

Showing less enthusiasm than if he faced a firing squad, Brash made a very brief statement in the impromptu press release. Steadfastly declining to answer any questions, he encouraged the reporters — and the crowd — to go home and await further information as it became available.

He did not approach Madison until he was satisfied that most of the people heeded his suggestion. The crowd finally thinned, and the news crews packed up and headed out.

Nick Vilardi noticed his approach before the women did. He shot off the porch railing and met the police chief as he started up the steps, bombarding him with questions. "Do you have any idea how long we'll be delayed? We have a very tight schedule. Will we be able to work tomorrow?"

Pushing the brim of his cowboy hat up with a flick of his finger, Brash gave the dark-haired man a cool look of assessment. Tension already simmered between them, thickening the air whenever they were thrown together; both were aware of the other's interest in Madison. More than once, their respective jobs had put them at odds. Nick had the best interests of the show at heart, whereas Brash was there to protect Maddy and the residents of the towns. If he happened to protect his own interest in Maddy in the process, all the better.

With slow, deliberate movement, Brash took the final step onto the porch, therefore exaggerating his height advantage. He looked down his nose at the other man, best he could; with only a two-inch cushion, the gesture was not nearly as intimidating as he would have liked.

"I'm sorry if finding a dead body doesn't fit in with your schedule, Nick." The words were amiable enough but delivered with an edge.

"It's a skeleton, Brash." Nick's voice was every bit as condescending as the officer's. "A good thirty or forty years past a dead body."

"Yes, but it belonged to someone. It's my duty to find out who that someone was, and I don't need a dozen or so extra people milling around, hampering the process."

"Surely you don't expect to find any evidence after

all this time!"

In answer, Brash crooked his brow in his signature expression: half frown, half-arched eyebrow, nostrils slightly flared. He had perfected the look years ago, during his days as a college football coach. One crooked brow could silence the most vehement outburst. The imperial gesture had served him even better as an officer of the law.

To his own credit, Nick met his domineering gaze straight on.

"Brash?" Madison's voice broke through the men's silent standoff.

"Maddy."

Other people surrounded them, but something in the low timbre of his voice made the greeting intimate. She rewarded him with a shy smile.

Mindful of the two other women on the porch, Brash forced his hungry gaze off Madison's pale face as he moved their way. "Hello, ladies. Genesis, Amanda." He nodded to each woman as he spoke, but his eyes soon returned to Madison. "It's been an eventful day. I suggest you all go home and relax for the rest of the day."

Madison's hazel eyes flew to his. "Relax? There's a dead body beneath my house."

"Not anymore," he reminded her. "And it's obviously been there for quite a few years, whether anyone was aware of it or not."

She ran her hands up and down her arms, warding off the chill only she could feel. Someone had called her to the porch earlier, so here she still sat, above the spot where someone had died. "I know," she conceded. "But it's still rather creepy, knowing someone died down there. And knowing that the secret staircase led up to Miss Juliet's bedroom..."

"It is rather curious; I'll give you that."

"I wonder if we'll ever know why she had all those secret passages," Genesis said, shaking her head in contemplation. "What does this make, Nick, like three or four so far?"

"At least," the carpenter agreed.

Amanda Hooper joined in the conversation. "This house was built in 1915, far too late to be a part of the Underground Railroad. I'm not familiar with Texas history, but was there anything happening in the state around that time that would have warranted hidden passageways and secrecy?"

Brash searched his memory banks. "Nothing major that I can think of," he said. "Oil production was growing, cotton was still king, and railroads couldn't lay tracks fast enough. If I remember my history right, the biggest issues of the day were pushing for prohibition and the women's right to vote."

"Prostitution and the Klan were still big then," Madison added. She was a bit of a history buff. "And there was some sort of threat posed by the Mexican Revolution, where there was a radical scheme to kill all white men over a certain age. But most of that trouble was down along the border, not here in the Brazos Valley. I can't imagine Miss Juliet being affected by any of the issues of the day. Certainly not enough to put in all these secret passageways."

"She must have had her reasons, imagined or otherwise," Nick rationalized. He turned to give Brash a direct look. "The real question is, how is this newest discovery going to affect our schedule?"

Brash barely contained his sigh. "I have more investigating I need to do, more photos I want to take." He glanced Madison's way, noting the worry written upon her face. He couldn't care less about disrupting Vilardi's tight schedule, but it was Madison and her twins who would suffer because of a delay. Besides, the sooner Nick Vilardi finished this job, the sooner he would be gone from their lives.

Hoping to reassure her, Brash offered Madison a wink that the carpenter could not see. Then he elaborated. "The master bedroom, staircase, and cellar will be under strict quarantine. But if you can guarantee your workers will not interfere with the investigation, I see no reason why work can't resume tomorrow morning."

Nick was not appeased. "We're scheduled to start work in the bedroom by the end of the week."

"Then re-schedule it."

"You obviously don't understand how the re-modeling process works. We have coordinated specific workers, deliveries, even television crews, all based on a very carefully constructed schedule. One change in that schedule can disrupt the entire thing."

Brash was unaffected. With another crook of his brow, his reply came out with a note of finality. "And you obviously do not understand how the process of the law works. I can shut down specific portions of the house, or I can shut down the whole thing. Your choice."

A nerve twitched in Nick's tightly clenched jaw. He stared at the lawman for a long moment, trying to find a chink in the granite facade.

"Fine," he said at last, his tone clipped. "I'll see to it that your investigation is not disturbed."

"Excellent." Brash turned toward Madison, all but dismissing the other man. "Maddy, may I have a word with you?"

She glanced down at her watch. "Sure. I want to pick the kids up from school anyway. We can talk on the way to my car."

He offered his hand as she stood from the chair. He knew cameras were rolling in the background, recording their every move. He knew Genesis watched the process with a twinkle in her eye. The light in Vilardi's gaze was not nearly as friendly, nor was the slightly wounded look in Amanda Hooper's pretty face. He knew the producer had a bit of a crush on him, even though he had never encouraged her. Dinner last week had been strictly business.

In spite of it all, Brash very deliberately wove his fingers through Madison's and guided her off the porch. He could not worry about the consequences.

Public or not, he was staking his claim.

Earlier declarations to herself aside, it felt so *right* when Brash took her hand. His touch steadied her nerves and made her feel grounded. Madison murmured a goodbye over her shoulder, allowing the chief of police to lead her off the porch and into the yard. Her car was still across the street.

"How are you holding up, Maddy?" he asked when they were out of earshot from the others.

"I'm okay," she said, but her voice lacked conviction. "Like I said, it's a little disconcerting, knowing someone died down there and simply... rotted away. But as selfish as it sounds, that's not what bothers me the most. It's all the added drama and hoopla of the press and the gossips and the onlookers." She gestured to a few relentless stragglers, still standing along the street watching as the last of the news crews drove away.

"You know how it is. Big news in a small town." He pushed the gate open, releasing her hand as they went through the opening single file.

She felt lost again without his touch. Not stopping to think the action through, she covertly slipped her hand into his once again. She refused to look his way or to acknowledge the surprise she knew would spring onto his face. Brash made no comment, but he gave her hand a gentle squeeze.

"Did you find any clues at all down there?" she asked.

"Not a single one. Tomorrow, we'll rig up better lights so that we can really look around, but to be honest, there isn't much to see. The room was practically empty."

"Except for a skeleton." A shiver accompanied the words.

"Except for a skeleton," he echoed, squeezing her hand again.

"What if it was something bad, something sinister? What if I can't bring myself to live there? We might find out Miss Juliet was hiding some horrible secret all these years."

"You'll cross that bridge when you get to it. Remember, that body has been there for a very long time. If I thought for a single minute you were in any sort of danger, I'd never let you live there. You know that, don't you?" He looked down at her, an intent light in his brown eyes.

The words from earlier echoed in Madison's mind. *I saw him having dinner the other night with that pretty, blond producer... They looked mighty cozy if you ask me.*

She forced the echoes away, reminding herself it was gossip. The unseen person talking about Brash and Amanda Hooper had also insinuated that Madison was somehow responsible for not only the skeleton's discovery, but its actual existence. Given that the skeleton had been there for decades, the implied accusation was ludicrous. Perhaps the rumored dinner date was, as well.

Another voice echoed in her mind, this one warm

and deep.

You're the only woman I'm interested in... I want a future with you, Maddy...

Two months ago, Brash had asked her to trust him. Perhaps she could start trusting him now, giving him the benefit of the doubt. Heavens knew she had been too quick to judge him in the past.

Madison moved a bit closer to his side, tipping her head to rest against his arm. "Yes, Brash," she said quietly. "I do know that."

"I'll keep you updated on anything I find."

"I appreciate that."

They reached her car but lingered with their hands still clasped. "If you're picking the kids up from school, I guess you'd better be going," he said with obvious reluctance.

"I think I should be the one to tell them about this latest body."

He heard the self-censure in her voice. His own held a note of exasperation. "For heaven's sake, it's not your fault, Maddy. You have nothing to feel guilty about."

"The gossip has already started, you know. *'She shows up, and dead bodies start popping up like weeds!'*" She mimicked the words with a sour note.

"Gossip, Maddy. Nothing but gossip."

"I know, but it's still hard to hear."

"So stop listening."

"You make it sound so easy."

A mischievous glimmer slipped into his eyes. With a heart-melting grin, Brash stepped closer and dipped his head, murmuring a few tantalizing words. "We could always give them something else to gossip about..."

She all but groaned. It was so tempting to step into his arms and accept the kiss that eluded them with infuriating seduction.

One of these days, they had both promised. One of these days, they would get around to sharing a kiss. Somehow, something always seemed to get in the way; their fear, perhaps, was the biggest obstacle of all. They instinctively knew that a kiss between them would be magical. That kiss, they both knew, would change everything.

Her voice came out sad. "I think my life is complicated enough right now, without adding more fuel to the flame."

For a moment, she thought he was going to ignore her words and kiss her anyway. Part of her hoped that he would. He cupped her cheek with his large palm and studied her mouth, fascinated by the tip of her tongue as it darted out to moisten her dry lips. "Funny you should say flame," he murmured.

There was nothing amusing about the flame that shot through her now, licking around her with its wicked blaze. Madison struggled to breathe normally, when inside, her lungs were choked with temptation.

A tricked-out pickup truck rumbled along the road behind them, its motor loud and rough. The smoke from its exhaust mingled with the flames that smoldered between them. Blinking away the disappointment of another lost opportunity to kiss her, Brash dropped his hand and moved away with a muttered curse.

"I swear, Maddy," he said thickly, "one of these days, I don't care where we are or who's looking, I'm going to just grab you and kiss you, and get us both out of our misery!"

She surprised herself, being able to laugh at a time like this. Nerves, she supposed. That, or the sheer joy of knowing she had not lost him, after all. She put her hand onto his chest, a bold move in itself. "So you think kissing me would be miserable, do you?" she teased.

He did not share her humor. He rubbed a hand along his neck, easing away the tension gathered there. "Can't be any worse than *not* kissing you," he grumbled.

Madison laughed again, patting his chest. "One day we'll test your theory," she promised. "But not now. Now I'm late to pick up the kids. I have to go."

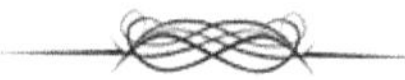

"No fair!" fifteen-year-old Blake grumbled as he folded his lanky form into the backseat. "I called shotgun."

"Yes, but you're all talk," his sister smiled at him with Saccharine sweetness. "I, on the other hand, am all about action!" She rolled her hands to emphasize her place in the front seat.

"Mo-om! I said it first," Blake insisted.

"You rode in the front seat this morning, so it's your sister's turn."

"I am so ready to get my own car," the boy muttered thickly. "Then I won't have to put up with her smart mouth." Curling his cute face into an ugly grimace, he mimicked his twin's words with an exaggerated flair. "Look at me, I'm all about action! They call me Miss Action. I'm like a real-life action figure, only clumsier. My super talent is tripping over my own feet in the cafeteria."

Bethani whirled around, blond hair flying and blue eyes snapping. "Shut up, you moron! And I only tripped because your friend has, like, size twenty-four feet. He stuck his foot out on purpose, and you let him!"

Ignoring the insults that flew back and forth over the seat, Madison concentrated on pulling out of the school's circular driveway. She waved at another parent and maneuvered her way around two drivers stopped in the middle of the road for a chat. As she pulled out of the school property, she tuned back in to the argument.

"I can't wait until we move into the Big House, so that I can have the entire third floor to myself!" Bethani declared, stuffing her arms across her chest as she flounced back around to face the front.

"Yeah, the crazies always live in the attic," her brother retorted.

"What is wrong with you two?" Madison demanded. "This isn't like you two to argue. What's going on?"

They immediately launched into their own animated version of the problem, both talking at once. Madison could only pick out a few words, here and there. Most of their complaints were wide and varied. She finally interrupted with a shrill whistle, a tactic she had not used since they were twelve.

"One at a time," she insisted. "Ladies first."

"It's like we live in a fishbowl, Mom," Bethani whined. "We can't even have a good, decent argument at home, because cameras are everywhere. I'm sorry, but I can't live with a goofball like your son and not let off a little steam now and then. It's just not natural."

"At first I thought it would be cool, being on television," Blake pitched in. "But I didn't know it would turn all my friends into jerks. They keep asking if they can come over, hoping they'll wind up on TV. If I let them come, I know they'll act all uber-cool and sophisticated, which will just come across as stupid. But if I don't invite them, they accuse me of being stuck-up and hogging all the fame for myself."

Guilt riddled Madison's heart. "I'm sorry. I guess this is all my fault. I never realized how hard this would be on all of us, living under the microscope like we are."

"There's no privacy," Bethani lamented. "I can't walk around in my cute little pajamas without a robe. I have to fix my hair and makeup before I even come out of my room every morning. I —"

"So she won't wind up on the next *Bride of Frankenstein* movie," Blake interjected.

"— have to be careful of what I say while I'm on the phone." Bethani ignored her brother's comment as she continued to bemoan the downfalls of fame. "I almost let it slip the other day that Kevin Johnson asked me out, when everyone knows he's supposed to like Kaci Gill. She's breaking up with Jeff just so Kevin will ask her to prom."

"You are not going to prom, young lady. You are only a freshman." Madison was quick to set the matter straight.

"I would never do that to Kaci. We're cheerleader sisters. And by the way, I heard the movie comment, moron. They'd never cast me as your bride. That would be sick."

They bickered again, requiring more interference from their mother. "Do the cameras really make you this tense?" Madison asked. "Maybe I can talk to Amanda and have her take them down at home. Surely, they can get enough footage from the cameras at the Big House. I'm sorry. I had no idea how miserable you two were with this."

"It's not your fault, Mom," Blake admitted grudgingly. "We all agreed to this. We all decided this was the best way to get the house remodeled."

"It was the *only* way," Madison corrected softly. "But you're right, it's hard to act natural when you know anything you say or do might end up on national television. And whether I like it or not, arguing is a natural part of being brother and sister."

"So are you saying you'll pull over on the side of the road and let us duke it out?" Bethani grinned, her blue eyes twinkling. "Because I can totally take him, you know."

"I didn't say a thing about fighting, just arguing. But enough of all that. There's something I need to tell you two. Something happened at the Big House today while we were filming."

"What? You found another secret passageway?" her son asked.

"Actually, yes. And that led to the discovery of a... well, we discovered a dead body. A skeleton."

"Another dead body?" Blake all but shrieked. "Are you kidding me? I've heard of chick magnets. I mean, you're looking at one." He indicated himself, of course. "But you've gotta be like some kind of corpse magnet. Seriously, Mom, this is the third time!"

"Yes, dear, I am aware of that."

Bethani was much more subdued. "A skeleton? Like, a real-live-but-not-anymore *people* skeleton?"

"Yes, Beth, a people skeleton."

The teen crossed her arms in front of her again. "If you found it in the attic, I'm switching rooms with Blake. I swear, I'm not staying on the third floor, that close to the attic."

"We didn't find it in the attic. We found it in the cellar. In a hidden room, more or less *under* the cellar, in fact."

"A hidden room? Cool!" Blake's blue eyes lit with interest.

"What's with all the crazy secret passages? Was Miss Juliet like a spy or something?" Bethani asked.

Madison laughed. "No, I don't think she was a spy."

"Did it reek? Did it smell like a dead rat?" Blake wanted to know.

"It was a skeleton, Blake. Decades past the reeking stage."

"So why was there a body down there?" Bethani asked.

"That, my dear, is the million-dollar question."

"Maybe Granny Bert remembers something."

"Looks like we can ask her. Her car is home. And it looks like Miss Sybille is here, too."

"Please, Lord, don't let them be doing granny aerobics again," Blake said, pressing his hands together as he issued the brief prayer. "My eyes are still scarred from the last time."

Bertha Cessna came to the door, watching them pile from the car as she sipped on one of her infamous smoothies. Her shrewd eyes were trained on her granddaughter.

"Is it true?" she asked before Madison even came through the door.

Huffing out a sigh, Maddy nodded. "It's true. One of the workers found a skeleton, in a secret room accessed from Miss Juliet's bedroom."

"Male or female?"

Madison lifted one shoulder. "Who knows?"

"So maybe the old prude wasn't as prudish as we all thought, eh?"

"She definitely had a thing for secret passages. Blake, don't leave your backpack in the middle of the floor."

Technically obeying his mother's directive, the fifteen-year-old shoved the bag against the edge of the sofa with the toe of his shoe. "I'm starved," he announced on his way toward the kitchen.

"There's a little of my smoothie left in the blender, if you want it," Granny Bert offered.

"Thanks, but I'll leave that for Beth. By the way, what's for dinner? All this talk about skeletons has made me hungry for ribs."

"You are so gross, Blakely Grayson Reynolds," his sister declared, following him from the room.

"They've been like this since I picked them up from school," Madison sighed. She dropped wearily into an armchair, lifting her hand in greeting to the elderly woman on the sofa. "Hey, Miss Sybille."

"And hello to you, Miss Dead Body Collector." Her grandmother's best friend half-snickered, half-snorted at her own witty attempt at humor. "I don't think I've ever known anyone with quite such a talent as yours."

"Why does everyone keep saying that?" Madison moaned. "I didn't even find this body, a worker did. And it's not really a body. It's an old pile of bones."

"Still, it's the third time you've been at the scene of a discovered body."

"I think it's more of a curse than a talent," she muttered. "Granny, did you know anything about a sub-cellar?"

"Miss Juliet didn't like us playing down in the basement," her grandmother recalled. "There was an old cistern down there, and she said it was dangerous. I remember going down there a few times with Mama to gather root vegetables and to store foods for the winter. When I was very young, the maids still did some of the laundry down there, and I got to watch a few times when they boiled sheets. That was before Miss Juliet went high-tech and bought a wringer-type washing machine."

Boiling sheets? There were times, like now, when Madison forgot that her grandmother had lived through eight decades of modern invention. Back when Bertha Hamilton Cessna was a child, doing the laundry must have been quite the chore. Lucky for Madison, renovation plans called for a state-of-the-art washing machine in not one, but two new laundry rooms, compliments of Valco Incorporated.

"It was at the back of the cellar, behind the cistern and a big area used as storage," Madison explained. "Hidden behind a wall and apparently dug at a later date. Compared to the rest of the space, this room was very primitive." Madison shivered, recalling the cold earthen walls and the crude bed, bearing bones.

"Never knew it existed. Apparently few others did, either, or the body would have been discovered long ago."

"Remember those grand parties Miss Juliet used to throw on Founder's Day? Wanda and I were talking about them just the other day." Miss Sybille's wrinkled face transformed with a smile. "That old house was really something in its day!"

While the two women reminisced over past days of glory at the Big House, Madison all but tuned them out. More relevant matters occupied her mind, namely a pair of bickering teenagers, upcoming jobs she had to prepare for, and what, indeed, was for supper. Ribs did not hold the same appeal to her right now as they did to her ever-starving son.

"So what will you do about it?" Granny Bert asked. When she repeated herself, Madison realized the question was directed at her.

"I'm sorry, what was that?"

"I asked what you were going to do about the skeleton."

"I-I don't suppose *I* will do anything. As far as I'm concerned, it's a matter for the authorities."

"No clues to the identity?"

"Not really. It was obviously very old. It looked to be average size, average height. Just bones." Madison shrugged.

"Sounds like half my friends," Granny Bert mused.

"Brash said we could resume work, as long as no one disturbed certain areas, the master bedroom included." She paused to frown. "Of course, given that we discovered the hidden staircase leading down to the room with the bones, I might have to rethink my choice of master. I don't like the thought of someone being able to access my bedroom from the basement."

"That is a bit curious," Granny Bert said. "I wonder what Miss Juliet was thinking when she put in that secret passage..."

"Was she already married when she had the house built?"

"No, Darwin Blakely didn't come along for another year or so."

Madison was familiar with the story. Saddled with spoiled and jealous offspring, the only way Bertram Randolph could keep peace within the family was to separate his feuding daughters, giving them each the land and opportunity to develop her very own town. The town of Juliet formed on the south side of the railroad track, Naomi to the north. A strip of common ground remained between the two, designated for a shared water well, train depot, school, and other such municipal necessities. The wealthy cotton baron built identical houses for his daughters, but let each woman develop her namesake town to her own liking. Soon after, Bertram Randolph took gravely ill and called in a specialist from Philadelphia. Both women promptly fell in love with the handsome dandy. In the end, Juliet won his hand in marriage, but Naomi bore his child. The doctor died in an accident before the child was even born, leaving both women to grieve alone. To this day, the two towns were divided by social stigma and bitter rivalries.

"Maybe Miss Juliet had a secret lover?" Madison speculated.

"I don't know about that," her grandmother frowned. "Miss Juliet was a bit of a prude. All prim and proper, all about show. I was fond of the ole gal, but to tell you the truth, she was a bit boring. I don't think she had it in her to do anything as daring as take a lover."

"There had to be some reason for all the hidden

passages."

"True, but I doubt it was to sneak in a lover."

"But it was definitely to sneak *something*, or else there was no need for secrecy."

"I guess you'll never know. The men who built that house are long since dead and buried," Miss Sybille ruminated.

"Or they might be stuffed in some other secret room we haven't found yet." Granny Bert's voice sounded surprisingly hopeful.

"Granny! What a terrible thing to say," Madison chided.

"Madison, sometimes you are so much like Miss Juliet I could swear you two were blood related. You worry too much about what people think, what looks proper and 'politically correct.'" Her grandmother's gnarled and bony fingers made air quotes around the words, before she propped her hands upon her hips. "Admit it. Didn't finding that skeleton make you feel more alive? Wouldn't you just love to sink your teeth into another really good mystery?"

Fully exasperated, Madison rolled her eyes. "I have enough going on in my life right now, thank you, without worrying about a death that obviously took place fifty to a hundred years ago. And for the last time, *I* didn't find the skeleton!"

"But you have to admit," her grandmother insisted gleefully, "getting to the bottom of this one is likely to be a doozy!"

4

"Thank you for agreeing to meet with me," Allen Wynn said. "I caught the news. I know you had a rough day yesterday." He pulled out a chair for Madison, waiting for her to have a seat before taking his own.

They met at *New Beginnings*, which had become Madison's unofficial office. Actually, her *official* unofficial office was normally the back booth, but a man currently occupied that space, forcing her and her client to sit at a nearby table. It lacked the feeling of inclusion, but given that they were, indeed, meeting at a public place of business, Madison knew she could not complain. She looked forward to the day when her office was completed at the Big House and she could meet with clients there.

Ignoring the reference to the day before, she smiled at her former classmate. "I'm happy to help, Allen. What can I do for you?"

"It's Hank Adams. The man is getting more cantankerous by the day." Allen shuffled a hand through his light brown hair, reflecting his frustrations. "We've been neighbors my entire life. He's normally a nice enough guy, but the older he gets, the meaner he's become. He's being downright unreasonable about this property dispute."

Allen was a member of the 'old' Wynn family, which was as much an institution in Juliet as the Cessna and Hamilton families were. The 'new' Nguyens — spelled differently but pronounced the same — had been in the area for less than ten years. Like Bertram Randolph, the Wynn family had settled in River County during the 1800s. Much of their property edged the eastern boundaries of Juliet, and some butted up to Hank Adams' land.

"If I remember correctly, it's just one specific strip of land that's causing the problem, along the foot of Pine Bluff." Madison had worked on this very case during her brief and miserable six-day stint for the local surveyor.

"Yes, that's right," Allen confirmed. "You know how folks have always done things around here. If they were building a fence in a wooded area, they just attached the barbed wire to the nearest tree. Technically, one or the other of the landowners might lose a foot here, gain another two feet there. The next time the fence was repaired, the line might shift a bit more, but by silent code of ethics, it was always in the opposite direction. That way, no one person repeatedly lost footage. It's been done that way for years."

A waitress slid up to the table, offering menus and a friendly smile. "Hey there, Miss Maddy. Mr. Wynn. What can I getcha?"

"I'll have a glass of water, Shilo Dawne," Madison smiled.

Allen waved away the menu. "I'd love a glass of Genny's sweet tea."

"Can I bring you a couple of Gennydoodle cookies?"

Maddy's voice sagged with regret. "Not for me, I'm afraid."

"Not for me, either. Gotta watch my girlish figure." Allen winked as he patted his generous waistline.

Once the waitress was gone, he turned back to the topic at hand. "Back about fifty years ago, Dad put up a new fence around the back of the property. There's a gully at the bottom of the bluffs, and Dad remembers that Hank and his son stirred a real to-do, insisting the fence be built around the gully, even though it made it as crooked as a snake.

"Three years ago, Dad divided his land between we three kids, so he had the property surveyed. No real surprise, but it turned out the fence line wasn't in the exact spot it should have been. In one thicket, Hank's fence came over onto our side by as much as six feet. In another, we had five feet of his land under our fence. In all, it amounts to less than seven or eight acres, most of it a useless gully and thick woods. I ended up with the section of land that joins Hank, so I tried talking to him about straightening out the fence to make it a bit more uniform."

Madison remembered the property all too well. She had accompanied Darla Mullins on the survey — one day of it, anyway — and recalled the heavily wooded thickets and bushy tree lines that dotted the land.

"Let me guess. He thinks you are being unfair, taking the quality land for yourself and giving him the thickets and gully."

"You would think, but actually, it's quite the opposite. He wants the woods around the gully. He insists that the trees belong to him and he refuses to acknowledge otherwise."

"Is there anything special about these trees? What kind are they?"

Allen shrugged. "Just like the rest of the trees on the place. A mix of post oaks, elms, pine, a few ash, maybe a blackjack or two. Nothing special. He and his son were so adamant about it, they almost convinced me the first survey was wrong. So I paid for a second one to be done, this one by Boundaries Surveying. Unfortunately, Darla Mullins died before the final paperwork was filed."

"And while I'm happy to take you on as a client, I'm not sure what it is you expect me to do," Madison interjected. She smiled up at Shilo Dawne as she delivered their drinks.

"To be honest, neither do I, but I know I have to do something. Hank has become so paranoid, he filed a restraining order against me. I'm not allowed to step foot on his property, even the part that is, in fact, my own land."

"It sounds like you need a lawyer, Allen, not me."

"And I plan to get one. But not until I find out what's so special about that particular piece of land. That's where you come in."

"I'm listening."

"I just want you to go over the fence, look around, see if you can tell what's going on. I don't know, maybe he's growing marijuana over there. That would explain the paranoia."

"Hank Adams is almost as old as my grandmother! You don't honestly think he's growing marijuana, do you?"

"I have no idea. Greed does strange things to people of all ages. Why else does he refuse to let anyone over there, even the survey team? Both surveyors had a heck of a time, getting permission to access his land in order to do their jobs properly. He's being entirely unreasonable. Not to mention flat-out wrong."

"If it's so cut and dry, why not just let an attorney argue the matter for you?"

"He's my neighbor, Maddy. I've known the man my entire life. And like you pointed out, he's close to eighty years old. I don't want to sue him, not if I have any other choice. I'm trying to be reasonable. If he would give me a legitimate reason, or even just talk to me, I would drop the whole thing. It's not a lot of land in question, after all. But most of our correspondence is done through his son and grandson. According to them, Hank has dug in his heels and refuses to budge."

They discussed strategy as they sipped their cold beverages. Several people spoke as they passed their table, reminding Madison that she really needed an office. It was one of the first rooms scheduled to be finished in the renovation. Given that a television show would be filmed all around it — though not inside the office, once completed — Madison wondered if it could offer more privacy than meeting here at the café. She hated to admit it, but she might be forced to rent an office somewhere in town, even though she had no budget for such a luxury.

"So we're set?" Allen confirmed with a smile. He pushed the signed contract toward her, the all-important check for the down payment lying on top. "You think you can do this?"

"I can tell you that I'll give you my best efforts."

"And that's all anyone can really ask, now isn't it?" Allen tapped the table. "Good meeting. I'll be in touch."

Before Madison could gather her paperwork and leave, an unfamiliar woman timidly approached her table. "Madison Reynolds?"

"Yes, that's me."

The woman tucked a string of brown hair behind her ear and shifted from one foot to the next, then back again. She was small, thin, with pale skin, and watery blue eyes that skittered away when Madison's gaze made contact. Her lackluster hair hung around her gaunt face in dejection. Although the woman was well dressed, Madison's first thought was *drug addict, begging for money.*

A long moment stretched between them, before the

woman finally blurted, "I-I need your help."

Madison bit back a sigh. *Definitely a druggie.*

To her surprise, the woman continued. "I need to hire you."

"Hire me?"

A flash of bravery flared in the woman's eyes as she looked directly at Madison. "That's what you do, isn't it? Take on odd clients?"

"Well, yes, we are a temporary employment service..."

Her chin lifted a notch and her voice grew stronger. "I have the money, if that's what you're worried about."

"No, it's not that. I was simply surprised..." Realizing she fumbled matters, Madison stood and extended her hand. "I'm sorry. Let's start over. Hi, I'm Madison Reynolds. And you are...?"

"Lisa Redmond."

She recognized the last name, if nothing more. "Ah. Please, have a seat and tell me how I can help you."

Once settled, Lisa Redmond dropped her eyes again and studied her bitten nails.

Madison prompted the conversation with a friendly, "So? Are you related to the Redmonds here in Naomi? I don't believe I've seen you around before."

"Oh, I live in Naomi," the woman confirmed with a nod. "And yes, I'm related. In a way. I'm married to Barry Redmond."

Madison tried to hide her surprise. She had gone to school with Barry and remembered him as being quite the jerk. A typical misfit with money, he liked flashy cars and flashy girls. Back in high school, he would never have given a second glance to the pale, washed-out woman before her.

Lisa caught the look Madison unsuccessfully tried to disguise. A sad smile flitted over her face as she misinterpreted. "You're remembering his first wife.

Vivian, the blond bombshell."

"No, I—"

"Or his second wife, Melanie. Same figure, different coloring?"

"No—"

"Third wife? Kilala, the one that spoke no English? He met her in Japan and brought her home for three months of wedded bliss. No talking, just... well, you know." She blushed before repeating the crass words she no doubt heard too often. With a resigned sigh, she explained, "I'm wife number four."

"Actually, I lost track of Barry after we graduated from high school."

"I doubt he's changed much in twenty years. He's still into fast cars and women." With a twist of her lips that could have been a wry smile, Lisa Redmond explained further. "That's why I want to hire you. I think Barry is looking for wife number five."

"I'm not sure how I can help you, Mrs. Redmond."

"I just confided a very personal matter to you. Please, call me Lisa."

Thinking this conversation sounded too familiar — much like the one with George Gail Burton two months ago — Madison felt the need to explain her company's primary goal. In her head, she shuffled through previous assignments, trying to find her focus area. Unfortunately, she was desperate enough to take on the oddest of jobs, meaning there was not a single common thread among her previous clients, other than the paycheck in the end. Before she could start to feel sorry for herself, Lisa pushed an envelope toward her.

"Lucy Nguyen and George Gail Burton both say a thousand dollars is hardly enough for the excellent work you do. So I put twice as much in there. Is two thousand enough for a retainer?"

Trying to look professional, Madison tamped down

the ridiculous giddiness bubbling inside her. *Two thousand is enough to have me dance at your next wedding.* "I'm sure it will be," she said with a demur murmur. "However, I still don't know what you're hiring me to do."

"Gather evidence that my husband is having an affair."

Madison almost groaned aloud. *This sounds exactly like George Gail's case. And look where that got me. Almost killed.*

Still, it was two thousand dollars...

"Well—"

To be so timid, Lisa Redmond had a habit of breaking in whenever Madison tried to speak. "I want photographic proof that Barry is seeing someone else. I know for a fact that he divorced both Kilala and Melanie without paying them a dime, claiming they were the ones at fault. I don't want that to happen to me. I hear he's been seen around town, even at this very restaurant, with more than one woman. I want you to take pictures, record conversations, gather as much evidence as you can to make certain I leave this marriage a wealthy woman."

So much for timid.

Remembering that Genesis had reported seeing Barry Redmond here with Angie Jones, Madison decided the task shouldn't be so difficult. Within ten minutes, she had a signed contract, another new client, and a satisfied smile upon her face.

On a roll, she pulled out her phone and scrolled through her list of recent contacts. Spotting the name she needed, she tapped the number and waited for the phone to ring.

By way of greeting, the man on the other end answered with, "Hey, dollface, what's up?"

"I need a favor, Derron."

"Anything for you, boss lady. Name it."

"I need a file. I need inside Boundaries."

"Anything but that."

"Please, Derron? I know it's painful for you, going back into the office, seeing your mother's things. But you know that sooner or later, you have to do something with all those files."

There was a heavy sigh on the other end of the line. "Yes, I know. But I much prefer the 'later' option."

"I'm actually trying to help you out here," Madison wheedled. "I'll relieve you of at least one of those files."

"Make it an entire filing cabinet, and we have a deal."

"I-I don't know about that…"

"Please, please, please?"

"You're doing the puppy dog thing, aren't you?"

"Yes, is it working? My eyes are big and soulful, and just a tad bit adoring."

Madison could not help but laugh. "Oh, all right. But you owe me."

"And I know exactly how I can repay you. I'm going to take you shopping. Your wardrobe is atrocious, girlfriend."

"Hey, what's wrong with my—" She glanced down at her navy slacks, sensible flat-soled shoes, and pale blue sweater set. She didn't even bother with her protest. "Never mind. Just meet me at Boundaries. Three o'clock sound good?"

"Blake has a baseball game, remember?"

"Oh, shoot, I almost forgot!"

On the other end of the line, Derron Mullins laughed. "You *did* forget." He called her out on the fact. "Whatever would you do without me, fair lady?"

"Be late to half the games?"

"Let me finish this last section of fence, and I'll meet you there. Give me a half hour."

"Thanks, Derron, I appreciate it."

"Tootles, dollface."

"Tootles," she echoed, pressing the *End* button with a satisfied nod.

At least if she had a copy of the survey, she would not be going onto Hank Adams' land blind. He might still accuse her of trespassing, but if she followed the survey exactly, it might come down to a matter of technicality.

And Madison was all about the details.

5

Two days later, Madison donned her hiking boots and headed out to the Wynn/Adams boundary line. Using the old farm truck Allen Wynn left on the property, she drove to the back of the place. Pine Bluff loomed in the near distance, guiding her way to the property in question. While not technically a mountain, the local landmark was high enough to be seen for miles around.

From all accounts, the high ridge itself sat on Adams' property. There was no dispute over ownership of the limestone mesa dotted with scrubby pines. The problem arose a hundred feet from the base of the bluffs. According to Allen, the fence line over-extended its boundaries by as much as six feet in places.

Gathering the laser distance meter she had borrowed from Derron, brightly colored orange chalk, a standard measuring tape, and her cell phone, Madison crawled from the truck. As an afterthought, she grabbed her jacket. It was springtime in Texas, meaning the afternoon would warm quickly, but for now, the morning air was still cool, particularly in the shade. Besides, the pockets came in handy.

After tucking her jeans legs into the tops of her boots to protect them from potential sticker burs and bull nettle, Madison set off toward the woods. Just as Allen claimed, the strands of barbed wire wove a crooked path along the southwest boundary of the tree line.

"Looks like it was done by a drunk Indian," she muttered aloud.

Madison snapped a few photos with her cell phone before crawling through the fence and into the dense thicket on the other side. It took a moment to find a chink in the solid armor of trees. When she deciphered a faint trail into the woods, she hoped it was forged by deer, not the feral hogs known to inhabit the area. The tusked beasts were notoriously mean and dangerous, and not something she wanted to meet up with.

She had to turn back twice. One path was blocked by thick underbrush, another led to a cavernous nest of briers and scrub that she dared not disturb. She tried to take a few measurements, but the limbs tangled low, causing her to duck and hunch most of the way. By the time she reached the other side, her back ached, her jacket ripped, and an array of twigs and leaves rode piggyback in her hair.

Good thing she was watching her step as she exited the thicket. Otherwise, she might have fallen into the deep gully that yawned between her and the base of the bluff. The perimeter of the ravine was as jagged as the fence had been, but it so happened she stepped out at the gully's widest point. Directly at her feet, the ground dropped sharply away, falling to a depth of at least twenty feet.

With great caution, Madison skirted the deep hole and stepped to her right, where a larger patch of earth offered solid footing. She would make her observations from here, thank you very much.

"Geez, no wonder Hank Adams wants to leave the fence where it is," she muttered aloud. "Who in their right mind would want to build a fence down there?" She peered into the ravine, noting the steeply banked sides, the shrubs and young trees poking from the embankment at odd angles, the boscage of crooked trees and bramble that littered the floor of the cavity. "And why would Allen care about the gully, anyway?"

Madison took a few more measurements, making her way along the crooked line of the gully. True, in places there was plenty of room to build a fence. So why did Hank Adams refuse to give up his claim to the trees? She had seen nothing special about the thicket, other than it being dense and prolific. According to the survey and her amateur skills with the meter, the copse definitely fell on Wynn property.

Personally, she did not understand why either man would want to claim the wasted acreage. Between the washed-out earth and the thick undergrowth, the disputed property was unusable. Did it really matter which man had it under fence?

After taking a few more measurements and a half dozen more photos, Madison decided she had done all she could. There was no readily visible reason why Hank Adams wanted the disputed acreage; no marijuana plants in sight, no secret outbuildings, no hidden treasure boxes that she could see. The most interesting thing she spotted was a small cave-like den on the far side of the gully, tucked beneath the limestone walls of Pine Bluff. Most likely, the home belonged to a bobcat or fox. She should go, before the occupant of the den came out to stake its claim.

Particularly if said occupant turns out to be larger than a bobcat. Madison grimaced with the thought, imaging that the lair could belong to a bigger wildcat. Through the years — and definitely through local folklore — a few panthers and leopards were said to roam River County. Sightings were rare, interaction even less common, but occasionally livestock would come up missing, or be found mangled and ripped to shreds. Coyotes were a known threat to ranchers, but some locals insisted that cats did their share of the damage.

Just in case, Madison hurried away from the ravine and its mysterious residents. She wasn't sure that entering the deep woods was a better alternative, but the truck waited for her on the other side, and that was enough to spur her forward.

She did, however, choose a different route, this one a bit toward the southern edge of the boundary line, where the trees did not look quite as populated. It would be a longer walk back to the truck, but hopefully less resistant. As an added bonus, she was able to walk almost the entire way without stooping and bending, other than to dodge an odd limb or two.

Without fighting the undergrowth and thick foliage, Madison could enjoy her walk through the woods. She remembered traipsing through similar woods as a child, joined by her cousins and a grand sense of adventure. Before her grandfather passed away, he taught them all how to identify some of the native trees and plants. To this day, Madison knew to be wary of the deceptive beauty of plants with shiny pointed leaves; Granny Bert's anecdote for poison ivy was to slather the victim in a thick coat of calamine lotion. Madison often wondered which was worse, the itchy whelps left by the plant, or the pasty pink, crackled coating her grandmother applied.

As the trees thinned even more, a quick look down at her GPS coordinates told her the tip of the property line ran roughly where she was standing. She marked the nearest tree with her chalk, on the side that faced Allen's property. "You could build a fence through here easily enough," she determined aloud. "Yet there it is over there, a good ten feet from here... Hmm. Maybe Allen is right to pursue the issue. There's no good reason why Hank Adams should have Wynn property under his fen—"

A rabbit darted across her path, interrupting her narrative as she squealed in surprise. As she laughed at her own foolishness, she heard a snap to her left. The sound was out-of-place in the woods, echoing with a distinct electronic swish. Madison stopped mid-step, looking around cautiously.

There. Up in the tree, almost directly above her. A red light blinked on the game-cam as it captured the rabbit's escape.

Madison glanced around, looking for signs of a deer-stand. Why else would Hank Adams have a game camera set up in the woods? She followed the projected scope of the camera, realizing it aligned directly with the path of least resistance to the fence line.

So it's not a game-cam, it's a spy-cam. He's trying to catch Allen Wynn if he comes onto the property. Geez. Maybe the old man really is paranoid, after all.

Madison recalculated her path, choosing to push through a denser stand of trees to the right, far from the reach of the camera. She scanned the tree for additional cameras, but the one device seemed to be the extent of the old man's paranoia.

Or not. With the next snap, this one distinctly louder, Madison cried out in pain as she wrenched to the ground. Confusion raced through her pain-riddled mind. Had she turned her ankle? It throbbed like the devil. She did not remember a misstep, yet she heard the snap. Was the bone broken? Her palms hurt where she caught herself, and she was fairly certain a stick punctured her knee. But none of that compared to the pain and pressure around her left ankle.

Madison managed to turn herself around and sit

up, so that she could take stock of her situation. She was vaguely aware of dropping the distance meter and cell phone when she fell, but she would worry about that later, after she accessed the damage to her ankle.

"You've got to be kidding me!" she cried in disbelief.

A shiny steel trap clamped securely around her booted foot. *A bear trap?* More likely, a panther trap. She tugged on her foot, but there was no give in the smooth steel jaws. She pulled harder. The only thing she succeeded in moving was the trap itself, pulling it from the hole in which it hid. Her eyes searched for the chain, finally spotting the first thick links as they disappeared into a small trench in the ground, covered well by fallen leaves. After that, the chain seemed to disappear. She overlooked it twice, before she finally realized the thick vine wrapped around the perimeter of a sturdy oak five feet away was actually the chain, cloaked in disguise.

Were panthers smart enough to decipher the threat of a chain? A shiver of apprehension worked its way down her spine. Instinctively she knew. *This trap was meant for a person, not an animal.*

She knew it was fruitless, but she reached for the chain with both hands and tugged with all her might. Her reward was a slight rattle, nothing more. Certainly not freedom.

"Don't panic." Madison kept her voice calm and steady as she instructed her brain to stay focused. "There's got to be a way to open the trap and get your foot out." She looked around, spotted a sturdy-looking stick, and tried to use it as leverage to pry the trap open.

It snapped as easily as a pretzel.

"Okay, still no reason to panic." She tugged on her foot again, realizing that the trap had snagged her foot on an angle, catching as much of her heel as it had the leather uppers of her boot. If she kept trashing her foot around, she might make the situation worse. If her heel slipped, the steel would tighten even more around her ankle. Worse, a sudden shift might cause the mighty jaws to snap again, this time breaking the bone.

"How do you do it, Madison Cessna Reynolds? How do you get yourself into these predicaments?" she chided herself. For some reason, her mother-in-law sprang to mind. Wouldn't Annette find this latest situation distasteful: the wife of her beloved late son, wallowing around on the forest floor, bound like a wild animal to a tree? Madison had no idea why she thought of the woman now, not when there were more pressing issues at hand. Namely, how she was going to free her wild animal self.

She spied her cell phone, half-buried in the leaves several feet away. She could probably reach it if she tried hard enough, but she hated the thought of calling for help. And whom, exactly, would she call? She may or may not be trespassing, depending on whose legal side you were on, Wynn or Adams. The possibility — or probability — of breaking the law ruled out calling Brash.

Dear Genny would gladly come to her rescue, but the baker knew no more about throwing traps than Madison did. That excluded her best friend. Cutter would come, but that would more than likely involve sirens and firetrucks, which would, in turn, involve the law. So calling Cutter was out. Granny Bert would come, of course, but she would probably be too busy laughing to offer any real help. Derron was her most likely source of help, but he was out of town today.

As she ruled out her options one-by-one, her ankle continued to throb. *It's probably swelling, too*, she thought. She leaned forward to unlace her hiking boot, loosening the tongue. She tested her ankle, wiggling it a bit to see how badly it was swollen.

When her foot moved easily within the confines of the leather, an idea took shape. Still seated in the dirt, she searched the ground around her, until she found a suitable stone and a chunk of hard, dried wood. She squeezed them into the trap, alongside her wedged boot. It took additional twigs and more rocks, but after five minutes of intense effort, Madison had the space around her boot packed with trash. Satisfied that the trap was wedged wide open and could not tighten around her, she gingerly began to work her foot free. Lips pressed into a grimace, she made the slow and painful withdrawal. A final tug, and her foot slid free, just as the packing gave way and the trap snapped again.

Exhausted, as much mentally as physically, Madison lay flat-out on the twig-littered ground, allowing her muscles to relax. She might have lain there longer, but the sounds of movement in the underbrush brought to mind the hogs and rumored panthers of the area. Even when she spotted the harmless armadillo, rooting noisily among the leaves left from autumn, she knew it was time to go. Worse than the wild animals, what if Hank Adams found her here, on the side of the fence he claimed as his property?

She managed to stand, even though it hurt to put weight on her left foot. With a suspicious eye, she scanned the area in front of her for more hidden traps. Earlier, she had been too concerned with cameras to think about booby-traps, but now it seemed she had to search from top to bottom, just to navigate the remaining four feet to the fence. She found a long limb and poked it along the path before her, sweeping the ground for more pitfalls. Satisfied, she hobbled from one tree to the next, using the limb as a sort of crutch.

At the fence, she balanced on her right foot, trying

to determine the best way to go through. Should she lead on her good foot, or her bad? As she contemplated the issue, she made certain the items in her pocket were stuffed in good and tight, and in no danger of falling out when she crawled through the barbed wire.

Instead of tamping the items down more securely, she managed to jerk the distance finder out when she pulled her hand free. It fell onto the top strand of the fence and bounced to the second.

Great. That thing probably costs several hundred dollars, and –

Sparks flew as the instrument hit the barbed wire. Madison heard a pop, then a sizzle. A bit dazed, she realized there was an electrical hot wire running along with the second strand of wire.

Talk about paranoid! Electrical fences, spy-cams, traps... Hank Adams was either psychotic, or he definitely had something to hide on his side of the fence. But what? She hadn't seen a thing worth defending.

Judging from the smoke wafting up from the wires, the meter had shorted out the electrical fence, leaving Madison free to cross the boundary. She got down on her belly and crawled beneath the wires. It was hardly dignified, but she was fairly certain she lost all pretense of dignity the moment she stepped into the thicket. Her hair was littered with trash, her clothes were torn and dirty, she was missing a boot, and she had probably just broken the law.

She could see the truck parked a good fifty yards away. At least the terrain on this side of the fence was fairly flat. It was a slow go, but with help of the pilfered limb and the fine art of hopping, Madison managed to make her way to the vehicle.

The slow journey gave her plenty of time to think. Why did Hank Adams want the thicket and the useless gully beyond? From what she could decipher, all the trees and half the ravine belonged to Allen Wynn. She understood not wanting to build a fence down in the gully, although she was certain it was possible and done countless of times by others. Why not skirt the perimeter and build the fence at least *closer* to the property line?

It had to be something about the trees, or something within the trees. She hadn't gone through the entire thicket, after all. She entered at the densest point, the part closest to the gully and the point least protected. She had exited several yards down, in Rambo territory apparently, leaving the middle section of the trees undisturbed.

"Wonder what pitfalls awaited me there?" she muttered aloud. "A snare? I might have been snatched up and left hanging from a tree. That might have been fun."

She wondered how she avoided electrocution upon entry into the property. Did the electric fence not reach that far? And why no traps or cameras?

Because, you fool, no one else is feeble-minded enough to take the animal trails. A normal person would take the path of least resistance. Proving once again that you, Madison Reynolds, are not normal.

As she hobbled alongside the fence, careful not to touch it, she discovered why she had been spared an electrical shock going in. The wire was broken at a coupling, rendering that section of the hot fence impotent.

At least one thing had been going in her favor today. She tried to appreciate the small blessing as she hobbled the last few feet of the way. Her ankle throbbed, her insides were all shook up, and she was exhausted.

But she was finally, blessedly, back to the truck.

"What happened to you?"

Instead of warm concern, Granny Bert eyed her with suspicion when Madison bumped her way up to the front door. Having left the handy limb behind, Madison had nothing to prop herself upon as she juggled her purse, the borrowed surveying equipment, a box that had been delivered to the front porch, and the front door lock. Hearing the commotion, Granny Bert had come to open the door.

Without preamble, Madison shoved most of her load into her grandmother's arms.

"I turned my ankle." This much was true. She simply left out the part about turning it while stepping into a steel trap.

Granny Bert peered down at her stockinged foot. A bright red toenail poked through the ravaged tip. "Where's your boot?"

"My foot was swelling," Madison answered vaguely. When she got within falling distance, she threw herself onto the sofa and sank thankfully into its cushions. "Good grief, what a day!"

"Is this a new hairstyle I don't know about? Or were you undercover as a tree?" She plucked a twig from Madison's disheveled hair, dislodging a strand of moss. It floated down onto Madison's shoulder, followed by a piece of a leaf.

"Something like that."

"Let's see the foot." With no pretense of trying to be gentle, Granny Bert jerked Madison's pants leg up and inspected her ankle by twisting it painfully in every direction. "Doesn't seem too bad. But let's get the sock off and put some ice on it, just in case."

Madison shielded her eyes with her arm, trying to rest while her grandmother fetched the ice. She jumped when the cold cubes touched her skin.

"How did you say you did this?"

"I didn't."

"Confidential case, or not fit for public consumption?" Granny Bert tossed a glance toward the overhead cameras. It was clear from the eager glint in her eyes that she hoped for the latter.

Madison made a growling sound low in her throat. Amazingly, she had somehow forgotten about the cameras that were ever rolling, intruding into her life even at moments like this. She raised her arm above her head and presented her palm. Speaking to the room at large and its multiple audio devices, her voice was weary as she said, "This segment is strictly forbidden from the cameras and mics. Under no circumstances do you have my permission to air any of this."

The camera was allowed in the common rooms of the house, its purpose to capture conversations pertaining to the remodel. There was a loose agreement that no other scenes would be kept, but already a snippet or two had made its way into the final cut. So far, the random shots had been harmless enough, no more than brief, general scenes that showed a normal family doing normal, everyday things. But Madison knew it was only a matter of time before that changed.

Also by loose agreement, any member of the family could 'opt out' by voicing a disclaimer as Madison had just done. She made a mental note to get the agreement in writing. *Give them an inch, and they'll take a mile. Makes for good television, they say.*

Not certain she fully trusted the production team, even for the conditions listed on paper, Madison dropped her voice to a near-whisper. "Granny, what can you tell me about Hank Adams? You've known him for a long time, haven't you?"

"Only if you call eighty years a long time. Well,

maybe seventy-nine. I think he's a few months younger than me." She frowned as she readjusted the ice pack on Madison's ankle. "Why are you asking about him? Thinking of firing your carpenter and hiring a local team after all?" She flashed a wrinkled smile, reminding her granddaughter of her previous shenanigans. The shrewd older woman had used the threat of hiring Hank Adams and his rag-tag team of helpers to remodel the Big House, claiming it would be far cheaper than allowing Nick Vilardi to do the job. By the time she had finished, the celebrity carpenter was ready to agree to any terms to secure the job. After just a few weeks, he returned with an offer none of them had seen coming: to remodel the entire house at no out-of-pocket expense.

Just out-of-mind expenses, Madison reminded herself. *Stipulations.*

Deliberately speaking loud enough that the mics could hear her, she had a wry comeback. "Replacing them might make life easier."

"What does this have to do with your ankle? Hank is getting hard of seeing. He didn't cause you to have another wreck, did he? Because I don't know how much more your insurance company is willing to overlook, even if your cousin does own the agency."

"No, I didn't have another wreck," Madison snapped testily. "I told you, I turned my ankle."

"He bumped into you at the grocery store? Knocked you off the sidewalk trying to get a Gennydoodle cookie, hot out of the oven? I swear, he's gained ten pounds since Genny opened up."

"Nothing like that. I was just asking you how well you know the man."

Granny Bert shrugged her bony shoulders. "About as well as you know anybody, I suppose, without living with them or being family. We grew up together. Our mamas both worked at the Big House, so our paths crossed even before we started school. There was only a dozen or so students in our grade most years, sometimes as many as twenty, but not enough that you didn't get sick and tired of seeing the same old faces, day in and day out. Hank dropped out around the tenth grade, but he ended up marrying one of my best friends, so it seemed there was no escaping him. Not that I ever wanted to, mind you. Hank and Virgie have been good friends through the years."

"Jimmy Adams is his nephew, right?"

"That's right, Neville's son. Jimmy is partners with your uncle at The Sisters Sale Barn and Ag teacher at the school. One of Hank and Virgie's daughters teaches fourth grade. Their son owns the Gold and Silver Exchange. The Adams family has been in the area for years."

"So what's this about a boundary dispute with Allen Wynn?"

Normally full of all the latest gossip, for a moment her grandmother seemed to falter. "I'm sure it's just a misunderstanding. Both men claim ownership to a small section of land. I doubt it's enough to cause too big a ruckus."

"I wouldn't bet on it," Madison murmured. "From what I can tell, the land belongs to Allen, but Hank is being unreasonable."

"The man can be as stubborn as a mule, that's for sure and certain. But sooner or later, he'll come around."

"I don't know about that. He seems determined to keep Allen off the property in question. But for the life of me, I can't see why. It's nothing but trees and a huge gully that backs up to Pine Bluff."

"Sounds like you've seen the property," Granny Bert observed wisely.

"I worked that week for Boundaries Surveying, you recall. We were surveying that very piece of land when... well, you know." She did not want to re-live the events that led to her overnight hospital stay, nor did she want to mention them with the cameras rolling, disclaimer or not.

"Didn't think you made it quite that far into the place."

Granny Bert always could see straight through her. Madison's shrug was noncommittal. "I take it Hank Adams is hard to get along with."

"Not at all. Why would you think such a thing?"

"Just... an observation."

"Wouldn't have anything to do with the twigs in your hair and the swelling in your foot, would it?"

"That depends. Would you say he's a vindictive man?" A bit of worry seeped into Madison's voice.

"What have you done, child?"

Her eyes darted to the camera. "Nothing."

Lifting Madison's injured foot unceremoniously, Granny Bert held it aloft as she plopped down on the couch. Madison scrambled to move the other leg out of the way as Granny Bert settled in beside her. Only then did she drop Madison's leg to rest upon her lap. "Might as well tell me about it," she said, but she kept her voice conspiratorially low.

"I will. But first, tell me more about Hank."

Granny Bert considered her words before speaking, something she often neglected to do. "Hank grew up poor but honest. The Adams family had lived in River County for years, long before The Sisters existed. When the towns were formed and boundary lines drawn, the Adams' land fell on the outskirts of Naomi. His family, though, worked for Miss Juliet at the Big House. His grandfather, Truman Ford, was the butler, and one of Miss Juliet's most trusted employees. There was always talk that Miss Juliet would leave her estate to Truman and Lily Ford, or at least to their offspring. They died long before her, of course, but Ruth Adams was still living, and so were her boys, Hank and Neville. Fact is, Hank expected to inherit the house. He did odd jobs for Miss Juliet all the time, tinkering around here and there, fixing what was broken, but he never allowed her to pay him. Some say he was doing it because he thought it would all be his one day. Others said he was repaying an old debt his family owed. I never asked. But I do know that when Miss Juliet passed on and her will was read, leaving most everything to me, Hank took it mighty hard. Said a few things he later apologized for. Took years, mind you, but after a while he forgave me for inheriting what he thought should have gone to him."

"What sorts of things did he say to you?"

"I don't exactly remember, not after all these years. To be honest, Hugh Redmond and his bunch were making more noise than Hank, insisting the estate belonged to them. But Hank did say something about past deeds. He insinuated that I had something on Miss Juliet and bribed her into leaving her estate to me. I had no idea what he was talking about, and he refused to elaborate. For the first couple of years, it seemed Hank did everything he could to undermine your grandfather and me. So, yes, I would say that he could be a vindictive man, but his anger only lasted a couple of years. He cooled down, apologized, and we picked up our friendship right where it left off. You might recall, he was a pall bearer at your grandpa's funeral, and if he outlives me, I want him as one at mine." She winked as she added, "Honorary, of course. He's getting too old and feeble to carry even a box of bones. Don't want him dropping the casket and causing a scene."

"Speaking of bones... Have you thought of any

possible explanation for Miss Juliet having a secret staircase in her room? Particularly one that led down to a secret room in the basement?"

"Sybille and I have been chewing on that one. We've wracked our brains, but we can't come up with a plausible reason for any of the hidden passages. In fact, we were thinking of talking to Hank, to see if he had any notions on the matter. Other than me, he probably knows the Big House better than anyone."

"Hmm, that's a thought."

"I also know that Miss Juliet kept a journal, but I've never come across any of them. Of course, I haven't looked through all her books. She was a voracious reader and had a huge library. Which is now yours, by the way, to do with as you may."

"But some of those books are quite valuable!"

Her grandmother shrugged. "So sell them and collect the money. When I sold you the house, I sold you the contents, as well."

There was censure in Madison's stern, "Granny."

The old woman was having none of it. "Get that tone out of your voice. And stop making that face. It might freeze that way." It had been a favorite saying of hers when her boys were young, and it had worked while raising her granddaughter, as well. She waved her wrinkled hand around the crowded room. "I have a house full of my own junk, what do I need with someone else's?"

Knowing she fought a losing battle, Madison sighed and dropped the subject. Her mind was already backtracking. "Miss Juliet kept a journal, huh?"

"For as long as I can remember. I'm sure there must be several volumes, stuffed somewhere in that behemoth of a house. I'd start looking in the bedroom, if I was you. Tell that boyfriend of yours you need in there."

Forgetting to keep her voice low, Madison's outburst held a tad too much protest. "Brash is *not* my boyfriend!"

Granny Bert gave her a knowing look, but her words were scoffing. "Then you're not half as smart as I gave you credit for."

6

Brash gave one last perusal to the primitive room buried deep beneath Juliet Randolph Blakely's historic old home. It offered few clues to its origins, even fewer as to its purpose.

If he had to guess, he thought the room was created after the original structure. Certainly, the materials used were much cruder, suggesting they may have been smuggled in. How, exactly, an eight by ten-foot pit could be dug without anyone noticing was beyond him, but stranger things had been known to happen.

Things like allowing a body to rot away in such a pit.

It had been four days since the gruesome discovery, and still they had no answers. The remains were shipped off to Austin for analysis and DNA testing, but Brash had little hope of getting a hit. It was only bones, after all. Bones of an unknown person from an unknown time period. Where did you even begin on a case like this?

At this point, he had far more questions than he did answers. Whom did the skeleton belong to? A vagrant? Theoretically, someone could have sneaked their way into the underground room anytime within the past hundred years and died there without anyone having known. They could have been sick... injured... bitten by a spider... died of starvation or suffocation...

But if that were the case, wouldn't there have been an odor? Wouldn't it have wafted up the secret staircase into Miss Juliet's room, or out into the upper rooms of the cellar?

So perhaps the skeleton had been a victim. He or she could have been held captive in the tiny room... moved there postmortem... murdered on sight... abandoned and left to die...

If any of those scenarios was correct, this was a case of murder. At the very least, negligent homicide.

But who was the murderer? The victim? They might never know.

The meager clues from the room had all been bagged, tagged, and taken off site. Not that there had been much. The handmade bed was nothing more than four posts topped by a wooden platform. There were remnants of a single bed cover, the last remains of a patchwork quilt long since rotted away. What time had not destroyed, rodents had.

The clothes from the skeleton were in similar condition. Only tatters remained. Much of those had disintegrated upon touch, leaving questions about whether the gray fabric had once been a skirt or a pair of pants. Judging from the boots discovered tucked beneath the bed and the fact that the skeleton was barefoot, it was customary to assume the body was male. But Brash knew better than to jump to conclusions until the facts proved otherwise.

The other furniture in the room consisted of a narrow table and a set of shelves propped precariously against one earthen wall. Long ago, the middle shelf had caved in, sending four glass jars crashing down. A dark, slightly fragrant substance — probably molasses, Brash suspected — had dripped onto the bottom shelf before pooling into a dark stain upon the dirt floor.

Amid the shattered glass and zinc lids, little of the contents from the other jars remained: a few gnawed corncobs, what might have once been a pickle, a small potato now hard as stone. A tin of peaches and another of canned meat were still intact, their labels faded and worn, their contents decades past expiration. On the top shelf, they had discovered a pewter plate, one fork, one knife, and a porcelain teacup, their elaborate designs and fine craftsmanship at odds in the rudimentary setting.

The only other things found in the room were an undecipherable piece of cloth adopted by a family of mice, a tattered Bible, a pencil, and a dog-eared novel with half its cover gnawed away. Brash and his team had extricated the meager items with care and sent them to the state lab for analysis.

There was literally nothing else to see, nothing else to analyze. If someone had, indeed, been living down here, they had existed with minimal comforts and minimal food. Brash shook his head, unable to imagine living in the dark, cramped, windowless space.

The thought of dying down here was even worse.

He would send someone in to take down the lights. The fire department had rigged a string of illumination around the room's perimeter, so that every nook and cranny could be seen and examined. With no more evidence left to gather, Brash saw no reason to leave the lights in place. No one should be down here, anyway. It was still considered an active crime scene, even though an actual crime having been committed was still in question.

Come to think of it, the 'active' part is even more questionable, Brash thought with a grunt. *Doesn't seem to have been any activity down here in decades.*

On a whim, he decided to take the hidden stairway up. The string lighting did little to illuminate the tiny cavern winding its way to the second floor. By only the fourth step, darkness engulfed him. Brash paused in the passageway to listen. At least twelve feet beneath the ground floor of the old mansion, he could hear nothing from above. There was no thump of overhead movement, no echo of voices or machines, not even the sound of air whistling through the man-made shaft. All was silent.

Secret room aside, how did someone build a secret staircase? In the darkness, Brash put out his hand, feeling the rough planks of wood that lined the narrow chamber. He was still in the sub-cellar, still a few feet below the actual basement. Constructing a secret passage down here was conceivable. Dig a vertical tunnel through the clay, line it with wood to keep it from caving in on itself, add steps. Difficult, but doable.

But creating a staircase that passed through existing rooms and walls? How could someone manage that in secret? Brash was not convinced it could be done. That meant Miss Juliet was aware of the hidden staircase. Had probably traveled the steep and narrow passage herself. If that were the case, when was the last time she had come down to the cellar? Before the mysterious person had died down there? Or after?

Brash frowned. Surely, he was not suggesting that the prim and proper esteemed founder of the town was a murderess! Miss Juliet had been dignified and refined, a lady in every sense of the word. Even in the face of public humiliation — her own sister giving birth to her deceased husband's illegitimate child — Juliet Blakely had held her head high and continued to see to the duties of the town. Nor could he fathom Miss Juliet as an accomplice to murder, not even by way of neglecting to report a crime. Had she known of the body in the sub-basement, he was certain she would have reported it.

Flipping on his flashlight, Brash continued up the steep and irregular steps. Their very construction suggested they were a retrofit. In a home built with superb craftsmanship, fine materials, and attention to the most minute detail, he was certain that if the staircase had been in the original blueprint, it would have been much more uniform.

Not only were the stiles irregular, but the walls were not uniform. The higher he climbed, the narrower the passage. The laddered steps turned at random, squeezing into impossible angles. More than once, Brash had to curl his broad shoulders inward to make a tight turn. Forced to duck his head yet again, Brash suspected this segment of the stairwell must pass through the first floor of the home, where retrofitting space for a staircase — even a steep spiral such as this — would have been challenging.

Having lost his sense of perception in the steep and dark assent, Brash stopped and listened. Unlike in the basement, he could now hear the sounds of the house around him. An electrical saw buzzed. Music played from a worker's radio. Hammers pounded, battery-operated screwdrivers whirred. Voices drifted in and out. Feet shuffled above him.

Another frown tugged on the corners of his mouth. Directly above him was the master bedroom, a room he had put under strict quarantine. Hoping to catch the person who dared disobey his order, Brash killed the flashlight and crept his way up the last remaining steps. He paused at the door, listening for voices on the other side.

"I told you, I have no idea." A man was speaking, and he sounded irritated.

Brash strained to hear the reply, but none was forthcoming. When the man spoke again, Brash realized he was talking on the phone.

"It's a bit difficult to search the place, when it's crawling with cameras and workers and the damned fire and police departments," the man said testily. "I'm doing what I can, but this house is huge … You do it, then! … I'm in the old lady's bedroom right now. If I get caught, it will cost me my job, so I've got to make this quick. She said to look in here."

Brash knew the panel hiding the stairwell was disguised as a bookcase. From the bedroom, it opened by pulling a lever. From the inside, that same lever was pushed in reverse. He did so now, but nothing happened. He pushed harder. Still nothing. Thumping the lever with force, he shoved on the entire panel, but the bookcase refused to budge.

Brash had two options. He could bust down the wall, but if it took more than one blow, the noise would forewarn the assailant and he would be gone before Brash kicked his way to freedom. The other option was to retrace his steps down the winding staircase, take the slippery steps from the hidden room up to the main basement, cross through its maze of rooms, circle around to the front of the house, hurry up the main staircase, run down the wing where Miss Juliet's room was located, and, finally, slip silently into the room marked with crime scene tape. That option would allow the intruder enough time to do a quick search and *still* make a clean getaway.

Knowing neither plan was perfect, Brash strained to make out more of the conversation. Perhaps he could identify the man's voice.

He could hear the man rifling about the room, opening drawers and pushing furniture aside. He muttered incoherently as he searched, but Brash clearly heard him say, "I don't find a thing. I don't think it's here."

Opening up his phone, Brash kept one ear tuned to

the conversation on the other side of the wall, even as he sent a text to Nick Vilardi. He instructed the carpenter to find out who was in the master bedroom and to detain them until he got there. He listened for a moment longer, until he got the sense the man was getting nervous about the amount of time elapsed. Brash had to act now. As he hurried down the steep stairway, moving as quickly as his big body allowed in such tight quarters, he gave up texting and dialed Nick's number.

The call went to voicemail. He dialed Amanda's number. When it, too, went to voice mail, he remembered that the crew was filming again today.

Great. Just what I need today. He saw the low overhead and ducked just in time, but he missed a narrow step wedged awkwardly into a corner. As his foot slipped and he felt himself falling, a few choice words leaked from his angry mouth. He was trying to quit cussing, but *damn, if that didn't hurt*! He banged his way down at least five treads, traveling on his backside, until the steps turned again. His outstretched legs were too long to make the corner, effectively stopping his travel. Brash took a moment to gather his wits and settle his breathing.

Five seconds, and he was up and moving, intent to make it into the main house in record time.

It was a valiant effort, but he was too late. By the time he ran through the basement, into the house, directly in front of the filming crew despite their cries of protest and Amanda's obvious distress, up the grand stairway, and into the master bedroom, the unknown man was gone.

In fact, nothing seemed to be disturbed. After clearing the room for an intruder, Brash searched the rest of the second floor, finding only a handful of workers in a far bedroom. Covered in drywall dust and each in various stages of taping and floating the walls, the men looked fully engrossed in their work and surprised to see him. Since no trace of white dust led from the room, Brash marked the men off his list of preliminary suspects.

Back in Miss Juliet's room, he looked for evidence left by the intruder. Nothing was out of place. There was a slight disturbance in the dust pattern on one dresser; a jewelry box shifted a fraction of an inch. Using the tip of his pen, he flipped the lid open and found it full of costume jewelry. He supposed it was fake, but it looked valuable. It was a wonder no one had stolen it before now. He would make a note to talk to Madison about it.

He looked around again. Come to think of it, why was anything still in the house? Most of the rooms were as Miss Juliet left them, still cluttered with furniture, curtains, rugs, even nick-knacks. With the mess of construction, and all the different workers wandering in and out, wouldn't it make more sense to clear the house, putting the contents in storage until the renovation was done? Another thing he should ask Madison.

He would have to call her. Warn her of the possible security breach. Alert her to the probability of theft. Even though his heart lightened at the thought of seeing her again, he hated to be the bearer of bad news. But he had promised to keep her updated, and Brash was nothing if not a man of his word.

Even if — no, make that *especially since* — Maddy had trouble believing it.

First, however, he had to contend with the angry

Home Again team.

"What the hell was the meaning of that?" Nick barged into the bedroom, his handsome face flushed with anger.

Brash turned and gave the television host his imperial look. "That," he said coolly, "was me doing my job. What I would like to know is, why haven't you been doing yours?"

"I was trying to, when you barged through like a two-ton truck!"

"Nick," Amanda murmured, trying to defuse the tension building in the room. She tugged on his arm gently, but her big violet eyes tried to connect with Brash's.

"I'm not talking about filming. I'm talking about controlling your workers. Someone has ignored the do-not-cross line and been snooping around in here."

Nick's sharp gaze darted around the room, looking for signs of disturbance. "Nothing appears out of place."

"Exactly. Meaning they had ample time to go through things without making a mess. I'll need to see the camera footage for this room."

"There isn't any."

Brash frowned. "I thought you had cameras rigged all over the place."

Amanda was the one to answer, drawing the police chief's gaze her way. "Only in the areas where we're currently working. We move the cameras as needed."

"Is there a camera on the stairs?"

"Yes, we keep that one running."

"Then I'll need to see it." Hopefully the intruder took the main staircase and not the one designated for servants, but he wasn't betting on it.

"Why do you think someone has been in here?" Nick asked.

"I heard them talking on their phone. Not only were they in here, they were searching for something."

Nick bristled immediately. "Are you accusing one of our crew of stealing something?"

"Not yet. But I do know they were in here looking for something."

"How do you know it was a worker?" Nick challenged. "Maybe someone else came in. Maybe one of the local looky-loos slipped through security and came up here to snoop around."

"I overheard the man say if he got caught, it would mean his job."

"So why didn't you catch him?"

"I was in the hidden stairwell, but the latch wouldn't work from the inside." When the other man started toward the bookcase, Brash warned, "Don't touch anything. I'll have to dust for prints."

"I suppose this is going to delay us even longer." Nick was clearly not pleased, his mouth curling down into a scowl.

Brash's shrug was anything but casual. "Control your men. Do your job in keeping them out of my hair, so I can do my job and get out of yours."

When Nick would have made an angry comeback, Amanda stepped in. She said a few low words to Nick, who frowned again but nodded. He threw a reluctant glance at the police chief. "I'll talk to the foremen, see if all their men are accounted for. And I'll have them reiterate the consequences of crossing the police tape."

"That's a good start. If this happens again, I'll have no choice but to declare the entire house off-limits."

Before his temper could spark, Amanda waved her co-worker away. She practically shoved him out the door but was quick to turn back around. "Brash, may I have a word with you?"

"Sure. What can I do for you?"

Amanda took his amiable attitude as encouragement to cross the room. She came close enough to touch his arm. "Brash, I hope you know we aren't trying to be difficult. But we're on a tight schedule, with many factors riding on our ability to follow a precise timeline."

"I do realize that, Amanda. Unfortunately, solving crimes seldom follows a time schedule." He offered a smile to soften the edge in his voice.

"Are you certain a crime has even been committed? That unfortunate soul could have died of natural causes."

"That is certainly a possibility."

"Do you really think a clue still exists up here?" She glanced around the room skeptically, but her hand still rested upon his arm.

"I know it's not a high probability, but I have a job to do, Amanda." He dropped his head slightly, adding weight to his low comment.

Madison stepped into the room at the precise moment Amanda moved closer, lifting her pretty face up toward Brash's. Maddy gave the tiniest of gasps, pulling Brash's attention to her startled face. He read the hurt in her expression, the misunderstanding in her eyes. She thought she had interrupted an intimate moment between him and the producer.

Damned if he would jerk away guiltily, as if he had done something wrong. He had no interest in Amanda, but Maddy had to learn to trust him. Ignoring the awkward tension in the room and the way his blood revved at the sight of the tall brunette, he kept his voice neutral as he greeted her. "Madison. Thank you for coming down."

"Of course." Because it would be rude to ignore the other woman, Madison offered a cool smile to the television producer. "Good morning, Amanda."

Brash felt the blond woman stiffen, her fingers curling into his arm before she dropped her hand and moved slightly away. Clearly disappointed by the interruption, Amanda's smile was forced. "Not really," she sighed. "Filming hit another snag, so now we're behind schedule. Again."

When she cut her eyes toward Brash, Madison sensed trouble. "Is there a problem?"

Before he could answer, the producer excused herself. "I'll let Brash tell you about it, while I see if I can calm Nick down. Brash, I'll speak to Paul and get you that footage you asked for." She tapped his arm again, her fingers lingering a full beat longer than necessary.

"I appreciate it, Amanda." He smiled down at the other woman.

Madison felt the prickly green thorns of jealousy curl around her heart. The man's smile was potent enough to be considered a lethal weapon. The smile wasn't even meant for her, but she still felt its effects, standing on the edges of its radiance.

Ever since Genesis made the statement about Amanda having feelings for Brash, Madison's attitude toward the other woman had inadvertently changed. She liked the producer — *had*, anyway, and still *wanted* to — but now Madison saw the woman as a threat to the tenuous relationship she was building with the chief of police. They faced enough obstacles without throwing a smart, attractive, *likable* blonde into the mix.

She waited for the producer to leave, noting how Amanda was dressed in a fashionable yet professional pantsuit of dark plum, while she was wearing basic black slacks and a plain white blouse. Maybe she should take Derron up on his offer to go shopping...

Irritated at her own lack of fashion sense,

Madison's voice was a bit sharper than necessary. "So did you find something new?"

Brash arched a curious brow at her tone but answered the question. "No new evidence, but I did discover we have a new problem."

"I think I've already met my quota for the week."

"There's a quota?" The skeptical smile was just playful enough, just charming enough, to steal her breath away. "And I'm just now hearing about this?"

"Some of us have a lower threshold than others."

"Don't know if you've noticed," he said wryly, "but both of us seem to have a higher-than-normal problem threshold."

"Yes, I've noticed." When she limped further into the room and saw his questioning gaze, she explained, "Turning my ankle is just one example of this week's current problem quota."

"How did you do that?"

She waved away his concern with a vague, "Naturally clumsy, I guess. So tell me what happened here."

Brash gave her a quick recap of the morning's events. As expected, his report resulted in a huge frown upon her pretty face.

"To your knowledge, is anything missing?" he asked.

Madison pivoted around the room, doing a quick survey. She raised her hands in a helpless gesture. "Nothing glaringly obvious, but who knows?"

"I'm surprised to see that most of Miss Juliet's possessions are still in the house."

"Tell me about it," Madison muttered with a sigh. "When Granny Bert inherited the house, she took out the personal effects — clothes, medicines, that sort of thing — but she was admittedly so overwhelmed with the enormity of the gift that she left most of it intact.

Not knowing quite what to do with it, she left all the furnishings and decorations."

"I can understand Granny Bert leaving it all, but I'm surprised the network didn't ask you to clear it out before they started the remodel."

"Apparently, leaving it makes for better television. Reminds viewers this was someone's home. Makes it more 'personable,' I think Amanda called it."

"I was in another bedroom earlier," Brash recalled. "It was completely empty."

"We're clearing them as we get to them. They even film taking everything out, so that viewers get a sense of each step of the process." Madison resisted the urge to roll her eyes but let a touch of drama drip into her voice.

"And you've never had a problem with anything being taken?"

"Not that I am aware of."

"I see that the jewelry is still in the jewelry box. I wonder why Granny Bert didn't take that, when she took the other personal effects."

"I assume she took whatever was valuable and left the costume stuff. Maybe our would-be thief knew this stuff was fake."

"Maybe." Brash studied the room at large, casting overt glances her way. After a moment he asked, "So what's the worried look about? What's bothering you?"

"Last night, Granny and I were talking about —" she glanced at the open doorway, deliberately turned away from it, and lowered her voice as she continued "— a journal that Miss Juliet was known to keep. Granny said it most likely would be here in the bedroom. She thought it might hold a clue as to why Miss Juliet had the secret passages, particularly the hidden room in the sub-basement. You don't think—You don't think someone... overheard our conversation and tried to find the journal themselves, do you?"

"Where did you have this conversation?"

"In Granny Bert's living room."

"Where there are cameras and mics." It was a statement, not a question.

"But I very clearly stated the opt-out, marking the conversation as private and not for television."

"But it was still recorded, meaning someone could still hear what was said."

Madison worried her bottom lip. "I-I hadn't thought about that," she admitted. "We have a verbal agreement that those portions of the conversation are to be ignored and promptly deleted."

"You may have some sort of agreement with Nick and Amanda, but there are probably dozens of technicians who handle the audio first. Besides, just because they erase something, doesn't mean they can un-hear it."

"True. I'll make a mental note to be *very* careful of what is said, opt-out or not," Madison murmured.

"The question is, even if your conversation was overheard, why would someone care about the journals? Who would that someone be?"

Madison shook her head with a hopeless sigh. "I haven't the foggiest."

7

With the noon hour over and the restaurant thinning out, Genesis made herself a plate and declared it time for a much-needed break. It had been a busy morning and she was starving.

Normally, she ate lunch with her staff, choosing to sit with them at a back table after the lunch hour was done. Over the last few weeks, a new member had joined their little group. Cutter Montgomery was a regular diner at the café, but his schedule had recently changed. Since his later mealtime usually coincided with the work staff's, he had taken to joining them at their table.

Genesis suspected it had something to do with her youngest waitress, Shilo Dawne Nedbalek. The dark-haired beauty had an obvious crush on the young fire chief. After only a few days of eating together, Genny was convinced the entire table of women had succumbed to Cutter's charms.

She refused to dwell on the fact that she, herself, may have been included in that crowd. So what if he was young enough to be her cousin? She knew the analogy made no sense — there were no age restrictions on cousins — but to say he was young enough to be her little brother gave off a sleazy vibe; you couldn't have a crush on your own brother.

And like it or not, Genny suspected she did, indeed, have a crush on the firefighter.

She had always thought him handsome. Tall and slim, with nice shoulders and lean hips. He wore his dark blond hair short, but sometimes when he took off his cowboy hat, a thick shock fell across his forehead in charming disarray, giving him a rakish look. His hazel eyes sparkled with humor and he had a smile that engaged his entire face. Cutter was more than just handsome. He was downright sexy.

The foolishness had started with that silly dance on Valentine's Day. Genesis had hosted a big party at *New Beginnings*, her way of giving back to the community for making her business so successful. She and Cutter happened to be dancing together when the band honored her with a song, a slow and sexy rendition of *The Lady in Red*.

Perhaps it had been the spotlight, or the excitement of the evening. Perchance, it had been the overall hype of Valentine's Day in general. But something happened between them that night as they were dancing. Something unexpected. Something primitive. It had swirled between them, a live current of awareness that zinged the air and stole their breath away.

They had spent the first few days avoiding one another, each embarrassed by their own reaction to the sensual moment. By silent accord, the dance was never mentioned again. It had taken a few weeks, but they had finally fallen back into an easy rapport, the one that had once come so naturally to them. Genny was not about to risk it all again by dwelling on a silly and fleeting crush. Given time, this foolishness would run its course. And in the meantime, she would simply ignore it.

"You're eating early today," Cutter observed as she

settled into the chair across from his. Usually the last to be seated, she often arrived at the table as he was having dessert. Today, however, he was just starting his meal.

"This is breakfast."

He looked at the assortment of foods on her plate, none of them traditional breakfast foods. "I prefer bacon and eggs," he teased.

"Yeah, well, so do I, but I'm usually so busy cooking them for other people I don't have time to eat them myself. So I settle for the mess-ups. Someone ordered cheese enchiladas, not this chicken one I'm about to devour."

"What is that stuff?" he asked, pointing to the creamy white mound on her plate.

"Risotto."

"Riso-who?"

Genny laughed at the expression on his face, ignoring the fact that even twisted in mock horror, his face was gut-wrenchingly handsome. These were hunger pains flipping around in her stomach, not a reaction to him. "Risotto," she repeated.

He jabbed a fingertip into the mixture, curiously testing the texture. "What is it?"

"Sautéed bits of vegetables cooked into rice and heavy cream. It's delicious. You should try some."

He still looked skeptical. Genny laughed again. Scooping a bite onto her fork, she held it out for his inspection. "Here, try it. I promise you'll like it."

Instead of taking the fork from her as she intended, he opened his mouth so that she could feed it to him. Little erotic shivers of delight danced down her arm and played havoc with her stomach. Genny pretended not to notice. Not when his hazel eyes pranced with mischief.

"Mmm," he said. "Not bad. In fact, that's pretty

good."

"Have I ever steered you wrong?" she teased.

"Never. You're the best cook I've ever known." His eyes twinkled again. "Just don't tell my mama I said that. Here, give me another bite."

"How about you get your own bowl of it?" Genny pretended to grumble as she scooped up another forkful and fed it to him.

"What is this?" Shilo Dawne demanded, her voice dripping with sarcasm. "Are your hands broken?"

Seemingly unabashed, Cutter offered her a maddening grin. "No, but they are full." He indicated the half-pound burger he held with both hands.

"You spoil him, Miss Genny," the waitress complained. She splashed sweet tea into his glass, flipped her long dark hair over her shoulder, and stalked off from the table.

Genny knew that Shilo Dawne had a strange way of flirting with Cutter; half the time, it seemed, she was angry with him, or took offense with something he said or did. She had a cute pouty face, after all, and most men seemed to like that. Cutter, however, usually seemed baffled by her behavior and seldom took the bait. Instead of coaxing her into a better mood, he normally argued back or, like now, simply ignored her.

Shilo Dawne was probably mad at him now, Genesis realized, because of his antics with her. She did have to admit, his casual sharing of her food — by her own hand, no less — did suggest something... intimate between them. With a frown, she belatedly remembered the cameras. She hoped they had not caught the silly moment on tape. She certainly hoped they would not air the meaningless gesture and make more of it than warranted.

"Why the frown?" he asked.

"I forgot about the cameras. I can just see it now."

She panned her hand through the air, imagining a ticker tape at the bottom of a television screen. "'Local eatery force-feeds its customers,'" she intoned.

"Or it could be a good thing," Cutter shrugged. He traced his own imaginary ticker-tape feed. "'Best cook in Texas has customers literally eating out of her hand.'"

Genny grinned, showing off the dimples that she deplored but everyone else adored. "Okay, I like that one. We'll go with that." She dug her fork into the enchilada and took a bite, stringing cheese from her mouth to the plate. They both laughed at her messy endeavor and Cutter's clumsy attempt to help with a napkin.

After several minutes of eating in silence, Cutter nodded to the camera discreetly blinking in the corner. "So how's life under the microscope?"

"Believe it or not, I actually forget it's there. Those first few days, we all walked around on tiptoes, trying to pose and primp for the camera, but that grew old really quick. A busy lunch rush has a way of making you forget about smiling pretty for the cameras." She flashed another dimpled grin. "Now I don't give it another thought. Funny how quickly you can become accustomed to something."

"I've noticed a lot more strangers in town since they started filming. Guess it's good for businesses around here, but we've already had an increase in traffic accidents. Seems like we go on twice as many calls these days."

"The price of fame. Stipulations, as Maddy calls them."

"Speaking of Miss Maddy... any word on the skeleton?" For months, Cutter had used the same respectful label with her, referring to her as 'Miss Genny.' Somewhere along the way, perhaps even before the dance, he had dropped the moniker, symbolically narrowing the age distance between them. Now he simply called her Genny.

"Not really. Brash turned it over to the state lab, but who knows how long that will take? She did ask me to come over to the Big House this afternoon, to help her look for some sort of journal Granny Bert remembered Miss Juliet keeping. They're hoping it might have a clue as to why she had all the secret passages and the secret room." She glanced at the clock on the wall. "I hope Rudy hurries with my car. He's putting new tires on it. I'll head over there as soon as he brings it back."

"I can give you a lift."

"You don't have to do that."

"I don't mind."

Genny pursed her lips as she considered his offer. "I may just take you up on it. Maddy seemed a little anxious when I talked to her."

"No problem." He flashed his charming smile, doing that thing to her stomach again. "All you have to do is ask."

By the time Genny arrived at the mansion, Brash had finished dusting for fingerprints and turned the room over to Maddy for her search.

When she saw her friend, the homeowner broke out in a smile. "Ah, reinforcements."

"And I come bearing gifts." Genny rattled the white bakery bag with the Gennydoodle cookies inside. In the other hand she had two disposable cups of coffee.

"As always, you are a lifesaver, my friend."

Sipping on her coffee, Genesis surveyed the room at large. At one time, the room had been the height of fashion. Thick carpets covered the gleaming hardwood floors. Heavy drapes adorned the windows, their large rose pattern identical to that of the fluffy duvet. Everything in the room was color-coordinated and artfully arranged, the dark burgundies and forest greens softened with splashes of cream and pale pink.

"It looks like Miss Juliet must have had this decorated right before her death," Genesis mused. "This matchy-matchy color scheme has the hallmarks of the eighties. So do the ribbons and roses sprouting all over the room." She motioned to the walls and winced. "They're even on the wallpaper."

"Miss Juliet was nothing, if not fashionable."

"So what's the plan? Where do we even start?"

"I don't know, but if you come across anything that looks valuable, box it up to take with us."

"I thought Amanda wanted you to clear the room on camera."

"I'm more concerned with preserving Miss Juliet's legacy and the contents of the house than I am about being 'personable' for the camera," Madison retorted.

Genny grinned. "I think I detect a hint of green in your voice."

Not amused by her friend's astute observation, Madison denied being jealous. "A reflection off all these climbing vines, I'm sure," she said with droll sincerity.

Genny's blue eyes twinkled. "Why, yes, I'm sure that's it."

After an hour of fruitless searching, the twinkle had dimmed. "I don't know about you, but I'm not finding a thing," Genesis declared, shutting the bottom drawer of an antique oak chest.

"Me, either." Madison huffed out a sigh. She was seated in an upholstered wing chair, resting her swollen ankle.

"Where else could we look?"

"One or both of the libraries would be my best

guess. I assume the one on the second floor was more for her personal reading pleasure, the larger one downstairs more for reference. And, of course, for show."

"Of course."

"The sad thing is, who did she show off to? According to Granny, she had very few friends, even fewer visitors. She opened the house once a year for a Founder's Day celebration and a few afternoon teas here and there, but she wasn't exactly a social butterfly."

"So let's finish up in here, and then we'll tackle the library."

"Or they could be in her sitting room," Madison noted, gazing through the opened door of the adjacent room. "Or her dressing room. Her suite of rooms takes up this entire side of the house, you know."

"For all we know, it could be in one of her secret passages. Or another secret room we don't know about yet."

"As long as it doesn't have another skeleton stuffed inside," Madison muttered.

Her friend grinned, tossing a throw pillow her way. It bounced off Madison's shoulder and fell to the ground. "So off your seat and on your feet. We have another five acres of ground to cover, and that's not counting the library downstairs."

"Has anyone ever told you that you have too much energy?" Madison grumbled, gingerly getting to her feet.

"That's how I get so much done, girlfriend. Now come on. I'm cheap labor, and time's a-wasting."

"You missed your calling. You should have been a drill sergeant."

Genny flashed a dimpled grin. "But you love me."

In reply, Madison scooped up the pillow and tossed

it back. Without a doubt, she did love her best friend. More than once, Genny had saved Madison's sanity.

It was no secret that Madison's father had a chronic sense of wanderlust; by now, even she knew the man would never grow up. Her mother willingly followed behind, as eager for the next adventure as he was. When Maddy was thirteen, Charlie and Allie decided the crazy lifestyle wasn't suited for a child, so they did what was best for them. They left their only daughter behind. More importantly, it turned out to be what was best for Madison. Granny Bert gave her a good, steady home, and Genesis Baker became her true and forever friend. Without Genny, Madison was certain she would have gone mad.

The friends were inseparable. They even went off to college together for another two years of side-by-side adventures. After that, Genesis took a break in traditional study and went to France to learn to be a pastry chef, and Madison met and married Grayson Reynolds. Even as Genny began a career and Maddy started a family, they remained close. When Madison's marriage began to fall apart two years ago, Genny came to her rescue, offering the emotional support that she needed. Last summer, Genny moved back to Naomi and opened a café. When Gray was killed in an automobile accident a few months later and left his family penniless, dear Genny convinced Madison to join her back home. Once again, Genny was her salvation.

So here they were, both living in The Sisters again, both starting over. Madison returned with decidedly more baggage than her friend did. Gray's betrayal cut deep, stirring up old insecurities of being unloved and unwanted. If anything, she depended on her friend now more than ever.

"You finish up in here," Madison decided. "I'll start

on the library."

The cozy retreat was an extension of the grand master suite. Boasting its own balcony at the front of the house, it opened off the grand staircase with elaborately carved double doors. A smaller set of doors, tucked into an alcove, connected the repository to Miss Juliet's private domain.

As difficult as it was to comprehend, all of this was hers now. Every inch of the huge old house. Every pompous piece of furnishings still inside. Every outdated piece of floral wallpaper. All hers, even though little of it suited her tastes.

True, Nick Vilardi had grand plans for the master suite of rooms. Convert the original dressing room into a huge closet, complete with custom built-ins. Create a new master bath extravagant enough to fulfill her every fantasy. Update the sitting room nestled into the turret. Add double French doors leading onto the balcony. Allow in plenty of natural light. New floors, new paint, new bedding.

With spectacular ideas of her own, Amanda was already talking about decorating the room. She had the perfect person in mind, too: Kiki Paretta, a Texan with her own popular show for the network. Amanda was excited about the possibility of a huge crossover audience for *Home Again*. It would be wonderful for their ratings, she gushed. Reality home-makeover television at its finest. Without asking what Madison had in mind for the rooms, Amanda arranged for Kiki to visit next month. She then 'accidentally' leaked word of it on social media. Fans were already delirious with anticipation.

If I think it's crazy now, just wait until Kiki hits town, Madison bemoaned silently. *Maybe I'll just hole up in here.*

She could stay in here for days, Madison decided.

Although quite a bit smaller than its formal counterpart downstairs, the room was impressive. The private sanctuary was a treasure trove for the written word. Hundreds of books lined the walls, everything from hardcover classics to modern day paperbacks. There were books of every genre: mysteries and love stories, poetry and sonnets, self-help books and autobiographies. Just as Granny had said, it was obvious that Juliet Randolph Blakely had a voracious appetite for reading.

Maddy sighed. She planned to look through each and every book, searching for the missing journals. The task was daunting.

8

The oddities began that week.

Throughout the years, there had been rumors of ghosts within the old mansion. It was said Miss Juliet encouraged the rumors, perhaps starting a few of them herself. Granny Bert claimed it was done to keep noisy visitors away. Once Madison's grandmother inherited the house, she found the rumors to be a great deterrent for looters and would-be squatters. Only the bravest daredevils were adventurous enough to sneak onto the grounds and break into the house. The few who did break in seldom took anything. It was one thing to defy the spirits and walk among them; it was another to steal from them.

Over the past decade or so, the rumors had died away. Madison liked to think it was an indication of maturity. After all, ghost stories were fun for teenagers, offering harmless entertainment on a small-town Friday night. Many a teenager from her generation had kept the legend alive and well, often based on tales passed down from their parents and grandparents. But the arrival of the new millennium had brought new families into the sister cities, most of whom knew nothing about the rivalry between the Randolph sisters and the man they both loved. Rumors of ghosts and disgruntled spirits had slowly faded away.

Content to let the legend of the so-called ghosts lie, Madison never mentioned it to the *Home Again* team. She was afraid Amanda Hooper might exploit that aspect of the home's past.

The first few weeks of filming had gone smoothly, but soon after the skeleton was discovered, unexplainable things began to happen around the mansion. Madison suspected some prankster was at work, reviving the old superstitions of ghosts for the benefit of national television. The public seemed to love that sort of thing, after all.

It started with the tools. When the workers arrived in the morning time, things had been tinkered with. It was harmless enough — saws unplugged, batteries turned backwards, things moved from one spot to another — but it cost precious time on a schedule already stretched thin. After a couple of days of the pesky inconvenience, they arrived another morning to discover a wall had been painted overnight. The paint of choice had been bright red, reminiscent of blood, particularly when it was splashed upon the walls with long dripping tendrils.

The cameras were of no help. The permanent cameras, the ones left running twenty-four/seven, had been disabled, or re-aligned to record blank space. By the time the problem was discovered and alarms were installed on the cameras to alert tampering, more mischief had occurred.

Windows were opened, doors were locked shut. Radios came on at random. Furniture was moved.

More alarms were installed, these on the premises. Madison and her family had one code, Nick and a crucial handful of *Home Again* team members had another. The electronic tattletale recorded each entrance and each person engaging the alarms.

Yet still the oddities occurred.

Today's event had been the most disturbing of all. Nick was the first to arrive for the morning, only to find several messages written on mirrors throughout the mansion. The blood-red paint gave a chilling tone to the ambiguous words. *Leave well enough alone,* demanded one message. *Get out,* said another. *No more.* A fourth mirror's message was the most ominous. *Stop before you're sorry.*

Officer Perry had come to investigate. Madison would have felt better with Brash there, but he was out of town for the day. Official business, dispatch said, but she could not help but notice that Amanda was missing today, as well.

Stop it, Madison. You promised to give him a chance. You're learning to trust again, remember?

She kept reminding herself of that fact as she made another sweep through the upstairs library. After almost a week of looking for the journals, possible places to search — and her patience — grew thin. Add the cryptic messages and Amanda's sudden absence on the very day Brash was out of town, and her nerves were on edge.

It had been difficult enough this week, conducting a clandestine search in a house filled with dozens of extra people and cameras in various locations. As owner of the house, Madison had every right to be there each day, but she felt uncomfortable doing so. She found it easiest to come after the workers were gone and she had the house to herself.

She brought the twins with her one evening to search the library. As comedian of the family, Blake found amusement in the titles, particularly the British love sonnets and Edwardian-era poetry. With his flair for dramatics, he acted out titles such as *Whither Thou*

Goeth and *The Death of a Toad*. Between laughing at her brother and discovering her own proclivity for romance novels, Bethani was of no more help than her twin was.

Another evening, Granny Bert offered to help, but that, too, proved fruitless. Caught up in memories of days past, her grandmother spent more time reading favorite passages from books and relaying old stories than she did looking for the journals. Her grandmother's stroll down memory lane was interesting, but Madison could accomplish more when she worked alone.

So here she was this evening, giving the library one last opportunity to produce the journals. If she still came up empty-handed, she would move on to another room.

She was at the desk, making certain she had not overlooked a false bottom in any of the drawers. Nothing. She sat back in the elaborate executive chair, running her hands over the soft burgundy leather with its delicately rolled arms and decidedly feminine design. Miss Juliet had excellent taste, she thought distractedly. The chair fit Madison's weary body like a glove, coaxing her to sit back, relax. Stay awhile.

She gave in, but just for a moment. It was almost dark out. Even though she would soon be living in the house, she avoided being here late at night by herself. She was not exactly afraid, but the recent mischief had her uneasy. Would-be 'ghost' aside, there was the matter of the trespasser Brash heard in Miss Juliet's room.

Madison swiveled the chair from side to side, absently contemplating the matter. Perhaps it was all connected. Perhaps the intruder Brash heard was their prankster. Perhaps she or he had a trick planned for the master bedroom but was frightened off before implementing it.

It could be kids. Madison wasn't sure how they were getting around the alarms, but most kids these days were geniuses with electronics. So far, the 'ghostly incidents' had been innocent enough. A bit juvenile, in fact. So definitely the work of kids, she decided.

Or was it? A whispered thought echoed in her mind. It could be a marketing ploy. For all she knew, Amanda might even be behind it, trying to boost ratings for the show. *Nothing like throwing in a little ghost action to intrigue people.*

In case her deal with Kiki's show fell through, a good ghost story might appease the masses, Madison realized. Amanda would definitely know how to market such a twist, how to spin it to their advantage. Why, with only a two-hour pilot and a barrage of sneak-peak commercials, the producer had already stirred interest for their upcoming premier to a fevered pitch. It was practically a hit already, before the first episode even aired. A nice ghost twist would only propel it to new heights.

Yet something about that scenario felt off. Would Amanda stoop so low? And if the network and Nick knew about it, would it even be considered stooping? It could all be a carefully orchestrated plan. It slowed progress, that was for certain. They were already behind schedule because of the skeleton. Throw in a late start for most of an entire week, and Nick was ranting about lost time and added costs. There was talk of working overtime this weekend, pulling in extra workers if need be to make up for the delay.

Perhaps all of these scenarios were off. This could very well be about the skeleton.

Her lips puckered as she considered that theory. If someone wanted to hide the truth about the skeleton, he or she could be sabotaging the renovation project.

But why? What could they possibly hope to gain? Madison tried to imagine how stopping the renovations could be of benefit.

She could think of only one reason. There was more to discover, hidden somewhere here in the house. Unease settled between her shoulder blades. Another body, perhaps? A murder weapon?

Or information?

Information contained inside a journal, perhaps? Madison nibbled her upper lip. Were the messages meant for her?

'*No more.*' No more searching for the journal, perchance?

'*Stop before you're sorry.*' As far as scare tactics went, the events so far had been rather lame, but they did seem to be escalating. Was it because she was still looking? Because she might find the journals and discover a secret someone was trying hard to keep?

A new thought occurred to her. Did that make Miss Juliet somehow guilty? Not necessarily, she reasoned. But the journals might offer some insight into the secret room and its purpose.

Madison drew in a deep, calming breath. There was a chance she was completely wrong. The incidents might have nothing to do with one another. It could be coincidence that one day after Granny Bert mentioned the old journals, the intruder defied police orders and rifled through Miss Juliet's bedroom. It could be mere chance that the oddities started immediately after that. Random occurrences that just happened to coincide with one another.

But she didn't think so.

Her eyes traveled around the room, more of a mental exercise than a visual one. What was she missing? Not physically, although the obvious answer was the journals themselves. She was missing something else, something that could explain the sudden appearance of their message-writing-work-disrupting 'ghost.'

The saccade of her hazel gaze swept the room, snagging on a far corner near the window. Madison spied one last cubbyhole she hadn't searched. The small cabinet was tucked between a large bookcase and the heavy folds of the drapes. Thinking it would be a perfect place to hide personal items, her hopes soared.

She tugged on the lower cabinet door, only to find it locked. Seeing no keyhole, she determined it was merely jammed. She pulled and tugged, twisted and turned. The small knob refused to budge. After several minutes of trying, she banged the top of the cabinet in frustration. Maybe she needed a hammer.

Or not.

With an almost imperceptible click, the door swung open. Feeling certain she had located the journals, Madison wiggled in glee and bent to retrieve them, only to find the chamber empty. Disappointment surged through her.

"What is it with all the cloak and dagger stuff?" she muttered aloud. Since almost half of Miss Juliet's books were mysteries, it was safe to assume the woman had been enchanted with the genre. Perhaps her passion for mystery had played a dominant role in designing her home. The woman certainly had the opportunity, the money, and the space. On all three accounts, she could afford to add a secret passageway here, a hidden staircase there. Her new home could have secret chambers and hidden cabinets built in at whim, filling it with intricate caches and secluded hiding spots. Anything her clandestine heart desired.

This meant if there was one hidden cabinet, there were probably others. Madison looked around the room, paying particular attention to corners. In a room filled with alcoves, built-in bookcases, and elaborate woodwork, the options were many. Every breakfront held a possibility. A solid panel taunted twice the opportunity.

For the next thirty minutes, Madison retraced the room, tapping and shoving, trying to trigger hidden mechanisms and the secret spaces they protected. She discovered three more.

A slim vertical panel between two bookcases held an old gun. A single barrel shotgun if she was not mistaken. Leaving it as is, she made a mental note to ask Brash of its worth. A secret drawer tucked beneath a shelf of books protected a stash of old letters and loose papers. These, Madison removed for later perusal. Lastly, she discovered another small cabinet, this one high overhead, hidden behind an alcove's fur down.

She needed a chair to reach it. She was climbing atop the seat, stretching upward, when she heard a noise from downstairs. The workers had gone for the day. So who did she hear rummaging around down below?

With a glance out the windows, Madison belatedly noticed that dusk had fallen. When the uneasy feeling between her shoulders returned, she found herself abandoning the newly discovered cabinet to sneak her way to the door. She tiptoed out onto the landing and peered down. Darkness crept in from the windows. With no lights left burning, the area below was dark and shadowed.

Another shuffling sound. Someone was definitely in the house, most likely Nick. The lead carpenter often stayed over, long after the workers had gone home for the day. He was, after all, meticulous with details. Madison suspected he was a workaholic, always finding something else that needed doing, something that needed fine-tuning.

"Nick? Is that you?" she called out.

No answer, just a distinctive thump from below.

Without stopping to question her reasoning, Madison quickly crossed the second-floor landing, bypassed the grand stairway, and made her way to the servants' staircase at the rear of the house. She kept her footsteps light. Checking that her cell phone was still in her pocket, Madison quietly crept down the stairs.

This staircase was decidedly less ornate than its showy counterpart at the front of the house. Strung from the first floor to the third, the steps here were simple and steep, the walls narrow. The back stairway had none of the polished banisters and exquisite details of the grand centerpiece, just a simple handrail along one wall. Nor, Madison breathed thankfully to herself, did it have the stark but crude spiral of the hidden passage down to the sub-basement. Just one turn on this steep descent.

Madison was halfway down the flight, almost to the landing, when blackness engulfed her. The overhead bulb went off, snuffing the already dim light from the passage. She stopped mid-step, gripping the narrow handrail. Perhaps the bulb had burned out, reaching the natural end of its lifespan. Perhaps someone had flipped the switch at the kitchen entrance. Perhaps power had been lost to the entire house. All that mattered at the moment was that she was surrounded by pitch, and the steps were unfamiliar. She eased slowly down, settling one foot onto the step at a time, feeling her way to the bottom of the staircase. As her eyes adjusted to the darkness, she could see the faintest of glow behind her, weak light filtering down from the second floor, proof that the electricity was working. There was no such light below, meaning the kitchen lights were off. Most likely, whoever had been in the house had turned off all the lights downstairs, including the one to the stairway.

Okay, so they're energy conscious, she thought, trying to soothe her nerves. *Good. That's good. I'm sure whoever it was had no idea I was still in the house. Obviously, they didn't hear me call out. They were probably leaving, turning out lights as they went.*

She reached the bottom step at last and reached for the doorknob. When it did not turn, she rattled it vigorously.

"Hello?" she called out. "Anyone there?"

She heard another bump and waited expectantly for the door to open. She heard feet shuffle on the other side. She thought she heard someone breathing. But the door remained closed.

"Hello?" She banged on the door for good measure. "Excuse me, but I'm still in here! Please open the door."

This time, there was no doubt that someone was on the other side. Madison could hear their ragged breath as they pulled in a deep gulp of air. She nervously did the same, impulsively pulling back. Quite without realizing it, she took a step backward, onto the stile above her. Then she took another, and another, until she turned and fled up the dark passage, as quickly and quietly as the blackness would allow her. It was too reminiscent of being stuck behind the fireplace wall. Whoever was downstairs knew she was in the stairwell and had no intentions of helping her.

Finally at the top, Madison ran into the master suite of rooms, slamming and locking the door behind her. The rambling suite had too many rooms, too many doors. Madison raced to lock them all. She barricaded herself in the sitting room, locking doors on either side for a second layer of protection. Only then did she pull out her cell phone and call Nick.

"Good evening, Madison," came his pleasant voice.

"This is a nice surprise. I didn't expect—"

She cut off his pleasantries with a sharp, "Are you here at the house? In the kitchen?"

"No, I'm at the hotel. Everyone has gone home for the day. I locked the doors behind me, but you'll need to set the alarm."

"Someone is here. Could it be Amanda?"

"No, she's still out of town. What's this all about?"

"I heard someone moving around down below. I called out to them, but they didn't answer. I was coming down the back stairwell when they turned out the lights and locked the door."

"Paul or Roberto must have gone back for something. I'm sure they had no idea you were in the stairwell."

"Whoever is in the house deliberately ignored me. I called out to them and could hear them on the other side of the door, but they would not answer."

Concern sparked in his voice. "Where are you now?"

"Locked in the sitting room in the master suite."

"Are you all right?" Nick asked sharply.

"A-A little shaken," she admitted.

"Stay where you are. I'll be right there!"

She did not argue. She was unaccustomed to having men rush to her rescue, but tonight she had no objections. Having never bought into the whole 'damsel in distress' thinking, Madison had more confidence in herself than she did in most men she knew. Between her own streak of independence and her late husband's rare show of protectiveness, she was used to fighting her own battles. She had to admit, however, that if Brash were available, she might have called him, and not necessarily because he was the chief of police. But he was out of town and Nick could be here in less than ten minutes.

"Hurry," was all she said.

It took eight. Eight minutes of pacing, straining to hear sounds of someone in the outer rooms. Eight minutes of staring at either doorknob, thinking she saw them jiggle more than once. Eight minutes of deep breathing techniques and trying to soothe her jagged nerves.

"Madison! Madison, are you all right?"

She heard Nick's voice as he burst through the front door. She did not immediately answer, lest she give her location away to whomever else had been in the house. Another two minutes ticked painfully away, until she heard Nick's voice again, this time closer.

"Madison, it's okay. It's Nick. You can come out now."

Madison took a moment to calm herself, running her hands over her fluttering stomach. She smoothed the wrinkles from her clothes, as surely as if she smoothed her ragged nerves. A final pat to her hair, a deeply indrawn breath, and Madison unlocked the door.

"Are you all right?" he asked anxiously, reaching for her hands.

"Yes, I'm fine." She tried laughing, but the sound was nervous and tight. "Feeling a bit silly, to be honest. I'm sure I overreacted. It's just that this week has been so strange..." Her voice trailed off, but she noticed the tight lines around his mouth. "What? What is it?"

"I don't think you were overreacting," he told her solemnly. "Come with me."

When he tugged on her hand, she followed without question.

Nick led her down the grand staircase, where the lights now gleamed brightly. They crossed through the formal dining room with its fabulous murals, passed through the butler's pantry, and stepped into the kitchen. With half the room gutted and bare, the other half covered in tools and sawdust and general disorder, it took Madison a moment to focus. Nick pointed to the door leading to the back stairwell, drawing her attention to the kitchen's newest guest.

A three-foot skeleton, the kind used for Halloween decoration, dangled just in front of the portal. Had Madison gone through the door earlier, she would have no doubt run directly into the plastic bones. She shivered slightly, imagining the fright it would have given her.

Just as someone planned, she realized.

Nick looked angry. "deCordova had better get control of these teenagers around here! If this persists, the show will be forced to press charges."

Madison looked at him sharply. "You think kids are behind this?"

"Equipment unplugged, cameras turned off, writing on mirrors. Now this."

Madison studied the indicated skeleton, strung in the exact spot she had heard the intruder. It was a message, she was certain of it. No matter the originally intended location for the frightful toy, the intruder left it here when he or she realized Madison was in the stairwell.

Nick still ranted. "I don't have time for this. We are pitifully behind schedule as it is. These kids have to be stopped. And of course it's kids. Who else would do such juvenile foolishness?"

Madison had no answer.

Who else, indeed?

9

If Nick was angry that evening, he was livid by morning.

Additional spooky guests appeared overnight. White sheets were strung up to look like ghosts floating through the air. Their precise placement — Miss Juliet's bedroom, the upstairs library, the basement stairway — reinforced Madison's suspicion that someone was sending her a message. But the dead chicken left in the quarantined sub-basement room sent the most threatening message of all. There was no note, but Madison heard the message loud and clear. *Remember what happened at Ronny Gleason's chicken houses. Your life was in danger then. It still is.*

Brash immediately declared the entire house off-limits. Back in town, he took over the scene and declared a three-day weekend at the Big House. He was immune to Nick's outrage and Amanda's pleas. He ordered everyone off the property. Even the cameras were ordered turned off.

Banished from the premises, Madison had no choice but to obey. While Brash and his crew did a thorough search of the old estate, she abandoned her search for the journals and turned her attention to duties at *In a Pinch*.

It was Friday, the day she ran errands for Miss Sybille. She had a half-day gig at Dean Lewis Insurance Company, but her afternoon yawned free, leaving her time to work on Allen Wynn's property dispute.

A quick check with the county tax rolls confirmed Allen's claim that his family kept the taxes up to date on the acreage in question. With two surveys, tax receipts dating back over a century, and the rule of the law behind him, Madison thought Allen should pursue legal action. She admired his hesitance to sue a neighbor and appreciated the job offer, but it appeared her services were not needed. She told Allen as much when she called him.

"I know, Maddy..." He was still reluctant to bring in a lawyer. "Could you just go out there one more time, see if there was anything you missed? Did you go over the entire property?"

"Well, no," she admitted. "I didn't explore the gully or the thickest area of the trees."

"The exact spots he is challenging," Allen pointed out.

"Did you know he has a spy-cam up? Traps set?"

"You've got to be kidding."

"Unfortunately, no. I still have the swollen ankle to prove it."

"Obviously the man is out of control. Maybe I should call the sheriff and let him handle it. I just hate the thought of sending an old man to jail."

Madison's defeated sigh carried over the phone. "Oh, all right. I'll go back out there, see if I can find any possible reason that he's being so mule-headed."

"Thanks, Maddy. I'll tuck a little something extra in your envelope."

So with Derron in tow as backup, Madison returned to the base of Pine Bluff.

"Tell me again what we're here for," the young man

said as he bent to tuck his skinny-legged jeans into the tops of bright red rubber boots. Ever the fashionista, his chambray work shirt was also red.

Maddy refused to look down at her own wardrobe. Now minus one boot of her own, she was wearing an old pair of Bethani's. The turquoise leather uppers clashed with the mostly blue T-shirt she wore; mostly, because it sported two large bleach spots down the front. She had on the same torn jacket from her first visit, not wanting to subject any more of her wardrobe to prickly vines and limbs.

"Because I obviously missed something before. Something that makes this thicket of woods worth protecting, even by nefarious means."

Derron studied the dense woods directly before them. "We aren't actually going *in* there, are we? Because these are Dolce & Gabbana."

"I told you what we were doing before we left. I can't help it if you wore designer jeans." Madison shook her head. Sometimes it felt like Derron was her third child.

Despite his flair for dramatics, the petite man was a true asset to her fledgling business. Over the past four months, Madison had accepted a wide range of jobs. Walking dogs. Running errands and providing taxi service to and from doctor appointments. Filling in at various offices and retail stores around town. A commercial chicken farm. Gathering information and providing surveillance for a private detective, a jealous wife, and a mother desperate to prove her son's innocence. But Derron brought with him a different skill set, allowing her to accept jobs that were even more diverse. He had covered three manual labor jobs, lent his strong back to move furniture, and used his talents to build backyard fences. Slowly but surely, *In a Pinch* was gaining a reputation for being the go-to for odd and temporary jobs, and Derron Mullins was partially responsible.

Ignoring her scolding, the young man whipped a gadget from his pocket and waved it over the top of the fence. Without glancing her way, he knew she scrunched her forehead. "Checking for an electrical charge," he explained. "No need to be electrocuted, first rattle out of the box."

"I, too, came prepared," she announced proudly, producing two metal detectors. "Handy for discovering traps, hidden treasures of gold, and any other metal secrets these woods hold in store. Plus," she dug in her jacket pocket and pulled out a small device, "this snazzy little bug detector. Camera variety, not insect."

"Since this is show and tell time..." As Derron tugged on his shirt to raise it, Madison had a brief moment of worry. What, exactly, did he plan to show her? She was almost relieved to see the holstered gun snuggled flat against his rub-board abs.

The relief quickly evaporated. "A gun? You brought a gun?" she squeaked.

"Oh, please, girlfriend. You've lived in the city too long," he chastised her. "Guns aren't just for turf wars and to massacre innocent people. Guns don't always take lives; most times they can save your own. What if a wild boar rushes us? What if we see a skunk, or a snake? And don't forget the rumors of big cats around these parts."

"Is it legal?"

"I'm not a moron, Madison. Of course, it's legal. Legal, registered, and backed by a safety course." Offended by her still-skeptical look, he produced a deep scowl. "What? You thought I brought this in case we encountered Hank Adams?" Derron shook his blond head in disgust. "And you thought *I* was melodramatic!"

Duly reprimanded, Madison offered a meek smile.

"I'm sorry. Guns make me nervous."

"You're a woman living alone, you often dabble in investigative work, you've had several attempts made on your life, and you travel out and about in the countryside. You need a gun, Madison. Ask that hunky boyfriend of yours to teach you how to handle one."

"He's not my boyfriend."

"And whose fault is that?" When he turned his back to her, Madison childishly stuck her tongue out at him. "Saw that!" he claimed.

Bickering put aside, they slipped through the strands of barbed wire and made their way into the thicket of dense woods. "Here." Madison handed Derron one of the metal detectors. "Look for anything other than a normal forest. Flag it with tape if you find anything."

Without the heat of the afternoon sun, the air was cooler in the thickly shaded area, making Madison grateful for the jacket she wore. The lack of direct sunlight also made it difficult to see, slowing their progress as much as the underbrush and the precautionary measures did. The duo proceeded slowly through the woods, sweeping the ground with the metal detector, the air with the surveillance detector. They stayed within eyesight of the other as they widened their scope, looking for anything amiss.

"I'm not seeing a thing," Madison called to her partner. A slight whine clung to her words. "You?"

"Only if pinecones are considered valuable. If they are, we're walking across a fortune right now."

"I don't see any marked trees, any half-buried stakes, and not a single hidden treasure chest. There's no marijuana plants, no drug labs, no secret printing presses. Nothing but brush, twigs, trees, and more trees. A typical forest." Her voice was definitely whiny as she added, "These trees aren't even that special. So what's the big deal?"

Their separate paths had come together at the jumbled pile of vines and thistle that some unknown animal called home. Derron pursed his lips, studying the prickly mess. "If I had something to hide, I'd choose somewhere like this."

"Especially if that something was a litter of baby piglets or a den of wolves," Madison fretted.

Her worries gave him pause. After a pregnant moment he ventured with a hopeful, "I don't see any recent tracks."

"Maybe because you're standing ten feet away."

Derron edged closer. He waved the metal detector through the air rather uselessly. When nothing stirred within, he moved in another few feet. "Stand back," he said, but his voice lacked conviction.

It felt rather odd allowing a man to 'protect' her, particularly this man. After all, she dwarfed him in size.

Against a blank background, the first thing noticeable about Derron Mullins was his handsome face and his nicely sculpted physique. But in a real-life setting, his size came into focus. His body was well proportioned and in excellent condition, but the blue-eyed man had an unusually petite build. Madison felt as if she were allowing a thirteen-year-old to defend her.

A thirteen-year-old with a gun, she reminded herself. She wisely stood back as Derron poked the nest with the metal pole.

When still nothing happened, Derron moved in with more confidence. He circled the garbled mass, poking, prodding, and peeking inside. He came back with a defeated sigh.

"Nada."

Madison propped hands onto her hips and looked around. "So why does the man insist on keeping this mess under fence? This is one of the few places I can even stand up straight in here. Why does Hank Adams insist on keeping it?"

"Maybe he's a sore loser."

Chewing on her lip, Madison considered the possibility. "Granny did say he was known to hold a grudge. Steel traps and spy cameras are a bit much, but she mentioned he was mad at her and my grandfather once, and tried to sabotage everything they did. After a couple of years, he came to his senses, made nice, and they became friends again."

"So the man is a bit overzealous. Perhaps a tad paranoid. I say it's a case for the courts, not you and me."

"I agree, but for the sake of earning our paycheck — not to mention the bonus Allen promised — we need to make a thorough evaluation."

"We have. The old man is a borderline nut case. Mean and ornery."

"The thing is, I know Hank Adams. He's not like that at all."

"Your ankle begs to differ, dollface," Derron pointed out.

Because he had a point, Madison continued to nibble her lip. "So if it's not the trees themselves or something hidden among them, it could be what's on the other side of the trees," she speculated.

"Which is?"

"A deep gully that backs up to Pine Bluff."

"Unless the gully is deep enough to be standing in oil, I doubt that's it."

"There's only one way to find out."

This time, Derron whined. "You're just determined to ruin these jeans, aren't you?"

Wondering if he would even notice additional rips, she picked her way around the thick undergrowth.

"This way," Madison instructed, ducking beneath a low branch. "But be careful coming out of the woods. The ground drops off almost immediately. Fall into the gully, and those fancy pants of yours will be history."

Brash knew dusting for prints was a longshot. Taking into account the carpenters, show personnel, crewmembers, Maddy, her family, and all their visiting friends, literally dozens of people had access to the house and its grounds. He would give it a shot, but he had little hope of being successful.

Despite Nick's insistence that kids were behind the pranks, Brash had his doubts. This didn't seem like the work of teenagers. Known to instigate a prank or two of his own during his youth, Brash knew that most teens lacked the attention span to pull this one off. One prank, maybe. Two, tops. After that, it was on to something else, something with immediate gratification.

Something like turning a young wild boar loose overnight in the cafeteria at school. Something like listing the principal's home phone number on Craig's List with the photo of an underpriced vintage Corvette for sale. Something like spray-painting the trees around town blue and white to boost school spirit. Those were the pranks local kids favored, not the series of low-key events that had taken place at the Big House.

The pranks, however, were escalating. No longer so low-key. With each escalation, the random deeds shifted from being merely irksome to becoming downright illegal. Tampering with a police investigation and trespassing were only the beginning. With the messages left on the mirrors, the pranks had suddenly escalated to terroristic threats.

Not the work of kids, Brash was sure of it.

Brash had already made a running list of possible suspects, but he kept the list confidential for now. It was still a very fluid investigation.

Whoever was doing this knew something about electronics. He or she was able to bypass alarms, redirect circuits, and disrupt video feed. Instinct told him it had something to do with the overheard conversation about the journals, so the person had access to the cameras and audio inside Maddy's house.

The very thought tightened his gut and brought out all sorts of protective instincts. Most had little to do with his job as chief of police. Every one of them had much to do with his feelings for the homeowner.

By now, it was obvious that the old mansion harbored a secret. The perpetrator, Brash hypothesized, had one of two reasons for wanting to keep the secret buried: to protect the past, or to insure the future.

If it was about the past, exposing the secret must mean the potential for dire consequences. Brash's mind raced as he tried to imagine what those could be. The skeleton suggested a murder. A murder meant a victim and a perpetrator. They were already working the missing person angle, but it was a daunting task. They were working with a one-hundred-year timeframe, after all.

While there was no time limit on pressing murder charges, there *was* a time limit on lifespan. Logic told him that if the deeds were about protecting a murderer, then that murderer was still alive. He did some quick calculations in his head. Even if the murderer had committed the crime at the age of fifteen and was now in his or her mid-eighties, the crime could have taken place as many as seventy years ago. It wasn't much, but it meant they could narrow their search to missing persons during and after the mid-1940s.

The condition of the body and the deterioration of the clothing suggested the corpse had been down in the basement for years, probably decades. It would probably be safe to overlook the last twenty-five years, concentrating on earlier disappearances. That left a rough window of between 1945 and 1990, give or take five years or so. Still a daunting task, by any standards.

Of course, it could still be about the past and not include a murder. There could be another secret hidden in the journals, something potentially damaging to … whom? An entire community came to mind. As matriarch of the town, Juliet Blakely more or less screened every resident who resided here. No 'unsavory characters' were allowed to rent or buy property in her namesake. Not only did she know each family who called Juliet their home, but she also knew their past. That had to amount to at least a few juicy secrets.

Miss Juliet died in 1983. Brash could pull records, cross-reference the families who lived here then to those still in the area. That would narrow it down somewhat, but not much. Most families had deep roots in the community and chose to stay.

Nor could he rule out residents of Naomi. On more than one occasion, Miss Juliet had ruled a family non-worthy of citizenship, only to have that same family settle across the railroad tracks, warmly welcomed into the town of Naomi. Reasons for rejection could be recorded in those journals.

Brash groaned, knowing the numbers just doubled. Potentially, Juliet Blakely could have recorded secrets about anyone in the twin cities.

And if this was about the future? Those secrets meant someone had something to lose. He would need to give special attention to anyone with political, social, or financial significance. He made a few notes on his list, thinking of names to jot down.

The list was getting impossibly longer, and he had not even touched upon the more obvious possibilities. This could be a marketing ploy. Any one of the *Home Again* team — but most likely Nick or Amanda — could be behind the pranks, trying to drum up interest for the show. What was that saying in Hollywood? Any press is good press. People loved ghost stories. Throw in a little danger, and it made for great news coverage.

He had managed to keep things under wraps so far, but any day now, Brash suspected the media would get wind of the 'incidents' at the old mansion and swoop in like vultures. The first episode of the show was due to air soon. With help from the media, ratings were sure to soar for that all-important season premier.

The lines tightened around his mouth as he jotted yet more names onto his list. Just the background checks could take weeks. Months. He only had two officers. A third had been hired and was due to start next month, but that did not help now. And no matter how efficient Vina was, the woman could not do all this by herself. Not and do her regular job, which was to keep the police department on its toes and running smoothly.

A thought came to mind, curling the tightness into a smile. He could hire outside help, just as he had done before. And he knew just which temporary service to call.

Having successfully avoided falling into the gully, Madison and Derron skirted the perimeter of the ravine. They went opposite the direction Madison had previously taken, looking for anything amiss.

"See anything, dollface?" Derron asked.

"A healthy crop of bull nettle. My grandfather once

taught us kids how to harvest the nut, but unless that's become the latest health food sensation, I don't think these plants are what we're looking for."

"Agreed. So now what?"

"I suppose there could be something down in the gully." Her voice was rife with reluctance, not wanting to admit that might be their next course of action.

Derron pointed toward the bottom of the bluff. "Or in that cave over there."

"What cave? You mean that animal den?"

He shrugged his delicate shoulders. "Cave, den. Tomato, tomatto. Whatever you want to call it."

"I call it insane, if you think I'm going to crawl off in a hole where some cougar might live!"

"We're not dressed to crawl inside a cave." He glanced over at her wardrobe with thinly concealed disdain. "I'm not, anyway. But we could go closer, look inside."

"At what?" she asked in horror. Visions of gnashing teeth and vicious claws flashed through her mind.

"Haven't you ever heard the rumors?"

"About the cougars? Yes! That's why I don't want to go any closer."

"Not about the cougars. About the caves."

Madison vaguely recalled some old tales from her youth. A few of the daredevils of the day claimed to have spent the night in an old cave as part of a dare. She never put much faith in the validity of the claims. Particularly since one such claim had come from an old boyfriend, a habitual liar who had trouble separating the truth from his vivid imagination. It took her less than two weeks to discover his flair for duplicity and to break up with him.

"I heard a few rumors, but I never believed them," she shrugged.

"My mom told me about them. She said they're not

rumors; they are actually true. Something about an earthquake thousands of years ago. It left a fault-line through the edge of River County, allowing the formation of ancient underground rivers. The waters rerouted or evaporated centuries up, leaving behind caves and tunnels."

Madison stared at him. "You just moved here a few years ago. How do you know this, and I don't?"

He shrugged a delicate shoulder. "My mother was a surveyor. Land was kind of her thing. She liked to poke around on rocky hills and cliffs like these. One time, she found a cave that the landowner didn't even know about. Most of them are hidden, unless you know they are there."

Madison searched her mind, trying to think of other hilly formations in the area. Located for the most part in a river bottom, the terrain stretching out from The Sisters was relatively flat, but here and there a high peak formed, such as Pine Bluff.

Without another word, Derron led the way toward the indention in the rocks. Once they passed the gully, Madison knew they would be trespassing on land that rightfully belonged to Hank Adams. She ignored her conscience and followed anyway.

They made their way closer to the bottom of the bluff. Navigating the irregular rocks was tricky, particularly when a wrong step could land in a tumble down the deep ravine.

On closer inspection, the bluff was more a series of layers of stone, stacked one upon another. Madison thought the ridges and changes of color might mean something, but geology had never been her strong point. Nor had rock climbing. One rocky layer tilted this way, the other that. The 'cave' was wedged into a corner between two sheets of limestone, not as close to the bottom as she originally thought.

"Here, girlfriend, take my hand."

Just as Madison grasped Derron's fingers and began to step across a wide chasm in the stone, they heard it.

It started lightly, little more than a rumble. It quickly turned into a deep growl. Deep and long. And much too close for comfort.

"On second thought…" Derron said, his face losing its color. "Run!"

10

Her ankle protested when she tried getting out of bed the next morning.

"You, my sorry friend, are getting too old for this," Madison reminded herself aloud.

Beside her, Bethani groaned in her sleep. She mumbled some incoherent reply before turning over to slumber in undisturbed bliss.

Poor baby. She needs her own bedroom.

Not for the first time, Madison thought their current living arrangements lacked much to be desired. She knew it was difficult for a teenage girl, sharing a bedroom with her mother.

Soon, she reminded herself. *Soon, we'll each have a room of our own.*

Madison flexed her swollen joint as she mentally reviewed her itinerary for the day. Mail invoices for jobs completed. Write Derron's paycheck and hope it didn't bounce. Go to Blake's baseball tournament at eleven. Again at three if they won. Make a date with a bottle of wine and a good book. *Hmm, not too bad of a Saturday.*

She limped down the hall and into the kitchen, where Granny had a pot of coffee brewed and waiting. She inhaled with satisfaction and smiled. "Good morning."

Her grandmother harrumphed. "We'll see if you're still saying that when you get a glimpse of the morning news."

The smile melted away. "Please, not before my first three cups of coffee."

"Then you'd better drink fast," the older woman advised. She nodded to the small television on the counter, where a shot of the Big House filled the screen. She hit the remote to turn up the volume.

"Do you believe in ghosts?" the woman on the screen asked. "It's not Halloween, but sources in Juliet, Texas tell us that the historic home of the town's namesake has seen a recent infestation of so-called 'haunts.' If you recall, a little over a week ago, a skeleton was discovered in the basement of the old mansion. No word as of yet whom the skeleton belonged to, nor whether an actual crime was believed to have been committed, but these new disturbances have shut down restoration efforts while police investigate. According to our sources, odd things began happening around the so-called Big House shortly after the skeleton was discovered. Urban legend has it that the old house is haunted, and this week, 'ghosts' have started to appear. The one-hundred-year-old mansion is the centerpiece for the new season of *HOME TV's* popular *Home Again* television series and will introduce a new format for the network's top-rated show. The network says the new format will merge home restoration with reality television, giving viewers an in-depth look at what remodeling is like on a day-to-day basis. The first episode is set to air in just a few days, but no word yet on how long the ghosts will *spook* away cameras. And speaking of ghosts... In Detroit, a ..."

Granny muted the volume as the picture flashed to

another story.

"Great," Madison muttered. "Just great. Now we'll have ghost chasers underfoot and séances set up on the lawn."

"Don't look now, but there's already a van out on the curb. *Ghost Buffers,* I believe it says."

"Five minutes," she mumbled. "Five minutes was all it took, and my nice little Saturday is shot to smithereens."

"The stipulations of fame, my dear. The stipulations of fame."

The cameras followed her to the baseball tournament.

Maddy sat quietly in the stands, watching as the rest of the spectators made fools of themselves. By the time she came back for the three o'clock game, the number in the stands had doubled. People sported handmade signs and silly hats, anything to snag the cameras' attention. Cheerleaders appeared, decked out in their cutest outfits, eager to cheer their team on to victory. Never mind that it was the first baseball game they had attended this year. What better time to support your team than when you could appear on national television? A portion of the high school band showed up, blaring their horns and beating their drums in an off-balanced rendition of the school song. Countless of people stopped to greet Madison with enthusiasm, the very same people who snubbed her on the street when the cameras weren't rolling. And all around her, the air buzzed with talk of ghosts haunting the Big House.

A news crew conducted interviews under the bleachers. They snagged people as they went to the concession stand to get their cheese nachos and overpriced soft drinks, speaking with anyone willing to share their version of local legend. The team from *Ghost Buffers* handed out stickers and ghost-figure balloons, along with advice on how to best protect people's home from ghostly infestations. A preliminary assessment was only $49.95, but if the home team won today, they were offering a one-time discount of twenty dollars off. Another camera from *Home Again* took it all in, gathering plenty of footage for their ongoing background story.

Overall, there was a festive spirit in the air, more like that of a carnival than of a high school baseball game.

Perfect, Madison bemoaned silently as she went to her car. *My life has become a carnival sideshow.* She pretended not to notice Myrna Lewis waving at her with a fake smile plastered across her round face. The woman never came to games, and she was never friendly to Madison. Funny, how the chance to be on television could change all that.

"At least we won. And Blake made two homeruns, right there on camera," she muttered aloud. Glimpsing Sadie Bealls getting into her truck, Madison's lips dipped downward. "Not that it will make the cut. I'm sure they'll be much more interested in how Sadie once saw a ghost float through the window of the Big House, right as she was driving down Main Street. My son played brilliantly, but that won't make the news. No, sir, not when they have some really juicy news, like the time Dolly Mac Crowder was having tea with Miss Juliet and saw a saucer float through the air. That, I'm sure, will make the headlines."

When her phone binged with a message, she saw a link to another news story that ran this morning on a Dallas station. After mentioning the ghosts, the commentator rehashed discovery of the skeleton, and showed an unflattering picture of Madison from that day, huddled beneath the old pecan tree, her face pale as death itself. He went on to mention that she was the widow of Dallas' own Grayson Reynolds. Viewers might remember the investigation that surrounded Reynolds Investments and his sudden death last November in an automobile accident.

"It was so kind of everyone to send me the link," Madison grumbled, erasing the message with a jab of her finger. "This is only the fifth person to do so. Not a single one of them bothered to call after I left Dallas, yet they all are sweet enough to send me this link. So thoughtful."

By the time she wove through traffic and pulled onto the road, Madison's nerves coiled into a tight knot. Her plan was to go home, open that bottle of wine, and have a nice, quiet evening to herself. No phones and no television. The twins were both spending the night with friends and Granny had Bingo. With any luck, she might salvage what was left of the day.

The dream of a peaceful evening died a quick and sudden death as her phone rang. When she saw the caller ID flash across the screen, she took it as an omen.

"Mother Reynolds, what a surprise."

Her mother-in-law had not called in weeks. If she put her mind to it, Madison could probably count on one hand the total times Annette had called since Gray's death. Two hands would cover the past twenty-four months. Which suited her just fine.

Madison's relationship with her mother-in-law had always been strained. Annette Reynolds had lofty plans for her only son, and they had not included a headstrong college girl with no pedigree. Much to her dismay, Grayson married the girl and brought her home to Dallas, where Annette was forced to act the proper mother-in-law. She dutifully included Madison in family events. Made certain she was in the highly commissioned family portrait. Introduced her to the cream of Dallas elite and secured her placement into all the social clubs and organizations. Bought her expensive gifts at Christmas and on her birthday. But the one thing Annette never quite mastered was the way her lip curled downward, each time Madison referred to her as 'mother.' And from the wedding day forward, anything that went wrong had been ruled Madison's fault.

Not bothering with niceties now, Annette charged into the reason for her call. Her tone was accusing. "Is it true? I'm hearing sordid reports about you being on *television!*"

Not certain if her horror related to the ghost sightings or the scandalous fact that her daughter-in-law was the star of a reality show, Madison hedged. "Oh? What exactly have you heard?"

"Why, it's all over the Dallas stations. You have been implicated in some sort of murder mystery, and it is hardly the first time! You have only been there four months, Madison, and apparently, this is the third scandal you've been involved in. What sort of environment have you taken my grandchildren into?"

"And we're all doing fine, Annette, thanks for asking."

"You do not have to be snide, Madison. It hardly becomes you."

Madison could picture her mother-in-law, sitting on one of her plush designer sofas, most likely in the *salon,* as she preferred to call the pretentious room. Perfectly coiffed hair, tinted a flattering shade of pale gold, sprinkled with just enough silver frosting to look natural. Impeccable makeup. A neat and stylish wardrobe. Madison could also envision that sharp patrician nose undoubtedly stuck into the air. Even now, the disdainful sniff carried over the airwaves.

"And you have not answered my question. It is bad enough that you took the children away from us and everything that was dear and familiar to them. Their home. Their friends. Their school. You dragged them to the ends of the Earth, to some backwoods town in the middle of a cotton field, and now I am learning that there is a decided criminal element there, with which you are apparently quite familiar! I must insist that you bring the children back immediately. They can live here at Ivy Hall."

She was spoiling for a fight. That was the only explanation for the haze of red appearing before Madison's eyes. After a stressful week filled with pranks and ghosts and elusive journals, a ridiculous day filled with posturing fans and phony friends and pushy reporters, and a long history of snide remarks and ridicule from a woman who presumptuously named her four-thousand-square-foot home *Ivy Hall,* Madison was primed for a fight.

Maddy whipped the car onto the side of the road. She ignored the car behind her. Let them blare the horn. She shoved the gearshift into park and prepared for battle.

Out of respect for her husband, Madison had never confronted Gray's mother head-on. She stood up to the other woman in her own quiet, dignified way, admittedly allowing small matters to slide in the name of family unity. Throughout the course of her marriage, Madison had learned to choose her battles wisely.

But Gray was gone. There was no family unity left.

And, yes, she was spoiling for a fight.

Madison kept her voice deceptively cool and steady. "First of all, Annette, I did not take the children away from their home. The bank threatened to do that, when your son failed to make the mortgage payments on time. I was fortunate to get out from under the staggering debt he left me with, even though I sold our home at a loss." The coolness sharpened into frost. "You remember the house, don't you, Annette? I wanted the smaller, more affordable one in another neighborhood, but you insisted we needed a house befitting Gray's status as an up and coming 'mover and shaker,' I believe you called him."

"*Grayson* was a brilliant businessman. The markets turned on him, but he would have seen his way out of the slump. I'm certain it was only temporary. And *he* chose that house, not me. I merely put him in touch with my agent."

"We both know you pushed him into buying it, Annette. Not that it mattered in the long run. The children and I were forced to leave Dallas because your son left us penniless when he died. I brought them back to my hometown, where we would be surrounded by true friends and family. Yes, it is a small town, but I prefer the word *quaint* over backwoods. And it's hardly the ends of the Earth. We are three hours from Dallas, Annette, not that you have bothered to visit. And by the way, I'm not the one living in a gated community, locked away with alarms and deadbolts because I don't trust my own neighbors."

"I have some of the finest neighbors in the city," Annette sniffed. "Pillars of the community. Lawyers. Judges. A Congressman. Highly respected business people."

"And I live in the same house as the former mayor of Juliet, a pillar of *our* community."

"Hardly the same caliber of people," Annette intoned stiffly.

Even though her mother-in-law could not see her, Madison smiled. "I agree wholeheartedly. There are few people in this world with the honesty and integrity of my grandmother."

Annette ignored the comment and continued with the tenacity of a bulldog. "Dead bodies, Madison? Ghosts? Whatever have you gotten yourself involved with? Are my grandchildren in danger?"

"Of course not, Annette. I would never let anything happen to them, and you know it."

"And yet you somehow think it is acceptable to parade them across national television?" Her voice dripped with drollness. "A reality show, Madison? Whatever were you thinking?"

Ah, she should have known. Annette disguised the reason for her call as concern, but the truth was that she was appalled to have members of her family associated with something as tawdry and undignified as a reality television show. *As if what your son did was dignified,* Madison snorted to herself.

Her voice was amazingly calm as she replied to her mother-in-law. "I was thinking that I needed to provide for my children, since your son did such a poor job in that department. Did you know our new home is larger than yours, Annette? A historical landmark, in fact. It's being completely renovated and restored, at absolutely no cost to me."

"There is always a cost, Madison. I think your children's safety is far too high of a price, don't you?"

"If you are implying that I have put the twins at risk by being on television—"

"I am not implying anything. I am saying it outright. There are vile sex offenders in the world, Madison. Pedophiles. And yet you choose to parade your innocent children in front of them, right there on the television screen for the entire world to ogle. Charles and I will not stand for it. I insist that you end this ridiculous nonsense this instant."

Her control began to slip. Madison's voice wavered

ever so slightly, anger causing her growled words to tremble. "You and Charles have no say-so in the matter."

"I believe a judge may see things differently."

Madison clutched the steering wheel with enough force to turn her knuckles white. The blood draining from her face surged sure and strong throughout her flushed body.

"Are you *threatening* me, Annette?"

"Of course not, Madison. I am merely expressing concern for my grandchildren. Naturally, Charles and I want what is best for them. We happen to believe that we could provide a much more stable and secure environment than the one they currently live in. I urge you to allow the children to come live with us, in the manner in which they are accustomed."

"My children have always lived in a home filled with love and warmth. *That* is the manner in which Blake and Bethani are accustomed."

"You must consider what is best for them."

"I *always* consider what is best for my children."

"Charles and I can provide for their needs, Madison. If they have fallen behind in their studies, we can hire private tutors. They will be up to task in no time. I'm certain we could use our influence and have them accepted into Wiltshire Academy."

Madison's lip curled in distaste. "And I'm sure you would hire a five-star chef to prepare their meals and a maid to prepare their rooms and a chauffeur to drive them back and forth to their fancy school." Her voice took on a hard edge. "Allowing employees to raise your children may have been good enough for you, Annette, but it's not good enough for me, and it's certainly not good enough for my children. They deserve better. They deserve home-cooked meals and a mother who is there for them." Feeling particularly malicious,

Madison hit below the belt. "Having had neither himself, that was something Gray insisted upon when we started our family."

After a sharp intake of breath, Annette repeated, "Consider what is best for the children, Madison. You are practically living in squalor, and now you have sold your soul to national television. Why, you might as well have prostituted yourself!"

The haze of red thickened. *It's true what they say.* The vague thought registered somewhere in her rage-filled mind. *I can literally feel my blood boiling. Lordy, I hope I don't have a heart attack, right here on the side of the road.*

Madison chose to ignore the inflammatory remark. She could have said something like 'Your son might have preferred that. Perhaps then he would not have cheated on me.' It might even have been true, but she refused to dignify the horrendous insult with a reply. Instead, she concentrated on what was important: Bethani and Blake. Madison's voice trembled with the rage that built inside her.

"*The children* have names, Annette. Not once during this conversation have you referred to them by name. Not once have you asked how they were doing, how they are adjusting without a father. That's because they are nothing more to you than a possession, something pretty to set upon a shelf and look at once in a while, something to show off to your friends and neighbors while you *play* at being a grandmother." Madison stopped to pull in deep, ragged breaths, as spent as if she had fought a physical match.

"Why you —"

Accustomed to having the upper hand, Madison knew her mother-in-law could not abide dismissal. That knowledge became her most powerful weapon. Before the other woman could launch a counterattack,

Madison delivered her final punch.

"Goodbye, Annette." Madison ended the call with a decisive click.

She sat on the side of the road for a long moment, knowing she was unfit to drive. She tried deep breathing techniques. She tried counting to ten. Fifty. She tried running her hands through her hair until it spiked it all directions. She tried massaging her neck and tense shoulders. Her hands still trembled on the wheel.

After only a moment's hesitation, she picked up her phone and made a call.

"Hello?"

The deep voice warmed her. She spoke quickly, before she lost her nerve. "Does your offer still stand?"

"Offer?"

"You once offered me use of your thinking spot. Does the offer still stand?"

He countered with a question of his own. "Have you had supper?"

"It's barely five o'clock. Why are you asking me about supper?"

"Have you or have you not eaten this evening?"

"No, Brash, I haven't eaten," she replied testily.

She heard the smile infuse his deep voice. "I'll pick you up in thirty minutes. And don't spoil your appetite."

"Brash, what does —"

"Details, Maddy. Let me take care of the details."

Details.

A smile touched her lips. She liked details.

11

She refused to acknowledge her sudden change of mood. Her nerves were calmer now, calm enough to drive herself home, where she changed from her slacks and sweater set into something more suitable for the outdoors. Sliding into her borrowed boots, a pair of soft jeans, and a simple cotton shirt, she grabbed a light jacket in case the evening turned chilly. Resisting the urge to re-apply her makeup — this wasn't a date, after all — she ran a comb through her sassy new haircut, added a low-luster gloss to her lips, and waited nervously for Brash to arrive.

Had she acted in haste? He might misinterpret her call. What if Brash thought this meant she was ready to start a relationship with him? Perhaps she had not stopped to think this through.

Perhaps, she grudgingly admitted, *that is the point. I didn't stop to think.*

Determined not to overthink things now, Madison met him at the curb, away from the prying eyes of the camera. Best not to get this on film, after all. She slipped into the truck before it came to a full stop.

"I'd like to think you're eager to see me," the police chief said, his dark eyes twinkling with wry humor. "But judging from the worry lines, I'd say it's been a rough day and you're just using me as a means of escape."

As she struggled for an appropriate comeback, he gave a lighthearted laugh. "I'm just kidding, Maddy. I figure if anyone deserves an escape, it's you. I'm honored you chose me as your partner in crime, so to speak."

She started to warn him not to read too much into her call, but she wisely bit her tongue. Besides, her curiosity was piqued. "You mentioned supper?"

"Ah, so you're hungry," he teased. "That's why you jumped in while the truck was still moving. If you absolutely can't wait, there's an energy bar in the console."

A note of impatience slipped into her voice. She was hardly in the mood for his teasing. "What, exactly, am I waiting for?"

"Well, neither of us have had supper yet, so I figured we could have a bite to eat while we're solving all your problems through my highly scientific method."

"I'm not dressed for dinner." She glanced down at her faded jeans in dismay. If she had known this was to be their first date, she would have made more effort with her wardrobe. And she definitely would have touched up her makeup.

"Don't worry, you look as beautiful as ever." His brown eyes caressed her, warming her with their sincerity. "And as far as I know, there's no dress code for a picnic."

A goofy grin took over her face. "A picnic?"

He was obviously pleased with her reaction, but his shrug was casual. "Nothing fancy, just a couple of sandwiches I threw together."

She leaned her head back and closed her eyes, the smile lingering on her face. She had been right to call Brash. Somehow, he knew exactly what she needed.

They drove in silence, until she opened her eyes again, curious to see deCordova Ranch dressed in a different season. When she was here two months ago, winter had stolen the leaves from the trees and painted the ranch in shades of gray. With spring's arrival, those same trees were now adorned with crowns of green. Young cotton plants pushed up through the rich river bottom soil, dotting the neatly plowed rows with early color. Cattle and horses roamed through the fields, munching on tender grasses that swayed in the gentle breeze. Most spectacularly, the once-dormant fields popped with color, now a masterpiece painted with Texas wildflowers.

"I had forgotten what spring looks like here," Madison murmured, gazing at the beauty around her.

"We do seem to have a bumper crop this year," Brash agreed as they drove through the colorful fields. Indian Paintbrushes, Black-eyed Susan's, dandelions, and buttercups vied for attention amid the vibrant blue and purple hues of the renowned Texas bluebonnet.

"Absolutely stunning." Already her spirits lifted, just seeing the beauty of the wildflowers.

Brash maneuvered them through the fields until they were deep within the ranch and near the banks of the Brazos River. Madison thought she was prepared for topping the final knoll and braking just feet from the steep riverbank. Still, she knew a moment of panic when the truck's windshield revealed nothing but blue sky.

Brash took one look at her squinted eyes and laughed. "Don't you trust me by now?" The tone was jovial, but she detected the edge to his words.

"Yes, Brash, I do trust you."

His smile did funny things to her heart. She reminded herself she was no longer a lovesick schoolgirl, infatuated with the star quarterback. They were grown up now, and life wasn't as simple as dreaming of a stolen kiss beneath the bleachers. Her mind was fully aware of the differences, but her heart trailed a couple of decades behind. Especially when he smiled.

His smile turned into an all-out grin and his brown eyes lit with mischief. "Remember that," he said, shifting the gear into reverse. Still reeling from the bone-melting power of his smile, Madison missed the way he turned the vehicle around and began backing toward the river.

She came to her senses with a squeal. "Brash! What are you doing?" She grabbed for the dash. "We're going to fall!"

"We aren't going to fall," he admonished with a chuckle.

"Are you trying to kill us?"

"What?" he asked innocently. "Does this scare you?" He gunned the motor just a little, moving them ever backward, as his eyes twinkled over at her.

"Stop that!" Madison hissed, using both hands to hold on. As if clutching a falling dashboard would save her, should they go over. "Stop looking at me and keep your eyes on what you're doing!"

"Seriously, this scares you?" Another few inches back, another daredevil grin as his eyes remained trained on hers.

"As a matter of fact, yes, it does."

"Oh, ye of little faith."

"Oh, ye of show-off attitude," she grumbled beneath her breath. To her relief, he consulted the mirror as he made a final push toward the river's edge, set the emergency brake, and killed the motor.

As he opened his door, Brash informed her smugly, "We were never in danger of falling."

Madison took perverse satisfaction in hearing his

knee pop as he unfolded his long legs from the truck and got out. He was definitely too old to be showing off like some teenage daredevil.

Brash opened the tailgate and helped her climb atop. She would never admit it, but he had done an excellent job backing them close along the riverbanks.

Silence settled between them, broken by the sounds of tumbling waters below and the stir of the breeze. Madison took a deep breath of the fresh country air, allowing its calming powers to settle into her lungs. She released her breath slowly, pushing tensions out along with the air.

Only then did Brash take her hand and ask in a quiet voice, "So what brings us out here today?"

She liked the way he said 'us.'

"There's so much," she admitted. "I don't even know where to start."

He waited. After a moment, she took another deep breath and whispered sadly, "I hardly recognize my life anymore. It's out of control."

He offered a tender smile. "So take it back." He scooted closer, until their legs were touching. He leaned in and pointed to the water below. "You remember how this works? Pick out something you see floating in the water. Imagine your troubles piled down there on it. Let the river get rid of it, carry your troubles away."

She saw a small piece of wood drifting upon the water. "I'm already regretting this whole reality TV thing. If it were just my family, it would be one thing. But it's the entire town. I had no idea people would react so... so *foolishly*. You should have seen them today. It was like a bad carnival."

"You're not responsible for how other people act, Maddy."

"But I brought them here. I'm responsible for the

fallout. If our town is portrayed as some backwoods hillbilly hole-in-the-wall, people will blame me. It will be my fault."

"Being blamed for something and being at fault are two different things. So put the idea of being responsible for an entire town's behavior on that little limb down there and get rid of it."

"But—"

"If people choose to act the fool on national television, it's not your fault, Maddy."

"But what comes out in the final cut and what our community is really like aren't always the same. What if they edit out the good parts and only keep the hokey stuff?"

"Again, it won't be your fault. Let it go, Maddy."

Willing to try it, Maddy tossed that worry upon the bobbing limb. It took a while, but slowly the wood drifted downriver.

"Next?" His voice was slightly smug.

"Things are going too fast. It's so insane." She didn't mean for it to happen, but to her chagrin, a tear slipped past her lashes. "I haven't even had time to grieve Gray's death."

Voice rough with emotion, he forced himself to ask, "You still love him?"

"No," she admitted brokenly. "Yes," she whispered. She squeezed her eyes impossibly tight. "A part of me hates him. He hurt me, Brash. He left me broken, in so many ways. But he was my children's father. For that, I'll always love him."

"I can understand that."

"Can you? Because I'm not sure I do." Maddy leaned her head against his arm and admitted the secret she had harbored for so long. "I'm so angry at him. I'm angry with him for dying. For leaving me alone to fix the mess he created. For leaving our babies so shattered and brokenhearted." She bit her lip, admitting another hard truth. "I'm angry at him for the things he did before he died, for destroying our marriage and ruining our happy family. I'm angry because now I don't have a chance to fix what went wrong."

His voice slipped an octave. "Is that what you would do? Fix things, go back to how they were?"

She thought about her answer. Her voice was sad as she uttered a small, "No."

After a long moment, Brash spoke. "You have to let your anger go, Maddy."

She shook her head stubbornly. "I deserve to be angry. He destroyed our marriage, Brash. He destroyed everything. Our marriage, our family, our business. More than our past, he destroyed our future. And then he went and died, and he left me to pick up the pieces. I have every right to be angry."

"Yes, you do."

Another tear traveled down her cheek. "But do you know what makes me angriest of all? I can't tell them, Brash. I can't tell my children what their father did. They have already lost so much. I can't take this from them too. Not their memories, their respect."

Brash pulled her into a hug. "Aw, Maddy."

"I have to pretend, Brash. I have to pretend I don't hate him. I have to pretend I'm not angry. Even when I'm so angry I just want to scream, I can't let them know. I have to pretend." Her voice broke. "I am so tired of pretending."

He held her while she cried. After a long moment, he spoke quietly against her hair. "There is another option." She stilled, waiting for him to go on. "You could let it go. Let the anger go, sweetheart."

"I-I don't think I can," she whispered.

"Yes, Maddy, you can." His voice held the

confidence she did not feel. Keeping one arm around her, Brash used the other to point to a log slowly making its way downriver. "See that big log down there? This is your chance. Put your anger on that log, Maddy, and let it wash away. You are right, sweetheart. You have every reason to be angry. But Gray is gone now, and your anger can't bring him back, and it can't hurt him. But it does hurt you. You've got to let it go, honey."

"But— "

"But this anger serves no purpose. It's only hurting you, and eventually it will hurt Blake and Bethani. And once you let the anger go, some of the pain will go, too."

Maddy wanted to believe him. Her eyes found the log in question, bobbing up and down in the waters. Could it really be so simple? Just to let the anger go?

Her voice came out breathless. Hopeful. "That-That log down there?" she asked.

He nodded. "That's the one. Pile your anger up there on it. All of it. The things he did, the lies he told. The betrayal you felt. Pile it all on that log. Get rid of it. Let the river wash it downstream."

Maddy stared at the log, mentally loading it down with her anger. Surely one log could never hold it all, not without sinking. She heaped it with layer upon layer of bitterness and anger, old baggage she had carried with her far too long. The more she heaped upon the log, the lighter her heart felt.

She watched as the log rocked upon the waters, dipping and swaying, taking an uncertain path downstream. Her breath caught when one end of the log snagged on a sandbar, turned sideways, and stalled. A smaller limb floated downstream, bumped into the log, and wedged there beside it. Madison held her breath in anticipation.

"Let it go, sweetheart. No matter what happens to

the log, let the anger go."

Madison nodded, but her eyes were riveted on the scene below. Was she strong enough to release it, even when the log was clearly trapped? Would her anger be the same way, suspended indefinitely, collecting more trash with time?

They watched the log for a long moment, both knowing it was hopeless. Brash cleared his throat and started his pep speech. "Give it time, it will —"

Madison shook her head. "Doesn't matter," she decided softly. "I saw its load slip off, one chunk at a time. It's floating away on its own." She looked over at him, her eyes shimmering with unshed tears. Something else glimmered within their hazel depths. Something bright and shiny, like optimism. Hope. Best of all, freedom.

"I feel so much lighter." Her voice was wondrous. "I can't believe that worked. How did you know?"

"I've had my own share of anger, you know. Just when I had everything I ever wanted — a career in football, fame and fortune, a place on an NFL team headed to the Super Bowl — my girlfriend, or make that my *ex*-girlfriend, came up pregnant. For a very long time, I blamed Shannon for it all falling apart. I quit the team, came home to be a husband and a father, but I never let go of the anger. I let it ruin our marriage. It wasn't until after the divorce that I realized it was eating me apart. I let go of the anger, let go of the resentment, and suddenly Shannon and I were able to become friends and be the sort of parents that Megan deserved."

"Your *ex*-girlfriend?"

"Yeah. We had an on-and-off relationship for years. We finally realized it wasn't working and decided to call it quits, once and for all. Six weeks later, Shannon found out she was pregnant."

"Wow. That must have been rough," Madison murmured.

"Like a typical fool, I only saw it from my end. I thought she was out to ruin my life."

"So why did you marry her?"

One look into his soulful eyes, and she knew the answer, even before he said, "I may be a lot of things, sweetheart, but first and foremost, I try to be a man of honor. She was carrying my child. And in my own selfish way, I did love Shannon. But the truth is, I loved blaming her even more."

Madison felt something shift inside her heart. Her voice turned husky. "I-I don't think I've ever heard such raw honesty in all my life."

Brash turned a large palm upward and shrugged his broad shoulders. "The truth ain't always pretty, but it is what it is."

"You're a wise man, Brash deCordova," she whispered softly.

"Not wise. But smart enough to know we didn't come out here to talk about my problems. We're here to solve yours. So what's next, pretty lady? What other troubles do you have?"

She sighed, her heart burdened once more. "I have so many. You pick. My life is under the microscope, scrutinized by reporters who don't know the first thing about me. A murder may or may not have been committed in my new home. The house may or may not be inhabited by ghosts. And now with the rumors of ghosts recirculating, the crazies are coming out of the woodwork. I don't know that I'm strong enough for all that."

Brash took her hand again. "First of all, you are one of the strongest women I have ever known. You've been through a lot in the past few months, but you've managed to hold your life together, not just for yourself, but also for your kids. And second, while you raise some valid concerns, most of them involve the case. And I try never to discuss a case while on a date."

"Is-Is this a date?"

The look he gave her sent goosebumps all the way to her toes. His eyes settled on her mouth. "Oh, yeah, sweetheart. This is definitely a date."

Madison put both hands to her cheeks and tried to soothe her destroyed makeup. "Now you tell me," she grumbled, but her heart soared.

He merely laughed, the sound deep and warm and free.

Their legs dangled over the edge of the tailgate, swinging in the breeze. Brash shifted one long leg and hooked a booted foot around hers. Madison leaned into him, slipping her arm through his as she rested her head on his shoulder. They studied the rippling waters below, both lost in their own thoughts.

Something still troubled her, something she needed to get off her heart. Something she wanted to share with Brash.

"She threatened to take my kids away, Brash." She whispered the horrible words, somehow afraid that speaking them aloud would make them come true.

"Who?" he asked sharply, looking down at her ashen face.

"My mother-in-law. She called today. She insinuated I was an unfit mother. She said I was putting my children at risk, allowing them to be on TV and exposing them to the world. She said they would be better off with her and my father-in-law."

"Maddy, I don't mean to make light of this, but believe me, you have nothing to worry about. You are a wonderful mother. No one would ever take your children away from you."

"You don't know these people, Brash. They have

money. Power. They know a lot of influential people. Judges."

"Again, no judge would take your children away from you, sweetheart." He moved his arm to place it around her, curling her into his warm embrace.

She picked at a thread on her shirt. "Gray ... did something. Something not quite legal. My in-laws pulled a few strings, called in a few favors. Swept the entire mess under the rug. What if- What if they do that again? What if they use their influence to take my children away from me?"

"It will never happen, honey. Trust me."

"But what if-what if she's right? What if I am putting them in danger?"

He put his other arm around her, pulling her close. Brash rested his chin atop dark hair that was tossed and tumbled by the breeze. For a long moment, he just held her. "Every parent grapples with that, sweetheart. Are we doing the right thing? Can we protect them from all the evil in the world? And the answer scares us to death, because the truth is, we can't. We can't protect them from everything. We can only do our best, and that's what you're doing, Maddy. You're doing everything in your power to give them a good life. A safe life. So don't let anyone ever make you doubt that. You are a good mom, Madison Reynolds."

She nodded, trying her best not to cry again. Not now, now that she knew this was a date. She tucked her curled-under lips together, just as Brash lowered his head to kiss her. Their noses bumped awkwardly, and what was to be their first magical kiss fell woefully short. It became a lopsided effort, but when they tried to correct it, they only made it worse. Madison pulled away in disappointment.

"Not so fast," Brash murmured, his breath still warm on her cheek. "I think we can do better."

"I certainly hope so," she whispered with a wry smile.

His mouth covered hers, smile and all. Gently, but with purpose. He masterfully tugged her lips together, molding them to fit exquisitely against his own. His kiss was slow and thorough. Almost methodical, had it not been pure magic. He increased the pressure through a speculative test of push and pull. Tiny sips that turned into nips. Queries that became answers, answers of the delicious, toe-curling variety. Another masterful move, and he had nudged her mouth opened again, easing his tongue inside. His hands slipped into her hair, cradling her face close as he kissed her so deeply and so completely that Madison's world tilted and spun, and found a new axis. Brash.

Before the kiss became too heated, before he lost himself completely to the heady taste and feel of this woman, Brash tempered the kiss to a low simmer. He forced himself to pull away. Dipped back in for one more taste. Tried to settle his ragged breathing as he rested his forehead against hers.

"That," he whispered hoarsely. "That was..." He tried to find the words, failing miserably. There were none. The kiss was everything he dreamed it would be, everything he feared it would be. After this, there was no going back.

He peered down at Maddy to see her reaction. His heart stalled in his chest. For him, it had been nothing less than magic. Life altering. But— "Are you... crying?"

"M-Maybe." Her voice was small.

His heart hurt, thinking she did not share the same feelings of wonder. The same sense of *rightness*. Devastated, his arms dropped from around her.

"I'm sorry," he said stiffly. "That's not the response I was going for. I thought we got it right that time."

"We did."

"Then… why are you crying?"

She lifted her gaze, tears swimming in the bright hazel of her eyes. "Because it was so perfect," she whispered.

Relief washed over him, settling into his weakened knees. He had never felt so relieved — nor so exposed — in his forty-two years of life. He wanted to celebrate. He wanted to shout to the world that he and Maddy were… What? *Perfect together, that's what.*

Before he could swoop her into his arms, she continued. "That's what scares me. Perfect never lasts. Perfect's not real."

He tried to make light of the situation, but the warble in his voice was heartfelt. "Give me another chance. I promise not to do so well this time."

She reached up to finger the sharp line of his jaw. A tiny thrill shot through her when she felt him quiver beneath her touch. How could he possibly understand? She had dreamed of this kiss for over half her life. She had been half in love, half in awe, of this man since she was fifteen years old. This kiss had been everything she had dreamed of. More than she had hoped for. It fulfilled her every teenage fantasy.

Her eyes fell to his mouth. He saw the desire in her eyes. The temptation.

"Find out," he challenged softly.

She jerked her eyes back to his. "Wh—What?"

"You're wondering if it was a fluke. The one and only perfect kiss. You're thinking a second kiss couldn't possibly be as good as the first. So find out."

Madison drew in a sharp breath. Did she dare? And what if it weren't? What if it destroyed her fantasy? The romantic girl inside her heart begged that she be satisfied, to leave well enough alone. She could savor her one perfect kiss. Let it be enough.

But the red-blooded woman inside her body

accepted his challenge. Maddy raised her face to his, pressing her warm mouth against his, willing to take the risk. As she threaded her fingers into his dark russet hair and pulled his face to hers, she knew one kiss would never be enough.

A long moment later, Brash lifted his head. A confident smile tickled the corners of his mouth. "Well?"

"Damn it, Brash, that one was even more perfect than the first." She sounded slightly annoyed as she pulled her arms from his neck and straightened her shirt.

He chuckled at her discomposure. "Why, Madison, I've never heard you curse before," he teased.

"Oh, sorry." She waved away the blunder. Beneath her breath, she grumbled, "I can barely remember my name right now, much less my manners."

It thrilled Brash to see the normally cool Madison Reynolds so flustered. Does wonders for a man's ego, he thought, his chest puffed with joy. Not to mention his heart. With a twinkle in his eye, he playfully bumped her shoulder with his. "I tell you what. I'm willing to try this kissing thing over and over, until one of us finally messes up. What about it? You game?"

She gave him a scornful look and changed the subject. "I believe you mentioned eating?"

"That's right. Not a proper date without dinner." He scooted off the tailgate with ease, then offered his hand to help her down. She knew he would use the excuse to steal another kiss.

Even short and sweet, his kiss was perfect. "Yep, still got it," he teased.

Maddy rolled her eyes. "You're going to be impossible now, aren't you? I should have never opened my mouth."

He let his eyes trail wickedly down to the mouth in

question. "Oh, but I'm so glad you did," he rumbled.

Amazing how one look could burn like fire. Maddy's feet faltered and she felt herself blushing like a schoolgirl. Flirting with Brash deCordova — even better, having Brash flirt with *her* — was an exhilarating experience.

Brash reached into the backseat of his pickup and pulled out the essentials for a picnic. He tossed a ragged but colorful quilt her way as he carried the cardboard box. After selecting a relatively flat spot along the riverbank, they spread out the cloth and pulled their feast from the box.

"No picnic basket, I see," she teased.

"Baskets are for sissies," he claimed. "This is what a real man's picnic looks like." He pulled out a roll of paper towels and waved them in the air. "Dual purpose, less waste. Used as both plate and napkin." Next came a Tupperware container. "Sandwiches. My gourmet specialty, bacon and pimento cheese." He kept digging. "Saltines. Cookies for dessert."

Her eyes twinkled. "Homemade, I see."

"I just use the fancy printed wrapper to keep them fresh," he assured her. He pulled the final items from his cardboard box. "Red plastic cups. Good for sweet tea," – he pulled out a Thermos — "song inspiration, or the pièce de résistance, wine from our local vineyard."

"Not bad for a cardboard box."

The sun dipped low as they shared their simple fare. As dusk crept across the sky, the air turned chilly. Brash brought her jacket from the truck and curled it around her shoulders, allowing his hands to linger. He nuzzled her cheek with a kiss.

"I'm glad you called, Maddy. I was going crazy, thinking you might not."

It was a little late to warn him not to read too much into her call. Definitely too late to pretend she wasn't interested.

"It's been a crazy week," she opted to say. "Thank you for use of your thinking spot. You might be on to something with your 'highly scientific method' of problem solving."

"Just wait until I show you my stress relieving techniques," he murmured, blowing softly into her ear. When she shivered, he asked, "Still cold?"

She looked him directly in the eye and shook her head. "Not at all."

Brash swallowed hard and pulled away, readjusting himself as he settled close beside her. "Don't look at me like that, Maddy," he warned. "I might forget that I'm a gentleman, and that this is our first date."

"I'm not worried," she told him, brushing away a lock of his dark hair. "You are, after all, a man of honor."

It pleased him to know she finally thought so. He pulled her against him as they found a comfortable position upon the hard ground and watched the sun sink behind the trees. Vivid streaks of color painted the sky and reflected off the river below. Wildflowers scented the air. The wind lay low and only a faint breeze stirred the encroaching darkness. In the distance cattle bellowed and motors whirred, but the evening around them was quiet and still.

"Perfect," Madison pronounced.

"Mmm." His fingers trailed over her arm, tracing the lazy pattern of a lover's caress.

As darkness settled around them, Madison snuggled deeper into his arms. She sat within the curve of his body, her back against his chest, their long legs intertwined at the ankles.

"How did you manage to get away from the department tonight?" she asked. "Are you on duty?"

"Nope. Told 'em I was out of service for the night.

Not to call me unless there was a dire emergency."

"Did you remind them that a goat trampling Myrna Lewis' prized begonias did not qualify as an emergency?"

"Sure did. Neither does Miss Sybille's dog getting lost in the old sewer tunnels or Everett Howell's horse walking down Main Street because it knows how to open the stall door. I think there's a city ordinance against keeping animals within three hundred feet of the railroad tracks, but since he's mayor of Naomi, no one enforces it."

"So I have you all to myself this evening?"

"Yep, looks like you're stuck with me. Unless you have a curfew?"

Madison laughed. "Actually, I don't, not tonight. Blake went home with Jamal, Beth is spending the night with Megan, and Granny had Bingo. They usually go out to eat afterward, so there's no telling what time she'll drag in. Sadly enough, my grandmother has a more active social life than I do."

"Granny Bert is a pistol, that's for sure," he said affectionately. He dipped his head to nuzzle her neck, encouraged when she stretched the long column for his nibbling pleasure. "I'd be willing to help you out on that social problem. Can't have your eighty-year-old granny going out more often than you, after all."

"Mmm. That's thoughtful of you."

Brash moved his mouth near her ear, his warm breath fanning over her and sending delightful shivers over her body. "This is our first date, but I want a second. A third. A twenty-fourth."

When Maddy laughed, the sound was almost gleeful. "Getting a little ahead of yourself, aren't you there, Chief?"

"Like I told you before, sweetheart, I want a future with you."

The words sounded so beautiful in his deep, rich voice. So promising. Almost possible. Maddy hugged the arms that encircled her and deftly changed the subject.

"Something you said a while ago... I think I want you to help me buy a gun, Brash. A pistol."

She felt him stiffen behind her. "A gun? Why do you want a gun, Madison?"

"It's not that I want one. But I think I might need one."

He physically turned her around to face him. "Why? Has something happened? Something you haven't told me about?"

"No. Not really. But like Derron pointed out, I sometimes travel out and about the countryside, and there are known to be cougars and wild hogs in the area."

"I'll be sure and get you a pair of running shoes, too. If you're close enough to shoot either one of those with a pistol, you'd better be doing it on the run."

She could hear his sarcasm. She knew she was not fooling him. "So many things have been happening lately," she admitted. "And you have to admit, I've had a rather unusual series of . . . events since I moved here three months ago. I've been run off the road, rammed into a train, stuffed in an incinerator, locked in a room and now a stairwell, trapped in a wall, almost run over by a dirt bike..."

He stopped her before she could go further. "I'd rather buy you a roll of bubble wrap and keep you protected. It makes my blood run cold, thinking of how many times I've almost lost you."

"Bubble wrap. I haven't thought of that. Wonder if Blake and Bethani would mind if I wrapped them both up nice and tight..."

"I'm serious, Maddy. I've just now found you. I

don't want to lose you."

"Says the man who faces danger every day. I feel the same way, you know. You're a police officer, Brash. A special investigator for the sheriff's office. What if something happens to you?" She shuddered at the very thought.

"I'm glad to know you care enough to worry. But don't. I'm a big boy. And yes, I'll help you get a gun. *After* you take a gun safety course."

"Of course." She turned back around and took up residence against his chest once more. She curled her hands over his as he wrapped both arms around her. Being in his arms already felt so natural. So *right*.

"I know I said I don't like to talk shop while on a date, but I have something I want to run by you. I'd like to hire you again."

She didn't know which was more promising, the thought of an income, or the opportunity to see Brash each day. Either way, it was a win-win situation.

"I'm sure I could fit you in," she said in her most professional voice. "What did you have in mind?"

"I need someone to do a record search, as in plural. Over several decades. Again, plural."

"What are you looking for?"

"Anyone who might have something to lose if those journals are discovered."

"You think it has to do with the journals, too, don't you? That's my theory. I don't care what Nick says, I don't think kids are behind this. And I certainly don't believe in ghosts."

"I think it has to do with the journals and with that skeleton we found."

"Any word from Austin?"

"Nah. With hundreds of urgent active cases to process, identifying a fifty-or-more-year-old skeleton falls pretty low on the totem pole."

"But that body belonged to someone, Brash. And I think it has something to do with all those secret passageways. At the very least, with the hidden staircase."

"I agree. But unless we find those journals, we might never know what that is." They shared a mutual sigh. "Do you have any more ideas of where to look?"

"I found one promising spot, just as I heard the person moving around downstairs. To be honest, I had already forgotten about it."

She felt the tension coil within his body. A few moments ticked by.

To give him credit, he tried. He never moved, never shifted, but Maddy detected the faint twitch in his corded arms.

"Are you thinking what I'm thinking?" she finally asked.

She felt his sigh of relief. He had tried to stay relaxed, but the lawman in him was restless. "We have the keys," he reasoned. "I declared the premises off limits, but you *are* the homeowner."

"And you *are* the chief of police."

They had the picnic tidied up in no time. As he stuffed it all back into the truck, Brash had a moment of regret.

"Are we sure we want to do this? We have the evening to ourselves. That might not happen again anytime soon."

"I know. But I don't think either one of us could really enjoy ourselves. Our minds would be on the case."

Instead of crawling into the truck, Brash shut the door behind him and hauled her into his arms. "You see?" he said. "Our minds think alike. Another reason we're perfect together."

It was another ten minutes before they actually left.

One kiss led to another, and then another. Madison could have spent the entire evening in his arms, but the damage had been done. Even lost in the magic of his kiss, the thought of the secret location lingered in her mind.

"I'll call dispatch, tell them it's us at the house," Brash said as they pulled away from the river.

"Good idea. I don't want to be called in for trespassing on my own property." Thoughts of trespassing brought to mind her foray onto the Adams' land. "What's the penalty for trespassing, by the way?"

"It's punishable by fine. In some cases, jail time. A criminal record. Not something to be taken lightly." He assumed she was talking about recent activity at the Big House. "I made certain there were plenty of signs posted around the property, so that an intruder would have no ground to stand on, claiming they didn't know it was private property."

"So posting a sign is enough to press charges, should a person come onto your property?"

"Yes, ma'am."

Madison made no comment. She visualized the dozens of 'Posted' and 'No Trespassing' signs she had seen strung along Hank Adams' fence line.

Oops.

12

Across town, Bethani and best friend Megan deCordova piled onto the futon, fortified with a barrel of popcorn, Dr. Pepper floats, fashion magazines, cell phones, chocolate candy, and the remote control. Everything two fifteen-year-old girls needed for a Saturday night sleepover.

"Can you believe it?" Megan squealed with glee. "Connor Evans asked me to the prom! This is so unbelievable!"

"I thought Miley was going to pee her pants when she saw him talking to you. She is soooo in love with him. She's been telling everyone he asked *her* to go to prom. Now she has to suck face and admit she's been lying all this time."

Some of the joy fell from Megan's face. "My dad will never let me go. He says fifteen is too young to go to senior prom."

"I hear the same thing from my mother," Bethani commiserated. "Not that anyone has asked me. I was afraid Kevin might, but I sorta brushed him off the other day, so maybe he got the hint. I know Kaci likes him. But Connor Evans? You are so lucky, Meg! He's like The Sisters High royalty!"

"I know, right?" Megan pushed stylish purple-rimmed glasses further up her perky nose, sending a sheet of long russet hair over her shoulder with a flick of the wrist. Grabbing a frosty float, she leaned back into the cushions and dunked the ice cream up and down with the spoon as she contemplated her situation. "He's definitely hot. And maybe if I could go out with him, then maybe Russell might give me a second look. He's the one I'd rather go out with. I'd give anything to catch his eye."

"That might be hard to do. He's all about Miley." Bethani rolled her eyes at the injustice of it all. Miley Redmond was their archrival and a bane to their teenage existence.

Savoring the taste of rich vanilla ice cream mixed with her favorite soft drink, Megan closed her eyes in pleasure. They popped back open immediately, and a huge grin lit her face.

"You know what this is like?"

Bethani shrugged. "Karma? Miley likes Connor, Connor likes you."

"That, too. But no, this is exactly like our parents, back in high school!" She scooted up on the futon, her face shining with excitement. She loved a romantic story, and her parents spun a sweet one. It even had a happy ending. "Your mom always had a crush on my dad. He was a senior, big man on campus, just like Connor. But my dad had a crush on my mother. She was a cheerleader, like me. Instead of liking my dad all that much during high school, she liked one of his best friends. Just like I like Russell, who is Connor's best friend."

Bethani knew the story. "Momma Matt," she nodded. She had taken to calling Megan's stepfather the same affectionate name Megan did.

"That's right. But he had a huge crush on *your* mom. Sort of like Russell has a crush on Miley. And at the time, our moms didn't like each other very much, just like I can't stand Miley."

"Okay, I guess I see the similarities," Bethani said.

"Wonder if our love circle will turn out the same way theirs did? Everyone liking the other one, all at different times. Your mom and Momma Matt dated for a while, my parents married for a while, and then everyone broke up."

"And then, eventually, your mom married Momma Matt. So she still got her happily-ever-after."

"Yeah, I know. So maybe I'll get mine, too, with Russell. What do you think?" She smiled broadly, quite proud of her keen sense of deduction.

"It could happen, I guess."

"Of course it could! Just like your mom can still have her happily-ever-after."

Bethani shook her head, a shadow of sadness falling across her face. "She had hers already. But it didn't last ever-after."

"Not with your dad, I'm sorry to say," Megan said, her tone gentle. Her voice brightened. "But it still could, with *my* dad!"

"Your dad?" Bethani's blond hair whipped through the air as she spun around to stare at her friend.

"Yeah. Oh, come on, surely you've seen the way they look at each other! They are obviously into each other. Big time."

"My-My dad just died. My mom's not ready to date again."

Megan saw the look on her friend's face and knew to tread softly. "Maybe not right now," she quickly amended. "But when she's ready. You know, in a few months or so. But wouldn't it be cool if they got together? I mean, we could wind up sisters!"

Bethani stared at her blankly. "Sisters? You mean, like, if they got *married*?" Her voice was borderline hysterical.

"Not-Not any time soon. Eventually. Like-Like a few years from now."

"I-I don't know. I'm not sure my mother will ever get married again." Bethani liked Mr. D, she really did. He was pretty cool for a policeman. He had been a famous football player back in the day and had gone on to coach at big name colleges. He doted on his daughter and he was nice to Bethani whenever she came to visit at his house. She had nothing against the man.

As long as he doesn't trample my dad's memory. Her dad had only been gone five months. Not nearly enough for her mom to be interested in another man. Sure, her parents had fought a lot in the end. They had even had separate bedrooms. Bethani knew things hadn't been right between her parents for a long time, but as long as he was alive, there was always hope they could get back together and they could be a happy family again. His death had changed all that, but she wasn't about to dishonor his memory by accepting another man into her mother's life. Not even if it was Brash deCordova, her new BFF's own father.

A terrible thought occurred to her. What if her mom had always been in love with Mr. D? What if she had never really loved her dad to begin with? What if Bethani's whole life had been a lie?

"Beth?" Megan asked in concern. "Are you all right? You look a little pale."

"It's nothing," Bethani lied. "I'm just tired."

Megan tossed her friend a chocolate bar. "Here, have some energy. You're going to need it, if we stay up to watch the whole *Hunger Games* saga."

13

"This way," Madison instructed as they stepped off the grand staircase. "It's in the upstairs library."

"Hold on a minute." Brash put a hand on her arm, his voice hushed with caution. He cocked his head to listen.

A full ninety seconds ticked by. All Madison heard was an old house, settling in for the night. She watched his face for clues. What had he heard? Was someone in the house? And how was it possible that he had grown more handsome through the years?

Brash wore maturity well. His athletic build was still finely honed and muscular. His shoulders had broadened with the years and his chest had thickened. His stomach was still flat, his legs long and lean. The fine lines that edged his soulful brown eyes hinted at life lessons learned. A few strands of silver wove through dark russet hair still thick and wavy. And Madison needed no reminder of how sensuous his mouth was, nor how devastating his smile could be.

Madison blinked in dismay, appalled that she had allowed her imagination to run away with her. This was no time to be mooning over the man, even if he had fulfilled her teenage fantasy tonight. Kissing Brash had been everything she dreamed of, and so much more.

But there were more important issues at hand.

She saw the slight pucker of his brow. He was unsure as to what he did or did not hear. Another thirty seconds passed before he visibly shook off the concern. "I think it's okay," he said, but his words were still quiet. "Lead the way."

"I found several hidden niches in here," she informed him, pushing a button on the light switch. It was an old-school variety, an antique replica of the home's original push button switches. *Home Again* rewired the entire house and updated most of the switches, but in the formal rooms, Madison had chosen to remain historically accurate to the style of the day. "Including one niche that holds a gun."

Typical for a man, particularly one who worked with firearms and enjoyed hunting sports, Brash was as impressed with the old shotgun as he was with the hidden vaults. She almost had to pry him away to inspect the overhead cabinet in the alcove.

"You'll probably need a chair," she advised. "You're tall, but not quite tall enough to- Never mind." Before she could finish her sentence, his nibble fingers found the latch to the cabinet and the door swung open.

Brash gave a low whistle. "I think we hit pay dirt."

"We found them? They're really there?"

"Well, it has some sort of books, anyway. I'd say at least two dozen. The spines are leather, no titles. Looks like they could be journals."

"What are you waiting for? Get them down."

Brash hesitated, glancing around the room. "Are you sure there are no cameras in here? I ordered them all turned off, and we didn't find any when we were in here, but I need to be certain."

"According to your friend Amanda" — even Madison could hear the slight sneer in her voice — "they add cameras on an as-need basis. They haven't started on this room yet, so there's no need for cameras."

"My friend?" he questioned, arching his trademark imperial brow.

"You two seemed rather cozy the other day. And I heard you had supper with her a couple of weeks ago." She hadn't meant to bring it up, hadn't meant for him to know she still had her doubts. A few kisses, no matter how perfect, could not erase years of insecurity. And a part of her kept thinking that 'perfect' was most always too good to be true. Certainly too good to last.

"That's right," Brash acknowledged. "Both business related."

Madison shrugged, but the gesture fell short of indifference. "Like I said, your friend."

"It's the way you said it." He marched toward her, his words practically a growl. "Let's get one thing straight, right now."

She expected a fiery speech. Indignation. She didn't expect Brash to jerk out his arm and snag her in close. She didn't expect his mouth to plunder hers, stealing her breath away with the intensity of his kiss. She didn't expect her knees to buckle and her blood to catch fire. She didn't expect to melt.

He ended the kiss on an impossibly sweet note. His arms released her so that he could cup her face in the palms of his hands. He kissed her with exquisite tenderness.

At last he lifted his lips from hers, still so close the air from his lungs whispered across her face. "Do I make myself clear?"

Completely unraveled by his kiss, Madison could only nod.

His thumbs traced the contour of her cheeks. Brown eyes stared into hazel. Breaths quickened. Eyelashes fluttered close.

"Maddy," he breathed into her eager mouth.

"Brash," she responded.

The kiss heated, melding their bodies close. Just as his hand began a slow trail of exploration, a sound from downstairs interrupted their moment.

Brash jerked his head up, listening as a bumping noise came from below. He moved away so quickly that Madison swayed in surprise. By the time she got her equilibrium under control, he had opened the secret panel and pulled out the old shotgun.

"Still loaded," he confirmed, just before he thrust it into her arms. "If anyone other than me comes through those doors, pull the trigger."

"Where are you going?" she cried in alarm. He was already halfway across the room, headed to lock the door leading into the bedroom.

Task completed, he quickly moved to the main entrance. "I'm going down. Keep the doors locked and don't let anyone in but me."

"But—"

"It will be okay, sweetheart." His words were so full of strength, she almost believed them.

"Be careful, Brash!"

"I will be. And Maddy? If you have to use the gun, hold it tight against your shoulder. It's going to kick like a mule."

It seemed he was gone forever. Madison held the gun at ready, until the weight of it became too much for her sagging muscles. She lowered it to her side but remained vigilant, alternately watching the doors for any sign of movement.

The house was too quiet. Every little sound, no matter how innocent, made her jump. Was that the sound of footsteps on the stairs, or a clock ticking away each slow, agonizing moment? Was that a limb brushing against the window, or someone trying to pick the lock? Was that the sigh of an old foundation, or the sound of Brash lying hurt and broken at the hands of some unknown intruder?

When she finally heard his voice, a tiny cry of relief escaped her lungs. She ran to the door and fumbled with the lock before she finally tugged it free.

"Are you all right?" They barked the words simultaneously.

"What was it?" Maddy asked. "Did you see anything?"

Brash shook his head. When he stopped to shut and lock the door behind him, Madison knew they might still be in danger.

"Brash?" Her voice was worried.

"I didn't see anyone, but that doesn't mean they weren't there. This is a big house. And we both know it's filled with secret passages and plenty of places to hide."

"What are you doing? Why are you going to the bedroom?"

"I'll be right back."

Madison followed him to the door, watching as he crossed to the bed and pulled back the designer duvet. He shook two pillows free from their cases, and then deftly stripped the bed. He was back by her side in no time, arms full of linens, locking the door behind him.

"We need to take the journals with us," he explained. "But I'd rather not be seen carrying them out. So if anyone's watching, all they'll see is us carrying out dirty linens."

"Good thinking," she murmured.

His dark eyes twinkled with merriment. "I'm glad you approve."

"How can you joke around at a time like this?"

He dropped a quick kiss onto the tip of her nose. "You're just so cute when you're worried." As he situated the pillowcases to his liking on the floor, he chuckled over his shoulder. "Not so much when you make that face."

"You don't have eyes in the back of your head." To prove her point, she childishly stuck out her tongue to his turned back.

"Sure I do. I'm a dad. Not to mention a lawman. And as fond as I am of your tongue, you might want to put it back in your delightful mouth." He glanced over his shoulder to wag his brows suggestively. "Save it for later use."

"As many times as I've pulled that on my own kids, I guess I deserve it," she grumbled. "Let me do that. You start handing down the books."

"Use both pillowcases. I don't think I can carry them all at once."

"I'm not helpless, you know. I can carry one bundle."

"Fine. But make one smaller than the other." Seeing the exasperation on her face, he grinned. "What? I was going to give you the bigger one."

They worked quickly, transferring the books from the upper cabinet to the linens on the floor.

"This is them, Brash," Madison said excitedly, but she kept her voice low. "These are old journals, written in her hand. I recognize the writing from old letters and papers I've seen."

"Don't get your hopes up too high," he warned. "They may not tell us anything."

"Maybe. But then again, they might explain it all. At least why she had all the secret passages."

"It's going to take a while to go through all those," he said, stepping off the chair with the final handful of books. "How many is this, twenty-five?"

She took the books and placed them in the larger pile. "Twenty-six. Sixteen in that pile, ten in this."

"So each one must cover several years."

Maddy nodded. "That rose-colored one began in 1980. The last entry was dated '83."

"I'm thinking we need the early journals. Probably those plain black ones. They look the oldest."

"I can't wait to get them home and start reading."

"You can't take these home with you, Madison."

"Why not?"

"First of all, it's too dangerous. Someone has been going to an awful lot of trouble to keep you from finding these. Imagine what they might do to keep you from actually reading them."

She bit her lip. "I hadn't thought about that."

"And second, there are cameras at your house. Even if we manage to sneak these out, it wouldn't remain a secret for long."

"So what do we do with them?"

"We'll take them to the station. If I'm hiring you to do some work for us, no one will question why you're spending so much time there."

"Again, good thinking."

He flashed another charming grin. "Again, glad you approve." A twinkle lit his eye. "Or, we could take them to my house. Give you a good excuse to be over there, too."

Even now, at this inopportune moment with danger lurking near, his smile did crazy things to her insides. "The station would be safer," she muttered. "On all accounts."

"You're mumbling beneath your breath."

"I said I think the station is the better choice."

"Unfortunately, I agree."

Madison hesitantly turned to face him. She nibbled on her lower lip without quite meeting his eyes.

"Brash," she began. "About tonight…"

"Uh-oh. We haven't even slept together, and here I am getting the morning-after speech."

"What are you talking about?" she asked in annoyance.

"Isn't that what this is? You had a good time tonight, yada, yada. Picnic was fun, kisses were great, more yada, yada. But you don't need any more complications in your life right now." He crossed his arms and gave her a challenging glare. His jaw was set in a square of granite. "Isn't that what you were going to say?"

"No," she said stubbornly. A few beats went by. "Maybe. But it's not what you think."

"And what do I think, Madison?"

"You think I still don't trust you. That I'm still hung up on all my old issues and that they reflect directly on you. That's what you told me before, isn't it?" Her eyes lit with a challenge of their own.

"I told you that your distrust reflects on me, on my integrity. I told you a relationship has to have trust and respect, or it has nothing. And I told you I don't do halfway, Maddy. It's all or nothing. You trust me or you don't."

"I trust you, Brash."

"Maybe with your life, but what about with your heart?"

She could hear the pain in his voice. His vulnerability touched her to the core. Stepping close to him, she put her hands upon his crossed arms. "Yes, Brash, I trust you with my heart. This isn't about that. This is about privacy. About the cameras and the reporters and the way my life has become a public exploit. The truth is, I'm not ready for people to know about… about us."

She felt his arms give. While she marveled at the

sudden look of pleasure warming his dark gaze, his arms snaked around her waist and pulled her close. His smile was smug as he confirmed, "So you finally admit there is an *us*?"

She answered cautiously. "I could deny it," she said, picking at a button on his shirt. He stiffened at the words. With her own smug grin, she gazed up at him and her voice softened. "But we both know I'd be lying."

He tugged her a bit closer. "So where do we go from here?"

"Picnics are good. There are no cameras at the ranch."

"So basically, we have to sneak around to see each other."

Her lips curled into an unhappy twist. "I'm afraid so."

"I don't like it," he claimed with a frown. "I'm not ashamed of us, Maddy."

"I'm not ashamed of us, either. It's not about that. But can you imagine what the press would do with this story? How they would twist it around? I'm a widow, Brash. My husband just died five months ago. No one knows that our marriage died long before that. All they'll talk about is how I'm already moving on. And look who I'm latching onto, the town's most handsome and eligible bachelor. A former football giant and current chief of police, the man in charge of investigating the strange goings-on at my house. By the time they get through with it, they'll make it sound like we're both involved in some sort of shady venture to scam the public. Like we planted the skeleton and the ghosts, just so we could have the house remodeled as our little love shack."

"I make it a rule to never move in with a woman, at least not until our second date."

She swatted at his arm. "Would you stop joking

around? This is serious!"

"You're blowing this all out of proportion, sweetheart."

"You don't know what the press can be like, Brash."

"Actually, I do. I opted out of my contract with the NFL so I could come home and be a husband and father. Don't you think the press had a field day with that one? I was head coach at Texas A&M during not one, but two losing seasons. I was coaching at Baylor when they had that big referee scandal. The press ripped me to shreds both times. But that's nothing compared to what they like to do to police chiefs. Every time a crime is committed, every time an innocent person dies, the press makes it about the cops in charge, not the criminals. So, yeah, Maddy, I do know about the press." His voice held a hard edge. It was a reminder that even though he often joked and teased, he was a dedicated officer of the law and a formidable adversary.

Madison was duly chastised. "You're right, of course. I'm sorry. I'm just saying that I have had more than my share of persistent reporters, trying to find a story when there is none. They even ran a segment in Dallas this morning, rehashing old news about Gray's failed business and his 'sudden death.' The way they said it implied there was something more to his accident than a blowout on a slick road. I just don't want to give them something else to talk about. It would be like pouring gasoline on a blazing fire."

"Shh. Come here, sweetheart." He gathered her gently to him for a hearty hug. "I understand. I don't like it, but I do understand." He gave her another quick squeeze. "And while I'd love to stand here and prove to you what an understanding man I can be, we need to get out of here. There still may be someone in the house."

Worry sparked in her eyes. "So what are we going to do?"

Brash pulled out his phone. "Call for backup."

14

The last of the customers cleared out of the café. Genesis wiped down the counter as she called out a friendly goodbye.

She normally did not work on Saturday nights, but Shilo Dawne had asked for the night off. Even though Genesis had been here since early morning, it was the least she could do for one of her most dedicated employees.

"Here, Genny, let me get that for you."

"Thanks, Cutter, but I can get it."

"I insist." With no effort at all, the young man took the heavy tray from her and carried it into the kitchen. He stayed for a few minutes to talk with the kitchen crew, and then came out with a pleased smile, nibbling on an apple turnover.

"I see Thelma tipped you," Genny teased.

"Yep." He swallowed the rest in one big gulp and licked his lips. "That was good, but you didn't make them today, did you?"

"As a matter of fact, no. I let Shilo Dawne make them this morning."

"I can tell. Yours are the best." His blue eyes twinkled conspiratorially.

"You have a little something right here," she

murmured, touching the corresponding place on her own face.

Unabashed, Cutter's tongue made a swipe for the sugar still dusting the side of his mouth. Genny's traitorous eyes followed. He made slow work of it, licking his lips slowly, his eyes tracing the same curves of her own mouth.

Genny turned away, fire burning in her face. It seemed to be spreading to other parts of her, too, but she steadfastly ignored it. It was humiliating, being caught drooling over him like a silly schoolgirl!

She was thankful when the busboy came out from the kitchen for the final round of dirty dishes. "Hey, man," he spoke to Cutter. "What are you doing here on a Saturday night? No hot date?"

Cutter's reply was smooth, if not vague. "The night's still young, man."

"I hear ya. Well, have a good one. Don't do anything I wouldn't do."

Genny saw the men bump knuckles as she turned back around. It suddenly dawned upon her why the young firefighter was here on a Saturday night. "You thought Shilo Dawne was working tonight. Sorry, I took her shift. She had a paper to finish."

"Yeah, she was complaining about that yesterday. Says your professor gives too much homework." He sounded somewhat resentful. Genny supposed it was because college classes took too much of the waitress' time.

"*My* professor?" she asked, eyebrows arched.

"Yeah, the one that hangs around here all the time. The one with the crazy ties."

"You mean Professor Calloway?"

"That's the one. Shilo Dawne says you two are dating."

Genny laughed aloud. "We are *not* dating. He's

asked me out a time or two, but I haven't said yes."

"But you're considering it." His tone was slightly accusing.

She shrugged as she untied her apron and plopped it onto the counter. "I don't know. Maybe. I don't have time for dating right now."

Before Cutter could make a comment, his phone rang. "Montgomery," he said brusquely.

"Cutter? Brash. I need to ask a favor. You busy?"

"Nah, man, whatcha got?"

"I need you to swing by the Big House. Maddy and I are here, and I think someone may be downstairs. Perry is on a call and Schimanski isn't answering his phone."

"Sure, Brash, I'll be there in five."

"No sirens. Come in on foot, if you can. Text me when you get here."

"Miss Maddy okay?" Cutter asked in concern.

Genny immediately tuned into the conversation. She pecked at his arm as he hung up with the chief of police. "What's wrong? What's happened to Maddy? I haven't heard from her all evening. Something's happened, hasn't it?"

"I'm not sure. I'm headed over to the Big House to find out."

"I'm coming with you." She hurried to the door of the kitchen and called, "Thelma? Can you lock up if I'm not back?

"Sure thing, Miss Genny. Everything okay?"

"I hope so." She followed Cutter out the door. "I hope so."

"I wish you had stayed in the truck, Genny," Cutter complained. They slipped among the shadows of the old mansion's yard, working their way to the front entrance. Cutter had texted the police chief, telling him they were on the premises.

"No way. That's my best friend in there, and you thought it was serious enough to bring a gun. I'm coming with you."

"Stay behind me when we go in," he instructed firmly. "Hook your finger in my belt so I'll know you're there."

"What's going on, Cutter?"

"I'm not sure, but one thing I do know; there are no such things as ghosts."

Through coordinated efforts, Brash and Madison came down the grand staircase as Cutter and Genny came through the front door. After a brief greeting, they broke apart to search the house. The men ventured out on their own, while Maddy and Genny worked as a team. They met back at the foot of the stairs.

"Nothing," Cutter said, keeping his voice low.

"In a house this size, they could move from one room to the next and we would never know it," Genny interjected.

"I'm guessing they're gone by now," Brash said. "Although I have no idea how they got in or out. The doors were still locked, the alarms engaged."

"Brash, what is it this person wants?" Genesis asked, her blue eyes sharp with worry.

"I have a pretty good idea. Which reminds me, I need to bring down the sheets."

"You're doing laundry at a time like this?" She forgot to keep her voice low as she propped her hands on her hips. "Don't you think there are a few more important things to worry about right now, like keeping my best friend and her children safe?"

Brash merely winked and jogged up the stairs. He unlocked the library door, grabbed up an armful of extra sheets so that the journal-filled pillowcases could not be seen, and came back down while Madison whispered an explanation to their friends.

Knowing there could be a covert mic in place, Maddy spoke louder than necessary as the men carried the pilfered journals toward the front door.

"I appreciate your help, guys, carrying out the dirty laundry for me. That fingerprint dust left such a mess, and I don't want it to set in on these sheets."

"It's the least I can do, since I made the mess," Brash replied. "I'll even carry these to your house for you. Ready?"

She locked the door and set the alarm, wondering for a moment why she even bothered. So far, this person was able to bypass all their efforts.

"I'll call you later, Gen," Madison said as she hugged her friend. "Thanks for coming. You, too, Cutter."

"I'm glad it turned out to be nothing," the young man said.

"You need a ride, Genny?" Brash offered.

"I've got it," Cutter was quick to say. "My truck's over there."

As they waved goodbye to the departing couple and started for Cutter's truck, he grinned down at the café owner. "Did you see what I just saw?"

Genny made a blind guess. "She locked the gate remotely?"

"No. The way he put his hand on her hip. Low, like this." He moved closer, sliding his large hand along the small of her back, just low enough to suggest intimacy.

"I-I missed that."

His hand remained in place as they walked. "I think it would be cool if they got together," Cutter said. "They make a good couple."

"I think so, too. And so does Maddy, she's just afraid to admit it."

They reached his truck and his hand fell from her waist. As he opened the door for her, he asked suddenly, "It's a nice night. Wanna go for a ride?"

Knowing she should say no, Genny heard herself agreeing. "Sure, why not?"

Cutter jogged around to the other side of the truck, but instead of starting the motor, he sat staring at the house they had just left.

"What?" Genny asked, following his gaze.

"Just watching for lights. Movement of some kind. Something is going on in there, I just don't know what."

"I just hope Maddy will be comfortable living there, once the remodel is done. This has to be disconcerting, knowing someone can slip in and out of your home at will."

"We'll catch him," he said with confidence, including himself in the team. He started the motor and began backing out.

"So where are we going?" she asked.

He shrugged. "I guess we could do what all the kids do, grab a couple of beers and hit the back roads."

"Driving around drinking, even on dirt roads, doesn't seem like a very good idea," Genny said. "And it's not quite my style."

"Mine, either. At least, not anymore. I've made my share of back roads, though, back in the day."

Genny laughed. "What? Five years ago?"

"Nah, I gave that up with high school."

"So, what, six or seven years ago?"

He looked at her sharply. "How old do you think I am?"

"I don't know. Twenty-five, twenty-six?"

"Not sure if I should be flattered or offended," he mumbled. He turned the truck onto Naomi's main street, driving right past *New Beginnings*. It was soon obvious that they were headed out of town.

"So?" Genesis finally asked. "Aren't you going to tell me?"

"Tell you what?"

"How old you are."

They passed Genny's modest little house, the one she had inherited from her parents. "You really should leave your lights on, Genny," he scolded. "It's not safe to go into a dark house at night."

"It's fine." She dismissed his worry with a wave of her hand. "I have those motion detection lights that come on when I get out of the car."

"That's good. Never can be too safe." A mile or so down the road, he pointed to a house on the right. "See? I even left my lights burning."

"You live there? I didn't know that."

"Yep. Right here on the edge of the ranch." He turned into a cattle guard entrance that carried them onto a gravel road. "My parents live toward the back of the property. Cooper and his wife live over there." He pointed to a house lit up in the distance.

"So you're close enough to help out on the ranch, but far enough away to have a little privacy," she guessed.

"Having three brothers and two sisters didn't offer much privacy growing up."

"No, I guess not."

They chatted about his family and the different paths the Montgomery children had taken. They wound their way through the ranch, until they took a questionable path up a steep hill.

"Are you sure this is a road?" Genny asked skeptically, bracing herself against the dashboard as they rocked back and forth among the rutted lanes.

"Haven't gotten around to getting it rocked yet, but yes, it's definitely a road."

They reached the crest of the hill, and by light of the

moon, Genny saw the flat field sparsely dotted with mature trees. "I bet this is gorgeous by daylight," she said. "Can you see a long way?"

"All the way to the river in that direction, back to town in that," he pointed. He looked over at her hopefully. "Want to get out?"

She glanced down at her shoes. If they were good enough for waitressing, they were good enough for traipsing through an open field. "Why not?" she shrugged.

Cutter walked slowly for her benefit, knowing her legs weren't nearly as long as his. Nor was she accustomed to the terrain. He took her elbow twice, helping her over a clump of grass and an unexpected dip. They rounded the ridge of trees and she saw it. The skeleton of a house.

"Going up or coming down?" she asked.

He laughed. "A little of both. This was my grandparents' house. I'm gutting it down to the frame, then building it back up to suit my needs."

"This is yours?" she asked in surprise. "But that house is huge!"

"They had a houseful of kids," he shrugged.

"You'll need a half dozen kids of your own to fill it up," she predicted.

"I wouldn't mind. I like big families." He led her into the gutted house, through an opening she assumed was the front door. "What about you, Genny? You ever thought of having kids?"

A familiar pain squeezed her heart, making it difficult to breath. "Of course I've thought about it. What woman doesn't?" She moved ahead of him, using the watery light of the moon as her guide. "I like the stairs."

"Not as fancy as the ones at the Big House," he allowed. "This is just an old farmhouse, but it raised a happy family."

"I guess this is the kitchen."

"When it's time to plan it, I'd like to get your input in here."

"Aw, how sweet. I'd be honored, Cutter."

"Tell me what you'd do."

"Well, I'd put a bank of cabinets along this wall. Double ovens over here. A huge commercial refrigerator here. Oh, and a big working bar right in the center. With stools on one side, cabinets and appliances on the other."

"Appliances?"

"You know, a second dishwasher, warming drawers, that sort of thing." She could see it in her head. Her dream kitchen.

"Warming drawers?"

"Sure. You know how I love to bake. I'd have those babies full of all sorts of breads and pies and cookies." She laughed at her own silly notions. This wasn't her house.

"Apple turnovers, too, I hope."

"Of course. And I won't tell Shilo Dawne that you said mine were better than hers." Her blue eyes twinkled with mischief. "Your secret is safe with me."

"I'll tell you another secret, too. Did you know there is a cave beneath us?"

"A cave?"

"Yep. About forty feet down, there's a huge open cavern. It's a little tricky getting to it, but once you're down there you've got plenty of room to walk around."

"Maddy and I were talking about the caves the other day. I remember some of the kids used to claim to explore them, but I thought they were just full of it."

"Nope, there really are caves around here. I can take you down there one day, if you like."

Genny laughed. "No thanks. When we were down in

the basement that day, I realized I might be a tad bit claustrophobic."

"Maybe it was just the skeleton," he suggested.

"Maybe. Still, I think I prefer to stay above ground."

"Then I won't bother showing you the tunnels," he grinned.

"What tunnels?"

"There are actually a few tunnels around here, as well. Some natural, some man-made."

"Like I said, I believe I'll stay above ground."

They wandered through the rest of the house. Cutter told her a few of his plans for the re-build. Genny made a few suggestions of her own, most of which he liked. They argued good-naturedly over one of her suggestions, until Genny finally threw her hands up in defeat.

"Hey, it's your house, your money. I think my way is more economical, but that's for you to decide. If you like throwing away your hard-earned money, far be it from me to stop you."

"I think it's worth the splurge," he said confidently.

As they wandered back to the front of the house, Genny asked, "So how long do you think this is going to take you?"

"Probably a year or so. I'm not in a particular hurry, since it will just be me living here. I'm saving my money, so I can build it out of pocket, no mortgage."

"That's a very wise plan, but I'm not sure how practical it is."

"What, you don't think I can afford it?"

She sputtered with her answer. "Well, uh, I, uh, I know how expensive everything is these days. And without a college education..."

"Who says I don't have a college education?" he asked sharply.

"I-I meant no offense. A lot of people don't go to

college these days. There's nothing wrong with that, Cutter."

"I agree. None of my brothers went to college, and they are all quite successful. One has a taxidermy business, one is part owner in the feed store, one helps Dad run the ranch. I, on the other hand, am the lone son with a snazzy little college diploma hanging on his wall. Two, as a matter of fact."

"I-I didn't mean to offend you, Cutter. I just assumed..."

"You assumed I had a go-nowhere job like welding. A second job as a volunteer firefighter that doesn't even pay. So naturally I must be uneducated." His tone was defensive.

"Actually, it was more of the fact that you were still here in The Sisters. Most kids that go to college move away."

"It's a shame, isn't it?" he said, his voice calmer now, more philosophical. "Most of the ambitious ones can't wait to get out of here. Which leaves us with the slackers, the ones who are content to do little or nothing with their lives." He looked over at her, the moonlight revealing the passionate glow of his eyes. "I'm not one of them, Genny. I have dreams. Ambitions. I want to be more. I just don't think I have to sell out to do it. I can stay where my roots are, plant new ones. And I can make The Sisters a better place to live."

Moved by his enamored speech, Genny began to see him in a new light. He was right, of course: he could still live in The Sisters and be successful. She knew he was highly regarded within the community. His dedication to the fire department was admirable. He ran his own successful welding business, which was a testament to his initiative and drive. Now she discovered he was building his own house, mortgage free. Obviously, the young man was wise beyond his years. He was already making his mark upon the community, and he still had his entire life before him. Genny had no doubt that if anyone could be successful here, it was Cutter Montgomery.

They made small talk as they drove back into town. When the conversation fell into a comfortable lull, Genny wondered about the lucky girl who would one day share the home with him. Shilo Dawne? More than likely, it would be Callie Beth Irwin. They had dated on-and-off for a while now. Or perhaps it would be someone else, someone he might already be seeing. Shortly after Valentines, there was a rumor he had admitted to being bitten by the love bug, but so far, she had noticed no one new in his life. Not that she knew very much about him. She certainly hadn't known about his college degrees.

"Genny?"

"Yes?"

"We're here."

Lost in thought, she had not realized they were stopped in front of the café. "So we are." She laughed at her own wandering thoughts.

As she groped around to find her purse, inadvertently knocked to the floorboard from the rough road up to his house, Cutter came around to open her door. He put his hand on her back to usher her up the walk.

"I enjoyed that, Cutter." Her genuine smile revealed her dimples. "You have a beautiful house. Or least, you will."

"You'll have to keep up with the progress. Come out often and keep me on track."

"I might just do that."

"I hope so." They stepped up to the door of the café. Genny tested it and found it locked.

"Do you have to go back in?" he asked.

"Yes, I still have a few things to do."

"You want me to wait for you?"

"Thanks, but I'll be fine. I know you have better things to do on a Saturday night than watch me count down the register."

Cutter frowned. "I don't like the thought of you handling the money so late at night, all alone in there. I don't mind waiting."

"Cutter, I do it all the time. I'll be fine, really."

His reluctance to leave her there alone was obvious.

"Honestly, Cutter, I'll be fine." She gave him a gentle push. "Shoo. Go on. Like you told Benny, the night's still young."

"I don't late-date," he told her solemnly.

"Date?" She laughed, realizing he was teasing. She decided to play along. "Well, then, thank you for my lovely date, kind sir. I had a nice time."

He wasn't laughing. His eyes were thoughtful. "So did I." He nodded toward the door. "I'll wait for you to go in. Be sure and lock the door behind you."

"Yes, sir," she said obediently. She twisted the key into the lock, stepped inside, and disengaged the alarm. "See? Perfectly safe."

She stood in the door while Cutter backed his way down the sidewalk. "Thanks for going tonight, Genny. And thanks for the input."

"My pleasure."

He turned to go, then spun back around. "Genny?" he called, just before she shut the door. She looked at him expectantly, waiting for him to go on. "I'm no slacker."

His words surprised her. Apparently, she had offended him more than she realized. Though he stood halfway down the walk, she could hear the emotion in his voice. "I have no doubt of that, Cutter," she said sincerely. "And you'll make some lucky girl a very good husband, I am certain of that."

"I don't want to marry a girl, Genny. I want to marry a woman."

With those strange words, he turned around. Puzzled, Genny watched him go. When he reached his truck door, he stopped to look back at her, still standing there with the door half-ajar.

"And Genesis?" he called.

"Yes?"

"I'm not as young as you think. I turned thirty-one last fall."

15

Madison began her new job on Monday morning. It did not occur to her to wonder how Brash managed to get her salary approved so quickly. She had no way of knowing he paid it out of his own pocket, just as he had done before. All she knew was that she was bringing in a paycheck, she was helping with her own case, and she could spend more time with the man of her dreams.

"I hope you know what you have gotten yourself into," Brash said. He hefted a large cardboard box onto the desk he assigned as her temporary workspace.

"I don't suppose there's a picnic in there."

"Nope. Just tax rolls for the years 1945-1950."

"You mean they're on *paper*?" she cried in dismay. "Not computerized?"

"We're working on it. I know we're back as far as 1972. Not so sure about the other twenty-two years."

"Twenty-two?"

"I'm working with a loose theory that if the person in the basement was murdered, the crime occurred sometime between the mid-40s and early-90s."

Madison cast a horrified glance to the box brimming with files. "But-but this is impossible!" Madison sputtered.

"Nothing's impossible, sweetheart. All you have to

do is start with the computerized records. Search for families who lived in the area in '72 and remained here in the early '90s. Cross-reference that list with paper records prior to '72. You should be able to narrow it down somewhat."

Madison glared at him. "I take back anything pleasant I may have said or thought about you since Saturday night. I hereby change my mind. You, sir, are a slave driver. A monster."

Brash chuckled, zeroing in on only one part of her rant. He settled a lean hip on the edge of her desk and leaned in. "So you've thought about me since Saturday, huh? That's good. Because I haven't been able to get you out of my head."

"I thought we were going to keep this thing secret!" she hissed between her teeth.

"No one's listening. And no one will see us, when you meet me in the back interrogation room at noon."

"Isn't that the room with a two-way mirror?" she asked sweetly.

"Don't worry. We'll keep the lights off." He waggled his eyebrows suggestively.

Madison buried her face in her hands and groaned. "Brash! How am I ever going to go through all these records? And no foolishness. I have to keep my mind on what I'm doing. When am I supposed to look through the journals?"

"We agreed to a half-day's pay, remember? You'll have the afternoons free to read the journals, barring other jobs you have."

"Unfortunately, there aren't many of those."

"See? It's all working out." He flashed her a killer smile, but she felt oddly immune to his charm. Most of it, anyway.

"I'll be back around lunchtime," he said, moving off her desk with a creak of his knee. "Old football injury," he explained.

Feeling spiteful, Madison smiled sweetly. "Or maybe just old."

By lunchtime, she had a partial list of names. She swore her eyes were permanently crossed. Brash brought lunch from Genny's and they ate together in the break room. Fortified by the meal and a fresh cup of coffee, Madison tackled the first of the journals. That, too, was a slow process.

By the second day, she had found one journal of interest. With Brash's blessing, she disguised it with a paper jacket from one of his procedural books and carried it home as homework.

Work had resumed at the mansion on Monday. Running dreadfully behind schedule, Nick kept crews late in the evening to make up for lost time. Three days of the grueling schedule passed without any sign of 'ghosts.'

On the fourth day, Madison awoke to find Granny Bert's house had been wrapped. It was a common enough prank in small towns everywhere; nothing was safe from the streaming white rolls of toilet paper, particularly trees and yard ornaments. Regarded mainly as a favored Halloween tradition, pranksters could strike at any time.

While childish, there was a certain edge to the papering of the rambling craftsman house on Sycamore. The porch columns were wrapped in red crepe paper, the color of blood. Along with an excess of paper, white sheets were strung across the porch, tied at the neck to resemble a ghost. And as luck would have it, the cameras on the porch had been disabled, failing to catch the perpetrators of the prank.

Madison doubted luck was involved, particularly when the news van pulled up at the house at the same time she discovered the morning mess. The reporter confirmed an anonymous tip called in to the station, citing a new development in the case.

"Mrs. Reynolds, do you have any idea who would have done such a thing, or what their motive might have been?" The reporter thrust the mic into her face as she went to her car.

"No comment."

"Sources tell us you are conducting some sort of search at the mansion, looking for clues to the skeleton's identity."

"No comment."

"We understand you've been at the police station every day this week, demanding action from the police."

"No comment."

"What can you tell us about the new investigation the IRS is conducting on your late husband's failed business?"

Madison faltered. This was the first she had heard of a new investigation. "No comment," she said, but her voice was weak.

"Is it true he embezzled millions of dollars from his clients over the past five years? You were his partner at the investment firm, isn't that correct?"

"No comment."

"Were you aware of the duplicity? Has the IRS contacted you personally?"

Madison's voice gained strength. "No. Comment." She slid into her car, slammed the door with purpose, and jerked the gearshift into reverse.

She could smell it before she saw it. Sniffing the foul air inside the car, Madison glanced down at her feet. Had she stepped in dog doo? She looked into her rearview mirror, mindful of the news van parked behind her. When she saw the pile of dead chickens in her backseat, their blood and worse smeared across the leather upholstery, her foot slipped from the brake. In her horror, she jerked the wheel and her moving car rammed into the side of the van.

Not stopping to put the vehicle into park, Madison jumped from her car, screaming vehemently.

The news camera was there to catch it all on film.

"Can I bring you anything else, sweetie?" Genesis asked in concern.

"No, I'm fine."

"No you're not," her best friend challenged. "You are two inches away from having a nervous breakdown."

Madison stared up at her bedroom ceiling, willing the tears away. "More like one inch, but who's counting?"

"Have you taken anything?"

"I don't need drugs, Genesis!" Madison snapped. "I need a lawyer!"

"Why do you think you need a lawyer?" Genny pushed the covers aside to sit by her friend. The bedroom was one of the few places in the house they could have a private conversation.

"For starters, Brash is out there right now, arguing with Nick and Amanda about the cameras. He's threatening to get a court order to take them down. They are making counter-threats, saying to do so would void my contract with them. If my contract is voided, I have to pay for the work already done on the house. Money that I do not have, now nor ever."

"Don't worry, Maddy, they'll work something out."

"I don't know about that. Nick is livid. His face is all red and mottled. And Brash is so deadly calm and focused that it's scary. Remind me to never cross that man." She shivered.

"As in, not to break his heart?" Genny asked, her eyes alight with mischief. "Come on, Maddy, you've hardly told me a thing about you and Brash! Is this any way to treat your best friend? Don't you know I live vicariously through you? Your love life is my love life."

Madison buried her face beneath her pillow. "Just smother me. Go ahead, get me out of my misery. If I have to watch that stupid video of myself one more time, I swear I am going to shoot somebody. Then I truly will need a lawyer!"

"Come on, it wasn't so bad. Most of it, anyway. And at least Granny Bert convinced the network to pay for all the damages to both vehicles, in exchange for not charging them with trespassing."

"They just wanted rights to the video. So they could play it over. And over. And over, again."

"But at least your insurance rates won't go up. That's something."

"What does it matter?" Madison groaned. "I may be in prison soon. If it's true about the IRS, they may come after me. Annette and Charles won't even try to bail me out."

"They will if it means saving their precious son's good name."

"How did this happen, Genny? How did all of this go so wrong?"

There was a knock on the door. "What's the secret code?" Genny called playfully.

"Jack Daniels."

Genny grinned at her friend. "I love your grandmother." She hustled off the bed and opened the door for the older woman. She took two of the three glasses from her hands and sniffed appreciatively. "Heavy on the Jack, light on the Coke. Good call. Here, Maddy, drink up."

She curled her nose sullenly. "I prefer wine."

"This is stronger. Drink," her grandmother ordered. "It will soothe your nerves."

Madison took a tiny sip. It was strong, but the burn going down was oddly comforting. "What's going on out there? Dare I ask?"

"Your man is really giving them the what-for. Nick is doing pretty good at holding his own, but the woman has already folded. She keeps staring at Brash with this stricken look upon her face." Granny reported the scene in the living room with relish, her eyes twinkling. "The show out there is even more entertaining than watching you jump out of your moving car, screaming at the top of your lungs."

"You can go now, thank you," Madison said drolly, taking another sip of her drink.

"I came to tell you that your cousin Charlotte called. She'll be happy to represent you, should this thing end up in court." Granny cocked her head to listen. "Hey, the shouting has stopped."

A few minutes later, there was a sharp rap on the door. "It's me," Brash said. He didn't wait for an invitation. He came right in.

Madison flew off the bed and into his arms. She ignored the look of surprise upon Genny's face. She also ignored Granny's face, now split with pride and a smile bright enough to power five light bulbs.

"It's about time," her grandmother crowed. She slapped Genny on the arm. "Did you know about this?"

"Apparently not everything," she said under her breath.

"How you doing, sweetheart?" Brash asked, soothing Madison's hair as he held her.

"Humiliated. Horrified. Worried sick." She pulled away to look up at him. "Brash, I can't afford to break my contract. The cameras have to stay."

"The cameras can come back," he corrected. "*After.*

After we find out who is doing this."

"But—"

"We've already worked it out, sweetheart. We came to a temporary solution."

"Don't you think you should have consulted me first?" she snapped.

"Not really. This is police business, not a personal matter."

"I think this is where we leave," Genny said, seeing the standoff about to take place. Brash and Madison were already engaged in a staring contest. "Granny, we should go."

"Why? This is just getting interesting."

"Granny Bert, I have a favor to ask of you," Brash said, breaking his gaze with Madison.

"Anything for a friend of Maddy's." She wiggled her eyebrows, putting emphasis on the word *friend*.

"I want you and Genny to go out there and stage a conversation. Be talking about the lost journals. Say it was a shame to find out they had been destroyed. Moan about Maddy wasting all that time looking for them, when now we know they were destroyed years ago."

"How did it supposedly happen?"

"You're creative. Make up something."

Granny Bert slapped her hands together and rubbed them in delight. "Finally! Someone who appreciates my unique talents. Come on, Genny, let's go put on a show. Just follow my lead. And Maddy?"

"Yes ma'am?"

"You got a good man there. Don't mess it up."

Brash laughed as the two women hurried out the door. Both were obviously eager to play their part for the cameras. He turned back to Madison. "You heard the woman. We're supposed to kiss and make up."

"That's not what she said."

"Okay, it's what I'm saying."

"Wait a minute," she said, pressing her hand against his chest. "Why did you put my grandmother up to that?"

"I think whoever is doing this has access to the cameras and mics here at the house. Before we take them down, I want to feed them some wrong information. Let them think there are no journals. If they believe their secret is safe, maybe I can keep you safe."

"I suppose it's worth a try."

"Anything is worth a try. I'd do anything to protect you, Maddy. You know that, don't you?"

She nodded, stepping into the comfort of his embrace.

A while later, Granny Bert checked back in on them. Brash sat against the bedstead, holding a sleeping Madison in his arms.

"How did it go?" he asked quietly.

"We put on a show worthy of an Oscar," the older woman beamed. "I was so convincing, I started to believe it myself."

"Let's just hope someone else believes it, too. Someone who has been eavesdropping on conversations here in the house."

"When you find out who it is, I hope you string 'em up by their balls."

Brash's lips twitched with humor at the older woman's candid choice of words. "Could be a woman, you know."

She dismissed the notion immediately. "Too messy. A woman's not going to do that with chicken guts."

Brash considered her theory. "You might have a point."

"Of course I have a point. And by the way, the kids

are staying with friends tonight. Beth is over at your ex-wife's."

"That's probably for the best," he said. He looked down at Madison, still sound asleep. "I don't know how much whiskey you put in her drink, but she is out like a light."

"Doesn't take much with that one. Never could hold her liquor." Granny Bert pursed her lips, then announced, "Maybe you should stay the night. She seems to be pretty content in your arms."

Brash looked up sharply. He had wanted to suggest it but worried it might not be prudent. "You wouldn't object?"

"I don't want you to make a habit of it, mind you, but you're both mature adults."

"I can assure you, Granny Bert, I would never —"

"I know you wouldn't." She winked a wizened eye. "That's why I'll let you stay."

The patrol car parked outside all night was easily explained; Brash was providing police protection. No one had to know that he spent the night inside Madison's bedroom, sleeping there with her in her bed. For benefit of the cameras, Granny made some comment about him staying in Blake's room.

He slept on top of the covers, fully clothed. He tucked the sheet over Madison and held her the whole night through, knowing he was making matters worse. How would he ever sleep again, without her in his arms?

Very early the next morning, Madison awoke with a groggy, "Brash? What are you doing here?"

"Shh, baby. Go back to sleep."

She snuggled into his arms and smiled as she drifted back to sleep. "Thank you."

"My pleasure."

Two hours later, she awoke again, finding him gone. She felt oddly bereft. There was a note tacked to his pillow.

'Not the way I envisioned our first night together, but the best night's sleep I've had in ages. Stay home today and relax. I've got this.'

She touched the crease on the covers left by his big body. Her heart curled with tenderness.

For twenty years, she had been infatuated with the man. She suspected she might even be half in love with him.

But she was wrong.

She was fully immersed.

16

Madison spent the morning reading through Miss Juliet's journals. The three she now had at home covered a range of years. Written in beautifully flowing script, the passages reminded Madison of the lost art of a handwritten letter. She felt oddly sad, seeing the articulated thoughts put onto paper by the woman's own hand. Miss Juliet must have spent hours with her journals, recording her thoughts in solitary because she had so few friends.

One of the earliest journals started while Juliet still lived at home. Although it was interesting to read about life at the turn of the century, a large portion of the writings were dedicated to the rivalry between her and her sister. Page after page was filled with their petty differences. Madison skimmed over the entries, looking for mention of construction at the new house.

She found a few interesting entries near the end of the journal.

… Father is so good to me. Imagine! An entire town at my disposal! No more sharing milliners with my sister! Those petty women offer Naomi first choice on the latest Paris styles, all because she brings them treats. But no more. No more waiting for the train to carry me to civilization. No more living in the same

house with Naomi's temper tantrums. Father is generously building us each our own house in our very own town. I shall have mine constructed in the center of town, so that I might be surrounded with all the conveniences of modern day life.

...Clarence is simply brilliant! It was Clarence who first suggested we make alterations. Father brought the blueprints from Atlanta, but I abhor the thought of having the exact house as my sister. Clarence is full of wonderful ideas. A change here... a wall moved there... My home shall be unique.

...Clarence had the most delightful surprise waiting for me when I arrived today! First, he asked me to read a passage from The Manor. It was my favorite scene, the one in which Theodora slips into the secret passageway to escape Murdoch's wrath. As I finished reading, Clarence gently pushed on a panel beside the fireplace, and — voila! The wall slid away, to reveal my very own secret passageway! What a thoughtful, delightful surprise my friend has given me.

Excitement surged through Madison's veins. Progress, at last!

Yet who, exactly, was this Clarence? Madison searched back through the entries, trying to find first mention of the man.

... Father has hired a talented carpenter to erect my new home. His name is Clarence, and he has done work for Father before. He is actually Truman's son, although the Fords did not raise him. I think there is a scandal in his past, but such things are not spoken of in polite society. Suffice it to say that Clarence is a loner, a quiet soul with thoughtful, brooding eyes. Yet he seems to be brilliant with a hammer and nails, and Father assures me he will do a fine job building my magnificent new home.

...Today I made a new but unlikely friend. As I so often do, I took a book with me when I visited the new house. I adore sitting beneath the sheltering arms of the trees in the front yard, dreaming of what my home and my town will look like when done. I have such plans for my new city! When I tire of plotting streets and neat city blocks, I often read. I was doing so today when Clarence, the carpenter, stopped to greet me.

... We have only conversed on matters concerning the house, but I saw no harm in engaging in a light conversation with the man. He seemed genuinely interested when he asked what I was reading. I found myself sharing the plotline of my newest book, the exciting new mystery novel The Manor. I saw the spark of interest flare in his eyes. I do believe the man enjoys a good mystery as much as I do! Before I quite knew what was happening, he asked me to read the story aloud to him, while he worked on properly aligning an inner wall. He listened with rapt attention and absorbed the story with a sharp mind and eager ear. He may only be a carpenter, and in essence my employee, but by the end of the chapter, I knew Clarence Ford had become my new literary friend.

There were a few more scattered entries concerning Juliet's unlikely friendship with the carpenter. Madison discovered that while Juliet Randolph may have been a social snob, she had a different scale of equality for those sharing her love of reading. Intellectually, she considered the man her equal. Madison had no sense of a budding romance between the two, merely shared appreciation for a well-crafted story.

The other journals were not sequential, skipping ahead to later years in the heiress' life. Madison skimmed through them, but found nothing of particular interest.

She needed the journal written immediately after this one, but she had no way of getting down to the station to retrieve it. Her car had already been hauled away for repair, and Granny Bert was out running errands in the Buick.

Oh, darn. Guess I'll have to call Brash. She reached for her phone and dialed the number with a little rush of anticipation.

He answered with a brusque, "deCordova."

Her anticipation shriveled like a popped balloon. "Oh, sorry. Bad timing?"

She heard his weary sigh and imagined him rubbing his neck in frustration. "You might say that. Schimanski made a drug bust last night. Turned out to be a pretty big stash."

"That's good, isn't it?"

"Good that it's off the street, bad that we're no closer to finding the source. Drug labs are popping up all over the county, worse than weeds. I have a feeling this one is close by."

"I can call back."

"Nah, I can use the break. What's up?"

"Are you still coming over tonight for the 'premiere'?" He could not see the air quotes she put around the word, but he heard the slightly scornful note in her voice.

"Wouldn't miss it. Megan even made brownies for the occasion."

"Think you could smuggle me in some more reading material?"

"Uhm, yeah, sure."

"I need a specific one. I found a few promising entries, but the journal ended in early 1915, when the house was first being built."

She heard him sigh again. "I'll try to find the next one in the sequence, but I'm not promising anything. I have a full day if I want to be out of here in time for the show."

"If not, it's okay." She tried to sound more genuine than she felt.

"I'll do my best, Maddy."

This time the smile in her voice was real. "I know you will, Brash. I'll let you get back to work. See you tonight."

"Can't wait."

They made a party of the premiere.

What started as an intimate group quickly mushroomed into forty or so of their closest friends and relatives gathering at Granny Bert's to watch the first official episode of *Home Again: Starting Over.*

One of the stipulations for taking the cameras down was that the plug was pulled *after* tonight's event; Amanda wanted to record everyone's first impressions of seeing themselves on television. Tomorrow, the feeds would halt temporarily, until Brash was satisfied his investigation was not being compromised.

So tonight the cameras rolled, capturing the party and its well-dressed attendees. It amazed Madison how everyone primped for the camera, including her great-uncle Jubal; he broke out a new pair of overalls for the occasion, complete with a bright red shirt that still sported factory creases.

"Hurry up, Mom, it's almost time!" Bethani tugged on her mother's hand as Madison put out another bowl of dip. Even though everyone had pitched in and brought a dish, the food was disappearing at an astonishing rate.

"I need to put out this last tray of meats," Madison protested as she turned back to the refrigerator.

"Here, I'll take that." The police chief appeared out

of nowhere, swooping in to take the heavy tray from her mother's hands.

Megan hadn't mentioned it again, but Bethani could not forget her friend's claim that their parents were into each other. She watched them now, trying to read their body language. Mr. D certainly stood closer to her mom than necessary. His fingers brushed hers as he took the tray. And was her mom *blushing?* What was that look that passed between them?

She had to act fast, before this thing got out of control. "Come on, Mom, I saved us a spot on the couch." Bethani grabbed her mother's arm and pulled her from the kitchen.

They wove their way through the crowded living room, to their place of honor on the sofa. Blake squeezed in between his sister and Granny Bert. "Come on, Aunt Genny. You, too."

"Yes, Genesis," Madison insisted, her pointed gaze seeking out her friend. "You're as much responsible for this as Granny Bert."

Cutter nudged Genny's arm and muttered, "Somehow, I don't think that's a compliment. Better get up there before she demands blood."

The five of them lined up on the couch as the intro began to play. Nestled between Genny and Bethani, Madison grabbed a hand from either side and squeezed. She felt inexplicably nervous. This was their life, about to be broadcast before a national television audience. After the success of the pilot teaser, this first full-fledged episode was sure to draw millions of eyes. Was she ready for this?

If she wasn't, it was too late now. Her face flashed across the screen, set in a particularly poignant expression.

The next two hours were painful, almost physically so. Madison had to give Amanda Hooper credit: the producer certainly knew how to weave a powerful story. She played up Madison's sad past as a recent widow. Hinted heavily at her dire financial status. Twisted just enough key elements and rearranged just enough facts to portray Madison as little less than a saint, trying to provide a home for her poor children while preserving the pride and joy of the town, the aged old mansion on Main. According to the narrator, Madison had reached out to *Home Again* as a last resort, determined to do whatever needed to save the historical landmark and her family's future.

They even had a few unflattering clips of her to prove it. One caught her at the kitchen table, trying to make sense of her finances. The despair was clear upon her face. Another clip was from the day she hobbled in from Hank Adams' place, arms full of paraphernalia, one boot missing, hair disheveled and strewn with bits of leaves and twigs. Still another caught her in grubby clothes, cleaning out a closet at the Big House and hardly looking her best.

The final straw was an out-of-text clip of her and Nick. Madison remembered the day it was taken. They were discussing replacing the fretwork on the porches and as she stepped over a pile of rubble, she stumbled and almost fell. Nick had been there to catch her and help her stand upright. The clip omitted the rubble and showed her leaning into him, his arm tucked around her waist. The narrator mentioned something about new possibilities. Verbally, it was a reference to the trim, but Madison knew the visual clip was hardly random.

As the room broke out in chuckles and good-natured heckling, Madison stole a glance at Brash. He stared at the television screen as a nerve jumped in his clenched jaw. Beside her, Bethani bumped her shoulder and teased in a voice just a bit too loud,

"Oooh, Mom, you go, girl! He's hot!"

At the next commercial break, Madison murmured something about needing a sip of water and picked her way into the kitchen. She mingled along the way, laughing with friends over her newfound stardom and asking if anyone needed more to eat or drink. As the show came back on and all eyes returned to the screen, Madison quietly slipped out the back door.

There was a far corner of the backyard where the cameras did not reach. Madison headed straight for it, needing a few moments of obscurity.

Brash found her there, swaying on the old swing that dangled from a weathered A-frame. "Room for two?" he asked quietly.

It was a tight fit, but she had no complaints. She leaned into his strength, pulling the masculine scent of his cologne into her lungs.

After a moment, he tried consoling her with a half-hearted, "It's not so bad."

"It's not so good, either." Her voice sounded glum.

"Actually, I think it's pretty good. Amanda has a flair for storytelling."

Madison blew out a long breath. "If it wasn't my story, I might be inclined to agree. But that's *me* up there, Brash. That's my life. Some of the things she showed, some of the details she shared... those were personal. Not something I wanted a million or so people to know about. Like you said, so much for our opt-out agreement."

"All in all, you seem to be taking it rather well."

She lifted the shoulder that wasn't tucked beneath his. "What can I do? I agreed to this mess. The damage has already been done. I just have to find a way to deal with the humiliation of having my family secrets aired on public television."

"It really wasn't that bad, sweetheart."

"We'll know tomorrow, if Jerry Springer calls for an interview."

He chuckled at her wry attempt at humor.

"Brash, about that shot of Nick and me... It wasn't what it looked like."

"You mean that wasn't really a gleam in his eye? He wasn't leering at you like a wolf leers at a lost sheep?"

Madison scowled. "Leer? Really?"

"What else would you call that look?" he sulked.

"I nearly fell over a pile of lumber. We were both startled."

"He sure seemed eager to help you."

Madison put her hand onto his chest. "Brash," she said softly. "We only have a few moments, alone out here with no cameras and no party. Do you really want to spend it talking about Nick?"

He immediately saw her logic. "I don't want to spend it talking, at all."

The kisses were just turning interesting when the kitchen door creaked open and a patch of light spilled out into the darkness. Well beyond its splash of illumination, Brash was slow to release her from his arms.

"Maybe they'll go away," he murmured against her mouth.

"Mom? Are you out here?"

Hearing her daughter's voice, Maddy pulled away guiltily. Nothing like getting caught necking, particularly by your own child.

"Y-Yes, honey?" Maddy reached up to wipe Brash's face clean of any trace evidence. He caught her finger in his mouth and gently suckled, sending fire throughout her veins.

"The show is nearly over. Are you coming back?"

She much preferred the show out here, but she could hardly say so. "Sure, honey. Be right there."

Maddy pressed a kiss onto Brash's lips. "We'll continue this later," she promised on a whisper. "You coming?"

"Not yet."

Maddy smoothed her clothes and tried straightening her hair as she crossed the darkened yard to where her daughter waited. "Did I miss anything good?" She tried to sound more enthusiastic than she felt.

"They showed some pictures of the Big House back in the day and interviewed a few of the old-timers. Granny Bert put on quite a show."

"I'm sure she did," Madison laughed. "I'll watch the recorded version later."

Bethani peered out into the darkness. "I thought I saw Mr. D come out here."

Trying to sound casual, Madison forced another laugh. "There's so many people in that house, how can you keep track of them all? Come on, let's go catch the end of the show. Did they show that segment of you and Megan practicing your cheerleading?"

As expected, her daughter's attention was quickly derailed. "Yes, and it was so cool! You know how we do that double flip and split? We nailed it perfectly, and they caught it all on tape!" Her blue eyes twinkled with excitement as they stepped into the crowded house, leaving Brash alone in the dark.

17

Days passed before the shimmer and shine of stardom began to dim.

Everywhere Madison went, people talked about the show. Most were thrilled with the small part they played in the quest for fame, if only by being a part of the collective whole. There were a few, however, who took offense to some remark or some shot captured on film. Those were the ones who made special efforts to seek Madison out and complain. Loudly.

Home Again: Starting Over wasn't just the talk of The Sisters. The show had exploded on a national scale. The numbers were in, proving the first episode a bona fide hit. Like the pilot before it, the two-hour special broke more network records. Amanda was ecstatic. Nick was under more pressure than ever to perform. Eager to be a part of the momentum, Kiki Paretta wanted to push the date up for their meeting. Television stations as far away as Denver wanted to schedule interviews.

Old friends from Dallas started calling, eager to catch up with their 'dear, dear' friend. Madison let most of the calls go to voicemail, most of the text messages go unanswered. Where were those dear friends when she needed them most?

It was easiest to hole up at the police station, where she could numb her mind with old files and faceless names. Her list was coming along nicely, narrowed down to just a few dozen families. She hoped to pare that down soon, providing Brash a good, solid list from which to work.

A week after the fiasco with the chickens and the van, Madison got her car back, good as new. The garage rushed the job, spurred by quick payment from the network and hopes of getting their name on television.

With the cameras now turned off at home, at least for the time being, Madison took more of the old journals home to read at her leisure. She still had to sneak them into the house as before, but once inside she no longer had to hide them from the all-seeing eye of the camera. Granny Bert helped her pour through the entries, although her grandmother was often sidetracked down memory lane. She enjoyed reliving moments from the past, as told through the pen of her friend and benefactor.

"This might be something," Granny Bert said one evening, looking up from a book dated later in the years.

She read the passage from the old journal aloud.

I had a visitor today. I am still so angry my hands are trembling; I may be incapable of writing. Hugh Redmond had the audacity to step foot on my property! And he brought the children with him! Two little stringy-haired children with snotty noses and ragged clothes. He came begging for money. He claimed it was for food, but I could smell the liquor on his breath. He had the nerve to remind me that the children were Darwin's own blood. My dear late husband's grandchildren, borne by his illegitimate daughter. Naomi may have named her child the ridiculous name of Love, but she was not conceived in love, she was conceived in deceit. Not a day went by that Darwin did not regret his ill-fated night with my hussy of a sister. She tricked him into her bed, seducing him with strong liquor and evil wiles. He never loved Naomi. Never would have wanted her child, nor her children.

But I regress. This is not about the scandalous woman I have the misfortune of calling my sister, although I have no doubt she put her son-in-law up to his brazen visit. Since her daughter's unfortunate death, Naomi has become more spiteful than ever. I am certain she put the man up to this farce, filling his foolish mind with notions of claiming what is mine. Encouraging him to come here and humiliate not only me, but himself.

He threatened me. That lowly, filthy mechanic actually threatened me. Said he would get a lawyer and sue me, taking half of my estate for Love's children. He said it was their right as a Blakely heir. I immediately called Asa. He assured me I have no need to worry. Father gave everything to me. The land, the house, the town. In the brief but blissful time Darwin and I were married, he made no contribution to my wealth, so therefore his heirs have no claim to my estate. That filthy, desperate man will have to seek elsewhere for his next bottle and his free ride in life. He will never see a dime from me.

"Wow," Madison said when her grandmother finished reading the entry. "Miss Juliet was certainly bitter. Perhaps with just cause, but bitter, nonetheless. Who was Asa?"

"Asa Bryant, her lawyer. But if Hugh Redmond threatened to sue back then, he might still be hoping to make a claim against her estate. He tried fighting the will when she left most everything to me, claiming his children deserved it more than I did. He — or some of his rowdy brood — may be trying to torment you now, scare you off the property so they can swoop in and take over."

"Maybe," Madison said, chewing on her lip. "I'll run it by Brash, get his take on it."

"Is he coming over tonight for episode two?"

"Not that I know of."

"Why not?"

"For one thing, I didn't invite him."

"And why not?" her grandmother challenged. She glared at Madison over the tops of her reading glasses. "I warned you about messing things up with that man! I hope you haven't already blown it."

"It's not that. But we have decided to keep things—"

"Don't say slow. I never did understand why people always claim they want to take things *slllooowww*."

Madison frowned at her grandmother's dramatics. "Not slow, exactly. More like quiet. We both agreed that making our relationship public would only complicate matters right now. The press has enough to feed on without throwing out a juicy little tidbit like this."

"So you admit there *is* a relationship!" Granny crowed with pride.

Madison could not help but blush. "I think one is definitely in the works," she finally conceded.

"So why do you look so worried? That's the best news I've heard in ages!"

"I don't know. I get the feeling that Beth might not be too thrilled with the thought of me dating again. I think Blake would be okay with it, but Bethani was definitely a daddy's girl. I think it may be too soon for her to adjust to the thought of me with another man."

"Give her a chance. Ask her and find out."

Almost on cue, Bethani came bounding into the

room. "It's almost show time! Megan's on her way over. That's okay, isn't it?"

"Of course, honey. She's always welcome here."

"Is that hunk of a father bringing her over?" Granny Bert asked.

Bethani shrugged, but her eyes darted to her mother. "I dunno. I think he may be working. Or on a date. I think she said he was busy, so her mom is dropping her off."

At mention of a date, Madison arched her brows and sent Granny Bert an I-told-you-so look.

"Oh? Who is he dating?" Granny Bert prodded.

"Oh, I think he has lots of girlfriends. Megan says women are always calling him and chasing after him. Not that he runs away very fast. I think he might have a bit of a reputation as a lady's man." She glanced again at her mother, seeing if her words hit their mark.

Instead of getting upset, Madison chuckled. "Some things never change. You should have seen him in high school! All the girls were crazy over him."

"Including you, as I recall," Granny Bert broke in. "So you're right, some things never change."

Madison glared at her grandmother, not appreciating the prompt.

Bethani, however, paid them no heed. "From what Megan says, Mr. D only has eyes for her mom. That's why he never remarried. He's still in love with Mrs. Aikman, even though she's married to his best friend now." She looked her mother in the eye, slaying her with her desperate blue gaze. "It's like that with you and Dad, right, Mom? He was your one true love. You would never remarry someone else... Would you?"

Madison was at a loss for what to say. "Sweetheart, I did love your father," she started softly. That much was true. At one time, long ago, she had loved Gray, back before he had an affair and destroyed their marriage. "But he's gone now, sweetie. And one day, I may meet someone and decide to remarry. Not anytime soon, but one day. I'm still young, you know."

"Young? You're almost *forty*!"

Granny Bert bit back a snicker. Madison sent her another stern look before turning to her daughter with an indulgent smile. She touched the girl's long blond hair and played with the ends, arranging it where it fell over her shoulders. "Believe it or not, that's not so very old. And one day, if I'm fortunate, I will meet a man I love as much as I loved your father. You want me to be happy, don't you, sweetheart?"

"Yes, of course, but... but why do you need a man? Aunt Genny doesn't need a man to be happy!" she challenged.

"I don't, Bethani. I'll be perfectly happy, simply being a mother to my two wonderful children. You and Blake are all I need to be content with life."

The teen was not easily appeased. "Content," she fairly spat. "That's different than being happy."

Madison pulled her daughter in for a hug. Who was this stranger, and what had she done with her sweet daughter? "I love you, Beth. I love you and your brother with all my heart. I am more than merely 'content' being your mother. I am proud and thrilled and ecstatic. Over the moon. I don't know how we got on this subject, but you have nothing to worry about. I promise you, sweetheart, I have no intentions of getting remarried anytime soon."

But as she made the solemn promise to her troubled daughter, a shadow slipped into her heart. Another stipulation, this one to her own happiness.

Her future with Brash just hit a major complication.

A noise woke Madison in the night. Somewhere

along the side of the house, she heard a thud. Probably a stray cat, she thought drowsily as she turned onto her side and listened. Hearing nothing more, she bunched up her pillow and tried to reclaim her comfortable position.

Another sound brought her eyes opened. It sounded like wood gently sliding against wood. A chair, perhaps? Was Granny Bert awake?

Madison glanced at the clock. 1:08 a.m. She doubted her grandmother was rummaging around in the living room at this hour.

As silently as possible, Madison eased from bed. She tiptoed to the bedroom door and listened. Over the ticking of the ancient mantel clock, she heard a slight thud. Someone was definitely in the living room.

It could be Blake, she told herself. Even after eating two bags of popcorn during the show, he complained he was starving. According to her fifteen-year-old son, popcorn was little better than eating salted and buttered air. He might be raiding the refrigerator, tiding himself over until breakfast.

She eased through the half-opened doorway, stepping cautiously into the hall. Her bare feet made no sound on the hardwood floor as she crept down the darkened path. She glanced at the closed doors along the corridor. If Blake or Granny Bert were up, they had shut their bedroom doors behind them.

Trying to convince herself she was being silly, Madison paused when she reached the end of the hall. Tucked as she was in the shadowy safety of the hallway, she surveyed the dark room before her. Soft electronic light radiated from a half dozen appliances, casting circles of diffused light into the darkness. Weak moonlight filtered in through the window blinds and the curtain on the front door. Except for the clock, the room was silent and still.

She eased into the room, feeling more confident. She would check out the adjacent dining room and the kitchen beyond, just to be certain.

A patch of moonlight lay across the dining room floor. Light that normally was not there.

Madison's heart hammered in her chest. That window had been closed when they went to bed.

She groped behind her, her fingers curling around the baseball bat Blake always left in the corner. For once, she was thankful the boy ignored her constant pleas to put away his gear. She pulled the bat into swinging position as she inched closer.

A figure dressed in black stood over the table, quietly leafing through the journals she had so carelessly left there. The person's back was to her, blocking most of the soft light that spilled from a handheld device and illuminated the pages. This was no random prowler. He — or she — was here for the journals.

Madison tried to take in as many details as possible. The person was tall, several inches more so than she. Outweighed her by a good fifty or so pounds, too. It was difficult to tell much about the person's shape, as it was covered by a loose-fitting black jacket and dark pants. But on the air was a hint of Old Spice, giving Madison the distinct impression their intruder was male.

Even armed with a baseball bat and the element of surprise, Madison knew she was no match for a man who was larger and stronger than she was. Her best option was to back silently away and call for help.

Her plan might have worked, except for the fact that she bumped into the wall and knocked a picture off its nail. As the old family portrait crashed to the floor amid the shattering of glass, the intruder whirled around.

He shone the light directly into Madison's eyes, bumping up the beam's intensity so that she was blinded. By the time she thought to shield her eyes and peer through the slits of her fingers, the person had grabbed the journal, backed his way to the window, and disappeared into the night.

"Hey! Hey, you!" Madison yelled. She ran to the window and hung her head out, careful not to disturb any fingerprints he might have left.

Any further yelling was useless. The dark figure had already melted into the night.

"Let's go through this one more time," Brash said as Maddy and her children huddled together on the couch.

"We've already been through this twice. I've told you what little I can."

"You know what they say, third time's a charm." He flashed a smile that was full of its own unique charm, but Madison was in no mood to be mollified.

She replayed the night's events once more, offering as much detail as possible.

"Close your eyes. In the split second that he turned around and saw you standing there, before the light was in your eyes, what could you see?"

Madison closed her eyes in concentration, trying to recapture those brief moments in her mind. "He was silhouetted against the window. There was an odd point to his head, so he was either wearing a beanie or having a bad hair day. I think there was something between his ears and his jacket collar. Maybe his hair was a bit on the long side, or maybe curly." She fingered her own short ends, imagining her brief impression of the perpetrator. Her eyes popped open. "That's all. That's all I saw, before he shone the light in my eyes."

"But that's something," he said with a warm smile of encouragement. "That's good, sweetheart. Really good." He used the term of endearment as he jotted down notes in his ever-present notebook. If anyone noticed the slip, it was forgotten as he continued briskly, "So we know your intruder was a tall, average-sized man with hair that came below his ears. So now, off the top of your head, spit out the names of five men that fit that description. Go."

Madison blinked in surprise, unprepared for the rapid-fire demand. Sputtering for just a moment, she rattled off the first men that came to mind. "Uhm, uhm ... Cutter Montgomery. My cousin Darrell Hamilton. Uhm, uhm, Nick Vilardi. Hugh Redmond. Jimbo Hadley. Bart Nedbalek."

"Good, good. Now I'll call out a few names. Tell me if they fit the image, or why not. Say the first thing that pops into your head. Ready?"

Madison closed her eyes for better concentration and nodded. It was like a television game show. She rattled out her answers as quickly as he ticked off the names, even if they made little or no sense.

"Jerry Don Peavey."

"Too thin."

"Hank Adams."

"Too old."

"Rudy Dewberry."

"Too black."

"Luis Gonzales."

"Wrong kind of hat."

"Nick Vilardi."

"Too sexy."

With her eyes closed, she missed the infamous arched brow. Brash never missed a beat, but there was an extra bite in his voice as he called out the next name. "Don Nguyen."

"Too short."

"Derron Mullins."

"*Way* too short."
"Barry Redmond."
"Maybe."
"Arles Bishop."
"Maybe."
"Stewart Combs."
"Don't know him."
"Allen Wynn."
"Too pudgy."
"Nobles Baines."
"Not right."
"Marion Crowder."
"Too stooped."
"John Montgomery."
"Hair's too short."
"Tom Pruett."
"Too old and crazy."
"Bernie Havlicek."
"Too scrawny."
"Dirk Simon."
"Haven't seen him in forever."
"Enrique Hernandez."
"Who? Oh, no. Too stocky."

When a beat passed without a name thrown at her, Madison opened her eyes. The inquisition was apparently over.

"What-What was all that?" she asked, feeling like she had been caught in a whirlwind.

"Just trying to get a better description."

"But I told you, I didn't see him well enough to *get* a description!" she wailed.

"But you got an impression, Maddy. And this little exercise was all about split-second first impressions."

Still skeptical, she pursed her lips. "I don't see how it helped."

"But it did. Based on your first impression, the

intruder was a white male, somewhere between twenty-five and forty, in good physical condition."

Madison was in awe, amazed he could deduce anything from such random bits of information. "You're amazing," she murmured.

"So you've mentioned," he replied, his smile wicked and warm.

Bethani saw the look simmering between her mother and the police chief. Sitting so close beside her mom, she could practically *feel* the sizzle. Her stomach did a funny little flip-flop, just seeing the gleam in Mr. D's dark eyes. If a man ever looked at her with such open desire... Wait. Desire? That meant... Oh, no. This would never do. Not on her watch.

Bethani sat up straighter. Tipping her chin up a notch, she disguised the calculated statement behind the pretense of playful banter. "You forgot to mention he's not nearly as sexy as Nick Vilardi. Mom, if I didn't know better, I'd say you have a crush on your carpenter."

In spite of herself, Madison blushed. There was no denying that she found the man attractive. And yes, there was a certain chemistry between them. She still recalled the embarrassing way she had literally jumped, the first time their hands met. His touch had been electrifying. There was something magnetic about the television host, and, like most women, she was drawn to his dark charm and rugged good looks. If not for the auburn-haired police chief watching her now, waiting to hear her answer, Madison might be interested in pursuing that attraction.

If, Madison acknowledged. Her eyes wandered over the police chief, their hazel depths warming with a sudden rush of tenderness. This was one stipulation she had no objection to. Why would she settle for attraction, if she had a chance at true love with the man of her dreams?

"No, Beth," she answered honestly. Her gaze was still trained on Brash. "I can assure you, I do not have a crush on Nick Vilardi."

Brash's facial expression did not change, but she saw the pleasure that lit his dark eyes.

Some of that light dimmed as Bethani babbled on. "Oh, we know you'll never love another man the way you loved Daddy. I remember the way y'all would go away for your romantic weekends, and the way you came home, all starry eyed and dreamy. You had those silly pet names for each other. Do you remember that, Blake? The way they always made goo-goo eyes at each other when they thought we weren't looking?"

In the middle of slurping down a bowl of cereal, her brother looked a bit confused by the question. His attention was focused on oat and honey nuggets, not his sister's romantic babble.

Girls were so mushy. The same way his cereal would be, if he didn't hurry and eat it. Blake mumbled a vague agreement as he turned the bowl upright and drank the last of his cereal in a few big gulps.

"Blake!" his mother admonished. "Where are your manners?"

"What'd I do?" he asked defensively. "I answered her."

"I'm talking about your table manners. Use a spoon. For that matter, use a table."

"But it's off limits, right, Mr. D?" The teen looked to the chief for confirmation.

"As a matter of fact, yes, it is. I'll bring a team in first thing in the morning — actually, in a few hours — to take prints. You'll need to avoid that area as much as possible until we're done."

"That might be hard for our walking garbage disposal," Bethani said, eying her brother with derision. "Blake will want to eat at least once or twice more before breakfast."

"What? I'm a growing boy. I need my nourishment."

"You also need your sleep," Madison interjected. She mussed both their blond heads. "The intruder is long gone. We're perfectly safe now. You kids need to go back to bed."

"I'll wait for you, Mom," Bethani volunteered.

"That's sweet, babe, but you need to get some sleep. Don't you have an algebra test in the morning?"

"Not if you write me an excuse..." the teen said, batting hopeful eyes at her mother.

"Not a chance, sister. Now scoot. Off to bed, both of you." She gave them each a kiss and watched them shuffle toward the hall. "Love you bunches!" she called. She glanced at her grandmother, dozing in the armchair. "Granny, why don't you go, too? There's nothing else we can do tonight. Brash has everything under control."

"What is this world coming to?" Granny Bert grumbled, getting slowly to her feet. Tonight, she looked every bit her eighty years, and then some. "I've lived in this house for over fifty years. Half the time I leave my door unlocked. Never lock my car. This is the first time anyone has dared to break in. This world is headed to hell in a handbasket. You mark my words, one of these days..." She continued her mumbled rant as she ambled down the hall and disappeared into her bedroom.

Brash turned to Maddy as the grumbles faded away down the hall. "I'll get someone out here around nine to dust for prints. As long as no one disturbs anything, there's no reason to do any more tonight. Why don't you go back to bed, too, Maddy?"

"As if I could sleep." She rolled her eyes, but they stuck somewhere on a threatening tear.

His voice turned gentle. "You were right about what you told the kids. The intruder is long gone. He won't come back tonight. Especially since he got what he came for."

Scrubbing her face with her hands, Madison bit back a moan. "Why is this happening, Brash? I don't understand what it is this person wants."

"Obviously they think there is some sort of incriminating evidence in those journals."

"But what?"

Brash hesitated for a moment before taking the seat next to her. "Still haven't learned anything reading them?"

"Just what I've already told you. Miss Juliet was a kindhearted woman, but a complete snob. She had a ridiculous feud with her only sister. And she made an unlikely friend in the carpenter who built her house. He may or may not have been illiterate, because she was always reading books aloud to him. They particularly loved mysteries, especially the ones with hidden passages and tunnels and secret rooms. From what I can tell, all the hidden spaces at the Big House were built on a whim, as a tribute to her love of who-done-its."

"Sounds a bit over the top."

"From what I gather, Clarence may have had feelings for Miss Juliet, but I don't think they were reciprocated. I don't think she even realized how he felt about her. In her eyes, they were simply friends."

"How far along are you in the journals?"

"Not nearly far enough. She's met Darwin and fallen madly in love with him, but they haven't married yet. Granny has been leafing through some of the later volumes. In fact, there was one tidbit in the book that was stolen tonight. There may have been more to discover, but I guess now we'll never know."

"What did you find?"

"A couple of years before Miss Juliet died, Hugh Redmond and his children came a-begging. When she refused to offer them money, he threatened to sue her. He claimed half of the estate belonged to Love's children. Granny thinks it could be him, or at least his children, that are trying to scare me out of the house, so that they can claim it for their own."

Brash pursed his lips, contemplating the matter. "Actually might make a little sense," he admitted.

"What was with the names, Brash? You called them out so quickly. You already had them in your little notebook, didn't you? And Barry Redmond was one of them."

"Let's just say that some are potential persons of interest, some were purely for comparison measures."

"How so?"

"You know I can't discuss the case with you, Maddy."

"But it's *my* case!"

He hesitated a moment before caving to the pressure of her expressive hazel eyes. "I'm not making any accusations, any assignment of guilt. But some of those names are people with connections to the list you have been compiling. These men had family in the area around the time we think the death may have occurred. So, in theory, those people may have something to lose if the identity of the skeleton is discovered."

Madison was impressed. "Very smart, Chief deCordova."

He flashed a grin. "I have my moments."

Her eyes followed the curve of his smile, tracing his lips with distracted attention. "You most certainly do," she murmured.

He all but groaned. "I'm on duty, Maddy. And you should go back to bed."

She huffed out her frustration. "Okay, okay. I'll go to bed. I just can't promise to sleep."

"I'll drive by every so often, if it makes you feel any safer. But I can assure you, the intruder won't be back tonight."

He stood to leave and put out a hand to help her up. "Remember, avoid the dining room if possible. Don't touch a thing on the table or around the window. If we're lucky, he wasn't wearing gloves."

"Thanks for coming so quickly."

"First of all, it was my job. Second of all, you know you can always call me. I'll come, on or off duty." His eyes warmed with a smile. "Professionally or personally. Doesn't matter. I'm at your beck and call, sweetheart."

"Thank you."

He was about to gather her into his arms when Bethani's voice floated out from the hallway, sounding small and scared. "Mom? I thought I heard something outside."

With a rueful smile of resignation, Brash turned Maddy toward her daughter and gentle prodded her forward. "Take your daughter back to bed. I'll lock the door behind me. And I'll make a sweep around the perimeter of the house before I go." He smiled indulgently at the teenager lurking in the hall. "Will that help you sleep, Bethani?"

She nodded, her blue eyes large and luminous. "I-I think so. Thanks, Mr. D."

"My pleasure, ladies. Now off to bed with both of you. I'll check around the house, then I'll drive by every hour. There's no reason to be afraid. I've got it under control."

Madison put her arm around Bethani's shoulders and found her daughter was trembling. "Aw, honey, it's okay. Nothing else is going to happen. We're perfectly safe now." Over the top of the teen's blond head, she sent Brash a woeful look. She hated to see Bethani so frightened. "Thank you, Brash."

"No problem. Night, ladies."

He waited for them to shuffle down the hall before he locked and shut the door firmly behind him and stepped out into the night.

18

Somewhere between mornings at the police station, afternoons split in a half dozen directions, and evenings spent with her nose stuffed inside the journals, Madison managed to squeeze in the assorted responsibilities of a mother and business owner, as well as fulfill the promise made to Lisa Redmond.

She traced Barry Redmond's movements on more than one occasion, following him to several questionable destinations. He visited more than one bar, spent an hour and a half inside Angie Jones' house late one night, and frequented the adult video store in a neighboring town, dressed in dark clothing and an air of secrecy. The only photos Madison could snap were of him coming and going, and he was always alone. As far as incriminating evidence, she was coming up empty-handed.

When her phone binged with a message from Genny midday on Thursday, Madison's luck changed.

Hurry over here, and you'll get an eyeful.

Without hesitation, Maddy jumped in her car and hurried to *New* Beginnings, where she saw Barry Redmond and Angie Jones sitting in a cozy back corner. Although seated across from one another, they leaned inward to keep their conversation private. With few other patrons in the café at the odd hour, they were in little danger of being overheard.

Genesis was behind the bakery counter, drying dishes with a cup towel. Madison noted none of the plates showed signs of being wet. She arched a brow as her friend encouraged, "Come show me those pictures you were telling me about."

Playing along, Madison soon understood. From where Genny stood, she had a perfect view of the corner table and the activity that took place beneath it.

"Uhm, yeah, here, I'll show you." Madison fumbled with her cover for a moment before she fell into the spirit of the game. Taking out her phone, she opened the camera feature and made certain the flash was off.

"Did you see this one? Oh, and look." Pretending to show her friend pictures from her screen, she proceeded to snap off a dozen random shots of the brazen couple in the corner.

Angie's shoe was abandoned on the floor as her stockinged foot traveled up the length of Barry's leg. His eyes went wide as her foot wandered inward and found its target. Even across the room, Madison could hear the slightly strangled sound he made as he shifted in his seat and allowed her better access.

"Would you look at that?" Genny murmured, watching the scene unfold on the live screen. To anyone listening, it sounded as if she found the photos on Madison's camera roll fascinating.

"And look at this," Madison said. Barry slipped off his own shoe and began to return the favor, running his own foot up Angie's other leg.

"Absolutely stunning. I have no words."

Dropping her voice, Madison cautioned, "Unless you want a repeat of the scene from *Harry Meets Sally*, you'd better break this thing up. And I hope the cameras aren't recording this! This is definitely R-rated, heading very quickly toward X."

Genesis glanced up to the *Home Again* cameras, which were steadily recording the area just past the groping couple. "No, thank goodness. And I'm pretty sure we're the only ones that can see what's happening. The angle is all wrong for Reverend and Mrs. Brubaker, thank the dear Lord. Can't you just imagine what would happen if they knew this was happening, not fifteen feet away from them? But you're right, I need to stop this. Think you have enough pictures?"

"More than enough." Just to be certain, Madison hit another button and cruised through her photos. "Oh, yes, plenty." Her lip curled in distaste and she had to repress the slight shudder running through her.

Grabbing a water pitcher, Genesis came from around the counter, her face set with determination. She ignored the way Lavonne Brubaker pushed her water glass to the edge of the table expectantly. She was headed to the little love nest in the back corner.

Flashing a dimpled smile at the couple, she asked innocently, "Need some cold water?"

Barry Redmond jerked his head up and blinked in surprise, obviously having forgotten they were in a public place. Madison snapped off a final picture, but not before he sharply glanced her way. He may have even heard her gaffed snicker at Genesis' remark.

Quickly closing her camera app and engaging the lock feature on her phone, Madison pretended to be searching for a good signal.

Rudely pushing Genesis aside, Barry abruptly stood from the table and strode Madison's way. Without a word of warning, he snatched the phone from Madison's hand and whipped the screen around for inspection.

"Were you taking pictures of me?" he snarled.

Madison remained perfectly cool. "What? Who are...? Barry Redmond. Is that you?"

"Don't act like you don't know who I am, Madison Cessna," he spat. "Everyone knows who I am, and certainly you."

She continued to play her part with great innocence. "But I haven't seen you in years. Not since high school."

"Or since yesterday, when I saw you driving in front of my house," he accused.

"Oh? Where do you live?"

"You know damn well where I live. Just like I know where you live."

Madison's hazel eyes snapped with fire. "Is that some sort of threat?"

"Take it how you like it. I went twenty years without seeing your snooty face. Let's make it another twenty, shall we?"

"Give me my phone back, and we might have a deal."

He slammed the cell phone down on the counter, hard enough to do potential damage to the phone and the surface it collided with. "Stay out of my face or you will regret it," he threatened darkly.

A third voice broke into the conversation, every bit as dark and menacing.

"Apologize to both ladies, or *you'll* regret it."

Barry Redmond glanced over his shoulder. "Stay out of this, kid."

"I'm no kid, old man," Cutter said with an authoritative air. "Apologize to Miss Maddy for so rudely slamming down her phone, and to Miss Genny for pushing her out of the way."

"Who the hell do you think you are?" Barry raged, whirling around to face the angry firefighter. One look at Cutter's deadly scowl and some of his bluster died.

"I'm the gentleman that demands you show these ladies some respect. Now apologize, before I throw you out."

"You can't throw me out. This is her place, not yours." With a defiant twist of his chin, he indicated Genesis as she approached. The front of her apron was wet where he had jostled her arm and caused her to spill water from the pitcher she carried.

One step forward was all it took. Seeing the furious younger man move closer in, practically nose to nose with him now, Barry swallowed nervously and changed his tune. "This place is nothing but a dump anyway," he mumbled. Behind Cutter, Angie Jones slithered out the door. Barry's scowl darkened as he grudgingly muttered, "Sorry."

"Not good enough," Cutter informed him curtly. Although Barry was ten years his senior, Cutter took the other man's arm and turned him to face Madison, instructing him as if he were a child, "Say it like you mean it."

Seething with anger, Barry Redmond glared at Madison with malice in his eyes. "I am sorry, Your Highness. Please forgive me."

Letting the sarcasm slide, Cutter continued, "Now tell Genesis you are sorry."

"For what?" Barry demanded with indignation.

"You pushed her out of the way and made her spill water all down her legs. And you are disrespecting her place of business."

"You weren't even in here!"

"I came through the door, just as you pushed her. Now apologize." His voice brooked no argument.

"I'm sorry," he sneered. "You think just because you're her best friend, you're some sort of royalty. But you forget I grew up here, too. I remember your past and your little *adventure* right out of high school."

A gasp escaped Genny, along with all her color. As the blood drained from her face, she put a trembling hand to her mouth and held in the soft cry.

Cutter threw a protective arm around her waist, turning so that his body shielded her from the man spouting hateful jargon.

"Get out." Cutter ground out the bitter warning with a deadly gleam in his eyes. "Pay your bill and get out. And don't come back."

When Barry pulled a twenty-dollar bill from his wallet and would have considered it enough, Cutter plucked another twenty from the folds. Ignoring Barry's blubbered protest, Cutter took the money and handed it to a still-pale Genny. "This should make up for his rude behavior."

"That's the last money you'll ever see from me," Barry glowered, wagging his finger dangerously close to Genesis' face.

Genny managed a nonchalant shrug, even though her body still trembled. How dare he bring up the past the way he had!

With a very loud snort of disgust, Barry Redmond shot one last glare toward Madison and stormed out of the I. A small spattering of applause heeled his departure.

"Are you okay, Genny?" Cutter asked in concern.

"Yes. He didn't hurt me, just startled me." She leaned into his strength.

"He's lucky I didn't beat the snot out of him," Cutter said darkly. Genny could feel the anger still coiled within him. "Miss Maddy? What about you? Are you all right?"

"I'm fine, Cutter." She offered a small smile of reassurance, even though it wavered a bit. She picked up her cell phone and examined it for damage. "My phone survived, too, so everything is good."

Cutter gave Genny's waist an encouraging squeeze before he disentangled his arm from her waist. "I hope you didn't mind that I kicked him out permanently," he said as an afterthought.

"No. No, not at all. Good riddance."

"My thoughts exactly," he grinned, finally beginning to relax. "Come on, I'll buy you two lovely ladies some coffee."

Genesis held up the extra twenty. "How about some Gennydoodle cookies to go with it? Barry's treat."

He gave her a mischievous wink. "You're on."

"I think I found something."

Madison blurted out her announcement the moment Brash answered the phone. He picked up on the fourth ring.

"Maddy?" he mumbled in confusion.

"What other woman calls you this late at night?" she asked irritably. Belatedly, she glanced at the clock and felt a stab of remorse. "You weren't asleep, were you?"

"It's after midnight. Yeah, I was asleep."

"Sorry. You want me to call back in the morning?"

Sheets rustled on the other end of the line. Madison refused to let her mind wander down that path, even though his sleep-roughened voice was so sexy it conjured up all sorts of tempting suggestions.

He mumbled something unintelligible as he sat up and swung his feet to the floor. Even over the phone lines, she could hear his knee pop. "Nah, I'm awake now. Tell me what you found."

"I'm reading in one of her journals, and Miss Juliet is talking about a trip she and her husband have taken. A sort of honeymoon, I suppose. When they came home, Darwin had a surprise waiting for her. A custom-made bookcase for their bedroom, designed and installed by her dear friend Clarence."

Interest sharpened his sleepy voice. "How long of a trip did they take?"

"One month. They traveled by train to Philadelphia to meet his family."

"Hmm." She could imagine his mind working as he thought aloud. "That might explain how someone managed to build a retro-fit staircase within the walls. That's always bothered me. How could a person add a staircase without anyone knowing it?"

"A month should be enough time to build one, don't you think?"

"With time enough to start on a cellar addition, to boot."

"So maybe she really didn't know about the room. Or the stairs." The thought was oddly comforting. "That was what bothered me the most," Madison admitted, "thinking Miss Juliet might somehow be involved in that unknown person's death."

"I understand. I didn't like that theory, either, but I couldn't make any other scenario fit. But an extended trip would explain how a staircase was built without her knowledge. I'm not sure what the servants thought, but maybe they felt it wasn't their place to speak up."

"I think I read... yes, right here. She gave the servants the entire month off, a paid vacation to celebrate her marriage. The only ones to stay behind to keep an eye on things were Truman and Lily Ford. Truman was her butler and most trusted employee."

"So wonder why he allowed this Clarence person to build a hidden staircase in the walls?"

"Maybe because it was his son?"

"What are you talking about?"

"Apparently, Clarence was Truman Ford's illegitimate son. Miss Juliet didn't say so in such crude terms, but she alluded to the fact."

"Hmm. I did not know that. So either the good butler knew about construction, or he left the house in his son's care and was as ignorant about the staircase as Miss Juliet was."

"Are we thinking she lived there all those years, and never knew about one last secret passage?" Madison asked.

"I would say it is definitely a possibility. Unless you find information in those journals to tell you otherwise, she may have slept just feet away but been none the wiser."

"So maybe my instincts were right. Maybe there was a one-sided relationship going on, and Clarence decided to put in a secret passage so he could spy on her."

"Or maybe the staircase was Darwin's idea."

"Either way, the whole thing is creepy. A secret passage that feeds directly from the cellar into the master bedroom. Ugh." A shiver ran through Madison's shoulders. "If I haven't already given the instructions, I want the staircase boarded off the minute you are through with this investigation."

"Don't worry, sweetheart. I'll drive the first nail."

"Any word yet from Austin?"

"These things take time."

"It's been five weeks already!"

"We may have to wait five months before we get the official report. Even then, I'm not holding out much hope for identification. There are just too many unknowns," Brash warned.

"Still, I'd like some sense of closure."

"That's not always possible, Maddy, particularly in cold cases like this one."

"I know. I don't like it, but I do know it's a possibility." She paused only briefly. "Changing subjects, guess who I saw today in town?"

"No idea."

"Barry Redmond. It wasn't a pleasant reunion, to say the least."

"Madison, I told you not to read anything into those names. I pulled several names at random, without making any accusations. Don't make this more than it is."

"Ooh, I must be in trouble," Madison taunted. "You're calling me Madison, not Maddy. You only do that when you're miffed with me."

"Miffed?" Now his voice held a ring of amusement.

"So maybe I've been reading too many journal entries. Some of the vernacular is wearing off."

"Be careful. I don't want too much of the prim and proper town matriarch rubbing off on you." The amusement gave way to pure devilment. His voice slipped an octave. "Not when I have another moonlight picnic planned."

It had to be exhaustion. That was the only explanation for the sultry tone that infiltrated her voice. "You don't say. And just when is this picnic taking place?"

"You tell me. You name the time, and it's a date."

She loved the low timber of his voice, roughened now with undisguised desire. She closed her eyes and bit back a sigh. "Things are still so crazy, Brash. The cameras may be off at the house, but they follow me like a shadow everywhere else. Now we have all these requests for interviews and appearances. The third episode hasn't even aired yet."

"All the more reason you need a little escape. River therapy."

"This weekend, maybe? Oh, wait. It's Mother's Day weekend."

"That's Sunday. We could squeeze in Saturday

night.”

“The kids and I have a tradition. We make cookies and watch old home videos the night before Mother’s Day.”

“Sounds fun.”

“It is. Can I get a raincheck on that picnic?” she asked hopefully.

“You bet. Like I said, you name the time, I’ve got the place.”

“Thanks, Brash. I’ll let you get back to bed. Sorry I woke you.”

“I’m not.” His voice was wicked and low. “I was already dreaming about you. Talking to you was so much better.”

19

The kitchen resembled a disaster zone. Mixing bowls and measuring cups littered the countertops, crammed alongside opened canisters and an electric mixer. Empty eggshells dripped on the tile counter, flour dusted the hardwood floors, and a trail of oats scattered from the pantry to the sink. Cookie sheets and cooling racks dominated every inch of the kitchen table.

"These smell awesome," Bethani beamed as she took a batch of hot cookies from the oven. With her hair up in a ponytail and flour smudged across her cheek, she looked like a little girl playing dress-up. She wore one of Granny Bert's old aprons, the frills and gingham check at odds with her ripped jeans and rhinestone flip-flops. As she made her way to the table, she inhaled another whiff of pure heaven. "Move over, Goober, so I can put these down."

"I'm trying to open these sprinkles," her brother complained. "They seal these suckers with some sort of cement." He gave one last tug and the seal broke free. Tiny bits of colorful candy confections sprayed across the kitchen.

"Way to go, bro."

Ignoring his sister's sarcasm, Blake held the jar up

in victory. "Free at last. Free at last."

"Enough with the speeches," Madison advised. "Grab the broom and sweep those up, before we grind them into the floor. Beth, how many does that make now?"

After a quick count, the teen reported, "Two dozen and three Chunky Charlies, three and a half dozen sugar cookies, four dozen peanut butter bites, three dozen chocolate chips, less the two your son just stuffed in his mouth."

"So when we finish this last batch we should be done." Madison surveyed the evening's efforts with a satisfied smile. It was one of their favorite traditions, started when the twins were just toddlers. What cookies they didn't eat or save for later, they wrapped up and gave in small batches to friends and neighbors, particularly moms.

"Can we start decorating the sugar cookies?"

"Sure. Granny, is that frosting about done?"

Stirring the mixture to smooth perfection, Granny Bert pointed to three small bowls at her side. "Finishing the white right now. There's the blue, pink, and yellow."

"This year's cookies are going to be the best!" Bethani grinned with confidence. "I love these colors. They're more like turquoise and hot pink. Totally awesome."

"Amazing what Easter egg coloring will do for frosting," the older woman smirked.

"Not very manly," Blake complained, swiping the vivid pink frosting across his finger.

"Hello? It's Mother's Day, you goofball," his sister chided. "It's not supposed to be manly."

"Yeah, well, without dads, there would be no Mother's Day." He stuck his tongue out in contempt, but the bright pink stain on its tip killed the desired effect. Bethani dissolved into giggles.

A warm sensation of joy blossomed within Madison's heart as the teens fell into a playful rapport while frosting cookies. It did wonders for a mother's soul to hear her children laughing and working together. Madison stood back and watched their antics with a tender smile upon her face. Where had the time gone? The twins were almost sixteen now. In her mind's eye they were still babies, still two exuberant toddlers who tried her patience but brought her the greatest joy she had ever known. Of all her accomplishments in life, she considered motherhood her greatest contribution to the world. It definitely brought her the most pride and happiness.

"Come on, Mom. You too, Granny. Come help us," Bethani encouraged.

"I think you two are doing a fine job," Madison said, but she joined in to make it a true family effort.

"These cookies are great, but what are we doing for supper?" Blake wanted to know. He stuffed a Chunky Charlie into his mouth before applying a layer of yellow frosting to the cookie in his other hand.

Wondering where he put all the food he consumed, an indulgent smile touched Madison's face. "Why don't we order pizza? I'll run get it while you set up the movies."

"I wish someone would offer home delivery around here," Blake complained. "If I had one gripe about moving to a small town, that would be it. No pizza delivery."

Hear that, Annette? Blake is happy here.

Thoughts of her mother-in-law's accusation intruded on their special evening. In truth, the heated conversation shadowed her constantly, reminding her of Annette's competitive — and often combative — nature. Madison could not ignore the possibility, however improbable, that Annette might try to take her children away from her.

Pushing unwanted thoughts of her mother-in-law aside, Madison laughed. "If that's your only complaint, I'd say we're in pretty good shape."

"Don't eat all the Chunky Charlies or there won't be any left!" Bethani fussed at her brother as he popped another into his mouth.

"Happy might not be much of a cook, but she sure makes a mean cookie," Blake said with a satisfied smack of his lips.

"You are right, my mother isn't much of a cook," Madison agreed. She remembered eating a lot of macaroni and cheese as a child. At the time, she thought ordering out for pizza and eating soup and pasta from a can was perfectly normal. Looking back, however, she realized her mother — known to Bethani and Blake as 'Happy' — was too busy with adventures to bother with the mundane task of cooking. Her one claim to fame was her Chunky Charlie cookies, a mishmash of Charlie Cessna's favorite candies and nuts thrown together in an oatmeal dough.

"Do you miss her and Grandpa Charlie?" Bethani asked, tilting her blond head to one side. "We haven't seen them in forever!"

"Of course I miss them." Her answer was perhaps a bit too quick. "But I was lucky enough to have a surrogate mother, one who turned out to be more of a mom to me than the woman who gave me birth." She shot a quick glance to Granny Bert, who pretended not to be listening. Though the older woman was buried up to her elbows in soapy water, a ghost of a smile softened her wrinkled face.

"Do you think they'll ever settle down and come back home?" Blake asked.

"I don't know, honey. My parents love adventure.

I'm afraid River County is a little too tame for their tastes."

Bethani made a sound of disbelief. "Not anymore, it isn't! Between the ghosts and the skeletons and the television crews, this place is way more exciting than those foreign countries they like to visit."

"Oh! That reminds me!" Blake's blue eyes lit up as he dug in his pocket for his cell phone. "I found the perfect Mother's Day gift for you."

Granny Bert joined in the conversation with her own harrumph. "What? A guard dog to keep watch on her?"

"Almost," the boy grinned. "Or at least the *sound* of one, to scare off thieves and attackers!" He pressed a button on his phone, causing it to rumble with a long, low growl. "That should put the fear into someone, don't you think? You can hook it up to a motion detector and — voila! Your own vicious attack dog."

"That should do it," Madison agreed with a chuckle. "It sounds like... wait a minute. Where did you get that?"

"It's an app on my phone. Or you can get the barking Dobermans." He pressed another button and rattled the windows with the incessant sound of multiple dogs ready for attack.

"No, no, go back to the other one. Yes, that one." There was no barking in this recording, just a low and menacing growl, much like the one she and Derron heard at the mouth of the cave. Taken by surprise that day, they assumed they had disturbed a cougar in its den. They dared not linger long enough to make positive identification. Could it have been only a recording? One activated by motion, just as Blake mentioned?

Suspicions swirled in her head. "Can anyone get that?"

"Sure. I'll send it to you, so you can have it on your phone. If you ever get in an uncomfortable situation and think someone is going to bother you, just crank this little baby up and send them running." He pressed a few buttons and reported with a grin, "Done. Check your phone."

Hearing the bing that confirmed a new message, Madison pulled her phone from her pocket. She played the recording back, comparing it to the remembered sound at Hank Adams' place. She wasn't positive, but she thought it was a close match.

Only one way to be sure, she told herself. First thing Monday, she would call Derron and drag him back to the wooded property.

Blake hooked an arm around his mother's shoulders and gave her a big, loud, sloppy kiss on the cheek. "Happy Mother's Day, Mom. Love you bunches!" A rakish grin crossed his face, one that was sure to slay countless of girls over the course of the next several years. "So, what about that pizza?"

Granny Bert volunteered to pick up their meal while the three of them piled onto the sofa and started the first of a dozen or more home movies. It was a time-honored tradition for their family, an opportunity to look back at the past and remember the good times they had shared. It was particularly emotional this year. The first time Gray's handsome face flashed across the screen, Bethani burst into tears. After watching several clips that featured their father, even Blake brushed away a tear or two.

When a close up of her late husband's face filled the screen, Madison could not deny the catch in her heart. Bethani grabbed the remote and punched pause, freezing the image for a moment in time.

"He was so handsome," the girl whispered in a choked voice.

"Yes, he was," Madison agreed. "You two look so much like him. You have his blond hair and his blue eyes. And his smile. Your father had such a wide, open smile."

"Tell us the story of how you met."

"You've heard this story a hundred times, Beth."

"But it never gets old. Please? And tell us about how he proposed. About the way he took you up in the hot air balloon and you almost got stuck in the treetops. Don't leave out a thing." The teen curled against her mother's side, eager to hear the fairytale of her parents' romance one more time.

Madison hesitated, nibbling on her lip. Could she do this? Was she strong enough?

You let the anger go, she reminded herself. *It was a poison inside you, so you got rid of it. You watched it float away in the river. And Brash was right. When you let go of the anger, some of the pain slipped away with it.*

Brash. A smile touched her face as she thought of the auburn-haired man. One day, she might be able to tell their love story.

For now, however, she needed to concentrate on another love story. Despite its bitter ending, her romance with Gray had begun beautifully, and it lived on in the two warm bodies that cuddled beside her. Drawing strength from their presence, Madison allowed herself to remember the magic of falling in love with their father. She stared into the blue eyes on the screen and thought only of the good times. Her voice was soft and reverent as she launched into the tale of her courtship with Grayson Reynolds.

"It sounds so perfect," Bethani whispered after the last story. She twisted so that she could stare up at her mother. "You loved him, didn't you, Mom?"

Madison found that it no longer hurt to answer. "Of course I did, sweetheart."

"Do you think... if he hadn't died..."

Madison knew what her daughter was asking. Knew what the girl wanted to hear. The answer, of course, was no. If Gray had lived, their marriage would not have survived. It had suffered a fatal blow when he first started having an affair two years ago, but her children did not need to know that.

Madison had always tried to be honest with her children, but being honest now would break her daughter's heart. As she contemplated how best to answer, Granny Bert opened the door. The tantalizing aroma of hot, steaming pizza followed her inside. Madison hastily wiped away the tears moistening her cheeks and welcomed the intrusion.

"Ah, just in time for the skiing video!" she said with forced enthusiasm. "Blake, go help Granny. Let's get this show on the road."

She glanced back to the handsome man still dominating the screen, the picture frozen as it captured a smile on his face and a twinkle in his eyes. It was a good way to remember her late husband. A good image to tuck away into her bruised and battered heart.

Thank you.

The sudden wave of tenderness caught her by surprise. After all that had happened, she had not expected to feel gratitude toward this man. To her amazement, the pain that normally gripped her heart gave way to subtle acceptance. Peace settled into her soul.

Thank you for the good times, her heart whispered. *And most of all, thank you for Bethani and Blake.*

Gray had been gone for six months, yet her anger and resentment had kept the turmoil of his passing alive. Nothing was more final than death itself, but closure had eluded her. Madison felt it now, however. As a calm detachment filled her once-angry heart, she knew that chapter of her life was finally over.

Renewed strength surged through her. She was now ready to tackle the world.

Goodbye, Gray.

<h1 style="text-align:center">20</h1>

Tackling the cave, however, would have to wait for another day.

"Sorry, you have that meeting with Murray Archer today, remember?" Derron informed her Monday morning.

"Oh, shoot, I forgot!"

Madison could hear his smug smile over the phone. "That's what you have me for, girlfriend."

"As soon as I can afford it, remind me to give you a raise."

"I'll settle for a paycheck for services already rendered. Did I miss payday last week?"

Madison squirmed in the car seat. "You noticed that, did you?" she murmured in a small voice. Doing a mental evaluation of her checking account, she tried not to feel nauseous. "I'll pay you by Wednesday, I promise. Unless, of course, you could hold off until Friday. Friday would be better for all parties involved."

Derron's easy laugh loosened the knot of dread tying up her stomach. "Good thing I have my inheritance," he told her. "Friday will be fine."

"You're the best, Derron!" she beamed.

"And don't you forget it, dollface."

"Remember to wear old clothes when we go back to

the cave."

"I have my spelunking outfit already picked out. Tootles, dollface. Tell that hunk of a boyfriend I said hello."

Instead of denying her relationship with Brash as she normally did, Madison reminded herself of the new chapter in her life. Knowing she would shock her friend, she smiled brightly and agreed, "Will do. Tootles."

She was still smiling as she pulled into the police station. She parked at the rear of the old train depot and took the well-worn path to the front door, a decided spring in her step.

"Good morning, Vina," she called cheerfully to the woman behind the counter. Not so very long ago, the older black woman had intimidated Madison. It was something about her almost super-human efficiency and her sharp black eyes. Not much slipped past the woman of undetermined age. She was as much a fixture at the police station as the old depot counter, and every bit as solid. Vina Jones was the glue that held the department together, and beside her, Madison could not help but feel inadequate.

In too good of a mood to let those insecurities slip in now, Madison wiggled her fingers in greeting and sailed her way toward Brash's office.

"Good morning, beautiful."

Her smile grew brighter. "And good morning to you."

"So how was your Mother's Day?" Brash asked.

"Wonderful. And in honor of all the lovely gifts I received, I have a small gift for you." She whipped out several papers held together with a paper clip. "My list of families residing in The Sisters back in the day and still currently in the area."

"You're all done?" he asked in surprise. He took the

papers and leaned back in his chair, looking notably impressed. "Very nicely done."

"And it only cost me my eyesight, my sanity, and half a head of hair."

"Aw, even with crossed eyes and thinning hair, you're still beautiful to me." He flashed her a charming grin, his attention quickly returning to the names on the list. "Hmm, I never even thought about a couple of these. Some were a given, but not all of these... Good work, Maddy. Very good work."

She warmed under his praise. In truth, she was feeling quite proud of herself. It was a daunting task he had given her, but she had managed to pull it off.

"So now what?"

"Now the real work begins."

"Uh, excuse me. If you think putting that list together wasn't work itself—"

He held up his palms in defense of her sudden attack. "Poor choice of words. I know creating this list was all kinds of crazy. But this was only the beginning. Now comes the legwork. Now we have to go through these names, one by one, and see what connections and interactions they had to Miss Juliet. We'll need to do interviews, background checks, that sort of thing. Dig around a little. See what, if anything, these people would have to lose if some dark secret from the past should surface."

"I took the liberty of making a second list." She pulled a single sheet of paper from her files. "These are the names I think we should concentrate on."

Instead of taking the list she offered, Brash studied her for a long moment. She began to squirm under his thoughtful gaze. He toyed with a pen on his desk, obviously contemplating the extent to which Madison should be involved in the investigation.

He finally sanctioned her input with a small nod.

"Tell me what you have and how you arrived at it."

Feeling quite pleased that he valued her thoughts, Madison sank into the chair across from his desk.

"In no particular order," she prefaced, but the first name she called was Amanda Hooper's.

"And why her?"

"Think about it. She is a very astute producer and businesswoman. What better way to generate publicity for her show than to create *more* publicity? The skeleton's discovery made quite a splash, even on the national news. And everyone loves a ghost story."

His expression unreadable, Brash's tone was just as neutral. "So naturally Nick Vilardi's name is on the list, as well, for the very same reasons."

"Of course." She squirmed a bit in her seat, neglecting to mention she had added it at the last minute. While Amanda's name was at the top of her suspect list, Nick's was dead last.

"Go on."

"Hank Adams."

"Certainly old enough to have known Miss Juliet personally and perhaps have knowledge of the skeleton. Why else did you select his name to be on the list?"

"He has definite ties to the Big House. Both of his grandparents and his mother all worked there. This Clarence person who built the house was actually Hank Adam's uncle. So if it should turn out that Clarence built the secret stairway for nefarious reasons and Hank knew what those were, he might want to keep it secret."

"He's going to rather drastic measures, don't you think, to protect the honor of a family member who has been dead for several decades?"

Madison shrugged. "Recently, not all of his actions have made a lot of sense. As you know, he is in the middle of a property dispute with Allen Wynn, and some of the things he has done are rather… drastic, as you put it." She thought of the trap. Definitely over the top.

"I'm not doubting you," Brash assured her, "just asking your rationale. Next?"

A bit uncomfortably, she read from her list. "Allen Wynn."

Brash was clearly surprised. "Oh?"

"It's a longshot, but what if he was trying to frame Hank Adams, so that he had a clear claim to the acreage in dispute?"

Brash looked suitably impressed. "Good point. And worth a look."

"Arles Bishop."

"Because…?"

"Okay, I admit it started because you mentioned him the night of the break-in. No, don't give me that look," she cautioned, waving his protest aside. "I looked into it, and his family had a bit of a run-in with Miss Juliet back when the town was first founded. She did not feel they were worthy of citizenship, so they settled in Naomi, but their paths crossed several times after that. At one point, his grandfather worked for the city of Juliet as a gardener. And yes, she had a gardener on the town payroll. Anyway, she had to fire him. Something about bootlegging. She mentioned it in one of the journals. After that, the Bishops caused a bit of trouble in town. This pattern seemed to continue for several years. And there was some mention of one of the Bishop women going missing in the early 50's. Everyone assumed she ran away from home, but what if it turned out to be her skeleton we found? I think it's worth adding Arles, or at least the Bishop family, to the list."

"Anyone else?"

"Barry Redmond. It is no secret that the Redmonds tried to stake a claim against Miss Juliet's estate, claiming they had a right to it as one of Darwin's descendants. It is also no secret that the Redmonds have never liked my family, resenting the fact that Granny inherited what they felt should have been theirs. And judging from my recent encounter with Barry, I would say he is still very bitter."

At mention of her altercation with Redmond, Brash's jaw tightened. He remained silent, however, as he studied her with shrewd eyes. He finally responded with, "Good work, Maddy. Very good. I'll look into it."

Sensing her dismissal, Maddy frowned. "Please tell me I did not just work myself out of a job."

Brash looked uncomfortable.

"I want to help. I could do some of the legwork. You're always saying how busy you are, how overworked. Let me take some of the load." She could tell that he was wavering. "Please, Brash. What can I do?"

Her cell phone rang. "You can answer your phone," he replied smartly.

He studied the list again as Madison took the call. As she hung up, she looked at him with an apologetic wince. "My lunch meeting just got moved up. Would it be a huge problem if I left?"

"Not at all. You've done a great job here. I appreciate your hard work."

"Please think about letting me do more."

Brash studied her for a moment, looking thoughtful. As his eyes warmed, a devilish grin slid over his face. "I can tell you this. I do promise to think about you."

"We're going out to eat?" Bethani asked in surprise.

Her mother made the announcement while Blake raided the refrigerator for a pre-dinner snack. "What's the occasion?"

"Do we need an occasion?" Madison asked.

"Yeah, we sorta do," the teen said ruefully. "You always say we can't afford to go out."

Madison was thankful the cameras were no longer rolling at the house, else they would have captured her daughter's reply.

"Okay, so maybe there is an occasion. I'll tell you about it over dinner. Where would everyone like to eat?"

Granny Bert was easy to please, but the twins requested their favorite Italian restaurant in College Station.

"It's a school night," Madison protested.

"But apparently we're celebrating," Blake was quick to point out. He stuffed the last of a banana into his mouth. "We don't know what it is we're celebrating, but surely it's worth the drive."

Madison's hesitation was brief. "You know what? It is. Let's go."

When they reached the restaurant an hour later, she almost changed her mind.

"Look at this line," Madison said in dismay. They were buried at least a dozen people back from the door. "You two have school tomorrow."

"I don't mind going in late," Blake offered.

"I'm sure you don't. You're always so thoughtful that way." Madison buzzed the top of his head with a light tap.

"Hey, just thinking of you," the teen insisted innocently. "You could sleep in."

"Or we could go somewhere without a line two miles long."

Bethani looked up from her phone long enough to

whine. "You promised we could eat here!"

"My taste buds are all set on cannelloni," Blake said. "Maybe a side of spaghetti. With spinach and artichoke dip for an appetizer."

After a few moments of waiting in line, Granny began to cough. Madison murmured a small 'bless you,' but the coughing fit continued. The sound was so long and ragged, she was beginning to get concerned. Other people in line turned to look at the older woman.

Bending over at the waist, Granny caught her great-grandson's eye and winked as she went into another fit of coughing and hacking.

"Are you all right?" Madison frowned.

The older woman waved her hand in the air, presumably to brush away the concern. "I will be. I don't know what the big deal is." She stopped to cough again. Her voice was surprisingly strong and loud, easily carrying to the couple in front of them. "My fever is not all that high. I have a headache and weakness. I don't know why the doctors are so uptight." As she went into another long fit of coughing, the couple decided they were not in the mood for Italian.

"Two down," Granny Bert coughed into her fist.

"What?" Madison was thoroughly confused. What was her grandmother talking about?

Moving forward in line, Granny Bert pushed in closer to the family ahead of them. She coughed and noisily cleared her throat.

"I said calm down. I'll return their calls in the morning." She pretended to grumble beneath her breath, but her voice was plenty loud, especially turned as she was toward the other family. "All that nonsense about putting me in quarantine. Can't a mother go visit her sick son in Africa without everyone getting so uptight? And what do those letters, CDC, stand for? Center for Disease Control? Or Can't Doctors Cure?"

She dissolved into another fit of prolonged coughing, just before the mother tugged on her husband's arm. The family of five slipped quietly to the end of the line.

"Getting shorter," Granny Bert said with satisfaction.

Appalled when she realized what her grandmother was doing, Madison chided, "You should be ashamed of yourself!"

"Why? Because I went halfway around the world to nurse my sick son? I had to go check on my baby boy." She coughed again for good measure. Then she lifted a wrinkled hand to her forehead, pretending to check for a fever. "Do I feel hot to you? They told me the signs to watch for. Fever and chills. A cough. Weakness and muscle pain. Stomach cramps and vomiting. Eye troubles." She rubbed at her forehead, then bent at the waist as if with sudden pain. "Blake, bring me my sweater. It's so cold out here."

Amused by her act, the teenager did his part to play along. "Will you need your barf bag again?"

Her voice lost some of its strength. "No, not this time. I think I just need to sit for a while, and rest." She alternated between gasping for air and coughing, until the people standing directly in front of them melted away into the crowd. Granny Bert stumbled forward, brushing against a young mother's arm.

"Oh, pardon me, sir. I-I didn't see you there."

With a frantic look in her eyes, the young mother clutched her small child to her and stepped back. "Please, ma'am, you go on ahead. We're really not that hungry."

Two more coughing fits, and they found themselves next in line to be seated. As the crowd thinned, Granny Bert made a remarkable recovery. Her cough disappeared, she was able to stand upright, and she no longer switched between shivering from the cold and fanning herself for air. There was no more talk of a sick son in Africa or the CDC. Much to Madison's chagrin and Blake's amusement, the older woman was all smiles as the waitress seated them just moments later.

"I cannot believe you did that!" Madison hissed.

"Did what?" her grandmother asked with feigned innocence. "I had a little tickle in my throat."

"What was all that nonsense about Africa?"

Granny Bert lifted a shoulder in lame defense. "Your father travels so much I lose track of what country he's in."

"You know good and well he's not sick and you did not visit him! You deliberately let people think you had Ebola!"

From across the table, Blake watched the interaction between the two women with a huge grin and a sparkle of mirth in his eyes. Having his own flair for dramatics, he fully appreciated his great-grandmother's finesse.

Turning toward him now, Granny Bert wore a look of complete innocence upon her wrinkled face. "Did I once use that term? I can't help it if people jumped to conclusions. And you know I'm old and getting forgetful. Sometimes my dreams are so vivid..." She blinked as if to clear the confusion from her mind, giving Madison a look of lost helplessness. "Are you saying it was only a dream? I didn't really travel so far? Then why am I so weak and tired..."

"Because you are a con artist!" Madison hissed, leaning forward to scold the other woman. "It must take a tremendous amount of energy, thinking up these schemes to trick people with!"

This time, Blake hooted aloud with laughter. Bethani remained buried in her cell phone.

"Don't encourage her, Blake," Madison snapped. "She is simply incorrigible. And don't get any bright ideas about copying her. I expect we might be thrown out of here at any moment."

The waitress stepped up to the table just in time to hear her last remarks. With a confused look upon her face, she darted a nervous glance between the foursome.

Granny Bert was quick to cover the awkward silence that followed. "She thinks we're under-dressed," she explained in a loud conspiratorial whisper. "I told her she looks fine, even though her outfit is a bit dated. Houndstooth went out of style a while back, but you won't kick us out, will you, dear?"

Melting into an indulgent smile, the server was quick to put her customers at ease. She even touched Madison's shoulder. "Oh, no ma'am, you look just fine. My grandma had a blouse just like that when I was little. Don't you worry about that for one minute."

Her face flooding with embarrassment, Madison made a mental note to accept Derron's offer of taking her shopping. Maybe it really was time to re-think her wardrobe.

After they placed their orders and were munching on warm breadsticks, Granny Bert wormed her way back into Madison's good graces. "So tell us why we're celebrating this evening. You have some good news, obviously."

"Yes, as a matter of fact, I do. Bethani, please put away your phone." With a shy smile of pride, Madison made her announcement. "I signed a pretty big client this afternoon. A private investigator out of Houston by the name of Murry Archer who wants to put *In a Pinch* on retainer."

Bethani looked dubious. She had put her cell away for *this*? "What does that even mean?"

"It means he is willing to pay me a salary, even when I'm not doing a job for him."

"That doesn't sound very smart on his part. Why would he do that?"

"To make certain I will be available when he does need me. I did some work for him once before, and he was so pleased with how it turned out, he wants me to do more. And when I am working a case for him, he will pay me twice my normal rates, *plus* expenses!" Her children might not understand the importance of those particular details, but her checkbook certainly did. She swore she felt it doing cartwheels of joy during their meeting. *At least it can do something other than bounce*, she thought ruefully.

"What will you be doing? I mean, you're way up here, he's way down there. Will you have to travel back and forth?" Blake wanted to know. "Who will cook dinner every night?"

"Get that panicked look out of your eyes, sweetheart. I will be home to cook your dinner. If I do any traveling, it will mostly be in the general area, much of it here in Bryan and College Station. Mr. Archer says he often gets calls about jobs in the Brazos Valley, but he has to turn them away because he doesn't have the resources to accommodate them."

"I'm guessing you are the new resources," Granny Bert speculated.

"That is correct," Madison confirmed with a proud smile. "I already have my first assignment."

Granny squinted her eyes to inquire, "Can you legally spy on people without an investigator's license?"

"According to him, in many ways an average citizen has more freedom and leniency to 'observe' than a licensed PI does." Madison used air quotes. "He has over a dozen non-licensed contacts working for him, most in the Houston area. I'll be his only contact here in the Brazos Valley. And get this. He suggested I change the name from *In a Pinch Temporary Services* to *In a Pinch Professional Services*. He said it sounds more... well, professional. Not to mention more versatile. Apparently, after working for a year under a PI, I can take the test to become a licensed investigator myself. He said he would be happy to mentor me."

"You're going to become a private eye?" Blake asked. Excitement warred with worry in his blue eyes.

"No, probably not. But it might be something to think about, later on down the road. It seems that half of my current customers already want services that fall in that general direction."

"That might not be a bad idea," her grandmother said, eyes twinkling with excitement. "Together, we'd make quite a team."

Madison blinked in surprise. "To-Together? Team?"

"Sure. Can you think of a single reason I wouldn't make an excellent sidekick for your PI services?" her grandmother challenged.

This time, it was Madison who panicked. Teaming up with her unpredictable grandmother for undercover work? The thought was terrifying.

"Uhm, excuse me for a minute. I need to visit the ladies' room."

She stalled for a suitable amount of time, hoping her grandmother would have forgotten her question by the time she returned. As Madison washed her hands and took extra time drying them, a woman approached her with a shy smile. "You're her, aren't you? You're that television star with the huge old house."

"I-I'm hardly a star."

"Of course you are! I recognize you from the show. I just love to watch it. Can I have your autograph?"

Madison shook her head modestly. "Oh, I don't think..."

"Please? We watch your show every week!" The

woman thrust a slip of paper toward her. She even had a pen handy.

"Well, okay." Feeling a bit self-conscious, Madison wrote a brief note of thanks and signed her name. She laughed when the woman squealed happily and left with the autograph snagged in a tight fist.

She returned to the table just as their meal arrived. As they were eating, a familiar couple stopped by their table to say hello.

"Bertha, I thought that was you and your family."

Granny Bert greeted her friends with a big smile. "Hank Adams, you old coot! What are you doing over here in the big city? Finally giving your fine wife a night off from cooking?"

"Had to come over and do a bit of shopping at Wal-Mart," wife Virgie acknowledged.

They chatted for a few moments before Granny Bert voiced the question paramount on Madison's mind. Her grandmother was many things, but shy was not one of them.

"So, Hank, what's all this nonsense I'm hearing about you and Allen Wynn? Are you giving that poor boy troubles?"

"Not me," the old man denied. "I don't know what bee got under his belt, but the boy has gone plumb crazy on me. Never knew him to be so greedy, but he's demanding I turn fifty acres over to him. Even pressed charges against me. Gone crazy, I say, just like his old grandma on his mama's side. You remember Miss Gladys, don't you? Loony as a bat. They say she drank too much of her daddy's moonshine as a child." Hank shook his head in an odd mix of sympathy and disgust.

"Old man Rupert sure made some mighty fine 'shine, though," Granny Bert beamed.

Madison edged into the conversation. "Fifty acres?" she questioned.

Virgie Adams bobbed her gray head. "It's had us so upset, we just can't deal with it," she admitted. "We turned it all over to our son and grandson. When they saw how upset all this was making us, they advised us to not even speak to Allen. Gerald's boy has been away to college, you know. Smart as a whip, with a half dozen awards and degrees to prove it. They said they would take care of everything for us. Said if Allen wants to sue us and take our land, they'll deal with him." Virgie patted her husband's arm in a gesture of comfort.

Madison frowned. The Adams family told a completely different story than Allen Wynn. Allen claimed the dispute involved less than ten acres. He also told her it was Hank who pressed the charges. One of them was apparently mistaken or flat-out lying, but which one?

Obviously, she needed to do a little more digging.

"Mother, we'd best be going," Hank told his wife. "You don't like driving after dark."

Virgie sighed. "My eyes aren't what they used to be. And poor Hank can hardly see at all anymore, no matter how strong they make his glasses. We just can't get around like we used to."

Someone can certainly get around well enough to set traps and spy cams, Madison thought grudgingly, unconsciously rubbing her ankle with her other foot as the elderly couple shuffled away.

Blake turned to his great-grandmother with a speculative grin. "Moonshine? We're studying prohibition at school and the effects it had on the nation. Some people say there was a big moonshine industry here in The Sisters. Is that true?"

Granny Bert slapped her leg with delight, her eyes twinkling. "Hoo boy, was there ever! It may have cranked up during prohibition, but believe me, it lasted for quite a few years after that."

"Who was the person you mentioned to Hank?" Madison asked.

"Rupert Madden. He was one of the better-known 'shiners. He made some mighty fine corn liquor. I can attest to that from personal experience." She winked a wizened old eye, earning a giggle from the teenagers.

"And who did you say he was?"

"Allen Wynn's great-grand pappy on his mother's side. Gladys Madden married Claude Wynn when she wasn't no more than thirteen or fourteen. She was a sweet little gal, but a bit simple-minded. Didn't matter to her that she married a man twice her age and half her size. She was happy as a lark, raising a whole passel of young'ns there on the farm."

His curiosity piqued, Blake wanted to know more. "Who were some of the other moonshiners?"

"Well, the best-known ones were Rupert Madden and Judd Havlicek. Oh, and the Bishops. Their whole family ran a still for years."

"As in Merle Bishop who owns the tractor dealership? And his son Arles?" Maddy asked.

"Same clan. Back then, everybody had big families. His grand pappy, old man Howdy Bishop, must have had at least nine or ten kids. I suppose selling corn liquor was the only way he could keep 'em all fed and clothed. They had stills hidden in every nook and cranny round these parts, trying to outsmart revenuers."

"I read in one of the journals that a Bishop worked for the town as a gardener, but Miss Juliet had to let him go."

"It was over the moonshine," Granny Bert confirmed. "She said it wasn't proper, having a city employee bootlegging on the side. When he refused to give up the still, she fired him."

"That must have caused hard feelings."

Granny shrugged. "I'm sure he made more money off the liquor than he did the roses."

"We go to school with a few Havliceks," Bethani said, her nose wrinkling in distaste. "They're always getting into trouble. It doesn't surprise me someone in their family was a moonshiner."

"It was more like the whole clan. Every one of them lazier than the next. Why, the whole lot of them avoids an honest day's work the way a chicken avoids the stew pot."

"So where were these stills located, Granny Bert?"

She gave Blake a knowing look. "Thinking of trying to find them, hoping they're still in business?"

His shrug was innocent enough. "Just curious."

"The more successful ones kept on the move, one step ahead of the law. But rumor had it that many a still was set up in the caves around the area. Then they smuggled their moonshine out through the tunnels."

"Caves?" Blake's eyes lit with excitement.

"Tunnels?" Madison echoed.

"There are tunnels and caves all through these parts." She cocked her head to one side and mused, "I haven't thought about those tunnels in years, 'cept the ones where the sewer lines run. As mayor, I had to think about those a few times too many. Still have to hear about them some, every time Sybille's little white poodle gets free of the yard and goes a-wandering."

"I could use some extra credit in my history class," Blake said, acknowledging his fledging grades. "You think I could interview you? You could tell me what you know about the legends and the rumors."

"I can do better than that," Granny Bert said, her eyes twinkling. "I can give you first-hand knowledge of what it was like to run it."

Madison's gasp was audible. "Granny! You were a bootlegger?" she cried in dismay.

"Times were hard, Madison. We made a living any way we could."

Madison stared at her grandmother in amazement. "I can't believe I'm just now hearing about this phase of your life. You have been an elected official, several times over. Now I'm finding out you were a criminal first!"

Unconcerned, her grandmother offered a low harrumph. "Like the two don't go hand-in-hand most of the time," she grumbled. "Don't act so high and mighty, Madison Cessna Reynolds. You don't know what it was like back in the Great Depression and the days after it. Folks did what they had to do to survive. It took a few decades for the economy to pick up around these parts. Selling corn liquor kept many a family fed and sheltered, including my own."

"Why did they call it bootlegging?" Bethani asked.

"A bottle would slip down inside your bootleg smooth as silk. Or glass, as the case might be." Her wrinkled face dissolved into a huge grin as she made a motion toward her leg. "That was my job. I was a runner."

"Did you ever see the caves or use the tunnels?" Blake wanted to know.

"The only cave I ever saw in action was the one out on the Montgomery place."

"The Montgomerys were moonshiners, too?" Madison was crestfallen. She thought so highly of Cutter.

"At the time, the place belonged to the Maddens. There was a handy little tunnel that ran from the cave down to the river bottom. A long stretch, and mighty dark without a lantern, but it was plenty big. You could even get a wheelbarrow in there to make a nice haul."

Blake grinned from ear to ear, delighted to hear of his great-grandmother's nefarious past. "Did you ever get caught by the law?"

Seeing the fascination that gleamed in her son's eye, Madison broke in. "I think this is enough talk about moonshining. I'm just glad there are no cameras around to record all this! I could never show my face around town again."

Her grandmother gave her a hard look. "There you go again, worrying about what other people think, just like Miss Juliet always did. Besides, don't you imagine most folks already know?"

Madison's only answer was a deep scowl.

The server returned, wanting to know if they had saved room for dessert.

"There's always room for dessert," Blake answered for the group.

"Dessert? How can you possibly have room for dessert after all you just ate?" Madison asked. She turned to the waitress with a firm, "No thanks, we're ready for the bill."

"But I wanted ice cream," her son sulked as the waitress disappeared.

"I tell you what. If you're still wanting ice cream when we go past the Dairy Queen, we'll stop and get dessert." Celebration or not, even a trademark Blizzard would be cheaper than one of the restaurant's pricey offerings.

The waitress returned with the bill and a take-out box for Bethani. Madison glanced at the total and immediately blanched. "Uhm, excuse me, but I think there's some mistake. Our bill couldn't possibly be this much."

"Oh, that included the other table," the server explained.

"What other table?"

The girl presented her with a broad smile. "That was so sweet of you to buy their meal like that. I thought I recognized you when you came in, but the clothes distracted me. I guess you have to dress down to avoid calling attention to yourself, huh? Anyway, some celebrities aren't as nice as you. We get a lot of musicians who play here in town, and you wouldn't believe how stingy some of them can be." The girl rambled on, but the buzzing in Madison's head overrode the chatter. She swallowed hard, mentally counting the meager cash she had in her wallet. She hadn't had time to cash Murray Archer's check yet.

"Did Hank and Virgie pull a fast one on us?" Granny Bert fumed. "That sounds about like the cheap old buzzard."

Madison always kept a fifty-dollar bill tucked away for emergencies. She pulled it out now, hoping to avoid further embarrassment. Only then did she see the second receipt.

"It wasn't Hank," she said weakly. "It was the so-called 'fan' in the restroom."

21

Before starting on the new assignment for Murray Archer, Madison was eager to tie up some of her own work. She confirmed dates for a fill-in position at a business in Naomi and lined up two jobs best suited for Derron. She spent the rest of the morning making and returning phone calls and putting together files for her two current clients. She would return to the disputed property one last time before giving Allen her final report.

The other client she met for lunch, tucked away in her customary corner booth at *New Beginnings*.

"I suppose you have something for me?" Lisa Redmond asked as she slipped into the booth opposite Madison. She looked only marginally better today than she had before. At least her hair was groomed.

"Yes, I think I have a rather complete report to offer you."

After they ordered their meal and had privacy again, Madison looked her client in the eye. "Are you certain you want to know what I found?"

The other woman sighed. "No, I don't want to know. But I *need* to know. I need to have something to fight back with."

Madison hesitated a moment before handing the

folder to the other woman. "Please know that some of the photographs inside may be rather upsetting. You might prefer to view them in private," Madison suggested.

"I know my husband is cheating on me. I have my suspicions about who she is. All these pictures will do is confirm it for sure." Lisa sounded weary. Still, she did not open the folder immediately. "So what did you find out?"

"Everything is noted inside the folder. I provided dates and times for each incident I reported. Other than one rather public display" — *just a few tables away, to be exact* — "I have no photographic proof that your husband is having an affair. However, there is more than enough circumstantial evidence to support that theory."

"You talk like a lawyer," Lisa complained. "Just tell me outright, is Barry having an affair?"

The woman asked for honesty. "In my opinion, yes."

A look of resignation settled over her face.

"I'm not surprised. It's the kid I feel sorry for."

"You have children?"

"He does. Miley. She's a good kid, but she's been handed around too many times. I worry what another step-mom will do to her head."

Although she did not realize the girl was Barry's daughter, Madison was familiar with the name. She had heard it often enough, spewed with venom from the mouth of her own daughter and her best friend. She made a mental note to have a talk with the girls, explain that Miley's home situation might be responsible for her churlish attitude.

"It's not unheard of for a step-child to choose to live with a step-parent." Madison offered what encouragement she could.

Lisa Redmond perked up. "You mean you think I

could win custody of her?"

"I-I don't know about that. That's really not my area of—"

"It would take a lot of money to raise a child. But I suppose I would get alimony. And she would probably get some sort of allowance..."

Madison could see the wheels turning in the other woman's mind. She regretted her rash statement, uttered only as a means of comfort. Judging from the look in her eyes, she feared Lisa might use the girl as an income.

"I appreciate your help." In a sudden flurry of motion, Lisa swiped the file from the table, stood to go, and tossed an envelope toward Madison. "Here's a bonus for a job well done. I might as well spend Barry's money while I can."

"But... what about your lunch?"

"There's enough in there to cover the cost of my meal," Lisa assured her. "I have to go now. I need to contact my lawyer. Thanks."

Stunned at the surge of energy the weary woman suddenly displayed, an uneasy feeling settled into Madison's stomach. She had a bad feeling that she had somehow been used.

After eating alone and bagging Lisa's meal as an after-school snack for Blake, Madison went home, determined to finish reading the rest of the journals by night's end. With the exception of the stolen book, she had them all at the house, lined up in chronological order. She had yet to discover any earth-shattering news — certainly nothing worthy of murder or even theft — but there were still several entries left to read. She acknowledged that if the answers were not inside the diaries, they might never know the truth.

Having read a similar entry in an earlier journal, Madison paused when she read a particular passage in a journal dated 1922.

It happened again last night. For the third time this week, I awoke to the oddest sensation. I sensed that someone was watching me. This time, I thought I saw a shadow moving near the bookcase, the one my love had built for me as a special wedding surprise. I called out, but no one answered. No air stirred. All was quiet, so it must have been my imagination.

Still, I instructed Truman to go round the entire house and make certain all doors and windows were secure. This is hardly the first time I felt that someone was in the room with me, even though I know it is impossible.

At first, I drew comfort from the thought that it was Darwin's spirit here with me, watching over me from his perch in heaven. I first sensed I had a visitor soon after my dear husband's fateful accident. I was so certain that he was still here with me, trying to comfort me best he could during those stark, desolate days. But as the days passed, and as the months have slipped into years, I no longer feel comforted by the presence of my nighttime visitor. Nor can I admit to feeling frightened. (Surely, if someone meant me harm, they would have taken advantage of my defenseless state long before now.)

The best I can say is that I feel uncomfortable, no longer at ease in my own bedroom. I often lay awake at night, pondering the existence of ghosts. As an intelligent woman, I do not believe in apparitions... yet as a lonely widow whose only friend has suddenly disappeared and whose sole visitor comes silently in the middle of the night, I find myself wondering... do ghosts really exist? What other explanation could there be?

Madison empathized with the young widow. She could not imagine how horrible it must have been for Miss Juliet to lose her beloved husband, only to discover her sister would soon bear his child. With no other family to depend upon, she must have felt so alone.

With a frown, Madison reread the passage. She had written *'whose only friend has suddenly disappeared.'* Was she referring to Clarence?

Thumbing back through the pages, Madison did not see his name in any of the entries. She went back two months before she found mention of the carpenter. She read the passages in reverse order, reviewing the latest ones first.

... When Clarence returns, I will ask him to repair the squeaky board. I hear it most often at night, when the house is settled and still. If I did not know differently, I might think someone else was in the house, but I know that I am the sole occupant of this big, lonely mansion.

... I have not seen my friend in days. He borrowed my copy of The Manor while away on his business trip. Clarence has been a good friend to me over the years, and I am not ashamed to admit how much I miss him. I know I would never have survived the loneliness and desolation of losing first my father, then my beloved Darwin, had it not been for his friendship. I miss our talks and our long discussions about books. If not for sweet Rose in the kitchen, I might truly go mad without someone to talk to each day.

... Today, Clarence told me he would be leaving on a trip. He called it a business trip, although I am not certain of its nature. To my knowledge, the man is a talented carpenter, but he has no particular business acumen. I fear this impromptu trip may be the result

of the awkward moment that occurred between us last week. I am afraid that my dear, sweet friend, the man who has become like a brother to me in my heart, may harbor romantic feelings toward me. However, my heart will always belong to my one true love. There is no room for another.

So, Clarence did have feelings for Miss Juliet! Madison twisted her mouth in a self-satisfied smirk. She had suspected as much all along.

She finished the journal through to the end and started on another. Clarence's name was mentioned only a handful more times in either book. Twice she mentioned that he had not returned yet from his trip, but most entries referring to him were written in past tense. She recalled when Clarence built a new shelf for her, repaired something around the house, surprised her with a new book of mystery and intrigue. The final mention of her friend was written with a heavy heart.

... I fear something dreadful has happened to my friend. No one has heard from Clarence in over five months, when he left for his mysterious business trip. By now, surely he would have written. Or perchance he would have sent me a book, some small token of remembrance to let me know he is doing well and thinking of me. Truman is convinced harm has befallen him. I tend to agree. In my heart, I believe that my dear friend has perished. I will remember him fondly and smile each time I look upon one of the special intricacies he gifted me with. He wanted my home to be different from Naomi's, filled with mysterious niches, hidden passages, and delightful surprises. He said it was only fitting that my home should be special; like its mistress, he claimed. Goodbye, my dear friend. I will miss our lively literary discussions and our shared love for the written word. I pray you find peace in the ever after.

Madison's heart quickened with excitement. Could it have been Clarence's body they discovered in the secret room? Instead of going away on a business trip, what if he went to live in the cellar, where he could be close to his requited love? What if the man had a sick obsession with Juliet, spying on her at night by way of the secret staircase?

Before Madison could grab her phone and discuss her theory with Brash, her phone rang. Nick's name flashed across the screen.

"Hello?"

He did not bother with a greeting. "Madison, I need you to come down to the house."

"Can't it wait? I'm in the middle of something."

"Drop it. You'll want to see this."

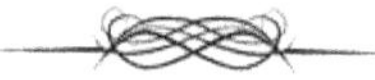

Nick led her into the far recesses of the cellar, into a corner opposite the secret room. The lighting was dim and the wooden wall in front of them absorbed what little reflection there was.

"You wanted to show me a wall?" she asked in confusion. Guessing at its significance, she all but groaned. "I can see it's not quite flush. Don't tell me this is a load-bearing wall that's eaten up with termites." Dismay slipped into her voice. "My entire house is going to fall in, isn't it?"

A smile stole over Nick's handsome features. "No, Madison, nothing like that. Despite its age, this house is surprisingly sound and sturdy. As is the foundation." His smile faded. "Even with all its secrets."

This time, she did groan. "Not another room," she protested.

"Well, not exactly."

"Then what?"

One section of wood jutted slightly forward, not

quite flush with the rest of the wall. To Madison, the wood appeared buckled, perhaps due to age or, worse, due to moisture. While she worried there was a water leak somewhere in the cellar, Nick tugged on the section in question. She braced herself, expecting to see faulty pipes or evidence of water damage.

She did not expect the wall to slide away and reveal a gaping hole in the earth beyond.

"What-what is it?" she asked in amazement.

Nick's voice was grim. "A tunnel."

"A tunnel? But... why? Where?"

"I have no idea why. This house just keeps getting stranger and stranger."

"I don't understand. Why haven't we found this before? How did you find it now? Why on Earth is there a tunnel in the cellar? And where does it go?" She peppered him with questions as she ran nervous fingers through her hair.

"It's well-disguised as part of the wall. The lighting is dim enough, and the workmanship good enough, that we never suspected a hidden door. Although, given the many hidden passages throughout the rest of the house, I suppose we should have."

"I-I can't believe this!" she murmured, still stunned.

"I discovered this passage quite by accident. I noticed how the wall appeared buckled. When I tried to secure it with a nail, I realized there was nothing behind it."

Venturing a step forward, Madison craned her neck to see inside the dark hole. It was surprisingly large. "This is uncanny. We were talking about tunnels, just last night. I never dreamed there could be one here, right beneath my own house!"

"Here's your flashlight."

"*My* flashlight?" she questioned.

"I thought you'd feel better having your own light."

"Wait a minute! Where are you going?"

Already half-swallowed by the dark cavern, Nick turned back to flash her a charming grin. "It's perfectly safe. I've already been through it. Follow me."

"But…" She felt a moment of panic. There was something spooky about being left behind, standing at the mouth of the big cavity. She had no idea what danger lurked beyond. Yet the thought of Nick proceeding without her was every bit as frightening. She wanted to be involved in the adventure, no matter the danger it posed.

"It's all right, Madison. The tunnel is safe."

Stepping into the cool recesses of the underground passage, she noted the ground beneath her feet. The earthen floor was well packed and free of debris. No snarled tree roots or stray stones to stump her toes upon. The walls and ceiling were neatly cut from clay, reinforced by columns of bricks and large beams every dozen or so feet. For a secret underground passage, the tunnel was neatly constructed and appeared quite sound.

As she followed Nick down the corridor — she barely had to duck, the passage was so large — Maddy wondered about its existence. Was it another of Clarence's additions? Had Miss Juliet known about it? Or was it, like the secret room, another result of his sick obsession?

They walked for what seemed a mile, though Madison suspected it was not nearly so far. The ground gradually rose on a slight incline. The ceiling, however, remained the same height, meaning she eventually had to stoop over as they approached the end of the tunnel. The atmosphere changed and a rank odor seeped into the crevices of the earthen walls.

"What is that smell?" she cringed.

"Drainage pipes. Possibly a little sewer gas. Watch

your step up here. This is the only part that gets tricky."

Madison detected the first hints of light. *Light at the end of the tunnel*, she mused with a slight smile.

At the first rumble, the smile fell away. As the sound intensified and the walls around her began to tremble, panic seized her heart. An earthquake?

No, even worse.

"Nick! The walls are caving in!" Madison cried, clutching his arm with frantic strength. "What do we do? Should we run for it?" She could see stronger light now, filtering in just ahead. They had to climb over some sort of obstacle, but daylight — and freedom — beckoned not more than twenty feet away.

The sound became a deadly roar. It rattled overhead. Echoed around them. Reverberated beneath their feet. Madison thought of being trapped inside the commercial chicken house while the pressure inside built, pulling at her clothes and her lungs and her sanity. This felt much the same. The roar alone was enough to push her over the edge.

"Nick!" she screamed, tugging on his arm. "We have to go!"

Why was he simply standing there?

"It's a cave-in!" she cried, pulling him toward the faint light. "Hurry!"

"It's not a cave-in." He had to yell to be heard, even though he stood so close she felt his hot breath upon her ear.

"It is!" she insisted.

"No, it's a train!"

She stopped tugging. "A-A train?"

"Yes," he yelled. "Just wait."

The echo was horrific. The walls shook with intensity and the roar continued to consume her, but Madison no longer cared. She sagged in relief against Nick. He gathered her close, offering shouted words of consolation. They reached her no stronger than a whisper.

Her body stopped trembling about the time the walls stopped quaking. The roar of the train finally retreated, chasing the cars down the rickety tracks and slowly fading into the wind. Madison whimpered in relief.

"Oh, my poor ears!" she moaned. "They're still roaring."

"I know," Nick yelled back in empathy. He was slow in releasing her. "Are you okay?"

"I will be." She was still yelling. It was the only way to hear above the ringing in her head.

"We're nearly through." They retrieved the flashlights they had dropped and he took her hand, pulling her along the final few feet. They had to scramble over a pile of dirt and rock, but beyond the rubble was an enormous drainage pipe. It connected to the tunnel on one end, jutting from under the train trestle on the other.

"Where-Where are we?" Madison asked. She gulped in a huge swallow of air, even though it was fetid, tainted with standing water and worse.

"At the edge of town. See, there's the water tower." He pointed to the landmark, helping her get her bearings.

"So we did come a long way," she murmured. She turned to look back into the mouth of the huge culvert. If she hadn't just come from it, she would never guess the dark recesses led to a tunnel.

As they retraced their steps, Madison stopped more than once to marvel. "This is absolutely amazing." She walked a few more feet, then stopped to shake her head. "I just can't believe this." She repeated the pattern all the way back to the house.

Before they reached the door to the cellar, Madison

held Nick back, placing her hand upon his arm. "Please, let's not tell the camera crews about this. They don't know, do they?"

"No. I wanted to tell you first, even though I'm sure Amanda will read me the riot act." He winced as he imagined that conversation. "I just ruined the perfect reveal on reality television."

"You have no idea how much I appreciate that," Madison told him with heartfelt sincerity. Amanda would, no doubt, be furious, having missed capturing Madison's stunned reaction on live footage. "We need to keep this between us, at least until I've told Brash and he's had time to investigate."

"He'd better hurry," Nick grumbled thickly. "Not only is this costing us in delays, but this is becoming increasingly dangerous. I'm worried about you, Madison."

She wanted to brush his concern away, but it wasn't so easy. Madison was every bit as worried. Instead of getting closer to the truth, they seemed to be sinking in deeper, discovering one layer of mystery upon another.

Nick reached out to tuck a strand of hair behind her ear. His hand lingered along her cheek.

"I worry you may be in danger," he confided.

Her heart thumped at his tender gesture, but Madison never hesitated. "Brash will keep me safe," she said with confidence. She knew that to be true.

"He may want to, but can he?" Nick challenged. "He hasn't been a police officer all that long, Madison. He's a football player. A coach. He may be a force to reckon with on the field, but how effective is he against criminals? He and his men shut us down for three days, so they could do a thorough search of this cellar. They obviously didn't do such a good job."

Madison pulled away from his touch, wanting to be free of his accusations. Free of the doubt he tried to plant within her.

"Like you pointed out, you and your team of experts missed it, too, while doing your structural examination. So let's just agree to keep it quiet for now."

Clearly displeased, the carpenter gave a jerky nod. "For now," he agreed. "But you'd better call your chief of police and get him down here. If this is going to cause another delay, I need to know about it now. At the rate we're going, we'll never make our October deadline."

22

Maddy hurried past the cameras and waited until she was in the seclusion of her car before calling Brash.

"deCordova," he barked into her ear.

She faltered. "Bad timing?"

He answered with a sigh. "You could say. There was a fender-bender in the Gas 'n Go parking lot. The out-of-towner is squawking for a lawyer and a neck brace, and the local jokel is showing definite signs of being high. I have a city council meeting in an hour and two reports to finish up before I go."

"Then I won't keep you. There was something I needed to tell you, but it can wait."

"Are you sure?"

"You have your hands full enough without this."

"Sounds pretty important. How about I stop by the house this evening? Maybe I'll be caught up by then, but I doubt it."

"That sounds fine." She hesitated for only a moment, then ventured, "Why-Why don't you come for supper?"

"Are you sure? I thought we were incognito." She could hear the teasing smile in his voice.

"It's just supper. We all have to eat, right?"

He wasn't fooled by her deliberately casual reply.

"Right. Listen, sweetheart, I have to go. I'll call you later."

She loved it when he called her sweetheart. It brightened the dismal shadow cast upon her day after discovering the tunnel. "Okay. Be safe out there."

She may have called it 'only supper,' but they both knew it was sort of a trial run. If Bethani was receptive to Brash being there, it might lead to other dinners and, eventually — hopefully — to dating. And if she wasn't...

Madison refused to think of that, even when she saw the stricken look upon her daughter's face when she announced they would be having a dinner guest.

"You have a *date*?" the girl practically hissed. "Mother, how could you!"

"It's-It's not a date," Madison was quick to say. "Brash is coming over to discuss the case. While he's here, he might as well eat dinner with us."

"But you put on makeup and fixed your hair!"

"I did both of those this morning, Beth, before I left for the day."

"*That* is fresh makeup and fresh perfume," the girl insisted adamantly.

"Okay, so I freshened up. I did last night, too, before we went out to eat."

"But you're wearing even better clothes tonight than you did last night," she wailed.

"Yeah, well, apparently I wasn't dressed so well last night." The server's comments still smarted. And she had even been wearing one of her favorite outfits.

"Can't you go change?"

Madison glanced down, almost afraid to ask. "Why? What's wrong with this outfit?"

"Nothing! That olive green looks really good with your coloring. Those khaki capris make your legs look long and lean, and that blouse makes you look boobier. Seriously, this is one of your better-looking outfits, Mom."

With an amused look on her face, Madison questioned, "Boobier?"

"Let's face it, Mom, you took after Granny Bert in the boobs department, not Happy. But this blouse makes you look... you know, boobier." She used her hands to indicate a fuller bosom.

Madison laughed outright, hugging her daughter with a spurt of delight. "Oh, Bethani, you are priceless!"

"I'm serious, Mom," the girl grumbled. "You shouldn't look so hot tonight. You'll give Mr. D the idea that you're interested."

It was the perfect lead-in. "Would that be so terrible, honey, if I was interested?" she asked softly.

"Terrible?" the girl echoed, her face crumbling. "It would be humiliating!"

Feeling as if she had been kicked in the stomach, Madison tried to disguise her dismay. "And why is that, sweetheart?"

"Be-Because!" she sputtered. "Just because! Because Daddy has only been gone a few weeks! It would be a disgrace to his memory. And because Megan is my best friend! How awkward would that be, if our parents hooked up?"

"Some best friends might think that was pretty cool," Madison suggested, "having their parents get together."

"Until their parents broke up!" she said with heavy melodrama. "Then they'd have to choose sides, and then their friendship would be ruined. Best friends one minute, mortal enemies the next!"

Madison dared not ask what would happen if the parents did not break up. What if it was an ever-after kind of love, the kind she suspected she already had with Brash? She wisely kept her thoughts to herself, even though her heart was breaking.

"Beth, I think you're being a tad bit—"

"Just tell me this isn't a date!" the teen broke in.

"This isn't a date."

"I don't believe you. This is terrible, just terrible!"

"Wait, honey, where are you going?"

"To my room. I've suddenly lost my appetite!"

Madison watched in stunned silence as the teen flounced down the hall, blond hair swinging adamantly in her wake. She was still staring after her daughter when the doorbell rang.

"Are you going to get that?" Granny Bert called from the kitchen.

"Uhm, sure." She made her way to the front door, her heart fluttering when she saw the handsome man on the other side of the threshold.

His eyes lit with appreciation when he saw her. "New blouse?" he murmured, eyes lingering on her 'boobier' silhouette. "I like."

The warm words slid over her, creating a thrill. Her laugh was only marginally forced as she pushed the argument with Bethani from her mind.

"Come on in, Brash. Supper's almost ready."

"You really didn't have to feed me, Maddy," he said. Then he gave her a heart-melting grin. "But I'm sure glad you are."

This time, her laughter was genuine. "Wait until you taste it first. Blake is such an indiscriminate eater I sometimes forget to test my culinary skills."

Ten minutes later, they gathered around the dining room table. Granny Bert looked at the empty chair beside Blake and asked, "Where's Bethani?"

Madison sighed. "She's not in a very hospitable mood this evening. I believe she decided she wasn't very hungry."

"Seemed okay earlier," Granny Bert said with shrewd observation.

Blake was clearly unconcerned about his twin. "More for me," he grinned.

Brash's forehead gathered in a wrinkle. "Is my being here a problem, Maddy?" he asked quietly.

"You're raising a teenage daughter, Brash. You should be familiar with the mood swings. Perfect angel one minute, complete monster the next." Madison tried to make light of the situation, even though her heart smarted. How could she be happy in a relationship with Brash, knowing her daughter was miserable?

This is never going to work, she moped. *Too many stipulations and complications.*

The conversation remained light throughout the meal. Blake offered comic relief and kept the adults in stitches. His re-telling of Granny Bert's Ebola act was so hilarious that even Madison had to laugh.

After supper, they all helped with the dishes and Blake carried a plate to his sister's room, while the adults settled around the table for coffee and serious conversation.

"So what did you want to tell me about, Maddy?" Brash asked. When he turned his eyes upon her, they lingered longer than necessary.

She warmed beneath his gaze, struggling to remember the topic that seemed so urgent earlier. "Nick called me down to the house today. He made another discovery."

"Another hidden room?" Brash asked in exasperation. "This is getting ridiculous!"

Instead of answering directly, she addressed her grandmother. "Granny Bert, what do you remember about the cellar when you were younger?"

The old woman shrugged. "Like I said before, not

all that much. We were never allowed to play down there. They said it was too dangerous."

"Dangerous?" Brash asked.

"I suppose with the cistern and all. And the fire. I still remember the days when laundry was done by hand. Miss Lily, Hank's grandma, insisted the only way to get the linens clean was to boil them. She insisted on using the old methods of a fire and cast-iron pot. She eventually used the wringer-style machine, but it wasn't much safer. Hardly a place for children."

Brash nodded as if he understood, even though the concept of boiling laundry was foreign to him. He barely had mastered the concept of separating the whites from the colors. He owned more than one pair of dingy underwear and bleach-spotted jeans.

Her turned back to Madison. "Why all the questions? What did you find?" he asked impatiently.

Again, she addressed her grandmother. "You know how we were discussing the tunnels last night? You said there were several in this area."

"That's what I hear. Only saw the one for myself, but folks say there are several."

Brash broke in. "You mean the sewer tunnels?"

"No, the bootlegging tunnels." Madison shot her grandmother a stern look.

"That's just old folklore." Brash would have brushed the statement away, until he saw the look that passed between the two women. His brow furrowed. "Isn't it?"

Madison crossed her arms in a prim gesture. "Someone I won't name — although she's sitting in this very room — assures me she has firsthand knowledge of the existence, and use, of said tunnels."

Brash hiked an eyebrow in surprise. "Granny? You were a bootlegger?"

"Depends. You asking as a lawman or a friend?"

His laughter was rich and definitely amused. "A

friend.”

"Then maybe I traveled down a tunnel a time or two, making a run.”

Before the conversation could get too far off track, Madison brought it back around with her stunning announcement. "We discovered a new tunnel today. New to us, anyway. From the looks of it, it has been around for quite a few years.”

"Where is that?”

"In the cellar of the Big House.”

For once in her life, her grandmother was rendered speechless. Even Brash had no immediate response.

"I beg your pardon?" Bertha Cessna finally sputtered. "My hearing must be going. I could have sworn you said in Miss Juliet's cellar.”

"I did. It leads from the far corner of the house, out to the railroad trestle on the edge of town.”

"That's quite a way," Brash noted. Madison had expected him to pepper her with questions, but he was oddly quiet, his dark eyes thoughtful.

"I can't believe there was a tunnel down there and I never knew it! Why, even though we were told not to, Hank, Jubal and I sneaked down there more'n once. Are you saying we walked right past a tunnel entrance and never even saw it?”

"It's covered by a wall. Or a door, I suppose it is. The entire thing is very well constructed and reinforced with brick.”

Granny Bert shook her head with a 'tsk, tsk,' clearly disgusted with her own lack of observation. "And we thought we were so smart, sneaking down there and playing in all those rooms. We liked to play pirates. Some explorers we were, too blind to see what was right before our very eyes!”

"So you had no idea there was a tunnel down there?”

"None whatsoever."

"What about Miss Juliet?" Brash asked.

"I doubt it. I don't recall her ever going down there. She always sent servants, even to fetch the wine for special occasions."

"I've found something new in the journals," Madison said, her voice edged with excitement. For the first time, she felt like they were close to solving the puzzle of the skeleton. "Now more than ever, I believe Miss Juliet knew nothing about the secret staircase, nor the secret room. I think Clarence was a sick man, obsessed with a woman who thought of him only as a friend. I think he built the tunnel, so that he could slip in and out at will and spy on Miss Juliet."

Brash did not seem convinced. "That's rather drastic, don't you think, building a tunnel when he could have just used the outside entrance?"

She told them of the journal entries and how Clarence had simply disappeared in the summer of '22.

"I suppose we could test the skeleton for a DNA match to Hank Adams or one of his off-spring," Brash thought aloud. "See if anything pops."

"I agree with Brash," Granny Bert said. "Sounds pretty drastic, even for a nutcase like this Clarence fella."

"But what other reason could there be for a secret tunnel?" She spread her palms upward in a sign of frustration. Then she glanced at Brash. "What? I see that look. You're thinking something, aren't you?"

"I'm just thinking."

"No, you're onto something, I can tell!"

"It's just a theory, mind you."

Granny Bert saw the same light in his eyes. "Yes, yes, spit it out." She used impatient hand movements to move him along.

"From what I understand, the cellar had a cistern as

a water supply. Plenty of copper tubing, too. A heat source for boiling laundry. Plenty of nooks and crannies, not to mention a secret room and a hidden tunnel."

Granny Bert's eyes glittered with excitement. "All the things needed to make moonshine!" she surmised.

Madison, however, was appalled. "What are you saying? That Miss Juliet was operating an illegal still, right in her very own cellar?"

"I never mentioned Miss Juliet."

"That's-That's even more insane! You think it was someone else, operating it under her nose? Right here in town, in the cellar of the city's most prestigious home?"

"You know what they say, hide in plain sight and no one sees you."

"But that's crazy!"

"About as crazy as a brick-lined tunnel and a hand-dug room."

His words gave her pause. Madison frowned as she considered them.

"It would have been the perfect set-up," Granny Bert mused. "They had everything they needed right there. They could have brought the corn in through the tunnel, literally by the trainload."

"And smuggled the finished product out the same way. The tunnel leads right to the train track, where it could have been loaded and shipped to parts unknown."

"But who would have done such a thing?" Madison posed the question to no one in particular.

"Could have been anyone. Maybe it was someone who worked for her. Or someone with a twisted sense of justice. Miss Juliet offended a lot of people with her highfalutin ways."

"But the servants would have seen. Great-Grandma

Rose would have seen!"

Granny shrugged. "I'm telling you girl, times were hard. Folks did what they had to survive."

"But your mother..."

"Who do you think sent me out to deliver the 'shine, girl? I did my fair share in making a living for the family. No one suspected a little girl with an elfish smile and braids in her hair." Her grandmother flashed a smile that still looked young and mischievous, and completely guileless. Madison, however, knew better.

Overwhelmed and completely frustrated, Madison slapped her hands onto the table and stood. She ranted quietly as she paced the room. "I can't believe this. My own grandmother was a bootlegger. The woman who taught me right from wrong grew up breaking the law. There are secret passages and hidden rooms in the house I'm going to live in, and now we discover a hidden tunnel! I have ghosts and unwanted visitors and a mystery that just keeps unwinding. And cameras! Cameras are everywhere, recording every little thing I do and say. I think I'm going insane. Definitely having a nervous breakdown. Maybe a heart attack. Maybe both. Who knows? Maybe there's a hidden cemetery down there, too, and they can just toss my body in with the rest of them."

Before Madison could come fully unwound, Granny Bert disappeared into the kitchen and came back out, thrusting a wine bottle into Brash's hands.

"Here. Take her out on the porch and calm her down."

Madison stopped her rant long enough to stab her grandmother with a hard look. "I'm not a child that needs to be mollycoddled, you know."

"If you were a child, I wouldn't be sending you out with wine. The night's still young," Granny Bert said, a devilish grin stealing over her features. "I'm headed to my room to watch some television. I won't hear a thing. Blake has his music playing and Bethani is bound to be buried in her phone. You two go on out and enjoy yourselves. The backyard might offer more privacy," she suggested pointedly.

Still keyed up, Madison snapped, "We're not teenagers, Granny. I think we can control our baser instincts."

Beside her, Brash offered a charming but maddening grin. "Speak for yourself."

Granny laughed with glee as Madison opened the front door and led the way out to the porch swing. Even though it faced the street, it tucked into a cozy little corner, shrouded by climbing roses and lattice panels.

Brash poured the wine and waited for Madison to settle within the crook of his arm. Her body was still tense.

"Try to relax, sweetheart. Things are going to work out."

"I don't know, Brash. They just seem to be getting worse, not better."

"Have some wine. Close your eyes and relax. There you go. Isn't that better?"

"Maybe a little."

Pushing the swing into a gentle rocking motion, Brash massaged her shoulder with lazy hypnotizing strokes. He felt the tension slowly ebb from her body. They sat in silence for a long time, soaking in the peaceful evening and each other's company.

As he refilled their wine glasses, he asked, "So what's this with Bethani?"

She could hear the concern in his voice. Some of the tension came back into hers. "She's still having a difficult time, Brash. You know how miserable she was when we first moved here. If not for your own sweet Megan, she might still be as miserable."

"They've become very good friends," he acknowledged.

"But you know how scary change is, especially for a child. Bethani not only lost her father, she had to leave behind everything that was safe and familiar. And now, just as things are calming down and she's beginning to feel settled, I throw a major wrench into the works with the earth-shattering news that thirty-nine is not too old to be dating."

"So she knows about us?" The low timbre of his voice, the way he said 'us,' was deliciously intimate.

"I think she suspects."

"So does Megan. She's thrilled, by the way. She thinks the world of you."

"This has nothing to do with how Beth feels about you, Brash," Maddy was quick to point out. "Please understand that. It's nothing personal."

"Feels pretty personal," he admitted lowly.

"She's young, Brash. Confused." Madison felt compelled to defend her daughter. "She adored Gray. Naturally, she sees me dating again as an affront to her father's memory. She's at the age where she has such romantic, idealistic notions. One forever-love and all of that. She still wants to believe in fairy tales, even though she knows, deep in her heart, that they don't exist."

Brash nuzzled his face against her hair. "I beg to differ."

She closed her eyes as warm sensations flooded her body. "You and I are both too old for fairy tales, Brash," she whispered.

"So are you saying I'm not your knight in shining armor?" His breath was warm against her ear, teasing her senses as surely as his words teased her mind.

"Maybe I'm saying... I'm not a damsel in distress." It was difficult to keep her train of thought when he blew so softly in her ear. Shivers of desire danced along her skin.

"The river, Maddy," he croaked hoarsely. "We need to go back to the river."

His lips nibbled an earlobe as he made his argument.

"No interruptions."

Began a slow path along her jawline.

"No case."

Hovered at the corner of hers.

"No kids."

Traced the perimeter of her mouth with the tip of his tongue.

"Just you."

Licked the seam of her lips.

"And me."

Pressed against hers.

"Beneath the stars."

Dipped inside.

"On a blanket."

And turned her world upside down.

Brash deCordova was many things. Star high school quarterback-turned-pro. College football coach. Sponsor of a football summer camp for disadvantaged youth. Officer of the law. Devoted father. Active member of the community and church.

Still reeling from his kisses, Madison added a few more titles to his impressive resume. World-class kisser. Slayer of dragons and demons. Knight-in-shining-armor extraordinaire.

Caught up in the magic of his kiss and the fairy tales spinning in her own head — worse, weaving their way throughout her heart — Madison imagined what it could be like, spending an evening in his arms, under the stars. His deeply rumbled reference to the blanket lured her with its seductive promise. Completely lost,

Madison whimpered deep in her throat.

All too soon, however, reality reared its ugly head. Maddy ignored it as long as she could, but she finally wedged a hand between them, gently pushing on his chest. "Brash, we- we can't."

He had known the protest was coming. He loosened his hold only marginally, tilting his forehead against hers. "I know." As if to remind himself of the reasons, he named them off in a resigned voice. "It's too soon. There's still too much going on. I need to keep my focus on the case. On keeping you and your family safe."

"And-And Bethani..." That was perhaps the biggest obstacle of all.

Their sighs in sync, Maddy moved out of his arms. After the slightest of hesitations, he draped his arm around her shoulders, the gesture one of comfort more than passion. "She'll come around, sweetheart."

"But what if she doesn't?" Maddy worried, her eyes revealing her deep inner fear. "Brash, we couldn't... I can't be with you, if it makes my daughter miserable."

"I know. We'll just have to give her time to adjust." He sounded more patient than he felt.

"I know you said you'd wait for me to get my life together. But what if... what if it takes longer than you thought? What if Bethani never comes around?"

He gave her an indulgent smile. "Honey, she's a teenager. Her 'never' won't last nearly as long as ours."

"I can't expect you to wait on me forever." The misery in her heart leaked out in her voice. "I see the way other women look at you, Brash. You could have your pick of them, including Amanda Hooper. They all throw themselves at you, practically begging you to have sex with them. How can I expect you to ignore them and wait for me, when I have no idea how long it will take before we can be together?"

Brash looked mildly amused at her sorry little rant.

"I imagine I'll get through it the same way I manage to walk past the bank every day."

His calm reply was so outrageous that she pulled away to stare at him. "What?" she asked, blinking in confusion. "What does the bank have to do with anything?"

"Yes, Maddy, I like sex. I like money, too. And the bank has plenty of it, just sitting there, begging me to come in and take it, by way of loan or theft. Right or wrong, either way can tempt a man. Yet every day, I manage to control myself. Somehow, I walk right past the temptation." His tone turned serious. "It doesn't matter what other women are offering, Maddy. I don't want them. I want you."

"But—"

He broke in, ignoring her protest. "Darlin', since the day I stepped foot on Ronnie Gleason's chicken farm and saw you there, covered in chicken poop and mud and so much worse, there has been only one woman in my whole world. You."

He was writing poetry again. Tears welled in her eyes. "Brash—"

"I'm crazy about you, Maddy. More than crazy. I—"

"No. Don't say it." She clamped her hand over his mouth, squelching the beautiful emotion she saw in his eyes, silencing the magical words she longed to hear. "You can't say it. Neither of us can. Not until..."

Brash drug his eyes away from hers, staring beyond her with a troubled expression on his face. When he spoke, his voice was resigned. "Bethani."

The teen stepped out onto the porch, allowing her eyes to adjust to the darkness. It was past ten. Surely Mr. D had gone home by now. Surely, they weren't out here on the porch, making a spectacle of themselves.

But she would check, just to make sure...

"Mom?" she asked tentatively. "Are you out here?"

Swallowing a gasp of dismay, Madison quickly ran her palms over her face. Teardrops moistened her fingertips. "Yes, honey, I'm here." Her bright voice cleverly hid the pain that invaded her heart.

"Why are you out here in the dark? Did he finally go home?"

Brash made a face that only Maddy could see.

"No, honey, he's still here. We were out here talking."

"Oh."

After a weary sigh, Brash brushed a soft kiss on Madison's lips and stood from the swing. "I was just about to leave, Beth," he said, stepping into the light. "Good thing you came out and reminded me of the time. I'm going in early in the morning, so I can get off in time to watch Megan's track meet. You'll be there, won't you?"

"Uhm, sure." She was taken back by his friendly attitude. She had been downright rude earlier, refusing to eat dinner with him there. So why was he being so nice? Guilt nibbled at her conscience.

"Why don't you take my place there on the swing and sit with your mom for a while? But not too long," he cautioned with a smile. "You ladies need to get to bed before long."

"Okay."

"Maddy, again, that was a delicious meal. Sorry you weren't feeling up to eating tonight, Beth. Hope you're better by tomorrow night, though. I promised Meg I'd take everyone out for pizza, and of course you're invited."

"Oh, well... sure. I mean, thank you."

Brash gave her a wink. "Have a good night, ladies. I'll talk to you both tomorrow."

Drying away the last of her tears, Madison patted the seat beside her. "Come sit by me, sweetie," she encouraged her daughter.

Bethani took the seat uncertainly, perching on the edge of the swing. Maddy did not say anything, waiting for the teen to speak first.

Her tone was defensive when she finally blurted out, "It's not Mr. D, per se. But it's too soon, Mom."

"It's been six months, sweetheart."

"I know. Entirely too soon. And Grandmother Annette agrees with me."

Madison's blood chilled. "When-When did you speak with your grandmother?"

"I called her tonight. I was upset, and I knew she would understand. She agrees that for you to see anyone so soon would be a disgrace to Daddy's memory. She says propriety dictates that you wait at least a full year before resuming a social life. I'm not sure about propriety, but I know what's decent and what's not."

"Beth—"

The teen charged on, unaware of her mother's breaking heart. "She's invited Blake and me to come for a visit, and I think we should go."

23

A restless night did nothing to improve Madison's spirits. Afraid she would disturb Bethani with her tossing and turning, she transferred to the couch shortly after midnight, but sleep was elusive. Long before six o'clock, she was dressed and ready to start the day.

She called Derron early, knowing she would wake him. "Are you ready for our outing?"

"Huh? What outing? Who is this?" the man replied groggily into the phone.

"This is the person who signs your paychecks," she retorted. Never mind that those checks came few and far between. "We're going back to the cave today, remember?"

"It's still the crack of dawn! Call back at a decent hour."

"It is a decent hour. It happens to be 6:03. I'll be there to pick you up in twenty minutes."

"You'll have to give me at least thirty," the younger man grumbled. "And you'd better bring breakfast."

She compromised. "We'll stop by *New Beginnings* and grab something to go."

"Remind me again. Why are we going back?" he whined.

"Because we missed something the first two times. Obviously, whatever it is, someone is going to drastic lengths to keep it hidden. Traps, cameras, restraining orders, motion detectors. It's insane. And I'm determined to get to the bottom of it, once and for all."

"What if it really is a cougar den?"

"Doesn't matter. Today I'm angry enough I might just tackle it with my bare hands!"

Derron was still mumbling when she hung up the phone, something about labor laws and employee abuse. She switched on the television in the kitchen, hoping to catch up on world events over another cup of coffee. Anything to divert her attention from her own troubles.

Just as she took a sip of the dark brew, her own image flashed across the screen. Hot coffee spewed from her mouth, spraying over the floor.

It was another fluff piece, something about the popularity of the television show and rumors of a spin-off. There was even something about a made-for-television movie in the works. It was the first Madison had heard of the ridiculous rumor, but the television station already had a survey started, asking viewers who they thought should be cast in the lead role. So far, the results were overwhelmingly in favor of Madison playing herself.

"Nonsense. Nothing but nonsense," she complained, turning the television back off. Was there no peace?

The house phone rang and she grabbed it on the second ring, not bothering to check caller ID. It was probably Derron, calling back to beg off for the day.

"Back off," a voice snarled on the other end of the line.

"Wh—What ?"

"Back off."

Madison gripped the receiver tighter. "Who is this?" she demanded.

"Consider this a friendly warning." The voice was anything but friendly as it ground out another dark order. "Back the hell off."

"I asked, who is this?" Madison snapped. "At least be man enough to identify yourself."

"Next time, the warning won't be so friendly."

The line went dead, buzzing in her ear long after the other person hung up. She finally slammed the receiver back into its cradle, muttering in frustration. "Problem is, I have no idea what I'm backing off from!"

She grabbed her equipment for the day and stalked out the door, as much angry as she was afraid. Enough was enough. Someone was messing with her, and she had reached her limit on tolerance.

"There has to be a better way to get there from here," Derron complained less than an hour later. They had crossed through the fence onto Adams' property, skirting the deep thicket of woods as they circled their way around to the bluff.

"When you think of one, let me know," Madison replied dryly.

"Do you have a back-up plan, just in case that wasn't a recording we heard? Besides your bare hands, that is?"

"You have your gun with you, right?"

"Yes."

"That's the back-up plan. But I'm certain that was the same recording. Just listen." She pressed the app button on her phone, filling the morning air with ominous sounds of a low, deep growl.

"Turn that thing off!" Derron warned. "You might call up a real animal, coming to investigate."

Madison pressed a button to stop play, but nothing happened. "I can't stop it," she fretted, jabbing more buttons. "Oh, here we go." New sounds roared from her phone. "Oops, not that one." Next, she unleashed dozens of barking Dobermans. "Not that one, either."

"Mute your phone, mute your phone!" Derron advised.

"I'm trying," she said, frantically trying to quiet the menacing noises she created. Halfway through a lonesome coyote's call, she found the mute button.

They walked along in silence for a few moments, but both kept looking over their shoulders. "You don't think we called anything up, do you?" Derron worried.

"I doubt it." She sounded more optimistic than she felt. "When I was little and we were out coyote hunting, my Grandpa Joe always used a wounded rabbit's cry."

"Good, no coyotes." They walked several more yards before he ventured with, "But what about cougars?"

"I don't know. We never tried to find any of those."

"Just for the record, we are not trying to find them today, either!"

"We'll know soon enough. There's Pine Bluff."

They paused to study the mini mountain. Like before, they would have to edge their way around the deep gully to reach the base of the formation.

"Let's go this way," Madison suggested.

"Lead the way."

She flashed him an evil look before proceeding along the treacherous path.

"What? I've got your back," he claimed gallantly, falling in single-file behind her.

"Fine, but you're going in the cave first."

"How did we come to that non-unanimous decision?"

"You're the one properly dressed for spelunking,"

she smirked, eying his attire over her shoulder. He wore hiking boots and a bright red jumpsuit, complete with a matching headlamp and several gadgets hanging from the tool belt cinched tight around his waist.

"Oh, all right," Derron grumbled. "Good thing I brought my knee pads."

They fell silent after that, concentrating on following the narrow cow trail around the mouth of the gully. Madison ignored the possibility that a pack of angry, hungry wildcats forged the path.

Like before, Derron gave her a hand and helped her over the uneven slabs of limestone that swelled beneath their feet. Before they reached the entrance of the cave, they paused to study their surroundings. Madison waved her hand experimentally, trying to engage the motion sensor that triggered the recording.

Nothing.

Derron took a tentative step forward and stuck his hand forward, waving it first high, then low. Still nothing.

"I thought this is where we were before," Madison said, beginning to get nervous. She had been so certain it was a recording...

"It is the same spot," Derron hissed. "I remember this exact rock. I helped you onto it, remember?"

"Yes." She stepped forward nervously, easing her way onto the rock and one step closer to the animal den.

The low rumble filled the still morning air. Even though it was a familiar sound by now, it caused them both to start.

Hand against his pounding heart, Derron nodded to her feet. "So the rock is the trigger."

"It appears that way."

"Sounds just like the app." He nibbled his lip worriedly. "Don't you think?"

"Definitely," she decided. But she was nervous, just the same.

"Step off, wait for it to stop, and do it again."

"Good idea."

They both breathed easier when she stepped onto the slab a second time and triggered sounds identical to those before.

"So definitely a recording, right?" A trace of doubt lingered in Derron's voice.

"Right," she confirmed.

"So what now?"

They looked toward the mouth of the cave's opening. The entrance was low, wedged into a crevice where two large boulders came together.

"And we're absolutely doing this, right?"

"Yes, Derron, we're doing this. And you're going first, because you're smaller."

"And because I'm wearing the proper clothes," he reminded her, tugging on his jumpsuit.

"Oh for heaven's sake, go already!"

The younger man crouched low and proceeded forward, curling himself into an even smaller profile. He paused only to activate his headlamp before thrusting his leg into the cavern. Before she lost sight of him, Madison scrambled to follow.

The entrance funneled into a narrow channel that sloped downward. Madison bit back hints of claustrophobia. Before she could rethink their mission, the channel broadened out and she was able to stand at her full height.

They were in the interior of the cave now, surrounded entirely by rock.

"What is that?" she hissed, pointing her own headlamp to a coiled object on the floor. "Is that a snake?"

"No. It looks like a cable of some sort."

By silence agreement, they talked in hushed tones, perhaps because they were on a clandestine mission and were afraid of being caught, or perhaps for fear of triggering a landslide.

She followed the cable's trail with her eyes. "Look, it strings out along that wall."

"Someone has been in here recently," Derron commented, seeing a few scattered bottles and pieces of trash.

She spotted matches and empty cans. "Kids?"

"Maybe."

She followed closely behind Derron as they proceeded forward. The floor was uneven in places, demanding they pay close attention to where they stepped. The walls narrowed again, and water trickled down along an expanse of jagged rock, making the path particularly treacherous.

"Lordy, what is that smell?" Madison put her hand to her nose. "It smells like rotten eggs."

"Uh, that's not good."

"I know. It stinks."

Derron came to a sudden stop in front of her. "Maybe we should go back."

She thought he was concerned about her delicate senses. "No, I'll be fine. I've worked in a chicken house and changed more dirty diapers than I care to remember. I'll be okay."

"That's not it," Derron hedged. "I know that smell."

She nudged him forward, whispering the entire time. "It smells like someone needs to change the cat litter. Is that sewer gas, you think? It smelled a little like this in the tunnel at the Big House, but not nearly as bad." She choked back a gag. "This is horrible. Almost like ammonia mixed with fertilizer and rotten eggs." She looked down at her feet. "You don't think we stepped in it, do you?"

"I doubt it," Derron said dryly. He paused again to look back at her. "You really don't know, do you?"

"Know what?"

"That's what a meth lab smells like."

When Brash visited the tunnel at the Big House early that morning, his trained eye noted details Nick and Madison had missed.

He was quick to spot the ancient torches set into the earthen walls at staggered intervals, a preferred source of light before flashlights.

He noticed the odd smell that lingered in the enclosed space, more offensive than mold and mildew.

Brash was particularly focused on the materials used to patch and reinforce specific areas of the tunnel. Sheets of corrugated tin spotted the walls and ceiling, but not all were the same age. Some were old and rusted, while others looked almost new. The newer pieces, he noted, were attached with the type of bolts and screws most often secured by a power drill. It did not take long for Brash to determine that the tunnel had seen recent use.

But he found the most telling piece of evidence at the mouth of the opening. Squatting to examine the dirt floor beneath his feet, ignoring the pop in his knee from an old football injury, Brash saw where the door scraped against the earth as it slid back and forth. Fresh marks told the story well enough.

Someone was still using the tunnel.

"A meth lab?" She squeaked the words, her steps faltering right along with her bravery.

"Yeah. Which would explain some of those containers I saw back there. Salt, cans of brake cleaner.

That crushed bottle was probably rubbing alcohol."

"How do you know these things?" she hissed.

"How do you not?" he countered.

He was right, of course. She was the mother of teenage twins. A would-be sleuth-in-the-making. She should know the signs of danger. And there was little else more dangerous than a methamphetamine lab.

"So what do we do?" she asked nervously.

"Get the hell out of here." He was already turning to retrace his steps, but Madison tugged on his arm.

"Wait. I think we should check it out."

"Are you insane?"

"If we could actually get a peek at it, we would know for certain and we could tell Brash."

"I don't know, dollface. I think we should go..."

"Come on, just a little further. Just to be sure."

"I have a bad feeling about this."

"I have a worse feeling about that meth, actually getting into the hands of people we know and love." She looked at him with her large hazel eyes, her worry obvious, even in the dim lighting. "I have kids, Derron," she whispered. "I can't just ignore this."

"We don't have to. We can go back up and call your boyfriend. He can be here in thirty minutes to shut it down."

"You go back, then. I'm going further in," she said stubbornly.

"Maddy!" he hissed to her back. "Madison, get back here!"

She kept walking, picking her way through the dark cavernous area. After a brief hesitation, Derron hurried to catch up with her. "Slow down," he hissed. "Stop. I think I hear something."

They waited for what seemed like hours. He finally shrugged and stepped forward to lead the way.

"That was probably my racing heart, echoing off the

walls," she whispered nervously.

"Then why are we doing this?"

"I just have to." It was the only explanation she could offer.

A few more feet and the tunnel curved. A faint light crept into the cavity where they stood, bathing the rocky walls with faint color. If she had not been so frightened, Madison might have noticed the beauty of the stalactites dripping overhead, sparkling with the slightest of illumination.

Using hand motions, Derron instructed her to turn off her headlamp. Darkness engulfed them. A sense of panic threatened to overtake her, but Derron's hand was strong and sure upon hers, offering her comfort.

As their eyes adjusted to the darkness, they saw the inky impressions of shadow and light, finger-painting the wall to their left. As quietly as possible, they inched forward, edging their way around the natural curve of the cave's granite wall.

A large room opened up before them, awash in bright electrical light. Utility lights swung from the ceiling, strung from thick cable like the one they saw earlier. The haze hanging in the air was thick and putrid, almost tangible. Determined not to gag, Madison pulled her shirt up over her mouth and breathed through the added layer of protection, for all the good it did her. The horrible smell was so intense she could taste it.

They hung back for a long moment, searching for movement within the cluttered space. With a sick feeling knotting the pit of her stomach, Madison surveyed the sorry scene before her. Two long tables were set up in the far side of the cavern room, littered with ordinary household items. She identified a dozen everyday cleaning products. Another dozen easily found in garages all across America. Bottles, jars, and containers of every shape and size were stuffed in among crockpots, coffee pots and portable butane cylinders. If not for the hazy stench that filled the air and the evil vibes radiating from the entire mess, it could have been someone's terribly messy house.

All of this is so easy to obtain, she thought with a sick realization. *There's nothing special about any of it. Anyone could do this, even kids.*

A sob escaped her at the very thought. Derron shot her a sharp look, reminding her of the need to remain silent. Just because they could not see anyone, did not mean they were not there.

Having seen too much to ever forget, Madison backed slowly away. Her feet were as leaden as her heart as she took a step in retreat.

It's not only that you can't un-hear things, she thought sadly. *You can't un-see them, either.*

Without warning, Derron jerked her arm and twisted her around.

She glared back at him, only to discover it was not Derron.

24

"Is Mom gone already?" Bethani emerged from her bedroom with a worried expression upon her face.

Blake looked up from the mixing bowl that doubled as his cereal bowl. "Yeah, she left early."

"Oh."

Granny Bert picked up on the teen's unease. "What's wrong, child?"

Bethani twisted a lock of blond hair around her finger. "I wanted to apologize to her about last night."

"Yeah, what was up with that?" her brother challenged. "I thought you liked Mr. D."

"I do. And I already told her I was sorry about that." *Hadn't she?* Bethani played the conversation back in her head, trying to remember if she had actually said the words.

"What else are you apologizing about?"

"I was a little harsh on her last night."

Blake gave her a wary look. "What did you do?"

"I laid the guilt on pretty thick," his twin admitted. "When I was talking to Grandmother Annette, it all made perfect sense. She helped me see things so clearly. But then I started talking to Mom. And I saw the hurt in her eyes..." Bethani slid into the chair, slumping onto the table with dejected gloom. "I think she really likes Mr. D. And it's wrong, Blake. It's just flat-out wrong. It's too soon since Daddy... died." She had trouble getting the word out.

"That's just it, Beth," her brother pointed out. "He died. Whether we like it or not, it's not like he's coming back."

"How can you be so cold?"

"I'm not being cold, Beth. Dad's gone, but Mom still has a life ahead of her. She deserves to be happy."

"Not with another man, she doesn't!"

"You're being childish," her brother accused.

"And you're being blind! Don't you remember how she treated him before he died? They slept in separate rooms, Blake. Don't you remember all the fussing and fighting? The way she gave Daddy the cold-shoulder?"

"I remember how he never came home until late at night. I remember how he missed all my games, and half your recitals. It was Mom who did everything with us."

Bethani leapt from her chair. "I can't believe you're dissing his memory like this!"

"I'm not dissing anybody."

"You are. You're talking bad about Daddy, and I won't stand for it! Do you hear me, Blake? I won't let you dishonor his memory like this!" She stomped from the room, leaving a confused brother to stare at her retreating back.

"What was all that about?" he muttered.

Granny Bert came to place a hand on his shoulder. Even though he pretended to be unconcerned, his body trembled with emotion. "She's just confused, Blake. She's having trouble processing her grief, and she's taking it out on the person she's closest to. Your mom."

"Yeah, well, I'm grieving too, but you don't see me blaming Mom for everything. And unlike Bethani, I remember how things were between them the last couple of years." His mouth turned down in a surly pout. "They tried to hide it, but their marriage was falling apart."

"And that's probably what makes this even harder for your sister. Girls see things differently than boys, Blake. They see with their heart, not just their eyes."

He simply snorted. As he turned his bowl up and gulped the remaining milk, his eyes fell on the gadget across the table. "What's that?"

Granny Bert shrugged. "Something your mom left."

Blake stretched out to pull the small device toward him. He fiddled with the buttons until it blinked to life. A series of lights flashed across the top, repeating the sequence every several seconds.

"What is this?" he wondered, turning it over to read the logo.

"Beats me. What are all the flashing lights about?"

With a worried look upon his face, Blake waved the gadget in the air. When he held the device high in the air, the dancing lights began to fade. Each time he lowered it, however, they flashed with persistence.

"Has that thing gone bonkers?" Granny Bert asked in amusement. "What is it, anyway? Some sort of radio?"

"No, but it does detect radio waves." He mouthed the rest of his answer. "It's a bug detector."

"Then why is it flashing like that?" his great-grandmother hissed.

Blake leaned over and peered beneath the table. Spotting the hidden mic, he sat back up, his eyes troubled. He pointed in silence, indicating the planted bug.

Still in a whisper, Granny Bert said, "But they were supposed to remove all the cameras and mics!"

She thought about the many unguarded topics they had discussed at this very table — many of them about the case and entries from the journals, some of them pure speculation and gossip, some of a more personal nature. If someone were up to no good and wanted to eavesdrop on Madison, they had gotten an earful. Even worse, if they meant her harm, they were privy to all her activities and schedules.

Unease settled into her bones, making her feel every bit of her eighty years. "Well, crap," Granny Bert groaned. "This can't be good."

Madison could not see the face of the man gripping her arm, but he was too tall to be her friend. Her wild gaze swung through the shadows, searching for Derron.

He had been right behind her. Where was he?

And who was this man?

Relief flashed through her as she spotted Derron in the semi-darkness, but the feeling died as quickly as it flared. A second man had him shoved against the cavern wall, his arm pressed firmly into Derron's throat. Even in the shadows, she could see her friend's face was turning a dangerous shade of scarlet.

Her immediate concern was for Derron. "Turn him loose! You're choking him!"

"Don't worry about pretty boy," snarled the man holding her. "You have bigger worries."

Madison struggled to free herself, but the man held her in a vice grip. "Be still!" her captor barked. "You're like a damned octopus," he complained, trying to contain her flailing arms and legs.

"Let my friend go!" Madison insisted, punctuating her demand with a jab of her bony elbow.

"Damn it, be still! And go easy on the dandy," he added to his friend.

The second man pulled his arm from Derron's

throat. He sagged against the rock wall, gasping for breath, but at least he was breathing.

Only then did Madison stop struggling. She transferred her gaze to the man bruising her arm with his harsh grip. He looked vaguely familiar, but with the light to his back, his face was cast in shadows. She judged him at six feet, tall and physically fit. Her eyes snagged on his silhouette, and the hair that curled just above his shirt collar.

The intruder from the house!

Adrenalin pumped through her veins.

"Who are you?" Madison demanded.

"I tried to warn you," he growled. "You were too stupid to listen. Too stupid to get the clues I left."

He shoved her roughly forward, keeping behind her as he pushed her into the large room. She coughed from the fetid air that invaded her lungs and stung her eyes. Judging from the shuffled sounds behind her, Derron was half-pushed, half-dragged into the space with her.

Using a booted foot, the man holding her kicked a plastic chair forward and plopped Madison roughly down upon it. With quick movements, he jerked a piece of excess cable and used it to tie her arms securely behind her back.

"Ouch! That hurts!" she protested.

"I'm so sorry, Your Highness. I know how delicate a princess like you can be." He cinched the cable even tighter. "All better now?" he asked with false concern.

"Much," she muttered. She would not give him the satisfaction of complaining again.

"Tie the other one up, too," the man told his companion.

"I need some rope."

"Pull the chair over here. Use the cable."

"But that's the electrical cable."

"Exactly." There was evil humor in his voice. "If they jerk too much, they'll pull down the lights and be left in the dark. Better yet, they might electrocute themselves."

His companion chuckled. Madison still could not see either man's face, but she guessed that the second man was the older of the two.

The men backed the two chairs together, using the same cable to bind both hostages' arms behind them. Each tug and twist sent the overhead lights dancing.

"Why are you doing this? What do you want?" Madison demanded.

"If you haven't figured it out by now, you're even stupider than I thought." Another sharp tug on the cable, another knot.

Madison could not help but sneer. "Obviously, you wanted to keep us from finding this cave and your pathetic little operation."

"This *pathetic* little operation nets me a nice profit every month," the man hissed near her ear. He was so close she could feel his hot breath blow across her cheek. When she tried turning her head, he twisted her neck painfully in the opposite direction. His voice dropped to an ominous hiss. "Which makes disposing of you merely a bonus."

He doubled his elbow and bopped her forcefully on the back of her head. Madison's neck popped forward. She bit down on her tongue as her chin banged against her breastbone. While she spat out a mouthful of blood and struggled to remain conscious from the staggering blow, the two men laughed and shuffled from the room.

Time sputtered down to a crawl. Madison's head was like a lead weight, sitting upon her shoulders amid a steady thrum of pain. A thousand needles pricked her arms as circulation ceased. Her back ached from the strained position. Her tongue was swollen and bleeding. She was too weary to chronicle the many other aches and pains that wracked her body. A sense of overwhelming fatigue seeped into her bones.

It was several minutes before she gathered enough strength to speak.

"D-Dewwon? You okay?" she asked around her thick tongue.

"I think so." His voice sounded hoarse. "You?"

The slightest movement set off fireworks within her skull. She grunted a sound intended as affirmation.

"Maddy?" Derron asked in concern. He twisted his neck around, desperate to see his friend.

"Okay," she said weakly.

"Who are these guys?"

"Don't know."

"We have to get out of here, Maddy, before they come back." When he tugged his hands, the overhead lights swung with a blinding strobe effect.

"Too ti'ed," she protested. How could she ever stand, with a head the size of a Mac truck upon her shoulders?

"Maddy, you have to stay awake. You can't go to sleep now."

"So sleepy." Her head lolled forward, but the movement triggered a round of roman candles in her brain. Lights flashed before her eyes as she jerked her head upright once more.

"Maddy, stay with me, Maddy," Derron said firmly. "All I can see is the wall. You're facing the room. Tell me what you see, Maddy."

She tried to focus on the table just beyond her reach. It refused to stay in place, floating haphazardly before her eyes. "Thwee tables. No, two. ... One? No, two," she decided, her eyes crossing with the effort to focus. She slowly named off items that she could see. With each listing, her mind seemed to clear. By the time she finished, she was almost capable of thinking straight. Her speech was improving, as well.

"Are you more rested now?" Derron asked.

"I think."

"Can you reach my hands? There, that's it. See if you can tug on my ropes. My hands are small. If you can loosen the cable, maybe I can work one of them free."

Her arms were half-asleep and her fingers clumsy. As Madison tried to coax a bit of give from the tight bindings, she thought about the men who had left them here. There was something so familiar about the first man, something other than their brief encounter during the break-in. She had the impression that she knew him somehow, yet even before he rendered her semi-senseless, she could not quite place him.

"I hear them coming back," Derron whispered, stilling his hands.

The men's voices echoed along the stone walls as they approached from the opposite side of the cavern.

"Looks like they're still here."

"Not smart enough to get free."

A third man was with them. His voice was not nearly as humored. "What do you plan to do with them?"

"I thought we could decide together."

"I say we shoot them and leave them lay," the second man said. He was the older one, the one who had tied Derron up.

"Can't do that, Pops. We need the workspace. We have to start on that big shipment for Waco."

As the men stepped into the cavern room, the large space seemed to shrink. Refusing to cowl to them, Madison sat up straighter in her chair.

"Aw, look at that. The princess looks as grand as ever, even all tied and trussed up like a turkey at Thanksgiving."

Madison eyed the man speaking, the intruder from the house. It was the first good look she had of him.

Seeing her confusion, the man's laughter had a bitter note. "Still trying to figure out who I am?"

"Yes," she admitted.

"You see me almost every day. Walk right past me, your Cessna nose stuck high up in the air."

Her forehead knitted into a frown. "Where do I see you?"

He snorted in disgust. "Typical." Without warning, his hand shot out to slap her across the cheek. "All you rich broads are the same. Every one of you!"

Rich? He has me confused with someone else! Had her cheek not been stinging so, she might have even laughed. But the movement had triggered the fireworks again, and those were no laughing matter.

"Cut it out, Paul!" the third man hissed. "We don't have time for this."

Paul. Madison's mind raced to recall having heard his name before. Hadn't Amanda mentioned him a few times? She thought perhaps he was one of the cameramen at the Big House, but she couldn't be certain.

"Why did you steal the journal?" she asked.

"To see what the old woman wrote about our family. To see if she knew about the tunnel."

"T-Tunnel? What tunnel?"

His short burst of laughter was brittle. "Don't bother playing dumb. I know you found the tunnel. In fact, I know just about everything you do."

"How—"

"That was a pretty smart little trick your granny played at the restaurant the other night. I'll have to remember that and try it myself."

Her surprise, this time, was genuine. "You were there?"

"No, but your son told the story so well," he sneered dryly.

Confusion showed in her eyes. "But how…"

"You really haven't figured it out yet, have you? You're nothing but a stupid old cow." He leaned close to her face and said in a loud, harsh voice, "I bugged your house, princess. With your permission, I might add."

"You-You work for Amanda." It was slowly making sense to her, penetrating through the throbbing pain in her head. She had a vague recollection of him being at Granny Bert's, helping install cameras for the show. She looked at him more closely. She was fairly certain he had come to un-install the cameras, as well. "But you took the cameras out."

He lifted his shoulder in a noncommittal shrug. "Could be I overlooked a mic or two."

"You've been bugging the house?" Madison asked in outrage. "Listening to everything we say?"

"Every boring word. Your daughter does like to go on, doesn't she? I know all the senseless gossip from The Sisters High, the words to every last cheer, and how her grades are slipping because she's worried about your new romance with the chief of police. She hasn't told you that she failed her last math test, by the way."

Before she could dwell on that piece of information, Paul the cameraman gave her a smug smile. "Of course, once in a while I hear something useful. Like the fact that the journals did exist. Hearing you hash out all your theories helped me to plan my next move. And of course it was quite handy, knowing you were coming out here again today."

"So it really was an inside job," Madison murmured. "You've been able to hear everything we say and do, because you had access to the cameras and the mics.

And you could get around the alarms because you work at the house.”

“I not only work there and have access, I’m the one who set it all up to begin with,” he told her smugly. “Even the alarms.”

“This-This was all Amanda’s doings?”

He snorted with disdain. “Look around you. She’s another one of you rich broads. Does this look like her style?” With an exasperated shake of his head, he explained what she was obviously too stupid to comprehend. “When I heard about the television show being filmed there, I made certain I was hired as a technician. A simple hack here and there, a few fake letters of reference, an altered document or two, and the head office suddenly sent a local expert in at the last minute.”

“How convenient,” Madison said drolly.

“Ain’t it, though?” His grin was diabolical. “As lead camera technician, I control where the cameras go. I made certain they stayed away from the cellar, until that nosy worker happened to discover the hidden staircase, and, hence, the secret room and its skeleton.”

A vague memory surfaced. “That was you that day, wasn’t it? You ran in with a second camera, trying to get in front of us.”

“I wasn’t sure where he was leading you. What he had discovered.”

“You thought he had found the tunnel,” Madison realized.

“But instead, it was just a skeleton.”

The older man beside him clearly blanched. He could not stop the dance of revulsion that shimmied through his shoulders. “All those years, we were down there with a dead body, and never even knew it,” he whined.

So no one had known about the skeleton. In her

estimation, this confirmed that the remains definitely belonged to Clarence. But so much else was still left unexplained.

"What-What were you doing down there?" she asked.

"What do you think?" Paul smirked.

Madison answered with a disdainful look and a question of her own. "Did Miss Juliet ever know?"

The second man answered. "That old broad had no idea what went on right beneath her own house." He spat out a stream of tobacco juice, not bothering to turn his head. It hit Derron, leaving a dark stain to trickle down the leg of his red jumpsuit.

With a high-pitched squeal, Derron jumped, causing the lights to bob merrily up and down. The other three men laughed and made crude remarks at his expense. The swaying lights gave Madison the perfect cover to jerk at her hands again, trying to wrest them free. She thought she felt one of the cables give, yet when she tugged, she found her hands were still firmly bound.

"Served her right," Pops continued. "Her and her highfalutin ways. It all started with my grand pappy. He cooked up corn liquor down there, right beneath her fancy dining room. Served it at some of her parties, too, though she never knew where it came from. All those years, and she never had a clue. Always acted so high and mighty, like she was better than our family. So it seemed only fair to replace the rinky-dink still with an even bigger operation. What's that they call it, Paul? Poetic justice?"

The third man was clearly losing his patience. During the entire confrontation, he kept to the shadows, his face never quite visible. His voice was sharp when he spoke. "Who the hell cares what they call it, as long as we call it a profit? You two have been yakking long enough. We need to start the batch for Waco. Do something with them and dispose of the bodies. Call me when it's done." He issued the brusque order before he turned on his heel and stomped away.

An empty silence stretched in his wake. Madison dared a glance at Paul. Given the thoughtful expression on his face, she guessed he was debating how best to kill them.

Stall! The urgent thought spurred Madison to speak up.

"I-I don't understand. Your grandfather had an illegal still in the basement of the Big House?"

Paul wasn't fooled. "You understand just fine. Your boyfriend figured it out last night. How they used the tunnel to bring in the corn and then cart out the liquor. My old granny didn't need a fire to do laundry; she needed a fire to make whiskey."

Maybe it was the headache, but Madison was having trouble keeping up. "Wait. I thought it was his grandfather." She cut her eyes to indicate the older man, knowing any movement would create starbursts in her head again. "But you're saying it was your grandmother?" Her eyes cut back to Paul.

"Technically, it was both his great-grandparents, my great-great."

"You're father and son?" she squeaked.

"Aw, so you're not quite as stupid as I thought," Paul grinned.

"Maybe I am. You'll have to explain it to me."

Actually, she thought she understood all too well. Miss Juliet had fired Ralph Bishop over moonshine. Apparently, the man had found a way to get even with her.

She recalled what else she knew about the family. Miss Juliet had not granted them residency in her namesake town, labeling them as unworthy of citizenship. In addition to firing one Bishop as town gardener, various journal entries had referenced conflicts with the extended family throughout the years.

Madison did not recognize either of the men, but she had admittedly lost touch with much of the community after moving away twenty years ago. Yet even though she did not know them, they obviously knew her.

She had to keep the men talking. The more time she killed — *poor choice of words, Madison!* — the more time she had to think of a solution.

She felt Derron's finger slip alongside hers, sending her some type of message. She half-listened to Paul, half-decoded the tap of Derron's fingers against her skin. One thing she definitely understood: Derron's hands were free.

25

"Do we have to spell it out for you?" Paul asked with a weary sigh.

"It looks like you might." Madison batted her eyes a few times, trying to look as stupid as he accused her of being. Would leaving her mouth hanging open help? Anything to get him talking and delaying the inevitable.

"You might say we've had a longtime family business, conducted in part in Juliet Randolph's cellar. Once the old woman finally died and left the house empty, we were able to expand our operation."

Judging from his speech and his overall demeanor, Paul was well educated and, in Madison's estimation, better than this. *This* was a despicable occupation on every level imaginable.

"So you left messages on the mirrors, moved things around, tried to revive the ghost stories to scare us away."

"But you were too stupid to heed the warnings."

"You stole the journal because you thought it had some big secret in it." She looked up at him with guileless eyes. "Whatever could it be?"

She understood Derron's sharp thump of warning. *Don't overplay the dumb act.*

The older man, however, fell for her ruse. "She

could have said something about the tunnel. About finding the still. If you ever made the connection to our family, you'd come looking for us."

This, she had to admit, was the part that truly did not make sense to her. Nor did the covert messages Derron scribbled on her palm with his finger. Confused by both, she did not bother to hide her frown. "I don't understand. Say it again." Let each man think her words were meant for him.

While Pops repeated himself, Derron started over with his own message. This time she concentrated on her friend's crude communication, understanding at least part of what he relayed. His hands were free and he had a gun. She had no idea what the rest of his plan might be, but it gave them a fighting chance.

It was more than these men would offer. Madison had the distinct impression that Paul's father was less educated yet more evil than his son was. He had a mean glint in his eye, whereas Paul's eyes glittered with greed and ambition. Paul, however, had a quick temper. He seemed to harbor some personal vendetta against her, if his 'princess' references were any clue. Despite education and ambition — or perhaps because of it — the son might very well be the more dangerous of the two.

"But the still operated years ago," Madison said. "How would that lead us to a modern-day meth lab?"

"You're here, ain't ya?" Pops snarled.

"Not because of the meth lab. I had no idea it was down here. I'm here because of the property dispute..."

It dawned upon her with sudden realization. She had it all wrong.

Perhaps she *was* as stupid as a cow!

"You're- You're not a Bishop." Her voice was faint.

Pops was clearly insulted. "Hell, no!"

Paul's lips curled downward with wrath. "You don't

even recognize me. Typical of a rich princess like yourself." He kicked the foot of her chair, jarring her with the force. "English Lit, Mrs. Bell's class?"

Stars exploded in her head from the sudden movement. Madison peered through them to the man standing at her side. A vague memory surfaced. "We were in the same class. You were a couple of years below me. We did a skit together for that literary meet."

"And you insisted on rewriting the classic," Paul spat. "You refused to kiss me like the scene dictated."

"It was a free interpretation skit. We were instructed to put our own spin on an old story."

"It was humiliating! The mighty Cessna princess, too good to kiss a lowly Adams. Wasn't it enough that your family had already stolen everything from mine? You already had everything. All I had was my pride. But you took that, too, in typical Cessna fashion."

It slowly sank in. "You're Hank's son and grandson," she whispered. "The ones with control of the land."

"That's right. The land was the one thing you didn't take from us. We're not about to let you take it now."

Pops — named Gerald at birth — joined the conversation, his voice bitter. "Truman Ford was my great grandfather. He was Miss Juliet's right-hand man. Everyone knew she would leave her estate to our family. Truman and Lily were already gone, but Grandma Ruth was next in line. My father after that." His face twisted in rage. "Me, damn it! Do you know how many times I heard my daddy say it would all be mine one day? He worked there for free, fixing up the place he thought would be his own. Then your granny stole it out from under us! Convinced the old woman to change her will. The Big House rightfully belongs to me and mine!" He paced the length of the tables littered with meth-making paraphernalia. "But we showed her.

We got even, didn't we, boy? We started the family business up again, this time bigger and better than ever. We didn't bother with penny-ante liquor. We went for the big-time." Gerald Adams spread his arms out, indicating his sorry enterprise.

While he continued to rant about the injustices wrought upon his family by the likes of her own, Derron tapped out frantic signals against her palm. Madison struggled to decipher them.

The swipe indicated all. All free. All done. All blank. All...

She gave up, concentrating on the next sign. An arrow sign, pointing down. All down?

The sharp rap upon her palm was like a pop. The pop of a gun? The pop of a fist? At any rate, a confrontation.

Derron repeated the message twice more before she understood. The swipe did not mean *all*, it meant movement. When he made his move, she was to get down. He would have his gun ready.

"I understand." She murmured the words intended for Derron. Clearing her throat, she spoke in a voice strong enough for the father-son duo to hear.

"Now I understand what all the traps and hot fences and motion sensors were about. Hank doesn't know, does he? That's why you told him it was more acreage than it was, why you claimed Allen was the one to instigate the boundary dispute. I understand why you played it up, why you so thoughtfully offered to take care of everything for him and Miss Virgie. You couldn't afford to lose the cover of the trees in the thicket. You couldn't expose the entrance to the cave."

"So surely you'll understand when we have to kill you." Paul's quiet tone belied the deadly intent of his words. "You know too much."

Behind her, Madison felt Derron subtly shift his

arm. She needed to distract the men while he covertly worked his arm around and reached for his gun.

She continued quickly, as if Paul had not made his intentions clear. "I still don't understand why you thought we would make a connection between the tunnel and this cave."

Paul shrugged. "If our family business started in one underground space, accessed by a tunnel, logic says it could likely continue in a similar space, different location."

"That logic makes no sense," she declared stubbornly.

"We weren't willing to take that chance."

The overhead lights swung wildly from the cable as Derron pushed from his chair. At the same time, he toppled Madison's chair onto its side, sending her down with a crashing thud and an expanse of cable. Momentarily stunned by the noise and the lights and the overall melee that followed, neither Adams noticed that their hostage was free.

Derron was small but quick. For all his diminutive size, he worked out regularly and was not only well muscled, but strong. Taken by surprise the first time, he had not fared well in their original scuffle, but the tables were turned now. He easily overpowered the elder Adams, twisting Pops' arm behind his back as he shoved the gun against his temple.

"What the—"

Derron jerked the man backwards, several steps away from his son. He glared up at Paul. "Move, and I kill the old man."

"You ain't got it in you, sugar britches," Paul goaded. He took a step forward, daring the smaller man to back his claim.

Madison worked frantically to free her hands. She managed to get one loose, allowing her to scramble from the overturned chair and untie her other hand. Her arms screamed in protest, awakening to the same prickling needles that had accompanied them to sleep. Her head throbbed from the original blow Paul had given her, compounded now by the fall to the floor. But there was finally hope, and it surged her forward, giving her the strength to stand.

She watched with dismay as Derron seemed to falter. His voice took on a slight whimper. "You're right, I can't kill him."

Both men laughed, mocking his lack of masculinity.

Both men misjudged her friend. When he spoke again, his voice had a calm, confident edge. "But I can certainly shoot you." Without a moment's hesitation, he jerked the gun down toward Paul's leg and fired.

The small caliber pistol was not nearly as deafening as the train had been, but between the sharp report of the gun, Paul's roar of pain, and Pops' yelp of disbelief, the combined sounds echoed off the cavern walls.

Madison feared a cave-in. A rockslide.

A nervous breakdown, at the very least.

"You shot me!" Paul wailed, writhing on the ground as blood gushed from his wound. "You freaking shot me!"

"And I'll do it again," Derron threatened. "Move over there to the chair."

"I can't move! I'm bleeding all over the place. You cracked my bone."

"Move, or I shoot again. Maddy, find something to tie him up with." Without taking his eyes off Paul or the gun off his father, Derron backed up and allowed the big man to drag himself toward the chair he had recently vacated.

Madison hurried to the table, shuffling through mounds of trash and assorted supplies. "Will a tie-wrap do?" she asked, holding up the thin white strips of plastic.

"Perfect. Paul, one hand at a time. Slow. No funny business," he warned.

Madison did not trust the man, even with a bleeding wound and a gun pointed at his father's head. She approached with caution. Derron instructed him to put one hand behind his back and grab the chair stiles. Still wary, Madison slipped the tie-wrap around his wrist.

Paul lunged toward her, grabbing for her arm. Madison never stopped to second-guess herself. She whipped out the other item she had found on the table and held it close to his eyes, depressing the button. Aerosol brake cleaner spewed into his face.

Paul dropped her arm and bellowed in agony. He clutched his blistered eyes with both hands, his cries loud and tortured as he alternately begged for mercy and cursed her existence. Madison dropped to her knees and bound his uninjured leg to the chair's leg, securing the hold with the plastic strip's lock mechanism. It might not do much, but it would surely slow him down.

Pops tried to wrench himself free of Derron's hold. The younger man used the butt of his pistol to whack the struggling man across the back of the head. He crumpled like a sagging heap of trash.

"Help me tie him to the other chair," Derron said. "Don't bother sitting it upright. Let him wallow around on the floor."

They made quick work of securing the unconscious man's arms and legs, fastening him at odd angles to the chair. There would be no easy escape for him, and certainly no getting through the narrow neck of the cave's entrance with a chair strapped to him so.

Paul, on the other hand, still presented a challenge. Blood mingled with tears, streaming down from his ravaged eyes. More blood saturated the leg of his blue jeans and pooled around his foot. His voice was hoarse and his skin was pale, but he managed to curse them both to hell. His head sagged onto his chest, but Madison feared it could be a trick. He might still have the strength to overpower her if she ventured close enough.

Derron solved their dilemma. Another quick rap with the butt of his pistol, and Paul followed his father into unconscious slumber. "Quick, tie him up and let's get out of here. We have to go before they wake up and the other one comes back."

Madison had forgotten about the third man. What if he heard the shot and came back? What if he was still here in the cave, in another chamber somewhere nearby? Her hands trembled as she secured Paul's thick wrists with the tie-wraps. Her efforts were clumsy and lacked finesse, but they should detain the man long enough for them to make an escape.

"Done!" she announced in a shaky voice. She refused to look back at the injured man, refused to feel an ounce of remorse for leaving him in such a condition. Once above ground, she would call for an ambulance.

Right after she called Brash.

26

The third man was long gone. Brash arrived within minutes of Maddy's call, but there were no signs of anyone other than the two men inside the cave.

Gerald revived and tried to escape, only to lodge himself and his bulky attachment in the back entrance of the cavern. Paul was still unconscious, more from the loss of blood than from the blow to the head. Both men would live to see prosecution, but Paul's eyes would never be the same.

Within days of the ordeal at the cave, life was back to normal in The Sisters. The new normal, the one with which Madison still struggled to adjust.

News crews camped out on their lawn again, begging for a story. Cameras clicked everywhere she went. Reporters dogged her every step. Fame came calling with a vengeance, proclaiming both her and Derron heroes.

Law enforcement agencies swarmed the area, sweeping through every known cave and tunnel in the county. Two more labs were found and confiscated. Brash and his officers worked overtime to track down every lead and every known associate. Some gave the chief of police/special investigator for River County credit for the busts, impressed with the speed in which he responded and the scope of his investigation. Others blamed him for not catching the criminals sooner. The third man from the cave was never found, and Gerald and Paul refused to give up his name. Brash pushed tirelessly on, knowing there were countless other criminals who managed to slip past the long arm of the law.

Life in the public eye rocked on, tossing back and forth with the tide of public opinion.

Hank and Virgie Adams were devastated by the actions of their son and grandson. They came in person to apologize, explaining they had no idea of the men's duplicity.

"I don't know where we went wrong, Bertha. We tried to be good parents to the boy, but he turned out rotten. He got it in his fool head that you and Miss Juliet had done us wrong, and he was hell-bent on seeking his own justice."

"Seems I recall someone else being a might bitter about it, too," Granny Bert gently admonished him.

"I'll own up to my mistake. I admit I took it hard at first. My momma, God bless her soul, always said I would inherit the house. I told my kids the same. But the truth is, it was Miss Juliet's house to do with as she pleased, and you were a good friend to her, Bertha. Maybe she found out my grand pappy was brewing liquor down there. Maybe she just changed her mind. Don't matter. It was hers, and she left it to you. It took me a while, but I came to realize that, and I didn't hold it against you and Joe. I reckon I forgot to tell my son and grandson as much. And for that, I am purely sorry."

"Don't go beating yourself up over it, Hank. You had no idea Gerald was brewing up something worse than corn liquor down in that cellar."

"I swear to you, Bertha, Madison, I had no idea. I never even knew about the tunnel until my momma was dying. She talked about it while she was out of her head, so I never knew if it was true or something she dreamed up. But I reckon Gerald checked it out. And you know the rest of that sad story."

Madison's heart went out to the grieving couple. Gerald's parents were not responsible for what he and Paul had done. It was bad enough that the elderly couple might never see their son and grandson again, except through prison bars. Two wasted lives, destroyed by bitterness, drugs, and greed.

She gently changed the subject. "So what about Clarence?"

"I tend to agree with you. He and my grand pappy were most likely in cahoots on building the tunnel, each for his own purpose: one to run moonshine, one to moon over Miss Juliet. From all accounts, my momma's half-brother wasn't firing on all four cylinders. He was a brilliant carpenter, but a bit shy on common sense and social skills."

"Hank did that DNA thing, to see if it was his remains you found in the cellar," Virgie added. "Only time will tell on that, but we all agree it's the most likely explanation to his disappearance."

Before they left, Hank turned back to his old friend, his weak eyes bright with emotion. "Bertha, you've been a fine friend through the years. I need to know the fool actions of my son and grandson haven't ruined all that."

"Oh, go on, you old fool," Granny Bert snorted, trying to hide her own emotions. "Takes more than a couple of young upstarts to ruin an eighty-year-old friendship."

He nodded, but his eyes were still moist. "Maddy, let me say again how sorrowful I am about what those two did to you."

"I don't hold you responsible in any way," Madison

assured the grieving parents. "And please, when the house is done, I want you to come for supper one night."

"We'll see," the old man promised.

"If we can see fit to step inside those walls, knowing what our family did there, we'll come," his wife promised. "And we thank you for the gracious offer."

Annette Reynolds, however, was not nearly as gracious. After threatening to sue everyone involved and even many who were not, she demanded that 'the children' return to Dallas immediately. A heated confrontation ensued, Maddy's side of it running along the lines of 'when hell freezes over and they bury my cold, dead body in the ice.' Madison slammed down the receiver before her mother-in-law could reply.

She was still quaking with anger when Blake plunked down beside his mother on the sofa. His blue eyes were troubled. "She can't do it, can she, Mom? She can't make us go back and live with her, can she?"

Madison put her arm around the teenager and hugged him close. "Of course not, sweetheart. She's just making noise."

"I don't want to go back. I like it here."

"Good, because this is where you're staying." Trying to make light of the situation — and angrier still at Annette for upsetting the boy with such nonsense — she tapped him on the nose and smiled. "I love you bunches. You know that, right?"

"Sure, Mom. And we love you bunches, too."

"And no one is going to come between us." Madison added the last as Bethani curled onto the couch on her other side. "It will always be the three of us, a united front against the world!" She encompassed both teenagers with her outstretched arms. She glanced at the clock. "Nick and Amanda are due here any minute. They want to re-install the cameras here at the house, but I'm standing strong. We are not going through that again."

"I thought you had a contract," Blake reminded her.

Madison tried to hide the worry in her eyes. "I do. But I may have to break it, because I'm not putting you two at risk again. They can do what they want at the Big House, but I draw the line here. No more cameras."

With the house quiet for the night and everyone else in bed, Madison curled up on the front porch swing and called Brash.

"How did your meeting go?" he asked, his warm baritone wrapping around her like a favorite quilt.

"Better than I anticipated. Amanda balked and tried to threaten me, but I stood firm. I took a page from Granny's rulebook and made noise about a lawsuit, playing up the fact that Paul was their employee and that the cameras put our lives in danger."

"Good girl." She could hear his chuckle. "I'm proud of you, sweetheart."

Madison wisely omitted how Nick had come to her rescue, arguing the case on her behalf. He did a far better job than she did, convincing Amanda to ignore their original contract. Using equal amounts of persuasive argument and charm, Nick insisted they would have enough footage from the cameras at the mansion and select areas around town.

The celebrity carpenter had too much invested in the remodel, both emotionally and physically, not to see the project through. He saw the neglected mansion as his own personal challenge and was determined to breathe new life into its faded floorboards and sagging beams. Madison knew Nick was largely responsible for securing the deal with the network and its many sponsors. She even suspected he had fronted some of the money himself, though she could not prove it. In truth, there were times—like that day in the tunnel, and this afternoon while arguing with Amanda—that Madison suspected his reasons might be of a more personal nature. She was not ignorant of the way he looked at her, nor was she altogether immune to the spark of attraction between them.

As far as she was concerned, however, that spark would never be kindled. Never ignited. Perhaps she should have made that point clear today. But she had learned enough from Granny Bert to know you never interrupted a man while he was speaking, at least not while that speech was in your defense.

Yet she mentioned none of that now, least of all to Brash.

"It wasn't without stipulations," she said. "I agreed to spend more time on-site, therefore more time on cameras at the Big House. I pretended to grumble, but to be honest, it was a better deal than I expected."

There was a lapse into silence. Brash broke it with an admission that sounded surprisingly like a growl. "I miss you, Maddy."

She was deliberately obtuse. "I-I haven't gone anywhere."

"It feels like it. It feels like we're having a long-distance relationship. We talk on the phone more than we talk in person."

She understood his complaint. She felt the same way.

Still, she hedged. "Things are so complicated right now..."

"Things?"

"My crazy life," she admitted. "The show. The media. My mother-in-law. And—And Bethani." Her voice took a sad tumble. "There's more to consider than my own happiness."

"That night on the porch," Brash recalled, his voice husky. "You wouldn't let me say what I wanted to say."

"No," she whispered. "I couldn't."

There was a pregnant moment of silence. "If I had…" His voice cracked, so raw that he had to start over. "If I had, would you have had anything to say back to me?"

Madison closed her eyes as a tear slipped from her lashes. He was asking if she loved him.

"Most definitely," she whispered.

She could hear his smile. It filled the silence between them, softening the hard edges and warming the void. "That's all I need to know." His voice was rich and deep.

She sniffed away a tear as he cleared his throat and went on to say, "We both have a busy summer ahead. You with the house and the job, plus any new assignments with Archer; me with football camp, a couple of law conventions, training a new officer, not to mention trying to track down the rest of the meth labs. Maybe this way is best. It gives Bethani more time to adjust to the idea of us."

"I want there to be an *us*, Brash," Maddy insisted softly.

Again, she heard his smile. "There already is, sweetheart." The richness in his voice was so deep and so warm it curled her toes. "You have enough to worry about, without this. I'll wait for you, sweetheart, until things settle down. I'm not going anywhere."

"No stipulations?" she whispered.

"None. Unconditional."

"Unconditional," she breathed. The thought made her smile.

Life always came with complications, but there were no stipulations to Brash's love.

Note from Author

Thank you for reading. I hope you have enjoyed my tale of *Stipulations and Complications*. If you did, please take a moment to share your opinion on Amazon, Goodreads, BookBub, and additional venues of your choice. Reviews are an author's best friend and play a major role in our careers.

The next installment of *The Sisters, Texas* is *Home Again: Starting Over*. I hope you'll read it!

If you would like to know more about my inspirations for this series and other books I have written, please visit www.beckiwillis.com or contact me directly at beckiwillis.ccp@gmail.com. I love to hear from readers and promise to write you back!

Questions for Book Club Discussion

1. What would you do if you found a skeleton in your house? Would you still live there?

2. Do you think Juliet Randolph Blakely knew about the hidden staircase down to the secret room? Madison assumed she never knew, but what do you think? Is it possible to live in a house and never know all its secrets?

3. Madison agreed to do the reality TV show because she felt it was her only option to restore the old mansion and provide a home for her children. Did she make the right choice? Is the cost of fame and the invasion of privacy too great a price to pay?

4. Madison kept the truth about her late husband from her children. What would you have done in her shoes? Would you protect your children from the truth about their father and willingly been seen as the 'bad guy,' or would you gently tell them of his deceit and help them understand that fairy tales don't exist in real life?

5. Now Maddy is caught between hurting her daughter and ignoring her own heart. What would you do in this situation? What do you think the next step is for Maddy and Brash?

6. Granny Bert is definitely a handful! Do you

have a relative (or friend) she reminds you of?

7. What character or characters do you most identify with in the series?

8. Which characters or situations would you like to see explored in future books?

ABOUT THE AUTHOR

Becki Willis, best known for her popular The Sisters, Texas Mystery Series and Forgotten Boxes, always dreamed of being an author. In November of '13, that dream became a reality. Since that time, she has published numerous books, won first place honors for Best Mystery Series, Best Suspense Fiction and Best Audio Book, and has introduced her imaginary friends to readers around the world.

An avid history buff, Becki likes to poke around in old places and learn about the past. Other addictions include reading, writing, junking, unraveling a good mystery, and coffee. She loves to travel, but believes coming home to her family and her Texas ranch is the best part of any trip. Becki is a member of the Association of Texas Authors, the National Association of Professional Women, and the Brazos Writers organization. She attended Texas A&M University and majored in Journalism.

You can connect with her at http://www.beckiwillis.com/ and http://www.facebook.com/beckiwillis.ccp?ref=hl. Better yet, email her at beckiwillis.ccp@gmail.com. She loves to hear from readers and encourages feedback!